Biking the Passage

a novel of reconciliation by

Keith McGowan

A note on the images and photographs contained in this book:

I have attempted to properly credit all images and photographs. If you claim copyright or believe that you have not been appropriately credited, please contact the author at the email address below. The image or photograph will be appropriately credited or removed.

Comments and questions about this book may be directed to the author via

keithmcgowan@gmail.com

Other Books by Keith McGowan

On a May Day, *a novel about neighbors*

Bucket Adventure Guides:

Rafting the Grand Canyon:
A somewhat accurate but highly entertaining account of the Perils of the Great Unknown along with biased suggestions on how to overcome such Perils without significant Loss of Life but probable Minor Damage to a limb or two

Hiking Machu Picchu:
Slightly Amusing Answers to Common and Uncommon Questions about Visiting the Lost City of the Incas including Important Insights on Dealing with Llamas

Driving
New Zealand:
How to
navigate
the wrong side
of the road
down under
without
running over a
kiwi
or
being
run over by a
Kiwi

A definition of reconciliation:

Restoration of friendly relations

An Unexpected Phone Call

My landline rings three times before I pick up the handset. I recognize the number on the caller ID. Although I know it well from years ago, I am surprised to see it — and I wonder why she is calling.

"Hello."

"Hey, Daddy."

The voice is the same, but different. Older, wiser. Still soft, but harder. My little girl has grown up. A flood of memories fills my head and twists my tongue into a knot.

"Daddy, you there?"

"Yes, I'm here," I stammer. "Just wasn't expecting a call from you."

"That's understandable. It's been a while."

I do some quick arithmetic in my head. "Eleven years."

I can tell she is doing her own mental math before responding. "Yeah, that sounds right." Still double checking me.

"At your graduation from Wake."

"I remember."

I recall how she looked on that warm spring day and wonder what she looks like now. We had been tight once — even through her teen years. Until college, it had been just the two of us against the world. My mind shifts to why she is calling after all this time.

"Are you OK? Is something wrong?" I was not able to hide the anxiety in my voice.

"I'm fine. That's not why I'm calling."

So why are you calling, I ask her in my head. The young woman I knew from her college days, the little girl in pigtails that I carted to soccer practice, always wanted something. And as a father, I was always ready to give my only daughter anything she wanted. She definitely wants something from me now, but she would make me wait, and the longer she procrastinates the bigger that something was going to be.

"So how have you been?" I ask. I really want to know.

"Great," she replies, "And you? How are you?"

I want more details. A lot more than a generic "great." But I would have to play along to get those details.

"I'm good. Can't complain."

She laughs.

I love hearing that laugh. It has been so long.

"That's not the father I remember. The father I remember *always* had complaints."

It was my turn to laugh. "Okay, I'll be honest. My neck is stiff this morning, the stock market has been down all week, and the kitchen faucet is dripping."

I can hear her smile. What would I give to *see* that smile again.

"That's the father I remember. Always complaining."

"So you called to insult your old man?"

"No, I have a question." She pauses. "Or rather a proposition."

Ah — I think — here it comes: the pitch for some money. I don't mind helping out. That's what fathers do. Considering my record as a parent, it was the least I could do. "What's the proposition?"

"Do you have a bike?"

A bike? She was calling to find out if I had a bike? "Yeah," I reply. "I got a bike."

"One that you pedal."

"Right."

"Take it out much?"

"Three times a day. It's in the way because I've got it parked in front of my freezer." I am trying to make her laugh again. She doesn't bite.

"Seriously. How often do you ride it, not just move it out of the way?"

"Every couple of days or so. The running was taking a toll on my knees."

"What kind of bike is it?"

"Kind?"

"Yep. Road bike? Mountain? Hybrid?"

"I guess you would call it a mountain bike."

"Brand? Model?"

"Fuji. Nevada model."

"I guess that would do. At least it's not a Schwinn."

"It's a nice bike, thank you. What's wrong with a Schwinn?"

"There are nicer bikes."

"I'm not going to pay $400 for a two-wheeled vehicle that I have to power myself."

"I guess I better not tell you how much I paid for my bike."

"How much?"

"I'm not telling you."

I think about playing the father card and demanding that she tell me. However, I had forfeited that privilege long ago. "You don't have to tell me. It was your money."

"True. I might tell you later. Depends on how things go."

"Okay." I decide to wait her out. I can tell that she is nervous. She wants to ask me something, something more important to her than what kind of bike I own. I hear her take a deep breath.

"I called to see if you would go on a trip with me."

I sit back in my chair, slightly shocked, but also excited. We had not seen each other in over a decade, but now my daughter wanted to spend time with me. A trip sounded like a great idea — an adventure where we could get to know each other again.

"Sure," I reply. "We always talked about going to Australia."

"I was thinking of something simpler." She hesitated. "A bike trip."

"Okay. I saw a brochure about some great bike trips in Europe. Outfit supplies the bikes, has a support van, includes most meals and nice accommodations."

"More simple than that. Just the two of us. On bikes."

My excitement ebbs, thinking she is talking about only a day trip — a brief spin around a park. Riding a bike is not my preferred method of spending an afternoon, but it is a start. Take it slow, I remind myself.

"OK, I'm game. Where do you want to ride?" I ask, trying to hide the disappointment in my voice.

"From Pittsburgh to Washington."

I pause a moment while I refresh my geography. "The state?" I ask.

"No. D. C."

I take in a deep breath. "That's a relief. What is that? 300 miles?"

"334 point 5."

My daughter always liked to be exact with her numbers. "Are you planning for us to cover that in a day?" I ask.

She did not laugh; her tone had grown very serious. "I think we can do it in six."

Six days? More mental math on my part. "About 50 to 60 miles a day. That's a bit of biking. Where are we going to stay?"

"There are lots of places to camp along the route."

"We're going to sleep in tents next to the road?"

"Not quite. Heard of the Great Allegheny Passage?"

"Nope."

"How about the C & O Canal?"

"The one that runs along the Potomac?"

"Yeah, you can bike on the old towpath. The Great Allegheny Passage is a converted railroad line that connects to it. No cars or trucks to deal with."

"All the way from Pittsburgh to D.C.?"

"Yep. Still game?"

I detect a tinge of excited anticipation in her voice, but I hesitate. The thought of trying to get my arthritic hip comfortable in a sleeping bag after spending the day sitting on a skinny bicycle seat gives me pause. Still, this was a chance to reconnect with Stephanie, and I could not let it pass.

"When did you want to do this trip?" I ask.

"I have a week of vacation at the end of July."

"July? Pretty hot in July." Perhaps I could persuade her to wait until the fall. It would be cooler then, and I would have more time to process this unexpected contact. *And* get in physical shape for it.

"That's when I have my vacation scheduled." She is very matter of fact. Take it or leave it, buddy. Her mother had often used the same approach with me. It was effective.

"I'm in."

—

"Really? You want to do this bike trip with me?" She sounds surprised, like she had expected me to turn her down. I guess she was used to her father disappointing her.

"Why not? Who wouldn't want to sit on a bike for six straight days in the broiling sun?"

"You don't have to come. It's okay. I would understand."

Sure you would, I think. And I would not hear from you for another eleven years. "It'll be great," I lie. "So what's the next step?"

"I'll be in touch in a couple of weeks. We'll talk logistics then."

"Logistics? When did you start using big words like that?"

"After I graduated from college."

An innocent phrase, but I feel the barbs in her tone. A sharp jab meant to prick without causing serious injury. I will have to pay for my shortcomings as a father to get my daughter back in my life, but I am ready to pony up.

"Will I need to bring a dictionary on this trip?" I ask.

"Maybe."

I can tell she is ready to hang up, but I am not ready to let go. Something in her voice tells me that she has spent lots of energy gearing up for this call.

"Is this the best number to reach you?" I ask, looking again at the familiar number on the caller ID.

"Yes. It's my cell. The same number I've always had."

"And you've got my number." I realize immediately how stupid my last statement sounds considering that she has just dialed my number. My desperation is leaking through.

"Yep."

"You're not going to forget it?"

"I never forgot it."

So why haven't you called before, I ask in my head. And why are you calling now? We sit in silence for a moment, each of us trying to think of what to say next. I think of her mother, and I wonder if my daughter is thinking of her as well. The extended silence grows awkward. Before I can say anything more, she cuts me off.

"Hey, I gotta go." She speaks rapidly into the phone. "Duty calls, but I'm looking forward to our trip. Bye."

—

I say, "Me, too," into the dial tone.

Round One with Hank

Unless one of us is in the hospital, Hank and I meet every Monday at Tomfoolery. We meet because we get tired of eating alone. We meet at Tomfoolery because a plate of burgers and fries is $5 on Mondays. Semi-retired guys have to watch their budgets more than their waistlines.

Hank is always late because he is in real estate. Or at least he thinks he's still in real estate. I will hear an excuse as to how he is about to close a big deal, but he never seems to close that big deal which will push him into full retirement. I seriously doubt Hank actually wants to go into full retirement as he likes the pretension of being close to the excitement.

But what do I know? I pretend to be a political consultant. Got one guy, a dark horse at the bottom of the polls, elected early in my career and then milked that for the next twenty years.

I met Hank when I was looking for a new place — the old one had too many memories. Hank found the house I live in now, a building that is in constant need of repair. Despite the fact that Hank represented me in the transaction, we remain friends.

I have sat down, perused the menu, and decided on the type of burger I want today — one covered in onions and mushrooms.

Hank rolls in on schedule, fifteen minutes late.

"Hey, buddy, sorry I'm late. Had to take a call from a Chicago investor. Looking for a large apartment complex."

It is his typical spiel. I ignore it. "Are you having your usual?" I ask.

"Yeah, sure. Why not?"

Hank is a man of habit. He likes eating the same meal, at the same place, with the same person. I appreciate guys like that, because I am that kind of guy.

Hank starts back in on his story. "So this guy from Chicago calls me and says that he is looking for a net, net, net

6

cash flow positive complex with at least 500 units. I could tell he hadn't done a lick of research, because there are no 500 unit complexes within 25 miles of here. And cash flow positive on a triple net basis? I haven't seen one of those in over a decade."

Hank pauses to take a gulp of water. I have no idea what he is talking about, but it doesn't matter. I like to listen to his patter as long as I only had to do it for an hour once a week.

"So I had to explain to this guy what the local situation was. We got to talking, and he explained his investment thesis to me. This generation coming up is not buying homes. They are mooching off their parents by living at home, or," Hank pauses for effect, "They are renting apartments."

The waitress appears at our table and takes our orders.

Hank resumes. "So he had these numbers. We are way short in this country on large rental complexes, and the demand is coming because mommy and daddy are moving into retirement and all these kids are going to be kicked out when the old homestead is sold. They are not going to be able to qualify for loans on houses because the home loan standards have been tightened and most of them have tons of student debt. That all clicked with my research."

"You did actual research?"

"Of course." He pretends to be insulted by my question.

Two Bud lights land loudly on the table. Sometimes, semi-retired guys have to watch their budgets *and* their waistlines.

Hank takes a quick swig to remove the foam from his brew. "I've got kids of my own. Both are living at home, and both have tons of student debt. And I'm ready to kick them both out."

I set my beer down. "I'd think long and hard before I did that."

"Hell, they're both pushing thirty. They've got decent jobs. Time they made their own way."

"Kids do need to make their own way," I agree. "Just be careful."

The waitress arrives with our food. Not only was the food cheap and the beer cold, the service was fast.

—

For once, Hank has stopped talking. He stares at me through the steam that rises in the air between us.

"You're right. I'll give it some more thought. So what's new with you?" he asks as he picks through his fries, selecting the longest one to eat first.

"I got a call from my daughter last night."

"That's great." Hank pauses in his fry search. "Wait, I didn't know you had a daughter."

"Until last night, I didn't think I did."

A confused look spreads over my friend's face.

"We hadn't spoken in eleven years," I offer as an explanation.

Hank's eyebrows pop up, and his eyes enlarge. "You haven't spoken to your only daughter in eleven years? What happened?"

"We had a difference of opinion."

"About what?"

"I've forgotten." I have not forgotten, but I do not want to discuss it with Hank, or anyone else for that matter.

"Okay, what did you guys talk about?" Hank asks.

"Going on a bike trip together."

"Eleven years go by, and she calls you about a bike trip?"

"I don't have the best relationship with my daughter."

Hank nods in agreement. "Daughters can be difficult. Even more difficult than wives."

"I think I was the one who was difficult."

Hank squints his eyes at me. "I can see that. So where is this bike trip?"

"We're going to bike from Pittsburgh to D. C."

Although Hank is about to consume a fry, his hand holding it stops in mid air. "Isn't that like 400 miles?" he asks.

"I am informed that it is 334.5 miles."

"What's the time frame? A month?"

"A week."

"A week? That's at least fifty miles a day. Have you ever ridden fifty miles on a bike?"

"Maybe in my whole life, I have."

"But in a single day?"

"No."

"And you're going to do this for seven days straight?"

"She thinks we can do it in six."

Hank shakes his head in disbelief. "Are you doing some kind of training?"

"Yeah," I smirk. "I've set up my bike in my living room, and I sit on it while I watch reruns of the Tour de France."

"Do you pedal?"

"Don't be silly! I would run into my furniture."

"Right." Hank rearranges the lettuce and tomato on his burger while removing the pickles. "Do you want these?" he asks, referring to the pickles.

"No, thanks."

Hank tosses them on my plate. He always offers his pickles to me, and I always decline. Then he gives them to me anyway. It was a little ritual we had.

I take another sip of beer and continue. "I'm getting my butt in shape for sitting on that skinny little seat."

Hank leans to his right and pretends to look at my derrière. "I can tell that part of the training program is working, but that bike won't move all by itself. You're going to have to pedal."

"It's mostly downhill."

"Pittsburgh is surrounded by mountains. You're going to be going up and down."

I shrug. "Maybe I should get one of those electric bikes."

"Is she riding an electric bike?"

"She didn't mention it. I have the impression she's into pedal bikes."

"So if you show up with an electric bike, she's going to classify you as a big time wimp."

I purse my lips. "Can't have that — better start a real training program. Are you offering to be my coach?"

"No." Hank emphatically chomps down on his burger and shakes his head.

"I pay well. I'll pick up today's check."

Hank continues to shake his head as he chews his burger. After he swallows his bite, he comments, "You could offer to pick up my monthly mortgage payment, and I still wouldn't do it."

"What kind of a friend are you?"

"A sane one."

"How about a once-a-week joint training ride?"

"On a bike?"

"I think that's the general idea."

"It's been at least 10 years since I've sat on a bike."

"Then it would be good for you as well. "

Hank cocks his head as he reaches for the ketchup and blatantly takes two large fries from off of my plate. "That would be a recipe for a heart attack."

"Stealing my fries and eating them is a recipe for a *physical* attack," I counter.

"Look, tell you what I will do, since I am such a good friend. You go on your training rides, and I will follow in my air-conditioned SUV."

"How will that help?"

"Whenever you slow down, I will open my window and scream insults about your manhood."

"Oh, that would be helpful," I reply scornfully.

"What are good friends for?"

"A few words of encouragement come to mind."

"Look, I think it's great that you and your daughter are getting back together after — what did you say — 11 years, but you need a reality check. Ask yourself a few simple questions."

"Like?"

"Well — first off — are you in shape?"

"Sort of," I say meekly.

"Have you thought about the weather? It's probably going to rain on you."

"I've been wet before."

"On a bike?"

"No."

"When are you going?"

"At the end of July."

Hank glowers at me in disbelief. "Last time I checked, it gets pretty hot in July."

"I'll take a dip in the river."

"How are you going to carry all your stuff?"

I smile as I say, "If my daughter is like most women, we will need a U-Haul."

"What if you get a flat?"

"That would be a problem," I admit.

"Where are you going to sleep?"

"She suggested we camp."

Hank starts laughing so hard I think he is going to choke on his food.

"Dude, you really need to think this through. Do some research. What is it you want to accomplish by going on this bike trip? Other than kill yourself?"

Talking to Hank has killed my appetite. I push back from the table and toss my napkin next to my plate. It is time to get serious. "I want to see my daughter again, Hank."

He nods in agreement. "I hear you, but there's got to be another way. Talk to her. Suggest some alternatives. She'll listen to you."

"I don't know. She can be stubborn when she sets her mind to something."

"Just like her old man?" Hank grins as he scoops up the remainder of my fries.

"Exactly like her old man," I reply with my own grin.

A Spin on the Computer

I fire up my old HP laptop and wait for it to slowly grind through its startup routine. It had been slow when I bought it, and every time I tried to use it, it got even slower, but it seemed important to Hewlett Packard that I know how much RAM the laptop had, that I had an out of date operating system, and that I needed to subscribe to an antivirus program.

When I finally get a screen, I type in "Great Allegheny Passage" into the search box and hit enter. The old machine whirls and groans at having to do something useful.

The second listing on the results page proclaims it to be the "official" website, so that is the one I click. At the top of the page, I scroll through multiple images, all inviting me to take the plunge: a flat roadway running through a forest, a scenic railroad trestle, a verdant green vista of rolling hills, a gently curving bridge. Sitting in my office chair, it all looks pretty easy. Below the scrolling pictures, a map traces out the route. The Great Allegheny Passage runs for 150 miles from Pittsburgh, Pennsylvania to Cumberland, Maryland. At Cumberland, the trail picks up the C & O Canal Towpath along the Potomac River for an additional 184.5 miles into Washington DC. The total mileage comes to under 335 miles; this trip is looking a little less onerous.

Little communities with colorful names like Confluence and Woodcock Hollow dot the route. There are familiar names like Boston and Hancock and odd ones like Ohiopyle and Paw Paw. There are also places with historic names: Homestead and Harpers Ferry. Within those communities, no doubt, are charming places to grab a bite to eat or slurp down a cold drink or seek shelter from the elements. The trail follows various waterways, offering scenic places to stop along the way. *I might even enjoy this trip,* I think to myself.

I see buttons to like somebody on Facebook or to follow them on Twitter. I have no idea how to do that or why I would want to. There are links for sponsors, but I click on the link for videos of people riding the trail. The weather is always beautiful, and everyone is smiling. This trip is looking more and more like a walk in the park than the ordeal through hell that Hank had implied.

I read along gaining encouragement with almost every word. That is, until I reach the description of the C & O Canal Towpath: "be prepared for ruts, tree roots, mud, and mosquitoes." That did not sound like fun at all.

I scroll back to a link entitled: "ABOUT THE TRAIL" and click. First thing I see is that no motorized vehicles are allowed. That rules out the electric bike idea. The trail is described as having a compact crushed limestone surface. I wonder if the limestone had been crushed by old overweight guys falling off their bikes. Good news is that the typical grade on the trail was less than 1%. The guide mentions a few tunnels. If it rained or got too hot, Steph and I could linger in them awhile and talk. We did not have to spend the whole time pedaling.

I can do this, I think to myself. All I need is a little training.

The First Training Ride

I have passed by an asphalt track numerous times that runs from Alapocas Run State Park to Bellevue State Park in northern Delaware. Although I have seen walkers, joggers, and bikers, I have never had the inclination to set foot on it. Today, I have selected it for my first training run. The internet said it was nine miles long. Perfect for an easy first training ride.

The track is known as the Northern Delaware Greenway Trail, and it hopes to someday link all of the state parks together. All I care about is that I can access it from my condo via a wide sidewalk.

I roll my bike out of the garage. The tires are a little flat so I pump some air in them. I give the brakes a quick squeeze. They sort of work, but I do not want to spend the time to adjust them. About to saddle up, I remember my helmet sitting on a hook back inside. Too much trouble to go fetch it, I reason. I'll wear it next time. The day is already warm and getting warmer.

I pull up to the light where I can observe the trail across the road. That is when I see him, blazing over the asphalt like a comet. He is all muscle, no fat anywhere in sight. Decked out in skin tight blue and gold spandex, he is riding fast on a matching bike. I can clearly see his top of the line equipment: an expensive helmet, more expensive sunglasses, and an outrageously expensive bicycle. He whizzes around a curve in perfect bike racing form -- a smooth steady pedal stroke that propels him past mere mortals. I label him "The Biking God", and I hate him.

The Biking God is gone as quickly as he came. I assess my own gear: stained t-shirt and old shorts; bike bought at Target on special; no helmet; and drugstore shades. Works for me — I think — as I set off, with the Biking God now out of sight and out of mind.

Heat rises from the hard pavement, but it offers a smooth ride. There is little traffic on the trail, and being in Delaware, one of the flattest states this side of Kansas, there are few hills. When I do encounter one, I just keep finding a lower gear. My bike has lots of gears, and I use all of them.

I am halfway up one hill, spinning furiously in my next to lowest gear, when I hear a runner coming up behind me. Typically on the trail, walkers are passed by runners, and runners are passed by bikers. I cycle faster in a vain effort to stay ahead, but I can tell the runner is gaining on me. Consoling myself with a reminder that today is only my first training ride and that the person behind me is probably some young collegiate track star training for the Olympics, I move to the right so that the runner can pass me. To my chagrin, the runner is female. Not only is the runner female, but she is well over thirty and pushing a double baby carriage filled with a pair of twins as she glides up the path in front of me. I hear a roaring noise and feel a sharp mental pain as my male ego is ripped out of my chest.

Although I pedal harder, I cannot maintain the pace necessary to even keep up with a mother of two pushing a stroller. When I reach the top of the hill, I stop and check my mileage. I have covered all of five miles, and I am exhausted. Hank is right: I need to talk Stephanie out of this bike trip.

The Call Back

The phone only rings once before Stephanie picks up.

"Hey, Daddy." The voice is cool, noncommittal.

I immediately regret calling, but I am committed. "I wasn't sure of the protocol, but I thought we should talk more about this trip."

"Protocol?" she asks.

"Yeah, whether I should wait for you to call, or if it was okay for me to call."

She laughs softly. "There should be no protocol for fathers and daughters. We should call each other whenever we feel like it."

"So, it's okay that I called?" I had never felt so insecure talking to a girl on the phone since I had called Mary Beth Decker to ask her to go to prom.

"Sure."

"You're not at work, are you? I don't want to bother you at work."

"It's not a problem."

"In fact, I don't even know where you work."

"Don't worry about that. I'm glad you called."

"You are?"

"Yes, I need sponsors."

"Sponsors?"

"Yes, I'm doing a charity ride this weekend, and I've procrastinated signing people up. I'm short on what I promised to raise."

"Well, sure, I'll contribute. How much do you need to make your goal?" I can see the headlines in tomorrow's family newspaper, "Father Rides to Rescue Daughter, Makes Generous Contribution for Her to Reach Charity Goal".

"It's a three day race."

"I thought it was just a charity ride."

"That's what I mean, but they will be recording times, so I do want to do my best."

"Of course," I say while I think: *just like her mother; always wanting to do her best.*

"So, if you could go a dollar a mile, that would put me over the top."

I am thinking a simple, short ride to raise money to benefit mankind, promote world peace, and save some whales. How far can this be over a long weekend? Maybe fifteen miles, twenty miles tops? How can a father in good conscience say no?

"No problem." I hear myself saying. "Sign me up for a dollar a mile."

"Oh, thanks, Daddy. I really appreciate it. I'm sure my friends would cover it, but I would have to spend time on the phone reaching them. Time I really don't have right now."

"My pleasure. So how far do you think you'll be riding?"

"The group I signed up for is supposed to complete 250 miles over three days."

I let out a low whistle. "That's over 80 miles a day," I remark.

"Yep."

And $250 out of my pocket when I thought I was only in for maybe a fifth of that. Fatherhood is expensive; I already knew that. But it was probably going to a help cure some terrible disease. "What's the cause?" I ask.

"We're raising money to end the inhumane treatment of mice in pharmaceutical research."

I am literally scratching my head on this one. "Can you explain to me how the treatment of the mice is inhumane? Isn't it *medical* research?"

"That's exactly the point, Daddy. They're raising these poor little animals for the sole purpose of injecting them with terrible diseases and watching them die."

"But don't they use the knowledge they gain to develop medicines to help humans?"

"To help humans, but not other animals. It's really criminal to treat animals this way for the sole benefit of humans."

I am left speechless. Somehow I have been snookered into donating $250 toward the ethical treatment of lab rats.

A slightly awkward silence ensues as I wrestle with where my hard earned cash is going.

Stephanie fills the gap with a question. "So did you call to ask me something about the trip?"

I clear my head of the thought of little white mice nibbling on Beaufort D'Ete cheese bought for $45 a pound with my donation; here is the opening I need. "As a matter of fact, I did want to discuss a few things with you about the trip. Just a few questions."

"Good, because I have been working really hard on the preparations."

"Yeah," I begin halfheartedly "I've been doing some reading on the internet and talking to some friends about this bike trip."

"Great!" she interjects cheerfully. "You should know before you go. That is what someone always told me. Find out what you're getting yourself into."

I recognize the phrase. I had used it often when raising her on my own.

Stephanie keeps talking. Growing up, she spoke as little as possible, but if she got excited about something she became a nonstop chatterbox. I think of that little girl as I listen to her ramble on.

"I'll send you a list of items to bring. Sunscreen, at least 50 SPF. Bug spray, but not anything with any DEET. A spare tube that fits your bike. I have a pump and patch kit so don't worry about that. We're going to need good flashlights for the tunnels. For cooking I have a neat little compact set. I have the perfect tent for us to take. Nice and lightweight. Do you have a sleeping bag?"

"I'll look, but I doubt it."

"Don't worry about it. I think I can borrow a friend's bag."

"Uh, listen Steph," I interrupt, "This sounds like a lot of stuff. How are we going to carry it all on two bikes?"

"Panniers." Her answer is simple and straightforward, at least for someone who knew what a pannier was.

"Yes, panniers." I try to sound like I know exactly what a pannier is while I desperately try to figure out how to spell it so I can look it up later on the internet.

Steph detected the uncertainty in my voice. "Daddy, do you know what a pannier is?"

"No, not really," I admit.

"It's the bag you attach to the frame of your bike to carry your stuff."

Oh, right, that makes sense. Nothing like sounding like an idiot when talking to your daughter, I think to myself. "Yeah, of course," I say aloud.

"Do you have a set?"

"No. Haven't needed them before."

"Here, I'll send you a link to a waterproof set. I know you will think they are expensive, but you want a reliable set that won't leak. You'll also need to install a bike rack over your rear wheel."

"Why do they need to be waterproof?"

There is a pause on the phone, and I know that I have asked a stupid question.

"In case it rains," she replies slowly.

"Uh, yes. Right. I guess the weather is a factor to consider." An image of me cycling for hours through a downpour washes through my brain. "I'm not sure I would know how to install these panniers."

"Any competent bike shop can do it, and it would also be a good idea for you to have them check your brakes, gears, tires, et cetera."

Sounds expensive, I think. "Look," I begin hesitantly, "Have you seen the elevation chart? The section from Cumberland to the eastern continental divide looks like we will need a rocket booster to get over it."

"Going from east to west?"

"Yeah."

"That's why we're going from west to east. More gradual climb going that way. Pittsburgh to DC, remember? But won't it be great going *down* that section?"

I think for a moment of hurtling down a narrow bike path at over a thousand feet per second sitting precariously on a two-wheeled vehicle heavily loaded with camping gear. Although I had not done extremely well in my high school physics class, I did recall that large mass items accelerated to something called maximum velocity when going downhill. I also recall that mass increased as an object approached the speed of light, and I was pretty sure from looking at the elevation chart that I was going to be getting close to that speed by the time I reached the bottom. I am definitely getting the brakes on my bike checked.

In the meantime, I need to talk Steph into a different trip — one a little less dangerous. So, I try a different tack.

"Right, right," I say as I think of my next objection. "Have you thought how we're getting to Pittsburgh? If we haul the bikes there on a car, we're going to have to drive back to retrieve it. Maybe a one-way rental, but drop off fees are outrageous. Or were you thinking of getting someone to take us up there? It would have to be a pretty big vehicle to haul the driver, us, our bikes, and gear."

"Got that all worked out," Steph replies confidently.

"Really?" I am surprised.

"Amtrak has a new service that will take our bikes to Pittsburgh."

A train, I think. I had not ridden a train in years and that had been in Europe. An American train? That could not possibly work.

"Is that safe? I just saw a Denzel Washington movie where a train was hijacked and crashed into a station."

"You watch too many movies."

"But won't we have to box up the bikes? Take the pedals and handlebars off? And then we'll have to put them back on."

"Nope. None of that. It's a roll on/roll off service. There are only eight slots so I have already reserved seats for us and space for two bikes."

"Oh."

I must not have hid the disappointment in my voice well, because Steph asks me, "Is there something wrong, Daddy?"

"Uh, no," I lie. My plan to dissuade her from this bike trip is not working. She has put a great deal of thought into it, but then I have another idea. "How long is this train ride?"

"That's the bad news," Stephanie admits. "Over seven hours. Leaves Union Station in DC at 4 pm and gets into downtown Pittsburgh at almost midnight."

"That's late."

"It is, and seven hours is a long time, but it will give us some time to talk."

I consider that. I could not deny that we needed to talk — for at least seven hours. "So the plan is for me to drive to DC and meet you at Union Station?" I ask.

"Actually, I live in Silver Spring. I was thinking you could meet me at my place, and then we can take the Red Line Metro to Union Station."

"We can take the bikes on the Metro?"

"As long as it is not rush hour."

She has thought of everything, except perhaps that her father was not physically capable of cycling 334.5 miles over six days. A long pause ensues as I try to think of another excuse to offer her.

"Daddy?"

"Yes."

"You're not saying anything. Are you sure you want to do this trip?"

"Oh, no, I want to do the trip. It's going to be a challenge, though."

"I thought you liked challenges."

"Well, in a way. At least challenges that I think I can do."

"You don't think you can do this?"

I can hear disappointment creeping into my daughter's voice. I had disappointed her so many times in the past.

Steph keeps talking: "If you don't want to do the bike trip, I'll understand."

I glance at the photo on the wall of my wife Nancy and I standing on a dock extending into the Chester River — a photo from happier times. Between us, a little girl stands — smiling — unaware of the arguments her parents were having. *No, you won't understand,* I think. You're young. Your body has not started giving out, and your mind still believes that it can do whatever it wants. My old mind has learned different.

"I just thought this type of trip would appeal to you," Stephanie continues. "You used to take me camping and we would go places and we used to have all sorts of adventures together — but we don't have to do this."

I hear her words hesitantly willing to let me off the hook, but I feel her emotions desperately trying to reel me in.

"No, Steph," I reply softly, "We have to do this. Just you and me."

"Yeah, Daddy, I really want to see you. Like old times."

"Maybe better than old times," I suggest.

Although I think I hear a sniffle on the other end of the line, I definitely hear paper being shuffled.

Sensing my daughter wants to end the conversation, I try to get a small concession. "Uh, I know there are a lot of things we have to work out, but I was wondering how strong you felt about the camping. I've done a little research, and I've found several places we could stay along the way. And we wouldn't have to haul tents and sleeping bags. Save a little weight."

"Sure, Daddy, we don't have to camp if you don't want to."

I feel a little relief. "Your old man is getting soft in his old age," I apologize.

"Listen," my daughter says. "I gotta go. Lots of work to do."

"Sure. We'll talk later."

I swear I hear her crying as she hangs up.

The Bike Shop

I am trying to remember the last time I had set foot in a bike shop as I prop the door open and push my bike ahead of me. The young guy sitting behind the counter looks up at me and then down at my bike.

His expression tells me why I did not like going into bike shops. It reminds me of the face on the waiter long ago when I ordered a burger at a little bistro on the Champs-Élysées. I would describe it as something between pity and disgust. On one hand, the guy felt sorry for me for not understanding the finer things in life; on the other, he reviled me for not enjoying them. Hey. I am just a guy who knows what he likes and does not want to spend a penny more.

"Can I help you?"

Probably not, I think, I am too set in my ways. Instead, I decide to throw myself on his mercy, and say, "I need all the help I can get."

That at least gets a thin smile.

I continue. "My daughter and I are going on a bike trip, and she suggested that I get my bike checked out."

He gives my bike a cursory once over with his eyes, and then says with a broadened smile, "Great, did you bring it with you?"

A jerk with a sense of humor — just like me. I decide then and there that we were going to get along fabulously.

With a smile just as big as his, I reply, "I'm afraid that this poor excuse is all I've got to take on the trip."

The guy steps over to a row of shiny new bicycles. They gleam in the light pouring in through the front window, looking sleek, light, and fast. With an open palm gesture, he suggests, "We could easily remedy that."

I know that if I follow him over to that row of new bikes, my bank account will be forever doomed. Instead, I stand my ground. "I'd like to see what you can do with this baby." I pat my old worn bike seat.

The guy shrugs. "Very well. We perform miracles daily. Where is this bike trip?"

"My daughter wants us to cycle the GAP." I intentionally use the acronym, thinking I can fool this bike shop clerk into thinking I am something of a cyclist, but it had no effect on him.

He bends down and examines my tires. "Your tread is getting a little worn here." He points to a spot.

"Yeah, okay," I agree.

"And did you know you have a broken spoke?"

I did not, but I was willing to be damned for all eternity rather than admit it to this guy. "Yeah, that was one of the reasons I brought it in."

"And the brakes need tightening. Can you find all your gears?"

"All the ones I need," I said coolly.

He nods and smiles. "The GAP, you say?"

"Yeah, the trail that comes out of Pittsburgh."

"Ahh," he said with a note of recognition. "The Great Allegheny Passage. I've heard that's a nice ride, not too challenging."

His tone is pleasant, but the "not too challenging" phrase at the end sticks in my craw. "We're doing the C&O Towpath while we're there," I add.

"The Towpath?" I can tell I have gotten his attention. "I've been on that sucker. Worst time I ever had on a bike."

"Really?"

"Just a day ride, but I was down in DC to visit a buddy. It had stormed the day before. Nothing but one mudhole after another. Several trees had fallen across the path, and we had to portage our bikes around them. We came in coated in mud."

"Wasn't much fun then?"

"Naw, it was totally awesome, dude." The guy laughs recalling his memories. "I'd suggest getting some knobby tires if you're going on the Towpath. Maybe some mud flaps so that none of that slop hits you in the face."

"I also need a bike rack and a set of panniers. To carry my stuff," I explain.

"Right over here." The bike clerk walks past the row of gleaming new bicycles to a wall display. He pulls a rack and a set of matching bags down. "How about these?"

I have no idea if what he had handed me would do or not, but I am pretty sure I can get the exact same items on Amazon for half the price. "So," I begin, "To install these on my bike, replace the rear wheel, check the brakes, and put on the mud flaps, what are we looking at?"

"That's going to take some of the mechanic's time. I'd say two to three hours, plus the price of the wheel, the rack, the panniers, and miscellaneous shop parts. Sure you don't want to look at one of the new bikes?"

I refuse to look in their direction. "I would still have to get the bike rack and panniers put on. How much an hour does the mechanic charge?"

"$75."

My lower jaw drops a little. "My lawyer doesn't charge that much," I protest.

The guy wrinkled his nose. "How old is your lawyer?"

"He practiced with Abraham Lincoln."

That, at least, gets a laugh out of the clerk. Just then, the bell on the front door to the bike shop tinkles, and another customer enters. I do not recognize him at first, but there is something familiar about him. He does not look at me or the clerk helping me but strides directly past us to the area behind the counter where a bike frame was on a stand. After looking at the bike frame on the stand and the other bikes strapped to the wall waiting for attention, he turns and glares at the bike shop clerk standing next to me.

The clerk loses what little interest he had in me. He exchanges his snobby demeanor for one of an absolute sycophant. "It's ready," he pleads as he scurries to where the new customer stands. "I locked your bike in the storeroom for safekeeping. I'll be right back with it." With that, the clerk disappears into the back nether regions of the bike shop.

I am left alone with the new customer. He does not look at me or otherwise acknowledge my presence, but stands with the mild irritation of a person who is not used to having to wait for what he had come for. Although he wears loose street clothes, I can tell his body is lean and muscled underneath. His facial features resemble those of a hawk, with a sharp nose and angular chin. I cannot detect an ounce of body fat anywhere as I wondered where I had seen him before.

"Here you go." The clerk comes out from the rear of the store pushing a sparkling blue and gold bicycle racing machine, and I remember where I have seen this new customer. He had been wearing spandex with the same blue and gold theme when he had raced ahead of me on the Northern Delaware Greenway Trail.

The Biking God grabs one of the handlebars to his chariot and carefully examines his ride.

The clerk practically prostrates himself, babbling, "We lubed the chain, adjusted the gears, and replaced the brake pads."

From where I stand, it looks like they have also vacuumed the bike, washed it with Dove soap, and then waxed the machine with a lambskin shammy to make it extra shiny.

The Biking God only nods before slowly reaching for the wallet in his back pocket.

The clerk holds up his hands. "No, on the house. It was our pleasure."

The Biking God glowers at him as if the bike shop should pay him for allowing mere mortals to touch his machine. Without a word, The Biking God rolls his chariot toward the front door.

Racing ahead of him, the clerk pushes the door open. As the deity leaves the building, the clerk says hopefully, "Come back anytime."

Such was the power of The Biking God. I still hate him, but I have to admire him for his ability to make the craven crawl in his presence. I doubt I will be able to display the same ability when I have to negotiate with the clerk my bill with the bike shop.

Dinner with Katherine

When a man lives alone for a number of years the way I have, he learns to appreciate how wonderful the presence of a woman can be. I love the way they look, the way they smell, the way they feel. Not that I want one around all the time, but every once in awhile, I enjoy being around one. And sometimes I need that feminine presence.

For years, Katherine and I have had an understanding. Not a commitment, but an understanding. Dropping in unannounced is not allowed, but we can call each other at any time of day or night, and the other will make themselves available.

I have to admit that Katherine calls me more than I call her. Her husband left her some years ago for a younger model, a travesty that left scars on Katherine that I am careful not to touch. Her daughter developed a drug problem in college, could never shake it, and has been in and out of rehab centers ever since. That ongoing situation has generated its own scar tissue that I try to avoid. Katherine's mother is still alive, and calls her every afternoon to complain that Katherine never comes to see her, forgetting that her dutiful daughter had stayed with her an hour that very morning. Like most women, Katherine does not deserve the life she lives. Unlike other women, Katherine never complains about her life.

She was surprised that I had called and invited her to dinner. We had seen each other only the week before. Our arrangement was that I would buy the groceries and that she would figure out what to cook from what I had bought. Despite my penchant for buying far more meat than vegetables, she somehow figured out how to prepare a balanced meal.

One of the things I like about Katherine is her patience. We chit chat through the meal preparation and the dinner itself. Not once does she push the conversation to why I had called her. After dinner, she sits at the bar drinking a glass of white wine while I clean up the kitchen. If I had a true complaint about Katherine, it was related to the number of pots and pans she uses when she cooks.

Holding up one pan, I ask, "What did you use this one for?"

"Hmm. I think that was for the cream sauce."

I pick up another one with remnants of the cream sauce still in it. "That was this one."

She shrugs. "Did you like the cream sauce?"

"It was delicious," I admit.

"Then stop complaining."

"Not complaining. Just observing."

"Then stop observing."

It is my turn to shrug. And smile. I pull the kitchen towel off my shoulder and dry my hands. I need to process Stephanie's call with a woman, a woman who is also a mother, and the mother of a daughter. Katherine fits the bill.

I look directly at Katherine, and she returns my gaze over the rim of her wine glass.

"My daughter called me last week." I try to sound as casual as possible, but Katherine was having none of it. She puts her wine glass down.

"I don't recall you telling me that you had a daughter."

"Probably because I never mentioned her to you."

"Does your daughter have a name?"

"Stephanie."

"That's a pretty name. Where does she live?"

I squint my nose. It was a simple fact I should know.

Katherine displays a disappointed look on her face. "You don't know where your daughter lives?"

"I think she lives in the DC area."

"What does she do there?"

I shrug. "Probably works for the government."

"Married?"

"Don't know."

"Any children?"

"Hadn't thought of that," I muse.

Katherine adjusts her seating position on the bar stool. I have learned that women often do that just before they unload on you. I steel myself for the lecture I know that I deserve but do not relish hearing.

"Okay, Tom. Let's recap our conversation here. You tell me you have a daughter, a daughter I didn't know about, and we've known each other over a year."

"A year and a half."

She ignores my correction. "You only have a general idea of where she lives — don't know what she does for a living — or if she is married — or if she has children. You could be a grandfather and not know it."

Damn women, I think. They were always concentrating on unimportant details.

Katherine must have read my thoughts because she continues, "I would say those are pretty *important* details a father should know about his daughter."

I need Katherine's help so I just nod in agreement. The interrogation resumes as Katherine picks up the wine bottle to refill her glass.

"How often do you talk?"

I reach for my beer as I am going to need fortification for the next part of this conversation. After a sip, I start with, "Based on how often we've talked recently, I would say — oh — on average, once every eleven years."

Katherine abruptly stops refilling her wine glass. "You haven't talked to your daughter in eleven years?" Incredulity drips from each of Katherine's words.

"Might have been even longer if she hadn't called last week."

"What happened?"

"Well, the phone rang — I picked it up — said hello — she said hello — and we went from there."

Katherine scowls at my attempt at humor. "That's not what I meant. What happened between the two of you that you didn't talk for eleven years?"

"She did some things; I said some things." I wave my beer from side to side as I speak. "One thing failed to lead to another — nor another — but time went on, and we ended up not speaking for awhile."

"Eleven years?"

"Yeah." I hang my head with regret.

"What sort of things did you say to her?"

"Basically, that I did not approve of some of the choices she was making."

"Choices about her own life?"

"Yeah."

"Didn't she have the right to make choices about her own life?"

"She didn't have the right to ruin her life."

"Who were you to make that determination?"

"I was her father."

"Interesting that you used the past tense."

Katherine's words cut across my chest and open old wounds near my heart. She immediately senses my pain and apologizes. "I'm sorry. I didn't mean for it to come out like that."

"But it did. Sometimes the truth hurts." I collect some spice containers sitting on the counter and put them back into the cabinet. Although I am now facing away from Katherine, I can feel her eyes on me. It was time to see if she would help me. "Katherine," I begin, "I need your help. My daughter has reached out to me. I don't deserve it, but I have a second chance with her. What I don't want to do is screw it up the way I did the first time." I turn to face Katherine. Her face is the most compassionate thing I have seen in a long while, but it contains tinges of worry.

Katherine sets her wine glass down and replies, "I'm not sure I'm the best person to ask for advice. From previous conversations we've had, you're aware of the issues I've had with my own daughter."

"But you still have a relationship with her."

"Of sorts. My therapist tells me I interject myself too much into my daughter's life."

"That's the opposite of me. If she was not going to follow my advice, I didn't see the point in talking."

"Another way to phrase that, Tom, is: 'If she didn't do what you told her to do, there was no point in having a relationship'."

"I guess so."

"If that was the message you sent her, that would explain why you never saw her."

"Could be." I ruefully admit to myself that Katherine is right. "Nothing like a pig-headed father."

"There are worse kinds. How old was she when she stopped following your orders?"

"Orders? You mean my well-reasoned, fatherly advice?"

"Advice can come across as orders to a young woman trying to establish her own identity."

"I don't know. She rebelled a little in high school. Dated guys she knew I didn't care for. Stayed out past her curfew a few times."

"All normal behaviour."

"I guess. We decided together where she was going to college."

"Did she want to go to college?"

The question startles me. "Of course, she wanted to go. Worked her little fanny off for good grades and took the SAT three times."

"Just checking. Sometimes our children do things just to try to please us."

"She liked college. Chose Wake Forest down in North Carolina. It wasn't until her senior year that the problems started."

"What sort of problems?"

"Stephanie was always good with languages. Picked them up easily. French, German, Spanish. Even a little Arabic. It was a unique skill, and I wanted her to pursue something in graduate school where she could use it."

"Did she want to go to graduate school?"

29

Another startling question. "Why not?" I demand. "A college degree by itself no longer cuts it in today's job market. You've got to make yourself stand out. She needed to go on to graduate school."

"Uh, huh."

I can tell Katherine disagrees with me by the tone of her voice, but I am on a roll.

"Stephanie kept refusing to commit to grad school. She put off taking the GRE. Wouldn't request her transcripts. Deadlines were coming up."

"But Daddy's little girl wasn't following your plan for her?"

Katherine is really starting to irritate me. "Look, after her mother died, it was just the two of us. She was the most important thing in my life, and I made sacrifices so that she could have the best possible life."

"But was it the life she wanted?"

I am taken aback; I had never thought of that question. "Why wouldn't she want to go on to grad school? Get it over with. Move on." I look at Katherine for empathy, but I cannot read her face. Women have a talent of disguising their emotions when they want to. She sits impassively, waiting patiently for me to continue spilling my guts to her. I carry on. "Things came to a head at graduation. I sat through the whole damn ceremony. The speaker, some CEO of an international company droned on and on about how this was the best moment of their lives and how they were all going to change the world. It wasn't the best moment of my life. It was hot, and I was sweating a river in a suit. I couldn't believe that there were so many kids graduating all at once and that they had to do it all outside."

Katherine nods. "That's the way those academics do it. Keep the kids in air conditioned comfort for four years, then force the parents to sit out in the heat to see them graduate."

"To top it off, her department gave her a special award. That especially annoyed me "

"Why?"

"She hadn't told me."

"Maybe she didn't know."

"Oh, she knew. She admitted later the department head had told her ahead of time. Claimed it was no big deal."

"Was it?"

"Yeeaah." I drag out the word as I slap my beer down on the counter harder than I mean to. Katherine's right eyebrow lifts, but I ignore it. "If she had had her grad school applications in, she could have gotten a full ride based on that award. By not getting her act together, she missed the window."

"Oh." Katherine's left eyebrow lifts to match her right. "And if she applied and got into grad school later, you would have had to pay full tuition."

"Not me. I made it clear that it was all on her. She had a golden opportunity, and she blew it."

"So you told her she had to pay for grad school?"

"Yep."

"How did she take that news?"

"Fine. Grad school was not on her event horizon."

"What *was* on her event horizon?"

"Learned about that when I took her to dinner that night."

"Did she bring the guy?"

I look at Katherine suspiciously. "How did you know there was a guy?"

"There's almost always a guy. I met my husband in college. All I'm going to say is that I did not graduate, and you know how that worked out for me. At least your daughter got her degree."

I hear the pain and regret in Katherine's voice, and I have to tread carefully. I had not wanted my daughter to make the mistake that Katherine had made, but I dare not say that to Katherine.

"To answer your question, she did not bring the guy. I sensed he was on stand by, though."

"Stand by?"

"A phone call away. Depending on how our conversation went."

"But the conversation at dinner did not go well?"

"We barely made it past the appetizers. When I pressed her about her future plans, she finally admitted to me that she had been dating an older guy who was now in med school. Her plan, as she called it, was to get a job waitressing to support him."

"And you told her that was not a good idea."

"Yes — except I think I used the word 'stupid' as I recall."

Katherine stares at me in horror. "You didn't!" she admonishes me.

I try to look repentant. "I'm afraid I did."

"Ah, I see. My father and I had a similar conversation my junior year of college. He was right, but I didn't listen to him."

"Well, I have no idea if I was right. It got pretty heated. I made the mistake of bringing up her mother and what she would say. That was too much for her, and she walked out. We didn't speak until she called last week."

Katherine whistles softly. We sit quietly for a moment thinking about long ago conversations. Finally, Katherine breaks the silence. "So you ghosted your daughter for eleven years because of that one argument?'

"Ghosted? I didn't haunt her. I left her alone."

Katherine shakes her head the way she does when I don't understand her. "Ghosting is slang for when you stop all communication with someone. It's usually a dating situation. Like when you want to stop seeing someone, but you don't want to hurt their feelings, so you just don't communicate hoping they will get the 'hint'."

"Oh. That's not what I intended. I feel stupid."

"You should." Katherine likes to hold my feet to the fire.

"Thanks," I say ruefully.

Katherine seems to be enjoying my discomfort. "What did the two of you talk about when she called?"

"She asked me to go on a bike trip."

"So, she's reaching out to you. That's a good sign. It means that she's forgiven you."

"Forgiven me for what?"

"For being a pig-headed father."

"Oh, that."

Katherine looks thoughtful. "A bike trip sounds like she wants to do something active so that the two of you are not just staring at each other. What are you going to do? Meet at a park and ride around for an hour?"

"Not exactly. She wants to bike from Pittsburgh to DC."

Katherine's jaw drops. "Isn't that like 400 miles?"

"334 point 5 is the official mileage."

"And you agreed to do this?"

"Yes."

"Are you insane?"

"You're not the first person to ask me that."

"Are you physically capable of biking that far?"

I take a long pull on my beer and swallow what little male pride I have left. "I honestly don't know, Katherine, but the way I see it, I don't have a choice. My daughter wants me to go on a bike trip, and if I want to have a relationship with her, I will have to sit on a bike for six days."

"In the sun."

"If necessary."

"And in the rain."

"Whatever it takes."

Katherine takes a sip of wine. "You do realize she's testing you."

"How so?"

"A bike trip like this is for someone much younger than you. She must know that and just wants to see how far you will go."

"So you think she will back out at the last minute?"

"Once she realizes that you are willing to do whatever to be with her, she'll let you off the hook."

"You don't know Stephanie. She would not have asked me if she did not want to do the trip. We used to do all kinds of outdoor things together: hiking, camping, whitewater rafting. We even did a high ropes course together. This bike trip is exactly the sort of thing she used to love to do with me."

"And you enjoyed it as well?"

"Oh, yeah!" I reply enthusiastically.

"When you were much younger."

"Yeah," I admit less enthusiastically.

"But you're older now, although not any wiser."

"Wise enough to ask *you* for advice."

"What sort of advice?"

"Advice on what I should talk to her about."

Katherine looks at me as if I had asked her to explain Einstein's theory of special relativity. "I haven't the foggiest idea of what you should talk to her about."

"But you're a woman — a mother. What do you talk to your daughter about?"

"It's not the same. I have mother/daughter conversations. Father/daughter conversations are quite different."

"Like how?"

"Like, to name just a few examples, my daughter and I talk about clothes, recipes, makeup, and guys."

"Ugh — sounds boring."

"It is," Katherine agrees. "Especially the part about guys."

"I need some help here," I plead. "I am not the world's most brilliant conversationalist."

Katherine cocks her head. "I don't know about that. I recall you talking me out of my clothes a few times."

"Okay — that's an entirely different conversation than the one I want to have with my daughter. I need some constructive suggestions."

"It's simple, Tom. Just ask her about her life. She will tell you what she wants you to know."

"What are some questions I should ask?" I pull out a pen and notepad to take notes.

Katherine shakes her head in frustration. "You really can be a nitwit. Ask her all the stuff you don't know. Ask her where she lives — does she like where she lives? — is she thinking about moving?. Ask her where she works — does she like where she works? — is she thinking about changing jobs? —"

"Could you slow down?" I interrupt her. I am writing furiously trying to get her suggestions on paper.

Katherine slides off her stool. She grasps my shoulders with both hands and shakes me. "You are hopeless!" She announces loudly. Then she punches me on the left side of my chest with her right palm. "Just talk to her from here." She

—

34

taps me gently on my forehead with in her index finger. "Not from here."

I look down at my shoes. "That's going to be hard for me," I admit.

"It is for most men." Katherine lifts my chin and cups my face with her hands. We stare into each other's eyes for a full minute. She kisses me on my forehead. "Now," she whispers, "Are you going to talk me out of my clothes tonight, or do I need to leave as a frustrated female?"

The Fourteenth Training Ride

I almost did not go this morning. It was raining. Not a hard rain, but enough moisture to make the roads slippery and my clothes damp. But both Hank and Katherine had predicted the distinct possibility that it was going to rain at some point during the trip. I needed to prepare myself.

After a couple of miles, I am glad I have ventured forth. The rain has cleared out most of the congestion on the bike trail. I do not see any parents pushing baby strollers or casual walkers meandering from side to side. Both hazards created obstacles that I really didn't want to navigate around on the slick path.

The rain stops, and the sun tries to come out from behind the clouds. Mud has washed up on the edges of the asphalt from the heavy precipitation that has fallen earlier, but the cooler air invigorates me. I push harder on my pedals, and the bike responds.

With my increased speed and few people about, I cut corners and fly down straight-a-ways. I pass two teenagers practicing tricks on their skateboards. The trees on either side of the trail become a green blur. *Nothing to this biking,* I think to myself.

I do not see him until I approach a particularly sharp curve to the left at a narrow portion of the trail. There is still plenty of room for two bikes to pass each other safely. However, I am moving fast (for me), and I have steered into his path to make the turn.

The Bike God is headed directly at me. He is dressed in bright yellow today. With his broad shoulders and narrow waist, his torso forms a muscled triangle. He is a giant yield sign bearing down on me. His head is up, and I know he sees me. I can see his thighs moving up and down in a steady rhythm. He makes no adjustments to his speed nor any attempt to turn. He is The Bike God. He is in the right, and I am in the wrong.

Slowing, I ease off on my turn and drift to the right. He thunders on, and I can feel the shock waves as he blows past me. I see no acknowledgment by him of our near miss, nor do I see the mud that blankets the right side of the curve in the bike path.

I clutch my handlebars in a death grip as I try to make a wider turn than I had planned but still remain on the asphalt. My front tire, though, finds no traction in the mud, and I continue in a straight line as the bike trail curves to the left.

In most parts of the Northern Delaware Greenway, my predicament would not have presented a major problem. I would have ended up cutting across a patch of grass or perhaps a concrete apron. Unfortunately for me, I had encountered The Bike God in a heavily wooded section. The green blur of the forest now becomes individual trees — large, hard immovable objects that rise from the ground to knock me off my bike seat. Trees are not my only problem. Fallen branches and rocks have created a malicious maze that I now had to navigate.

I squeeze between two trees that I did not think I would get through only to encounter a third tree with a thick trunk directly in my path. Steering around it to the left, I duck underneath an overhanging limb that swats my bare head as I pass underneath. I dodge one rock but hit another that launches me into the air. I come down hard just in time to turn to the right to avoid a fallen limb. During my whole flight through the forest, I have been squeezing my hand brakes as hard as I can with no discernible reduction in speed. I am fast approaching an area with boulders rather than rocks. In desperation I reach out and bear hug a passing tree. My bike and I come to a sudden — and abrupt — stop.

For some time, all I can hear is my heart pounding. I clutch the tree and take an inventory of my body parts. As far as I can tell, I have not broken anything on either the bike or my person. The only discernible damage appears to be deep scratches on my arms from the tree bark while the right side of my face feels raw.

"Whoa, dude, that was totally rad!"

"Totally!"

The words come from behind me. I twist around on my bike seat to see who is yelling at me. The voices belong to the two skateboarders that I had passed earlier. One was tall and lanky, the other short and on the beefy side. They are juiced about my little unplanned stunt and are talking over each other in their excitement.

"Man, I would never try that! It was totally sick."

"Not without a helmet. That was like insane."

"No way."

"Not me."

"But you bombed it!"

"Totally!"

They have followed me into the trees; their skateboards are tucked under their arms. Both wear helmets on their heads, although neither has the chin straps buckled. I did not know whether I preferred "sick" or "insane" as the description of my predicament.

"So you saw me go off the bike path?" I ask as I unwrap my arms from the tree trunk.

"Oh, yeah, we were looking for a place to do some jumps, and when you took off into the woods we thought you — being old school and local — might know some spots where we could catch some serious air. We followed you."

I start to ask them if they had seen The Bike God run me off the path, but I think better of it. "Following me can be dangerous," I comment.

"But, dude, you know where the jumps are."

I have no idea what he is talking about until the shorter one points at the rock that had launched me into the air. "You knew exactly which one to hit."

"And you totally nailed the landing!" his friend adds.

"Totally!" the short one agrees.

Pretending that I had planned my little cycling demonstration in the woods, I shrug nonchalantly as I unwrap myself from the tree and climb off my bike. I initiate a more thorough inspection of my bike. No broken frame parts. No flats. No dents. My ride looks good to go, but getting back to the path is going to be a slog.

"Grabbing the tree, dude, that was radly sketchy, but forget that, it was pretty clean." The shorter one stands next to me as if to help me with my inspection. "Yeah, snagging the tree cost you some sleaze points, but you more than made up for it with the raspberries there on your cheek. The chicks dig scrapes."

I gingerly touch my right cheek. My fingers come away with specks of red.

"Dude, you must be stoked. How long you been working on that?"

Pulling a bandana out of my pocket, I hold it to my face to staunch the bleeding. "Just today." I try to sound nonchalant.

"You gonna bomb it again? We could do a video."

I stare blankly at the shorter skateboarder. "I think I'm done for the day," I reply.

"Ah, dude, yeah, ABD!"

While I converse with the one skater, unable to decipher some of the terms he is using, the taller one has walked past us in the direction I had been headed. He stops a few feet away from the boulders I had grabbed the tree to avoid and called out, "You missed a big burly, dude." He is looking past the boulders where I cannot see.

Having no idea what he is talking about, I walk over to where the tall skater is standing. Just on the other side of the boulders, a deep ravine cuts through the hillside. If I had been able to navigate the boulders without crashing into them and destroying myself and my bike, I would have found myself cascading fifty feet or so down the side of this ravine where more large rocks awaited me at the bottom. I might have lain down there for hours waiting for someone to find me and haul my broken body to the emergency room — if not the morgue.

Instead, my two new friends help me haul my bike back to the path where we part ways.

As I pedal at a more moderate pace back home and work out the aches and pains in my body, I translate "big burly" into "big hurt".

Round Two with Hank

Hank and I have gathered for our weekly hamburger fix at Tomfoolery. He arrives late as usual.

"So how's the training coming along?" Hank starts the conversation with a smirk on his face.

"Great," I reply. "I'm up to watching five Tour de France videos a day. Pretty soon I will be able to watch it live."

"That sounds like progress." Hank tilts his head and examines the scratch marks on the right side of my face. "What happened to you? It looks like you got into a fight with a cat."

"A tree attacked me."

"Uh, huh." Hank settles into his seat and looks at my arms. I have wrapped my forearms in gauze and an ace bandage to prevent infection. Hank points at them. "Did the tree do that as well?"

"Yeah." Self conscious, I stick my arms under the table.

Hank purses his lips. "I suggest you stay away from dangerous things like trees."

"I was minding my own business," I protest.

"I'm sure you were."

The waitress stops by. "The usual, gentlemen?" she inquires.

I look up sheepishly at her. "Yes, we'll each have the burger special, and my friend will want his Bud Light, but I'll just have water."

"Okay," she shrugs and disappears into the kitchen.

A horrified look spread across Hank's face. "You're not having a beer today?"

"Nope. The alcohol dehydrates the body, and I need to get this body in shape. Even if it kills me," I add with a smile.

39

"Are you serious about doing this bike trip?"

"Afraid so."

"I thought you were going to talk your daughter out of this insanity."

"I tried. All I could do was convince her to skip the camping."

"But you're still going to do the biking?"

"Yeah."

"For six days straight?"

All I can do is nod my head.

Hank lays his forearms on the table, and his face gets serious. "Tom, the sun is going to fry the brains inside your skull into a gray mush. Then, the rainstorms are going to wash them out through your nasal passages."

"That's a pleasant thought," I muse.

"And have you thought of your butt?"

"Not recently."

"You are going to have that skinny little bike seat rammed up between your buns for eight hours a day. Your thighs are going to burn like hell from pumping those pedals all day."

"You make it sound like I'm going to be making a porno movie."

Our drinks arrive at that very moment, and I can tell that the waitress has heard me say "porno movie". While she smiles at Hank, she gives me the disappointed "I didn't think you were a dirty old man" look.

Thankfully, Hank switches topics. He is a diehard — some would say obnoxious — Philly sports fan. Others would say that all Philly sports fans are obnoxious. As it is summer, he is whining about the Philly pitching staff. I commiserate with him, agreeing that they are nothing but overpaid bums who wear their hair too long. Unfortunately for me, I make a comment about some of them wearing tattoos where the sun does not shine just as the waitress appears with our burgers. She refuses to look at me when she asks us if there is anything else we need. I have the distinct impression she wants to pour my glass of water over my head.

Hank grabs the mustard and ketchup and squeezes generous portions of each onto the buns of his burger. He offers them to me, but I decline with a shake of my head.

I — on the other hand — carefully remove the buns of my burger and set them aside. Making the lettuce, tomato slices, and pickles into a small salad, I pick up my knife and fork and start cutting up my burger patty.

Hank stares at me dumbfounded. "What are you doing?"

"There's at least 200 calories in that bun."

"Since when have you started counting calories?"

"Since I decided to go on a bike trip with my daughter."

"I thought we decided you were going to talk her out of that idea. Go on a cruise or something more reasonable."

"Yeah, well, that didn't go too well."

"And you think riding fifty to sixty miles a day on a bike for six days straight is going to go any better?"

I shrug. "A man's gotta do what a man's gotta do." I carefully slide my fries off of my plate onto his. "I won't be eating these either."

Hank looks from the cornucopia of fries that now cover his plate to the pitiful portions of food on mine. "You have totally lost your mind," he announces.

"Not really. I just need to lose some weight."

Shaking his head, Hank starts in on his — our — fries. "So tell me how it went. Did you get her to reduce the mileage or extend the number of days?"

"No. I think she's set on doing the whole distance, and she only has so many days of vacation. However, I did talk her into letting me sponsor her on a charity bike ride."

"Really?"

"Yeah. Apparently, I'm going to donate $250 so that lab rats are not harmed in cancer research."

Hank eyes me curiously with a fry hanging from the corner of his mouth. "I thought they sacrificed those mice to save human lives."

"Don't get me started."

"I should let you negotiate my next real estate deal," Hank suggests sarcastically.

"Dads never do well when trying to negotiate with their own daughters."

"True," Hank agrees. "So how many months do you have to get ready for this bike trip?

"I have weeks, not months."

"That's not enough time."

"Tell me about it. I'm going out on the bike twice a day. My legs are sore, but my lower back feels better."

Hank reaches into his pocket, withdraws a bottle of pills, and slaps them on the table. "I have one word of advice for you, young man."

My eyes dart from the bottle of pills to Hank's face and then back to the bottle. I feel like I am an actor in the scene from the movie *The Graduate* when Dustin Hoffman was told that the future lay in plastics. "And that word is?" I ask meekly.

"Advil."

"I see."

"You can have the rest of that bottle. Take one tablet every four hours. It will numb your body to what you are doing to it."

"Thanks."

"Don't mention it. I hate to see a buddy in pain."

I nod, but something puzzles me. "Did you just happen to have this bottle of pills in your pocket, or did you bring them especially for me?"

"That Advil? I carry a bottle with me everywhere I go. Helps me get through the day."

I push the bottle of Advil in his direction. "Here, take it back," I insist. "I'll get some of my own. I don't want to leave you without your meds."

"Don't worry about me," Hank assures me. "I've got back up." With a grin, he fishes another bottle of pills out of his pocket and flashes the Aleve label in my direction. "If the Advil doesn't knock out the pain, the Aleve will."

"Okay." I smile ruefully. "Any other pearls of wisdom?" I ask.

"Yeah, but they would be wasted on you."

Hank and I eat in silence for a while. That is fine with me, but being silent isn't in Hank's nature.

I have just about finished my meager meal when he asks, "Sure you don't want some of these fries?"

"Oh, I want them," I admit. "I just can't have them."

Hank slowly masticates one of his fries. Actually, it was probably one of *my* fries, and I say masticated because he was thoroughly chewing it. Hank usually inhaled his fries by the bushel. I can tell he is thinking. He is looking at me the same way a cow looks at you while chewing its cud and sees you stumbling through its pasture. It knows you're lost — and you know you're lost — and it's wondering why the good lord made two-legged creatures so stupid.

Hank finally swallows his bite and states the obvious. "This bike ride is real important to you."

I cannot tell if his sentence is a statement or a question. "It's my daughter, Hank. You know you will do things for your daughter that you will not do for anyone else. Not your son. Not your wife. Not even your own mother."

"How about your best friend?"

"Especially not *my* best friend."

Hank gives me a faux hurt look, but he nods his understanding. He picks up his beer and swirls around his last sip. I can tell that he is looking at the scratches on my face. "So tell me, will there be any trees near this bike trail you're going on?"

"Hundreds, if not thousands."

"You, my man, are headed for a world of trouble."

I nod in agreement.

Second Dinner with Katherine

When a man lives without female supervision for a number of years the way I have, he gets sloppy. He "forgets" to pick up his dirty clothes, to bathe regularly, and to eat vegetables. Instead, he watches too much sports, sleeps longer than he should, and wears whatever he first sees in his closet — which is usually what he wore the day before.

I enjoy living without female supervision; it feels liberating. Liberating in the way jumping out of an airplane feels. Not that I have ever jumped out of an airplane, but I can imagine what it feels like. Nothing between you and the ground far below. Nothing but air blowing past you. It must feel wonderful — something you want to do again. But to do it again — and not be smashed into tiny pieces — you need a parachute. A parachute that you know will open and that it will not have holes in it. Feeling liberated is great but you have to be able to survive it. You need a reliable parachute.

Katherine is my parachute — a smart, beautiful woman who can cook. She greets me at the door to her condo.

"What happened to you?"

She is staring at the scratches on the side of my face.

"I got into a fight with a raccoon."

"A raccoon? Where did you find a raccoon around here?"

"Could have been a cat — it was a furry critter with claws."

"Did these come from the cat?"

She points at my arms. I have removed the gauze. Angry red lines run down my forearms.

"Hmmm. 'Fraid so."

"What did you do to that poor cat?"

I have forgotten that Katherine is an inveterate animal lover.

"Actually, it was a tree."

"What did you do to the poor tree?"

I have also forgotten that Katherine is an inveterate tree lover.

"Nothing. I just wanted to give it a hug."

"When did you become a tree hugger?"

"When one of them saved my life."

Fortunately, she decides to drop the matter — at least for now — and lets me in. As I enter, my nostrils are overwhelmed with wonderful aromas wafting from her kitchen. "Smells good," I comment.

"I hope you like it. It's a new recipe."

I follow her into the kitchen.

"What's on the menu?"

"Wild rice, grilled asparagus, and a turkey tenderloin covered in a cracked pepper sauce."

"And dessert?"

"If you use your good table manners tonight, you can have me."

"I say we start with dessert." I reach for her, but she slips away with a little laugh.

"You need to eat a good meal first. I want you to have lots of strength and stamina tonight."

"Oh, really?"

"Most definitely." Katherine smiles at me as she pulls a frosted mug out of her freezer and starts to open a beer. It is one of my favorite microbrews, but I stop her.

"Can I have something else?"

Katherine looks at me as if I am a stranger. "Isn't this your favorite beer?"

"One of them," I admit. "But I'm trying to cut back."

She eyes me suspiciously. "Why?"

"Just trying to get in shape, that's all."

Understanding dawns on her. "For your bike trip?"

I nod sheepishly.

"In that case, how about a lemonade laced with mint?"

"Sounds delicious."

"It is." As she pours my nonalcoholic drink, she glances at me. "Do you know what you're going to say to your daughter?"

I take the glass she offers me and steal a taste before answering. "Whoa, that's tart."

"Too tart?"

"Almost, but still drinkable. I prefer my women tart — and my drinks smooth."

Katherine brushes her hand across my cheek, checking for beard stubble. "And I like my drinks tart — and my men smooth."

We kiss.

Neither one of us wants to stop, and dinner would have been delayed but my stomach starts growling. Our kissing ends with laughter.

"I think I better feed the beast," Katherine says. As she fixes our plates, she reminds me over her shoulder. "You didn't answer my question."

"Question?"

"Do you know what you're going to say to your daughter?"

"About what?"

Katherine turns around and menacingly waves a large carving knife in my direction. "About how you've been a schmuck for not contacting her for eleven years!"

Her eyes have gone from seeking love to contemplating murder.

"I guess I should start with an apology?" I suggest hopefully.

"And then?"

I think for minute. "Another apology?"

Katherine is shaking her head. "You are absolutely hopeless. What happened to the questions about what has happened in her life over the past decade?"

"Oh, yeah." I grimace. "I think I lost my notes. Can we go over the questions I'm supposed to ask?"

"I doubt that will do any good. Have you thought about why she called?"

I shrug. "She wants to go on a bike ride."

"After eleven years? I think this is about more than a bike ride."

"Is this a woman's intuition thing?"

"More of a mother's intuition."

"So what is your mother's intuition telling you?"

"That something has happened in her life that makes her want to reestablish her relationship with you."

I had considered that thought on some of my training rides. "Yeah, could be. I just don't have a clue."

"So you're hopeless *and* clueless?"

Katherine is still waving the large carving knife around as she speaks. I elect to be agreeable to avoid being stabbed. Sexually frustrated women can be dangerous. I learned that a long time ago from the movie *Basic Instinct*.

"Afraid so."

"Here's an idea: She's getting married and wants you to walk her down the aisle."

"Nice thought, but I doubt it. She could just have sent me an invitation."

"How about she's pregnant? She plans to keep the baby but not marry the father."

I sigh. "That happens a lot in our world these days."

"But it hasn't happened to *your* world. Makes a world of difference when it's *your* daughter."

I contemplate Katherine's suggestion. My daughter had observed first hand the struggles of an inept single parent. Perhaps she was reaching out to me for help.

"True. It's a possibility," I admit.

"Here's another possibility: She's been diagnosed with cancer and only has a few months to live."

My eyes widen. "Aren't you Little Miss Sunshine?"

"Do you know how many women die of breast cancer every year?"

"That statistic escapes me."

"Over 40,000 in the US alone."

"I did not realize the number was so high."

"It's a serious problem."

"Sounds like it."

"Speaking of which, have you checked with your doctor?"

"About what?"

To my relief, Katherine finally sets the large carving knife down. "About what we've been talking about — going on this crazy bike trip."

I carefully select a grape from the bowl on the counter and bite into it while I pretend to think about her question. "Nah, I don't think he would want to go."

Perturbed, Katherine grabs one of my scratched forearms to get my attention.

"Ouch!" I try to withdraw my arm, but she grips it tighter, her carefully manicured nails digging in slightly.

"I don't mean whether your doctor will go with you on this insane adventure, but whether he thinks *you* should go."

"Why shouldn't I go?"

"Because you might have a heart attack out in the middle of the wilderness." She squeezes my forearm, and I wince. I am thinking that I am going to have a heart attack in Katherine's kitchen if she puts any more pressure on my arm.

"I haven't seen my doctor in a while." I admit meekly.

"What? How long?" To my relief, she lets go of my arm.

"A year. Maybe longer."

"How much longer?"

Katherine has picked up the large carving knife again.

"Probably close to three years ago."

"A man of your age should be getting annual check ups." She is back to waving the knife in making her conversational points. "You could be the one with cancer, buddy, and not even know it."

The tip of the knife is pointing directly at me.

"Could we rewind this conversation to the point when we were kissing?" I ask.

"Not until we've eaten this delicious dinner I've prepared."

"And then we can get back to the kissing?"

"Only if I hear how wonderful the food is."

"And then?"

"Only if you promise to see your doctor before you go on this bike trip."

"Okay, then. If I promise to see the doctor and I tell you your cooking would make Martha Ray jealous, then can we get back to the kissing?" I carefully extract the large carving knife from Katherine's fist and slide it down the counter out of reach. Taking her in my arms, I ask, "Is that a deal?"

"Maybe."

Katherine is looking directly into my eyes. Her lips have parted slightly.

"I promise, and the food is delicious," I say softly.

"How can you say the food is delicious when you haven't tasted it yet?"

"I haven't seen the doctor yet, either." I say this as I move in slowly, anticipating a protest. Getting none, I proceed in. The kissing and its aftermath cause a serious delay to dinner. But I am watching my diet after all.

A Visit to the Doctor

I enter the Golden Horizon Medical Professional Building sharply at 7:30 AM, when the security guard opens the front doors. The directory has changed since I've been here, and it takes me a while to find my doctor's name. He's moved up to the top floor. Must be doing well.

I come out of the elevator and enter a massive waiting area. At the far end is a receptionist behind a glass window. I stride over and tap on the glass. The woman behind the glass slides open the window.

"May I help you?"

"Yes, I'd like to see Dave, please."

She gives me a puzzled look. "Dave? Do you mean Dr. Berman? As in Dr. David Berman?"

She emphasizes the last sentence, especially the title doctor.

I have always had trouble dealing with officious people, and this woman reeks of officiousness. Although I am sure that she is quite capable in performing her job — which is primarily to keep chumps like me away from important people like doctors — I need to get an "all clear" so that Katherine will speak to me when — if — I return from the bike trip with my daughter. I decide to invoke politeness and my little boy charm.

I smile as sweetly as I can before 8 AM in the morning and say, "Yes, that's the one."

"Do you have an appointment?" The receptionist is all business. She is smart enough to realize that I am trouble, and it is too early in the morning for trouble.

"Ah, no. Just tell Dave that I'm here, and I'm sure he'll be able to squeeze me in. That's why I came so early."

She is having none of my little boy charm. "Dr. Berman is a very busy man. If you don't have an appointment, he won't be able to see you today."

I decide to make a strategic retreat as I still have a week before the bike trip. "Can I make an appointment with you for the next available time slot for Dave — er, Dr. Berman?"

"Of course." I finally get something of a happy face. "May I see your insurance card and photo ID?"

"Why do you need to see that for an appointment?"

"Office policy."

"That makes no sense — " My voice trails off as I observe the bland smile on the receptionist's face. She is not going to budge until I produce the requested documents. I have trouble finding the insurance card in my wallet, but fortunately it is there. When I hand it to the receptionist, her happy face dims.

"This card has expired."

I frown. "Well, I know I pay the premium every month. Just call that number on the back, and I am sure they will confirm coverage."

"Okay, " she says slowly. "What did you want to see the doctor about?"

"I want to ask him how his golf game is."

The happy face disappears completely.

"Just a general physical," I say sheepishly.

The receptionist flips through a paper calendar, looks at a computer screen, and clicks on her keyboard. Then she looks up at me. "I have an opening with Dr. Berman the last week of October. Would you like to take that one?"

I feel my jaw drop slightly "But it's July now," I protest.

"Like I said, Dr. Berman is a busy man."

"Nothing sooner?"

She glances at her computer screen. "Some of his associates have openings in September."

I drop the little boy charm as it is having no effect on this woman. "October doesn't work for me. September doesn't work for me. I need to see *Dave* this week."

The receptionist does not bother to refer to her computer screen. "*Dr. Berman* does not have any availability this week."

"What if I had broken my leg, and I was here to see *Dave* for that?"

I am hurling *Dave* at her, and she is retaliating with *Dr. Berman.*

"Sir, if you have a broken leg, I will call you an ambulance immediately to take you to the emergency room."

A line has formed behind me, and I see the possibility of an opportunity for me. "I haven't broken my leg, but I will stop bothering you and let these fine people behind me have the pleasure of conversing with you if you will do one little thing for me."

"And that is?" She asks frostily.

"That you tell *Dr. Berman* that Tom Reynolds is here, and that he is going to break one of his legs unless he sees him today." I give her my broadest and friendliest grin.

"That would be my pleasure." The words come out in small chunks of ice.

"Thank you."

I turn, and the woman behind me looks horrified, probably because of my remark about breaking one of Dave's legs.

"He owes me money," I tell her.

I find a chair next to a pile of *Sports Illustrated* magazines. As I may be here awhile, I settle in. I am only halfway through an article about the mounting legal troubles of Lance Armstrong — a guy who truly fell off his bike — when I hear my name called.

The prim little nurse escorts me to the standard medical examining room. She weighs me and then asks my height. I lie, but she records the extra two inches I give myself without batting an eye. She takes my temperature and blood pressure. After putting them into the tablet she is carrying, she tells me the doctor will be with me in a minute and leaves.

I figure I will be sitting and waiting long enough for a quick nap. My eyes are barely closed when Dave barges in. He slaps down a bill with Alexander Hamilton's face on it.

"I thought you'd forgotten about that bet," he announces.

"I never forget a bet," I reply. "But it was for twenty bucks, not ten."

"I deducted my fee for seeing you without an appointment."

We grin and shake hands.

"How's Louise?" I ask.

"Louise is great. And you? How are you?"

My relationship with Dave went back — way back. Dave and Louise and Nancy and I did all kinds of things together. We bought houses across the street from each, had each other over for dinner, started families about the same time, took a ski trip to Colorado together. Louise and Nancy could walk and talk for hours. Dave and I could sit and drink beer for hours. I always knew I could rely on Dave, and Dave knew he could rely on me — well, most of the time he could.

Dave and Louise were a big help with Stephanie when I became a single parent. Steph spent quite a few afternoons and evenings at their house while I pretended to be off at work. As Stephanie transformed from a little girl in pigtails to a young woman who wanted a training bra, I relied on Louise to fill in the giant gaping hole left after Nancy died.

When Steph left for college, I knew I had to make a change. The house was too big for one guy, and it held too many memories of the women I loved — women who no longer lived with me. I got a smaller place, said goodbye to Louise, and promised Dave that I would see him once a year for my annual physical. It was one of many promises I failed to keep.

All of those years of memories flood my brain in the seconds that passed as I consider how to answer Dave's question.

"Steph called me," I hear myself saying.

"How is she doing?"

Dave is all smiles, wearing the expression of someone who has the pleasure of seeing an old friend showing up unannounced in his waiting room.

I pick at some nonexistent lint on my trousers. "I really don't know." I have to be honest with Dave. He's not just my friend — friends have to be lied to from time to time — he's my doctor. "We haven't spoken in years."

A look of concern replaces the smiling expression on Dave's face. "How many years?"

"Eleven." I try to sound matter of fact.

Dave sees right through me. He lets his glasses slide down the bridge of his nose so that he can look me straight in the eye. "What happened?"

"Nothing. As in I said some stupid things, and then I did nothing. So we stopped communicating."

"Oh." Dave's face is asking for more information.

"But we're talking now. She called me!" I try to sound perky. "And we're going on a bike trip together!"

I can tell that Dave also sees right through my feigned perkiness. "That's great. I guess that's why you're here to see me."

"Yes. That and I was ordered to appear before you."

"Ordered?"

"By Katherine."

"Katherine?"

As Dave and I have not been in communication, he does not know about her or our relationship.

"Katherine is my friend."

"Who orders you to see your doctor? Must be a special kind of friend." Dave seems bemused that I have a female friend.

"Katherine *is* special, but I prefer to use the term unique. She wants an all clear for me to go on this bike trip."

"Is she going on this bike trip?"

"Katherine? No, just Steph and me."

"And you haven't spoken to Stephanie in eleven years?"

"Yeah."

"Sounds like fun. I'll write you a prescription." He pulls out a pad, scribbles on it, rips the page off, and hands it to me.

I read it. The note states: "Go on a bike ride with Stephanie."

"That's it? You're not going to draw blood or something?"

"Do you want me to draw blood?"

"Not really."

"Then go on this bike ride with your daughter. Where is this trip?"

I glance down at my "prescription" and then back up at Dave. Despite being my friend, he's a smart guy. He's a doctor after all. I suspect he is setting a trap for me.

"Pittsburgh," I answer him.

"Lots of hills around Pittsburgh."

"So I hear. That's why we're biking to D.C."

"Isn't that like 300 miles?"

"334 point 5."

Dave whistles and adjusts his glasses. He sizes me up. "Can I see that prescription I just wrote you?"

I hand it to him. He writes one word on it and hands it back. The word "short" has been inserted between "a" and "bike". I nod and look at Dave. He is looking at me over the rim of his glasses. He did not have glasses that night at the hospital. We were younger and closer. He had sat with me for hours as a friend, not a doctor. He had heard the news about Nancy with me. We had cried together: grown men sobbing in a hospital waiting room. But that was decades ago.

This morning, he was sitting again with me as a friend and not a doctor. I can see tears welling up in his eyes. I struggle to hold it together.

"I miss Nancy," he says softly.

"I do, too."

We grip each other's shoulders, desperately trying to give each other strength.

"I have to go on this bike trip, Dave," I whisper.

"Then go on the bike trip," he replies.

"I don't know if I can do it," I admit.

"Sure you can. The Tom Reynolds I know will find a way."

We sit together for a moment as we try to regain our composure. I pull away first, tug on the sleeves of my shirt, and say, "Sorry, man, you've got real patients to see."

"True."

Dave turns away from me and starts tapping on a computer keyboard. "Who have you been seeing besides me? We need to get their records."

I start slightly. "Dave, you're my doctor. I haven't gone to anybody else. You make it sound like I've been cheating on you."

"If that's the case, the only one you've been cheating is yourself. Do you know the last time you saw me?"

"A couple of years ago?"

"Try over five years. A guy your age should get an annual physical. Your weight and blood pressure are tolerable, but I'll give you odds that you're triglycerides are off the chart. And have you had a colon screening?"

"Uh, no."

"Flu shot?"

"Don't like needles."

"Then I won't ask about the shingles vaccination. Let's get started. I have a long series of questions to ask you. And there will be a number of tests. As you said, I have real patients to see."

He has sprung the trap on me. Dave was always a clever fellow — quick with the appropriate repartee. He never failed to make Nancy laugh when we were all together. I will have to submit to his health inquisition, but there is something I have to do first — something I often fail to do with old friends — show a little gratitude.

"Thanks for seeing me, Dave."

He turns away from the computer screen to face me.

"You won't thank me when you get my bill."

The Thirty Something Training Ride

The day is gloriously sunny but oppressively hot. Dave (Dr. Berman) has cleared me for takeoff, and I am ready to get back to work on getting in shape. Although I had given a passing thought to wearing my bike helmet this afternoon, I much prefer a cooler baseball cap. In fact, I had not worn the helmet during any of my training rides as I had not taken the trouble to look for it despite my earlier encounter with the tree. Just another piece of gear to keep track of as far as I was concerned. Yes, I had chosen comfort and convenience over safety for not the first time in my life.

My ride goes smoothly, and I will soon reach the turnaround point of today's workout. For most of the time the wind has been in my face, and I am looking forward to having it at my back. Still, my mileage is improving with less than a week to go before I head over to D.C. to see Stephanie for the first time in eleven years. The thought of our meeting face to face makes me nervous, but I am also eagerly anticipating being with her for the next week. I have just got to be able to do the daily bike mileage.

Despite the protests from my aching thighs, I push down harder on the pedals. I am slowly picking up speed when I hear an ominous hissing sound coming from below me. My bike slows and grows sluggish. I glance down. To my chagrin, I see my rear tire collapsing. I stop. The tire rapidly loses all its air. I have a flat miles from home.

This catastrophe could not have happened at a worse spot. I am almost at the farthest point from my house. I chose a route today through a residential area with few if any commercial places where I might be able to get the flat fixed. I have ventured forth without my cell phone. I have no patch kit, no spare inner tube, and no pump.

Even if I had what I need, I doubt that I would remember how to pull off the wheel, remove the inner tube, find the leak, patch the leak, inflate the tire, reinsert the tube into the tire, and then reinstall the wheel. The thought that I am totally unprepared for a bike trip of over three hundred miles crosses my mind, but I try to stay positive. I have a long walk ahead of me — pushing a bike.

The day remains gloriously sunny and just as oppressively hot. Without the cooling breeze generated from pedaling the bike, I heat up, and rivulets of sweat pour down my back. I try to enjoy the day as I walk, bit I frequently scrape my calf on my pedal. *Walking is good exercise,* I remind myself.

I am about halfway home, still miles away, when I see him appear over a rise headed in my direction. He is wearing his trademark blue and gold spandex, and sunlight glints off the frame of his pedal-powered chariot. The Bike God will soon roar by me. Needing a rest and remembering what happened to me last time I encountered him, I pull off to the side and wait for him to whizz past.

The cadence of his pedaling is smooth and effortless, and it propels him forward with graceful speed. Such power cannot be impaired by a stiff headwind or a steep climb. I brace for the shockwave as he passes me.

To my surprise, he comes to a complete stop about ten feet from where I stand. I have a chance to size him up, mortal to immortal. He seems to be doing the same, immortal to mortal. With The Bike God stationary, I can see things that I could not when he was in flight. I observe two features of his face that I had not noticed before: his eyes resemble those of a peregrine falcon that instill fear in men and his chin has a dimple that women must swoon over. I feel myself unconsciously sucking in my gut and trying to stand more erect. He is still at least six inches taller than me.

We stand there observing each other for a few seconds, before he speaks.

"Flat?"

"Yeah." I shrug as I reply.

"Patch?"

"Not carrying any with me."

"Spare?"

"Don't have one of those either."

"Pump?"

"Nope."

The guy speaks less than Clint Eastwood in *A Few Dollars More*. Four one word questions that quickly summarize my predicament. I cannot tell from The Bike God's expression whether my human frailty amuses or annoys him.

He smoothly dismounts from his chariot and leans it against a tree. From circular motions he makes with his hands, I understand that he wants me to flip my bike upside down. I comply.

As his hands move quickly over my bike, I stand back and watch him work. He unhooks my brakes, flips the levers securing my rear wheel, and effortlessly frees my flat tire from the chain. His fingers compress the sides of the tire and then start separating the rubber from the rim.

"Don't you need a screwdriver or something to get the tire off?" I ask.

The Bike God ignores my suggestion. Instead, he uses his fingers like steel rods to pry the tire off the rim in about 35 seconds. I have accomplished the same task before, but I had had to struggle for fifteen minutes with two screwdrivers and lots of swear words. The Bike God had used his fingers and said nothing.

After pulling the flaccid tube from inside the tire, The Bike God runs the steel index finger of his right hand around the inside of the tire. I hear a faint grunt, and he produces an inch long thorn. He offers it to me for my inspection. While I am looking at the thorn, he is examining the limp tube, slowly going over every inch. I hear another faint grunt. He shows me where the thorn penetrated the tube.

The Bike God walks over to his chariot and extracts a patch, a small piece of sandpaper, and a tiny tube of glue from a pouch behind his saddle. I watch him scuff the pierced tube around the miniscule hole that stopped my ride. He applies a thin layer of glue where he has scuffed the tube.

Looking up from his work while he waits for the glue to dry, he stares at me. I try to meet his gaze, but I am ashamed of my incompetence and grateful for his help. His eyes reveal no emotion, neither disdain nor empathy. Without looking down, he applies the patch on top of the glue and holds it in place for what seems an eternity. Finally, he checks the edges of the patch and retrieves a pump that is attached to the frame of his chariot. With a few quick strokes, he has my tube partially inflated and inserts it into the tire. His steel fingers now pry and prod the tire back onto its wheel. He slides the wheel into place on my bike, deftly catching the chain into the correct sprocket.

The small hand pump would take me half an hour to fully inflate my tire, but he seems to accomplish the same feat in less than a minute. He flips my bike right side up and checks that my brakes are reattached. A curt nod indicates that he has finished his work.

I examine my repaired tire. It is good to go. I feel that The Bike God deserved something more than a simple thank you, but he might have been insulted if I offered him money.

"Thanks, man, I really appreciate this. You saved my ass."

The Bike God says nothing and does nothing to acknowledge my gratitude. Instead, he taps the side of his helmeted head. "You wear helmet, no."

"No -- I mean -- yes," I stutter. "I will wear a helmet." I had heard a foreign accent. Of course, I think, no god would be an American.

"Good."

I may have detected the hint of a smile, but it is hard to look into the face of a deity. The Bike God turns and seems to float back to his chariot. In one smooth motion, he remounts and is off.

Alone with my bike, I reach down and squeeze the repaired tire to check its inflation level. I could get home quickly now, but I also consider completing my ride. With a turn of my handlebars, I head back to finish what I had started, trying all the while to remember what I had done with my bike helmet.

Hank Round Three

Hank and I are having our last meal before I headed down to DC to join Stephanie for our grand adventure. While I nurse my burger patty and sip water, Hank is enjoying his burger and fries as well as my fries. All of which he is washing down with a frosty cold beer that I salivate over.

"So next week you're headed down to DC to start your bike trip," Hanks says with a big grin.

"That's the plan," I confess.

He leans forward and whispers conspiratorially, "You know you can call me."

I pause in my eating. "Call you?" I ask.

"Yeah — you know — if you find yourself in over your head."

"You think I can't handle six days on a bike?"

Hank raises his hands defensively. "Look, if any overweight, out of shape, over the hill guy can do this trip, you can."

"I'm not sure if that's a compliment or an insult."

"All I'm saying is that you just might find yourself in a situation where you need extraction."

"You make it sound like a military operation."

"If you find yourself under fire and taking casualties, I just want you to know that I'll come rescue you."

Hank has turned his head sideways and is looking at me out of the corners of his eyes. He is showing his caring side, and guys had to be careful when they did that. It makes them vulnerable.

"Thanks, Hank. I appreciate the offer, but I think I will be fine."

Hank relaxes and nibbles on one of his fries. He seems relieved that I have declined his offer. "Of course," he continues, "if I did have to come pick you up, I would feel compelled to remind you — during the course of our journey home — that I did not think this trip was a good idea."

"Yes, I imagine that you would deliver that message every ten miles."

"More like every five miles — and I like to drive *real* slow when I'm reminding people that I was right."

"Sounds like if you do come and pick me up, it will be the longest ride of my life."

"Just know that the offer is open."

"Comforting," I snort. "If anything, that offer will motivate me to keep pedalling until my feet fall off my legs."

"See," Hank smiles snidely, "I'm already helping you, but that's not all."

"I don't think I could handle any more of your assistance, Hank," I protest.

Hank waves his palms at me. "My pleasure. I need to do what I can for my best buddy." He pulls out his cell phone and swipes through several screens to find what he wants. "Here it is!" he announces triumphantly.

I think about retrieving one of my fries from his plate but think better of it.

"Would you like to know the weather report for next week when you go on your little excursion?" he asks.

"Not really," I reply. Giving in to my hunger pangs, I reach for a fry sticking out from the large pile on Hank's plate, but he slaps my hand away.

"No, you don't," he scolds me. "You're not breaking training on my watch."

I slump back in my chair and proceed to sulk like a teenager who has just been told he has been grounded and cannot go out on Friday night.

"Listen up, so you will be mentally prepared." Hank puts on his reading glasses and starts reciting the weather report on his cell phone screen. "A heat alert has been issued to include parts of 21 states as a 'heat dome' is expected to hover over much of the nation later this week, with some places forecast to reach up to a dangerous 115 degrees."

Hank pauses and peers at me over the rim of his glasses. "I'm pretty sure that's Fahrenheit."

I shrug, pretending indifference although I am weighing the odds of successfully snitching a fry from his plate while he is reading his cell phone screen.

He resumes. "The sizzling heat index — a measure of how hot it feels when humidity is factored in with the actual air temperature — will first hit parts of the central U.S. during the latter half of the week and will then spread toward the Northeast and mid-Atlantic late this week into the weekend."

Again, Hank pauses and peers at me over the rim of his glasses. "That means the time frame when you will be on your bike for eight to ten hours during the middle of the day."

I just glare at him; I have never seen anyone enjoy reading a weather report as much as Hank is. He goes on anyway.

"The intense weather is the result of an atmospheric phenomenon called a heat dome — a ridge, or high-pressure system, that traps hot air underneath it — creating unusually hot and humid conditions. Most of the eastern United States will continue to swelter with above-average temperatures into the end of the month. Highs during the last part of July typically range from the middle 80s to near 90 degrees Fahrenheit across much of the region. High temperatures in many areas will average 5-10 degrees above normal and will be close to 15 degrees above normal in some locations. With no strong pushes of cool air from Canada on the horizon, people from the mid-Atlantic to the Deep South can expect virtually no relief from the high heat and humidity."

I make a move for one of his fries, but my supposed good friend deftly slides his platter of fries out of my reach. Hank finishes his recitation of the weather report with an air of satisfaction and puts away his cell phone.

"So, to sum up," I say with only a tinge of sarcasm, "It will be hotter than Hades next week."

"Actually," Hank waves a french fry in the air as if to taunt me, "Hades will be a shade cooler than where you are headed."

"Thanks for the information."

"My pleasure."

"Anything else you want to share with me?"

"Yes, I have a gift."

"A gift?"

"To help you with the heat on your trip."

"You bought me a portable air conditioning unit?"

"In a manner of speaking." Hank places a small package on the table and slides it over to me. It is neatly wrapped in slick paper that utilizes every color in the rainbow. A large unicorn decorates the top.

"Did you wrap this?" I inquire.

"Of course not. I got my eight year old neighbor to do it. She's into bright colors and —"

"Unicorns," I finish his sentence. Using my dinner knife, I open one end of the package and pull out the box inside. The box has a picture of its contents: a battery operated fan. I pull it out of the box and hold it up.

"Do you like it?" Hank asks eagerly. "I think you're going to find it useful. There's an attachment where you can put it on the front of your bike."

The fan is in the shape of a tiny biplane piloted by a bear. The soft, rubber propellers serve as the blades of the fan. I press a small button on the side. The propellers whirl, and the resulting breeze blows our paper napkins onto the floor. The bear waves his right paw in time with the spinning of the propellers. Small red lights on the tips of the wings and the tail flash.

62

"You expect me to put this on my bike?" I do not try to hide my incredulity.

"Sure. Look, when it's hot, it will generate a breeze to keep you cool. And when it's not — like at night when you're pedaling — you can turn it around for extra propulsion."

"I don't plan on biking in the dark."

"If you're going to bike 334 miles in six days, I expect you'll be pumping those pedals until at least midnight."

"334 — point — 5," I correct him.

"All the more reason to put it on the front of your bike."

Switching the fan off and on and watching the waving bear and the flashing red lights, I consider my response.

"You know," I begin. "I think I *will* put this irritating fleabag of a bear on my handlebars."

"There you go," Hank encourages me.

"And every time I start to slow down, I am going to look at this bear — remember who gave it to me — and I am going to speed up."

"Whatever gets you back to D. C."

"Because I am going to imagine running over the asshole who gave it to me."

"Ouch!" Hank recoiled slightly in his chair. "That's a little harsh, isn't it?"

"Not for someone like you, especially when you know what a challenge this trip will be for me."

"It's all in the mind, my friend."

"I think it's all in the butt."

"For you — same difference."

The Reunion

As I crest the Chesapeake Bay Bridge, I say a prayer of thanks that I am headed toward D. C. and not away from it. Although it is only midday Friday, traffic headed toward the Eastern shore of Maryland and the Delaware beaches is slow and thick. I cannot blame them seeking the cooling breezes off the Atlantic in late July, but I do not envy them for sitting for hours on the road. Instead, I will be sweltering on a bike trying to make my way from Pittsburgh to D. C. and back into my daughter's life.

Steph had given me her address and told me to be at her place no later than one. We have a train to catch at four. The train would get us to Pittsburgh around midnight. After a night in a hotel, we would set out the next day. She had everything planned out. All I had to do was show up with my bike. What was it that Woody Allen said about life? Ninety percent of it was just showing up. I could do that, couldn't I? Just show up and be myself.

I hear a voice — strong and feminine — correct me: "He actually said 80%. Why can't you keep your numbers straight?" I ignore it.

The pace of the traffic picks up as I get closer to D. C. I glance in my rear view mirror and think someone is tailgating me until I realize that what I am seeing is my bike attached to the rack on the back of my car. Did I secure it well enough? What if it fell off? I could call Steph and tell her that my bike fell off the rack — that it was too damaged to repair. After calling off this crazy bike trip, we would just talk and have a nice dinner together. I could retreat back to Delaware later if things did not go well. If things went well, then we could talk about meeting again.

I hear the voice again: "Don't try to back out now. You've come too far." I roll my eyes, but I do not reply.

In the mirror off the driver's door, I watch the front wheel of my bike spin lazily as I whizz past cars and trucks. I was going to be depending on that wheel to get me back. Could I rely on it? Could Steph rely on me?

Absorbed in my self doubt, I almost miss my cutoff for the Beltway. I sweep across three lanes to get to it, ignoring the angry honks and gestures from my fellow drivers. Why am I doing this to myself, I wonder. Things will be fine. Just be myself, and speak from the heart like Katherine suggested.

I drive another mile before the self doubt returns. Who am I kidding? Being myself cost me eleven years of being with my daughter. And what did I know about speaking from the heart? Political consultants do not speak from the heart.

"Real fathers know how to speak from the heart." The voice is scolding. Although similar to Katherine's, it is slightly more throaty and brimming with confidence. For a brief moment, I think she is sitting beside me in the car. The last time that I had talked to her, she had been sitting next to me in a car. It had been a different car — a different set of circumstances — a long time ago.

I sneak a peek to my right to make sure she is not there. The seat is empty. I glance over my shoulder to make sure she is not sitting in the back. Although I am alone in the car, I feel her presence. I am certain I smell her perfume.

"Why are you such a coward?"

Yes, it is definitely Nancy talking to me. I can tell from the tone: high expectations with a tinge of disappointment.

"She's your daughter. She will accept you for who you are."

"She's *our* daughter," I point out.

"I gave birth to her, but you raised her. That makes her *your* daughter."

"That's not fair."

"Who ever said life was fair?"

"A liberal Republican."

"Always with the jokes that aren't funny. You haven't changed."

"I've changed a lot. I'm not the same man without you."

"Don't lay your troubles on me."

"You weren't there when I needed you."

"Just stop. You know why I wasn't there. And you know who is to blame. Now take the next exit and go see *your* daughter."

"Why is it always up to me? Why do I have to be the responsible one?"

Nancy's voice does not answer. I start to yell at her — to make her respond, but I hear the voice navigation on my phone say, "In a quarter of a mile take exit 30 for US 29 South/Colesville Road to Silver Spring."

I am in the wrong lane.

Horns honk as I maneuver, but I get to where I need to be. I exit and concentrate on my driving. Before I am ready, I find myself sitting in front of Steph's townhome.

The front lawn is freshly mowed, and the hedges in front are neatly manicured. A shiny new BMW rests in the driveway. On the small front porch, I see a bike fitted out with panniers. While I am taking this in, an attractive young woman comes out of the front door and puts something into the left pannier. She examines the bike, making adjustments. Her long light brown hair is braided into a single strand that falls down the middle of her back. Wearing a bright green top and matching biking shorts, I can tell she is trim and athletic. She is the spitting image of her mother, right down to her mannerisms.

After a deep breath and a long exhalation, I exit my car. I stand for a moment with the car door open, wondering what to say and whether I should shake her hand when we greet. My hands tremble at the thought of touching her again.

Stephanie looks up when she hears me close my car door. Her face brightens.

I see the familiar beaming smile, and she bounces off the front porch toward me. Walking toward her, I am struck speechless by her beauty and vitality.

I hear her say, "I didn't hear you drive up!", and I extend my right hand as the distance between us closes. Ignoring my hand, she throws her arms around my neck and hugs me tight. I hear her say, "I'm so glad you're here."

My hands reflexively go to her back, and I feel the little girl I once knew, hanging on to me for dear life.

"Me, too," I manage to say.

She breaks away. "Is this your bike?" She bounds to the back of my car for a look.

"No. I found that one lying on the side of the road on the way here."

She smiles at me. "I can already tell you haven't changed a bit." With ease, she unsnaps the restraining straps and lifts my bike off its rack.

I try to assist. "Here, let me help."

Holding the bike over her shoulder, she waves me off. "I've got it. Grab your panniers, and let's put them on."

Indeed, she has things under control. I might not have changed, but she has. Steph is stronger and more confident.

"Your car will be fine here. Just don't leave anything visible that looks valuable."

My daughter seems very comfortable issuing orders, even to men old enough to be her father. I grab my panniers, lock the car, and turn to walk toward toward Steph's townhome. The sight of a young man standing on her front porch holding a cat stops me in my tracks. He is tall and lean with close cropped hair and an angular jaw — everything I despise in a guy.

Steph sets my bike down and bounces up the stairs to him. She kisses him on the cheek and pets the cat before slipping inside.

So this is her family I think to myself: a man and a cat. She had not mentioned a guy in our phone conversations, but of course my daughter would have a male in her life. She's a smart, beautiful young woman, and smart, beautiful women always have men in their lives. The cat is not a total surprise. She had always wanted one growing up, but I'm not a cat person. Steeling myself emotionally, I stagger up the driveway lugging my panniers.

The guy does not move to help as he watches me approach. As I get close, the cat senses my disdain for its species and bolts from his arms.

"Hi, I'm Tom Reynolds." I drop the panniers and extend my right hand.

"Nice to meet you, Mr. Reynolds." He shakes my hand, but his response is lukewarm. "I've heard a lot about you."

I am dying to ask what he has heard, but I restrain myself. Although I like that he has used my surname with a title, I try to break the ice. "Just Tom is fine," I suggest.

He does not reciprocate with his name so I press the issue. "And your name?"

"Oh, Steve," he tells me. "I thought you knew."

No last name and an expectation that I should know it — not a good start to our relationship. Yes, I should know who my daughter is living with — but I don't. There are quite a few things I don't know about her current life.

The cat has repositioned itself on the railing of the porch. It is pretending that it does not know I exist.

I have a lot of questions for this guy — "Steve" — but I am struggling with where I should start. I have a habit of asking the wrong question at the wrong time to the wrong person. It's a special talent of mine.

We end up staring at each other until Steph returns.

"Oh, good, you two are getting to know each other," she says.

Both Steve and I smile. Yes, we are two guys getting to know each other by standing on a porch eyeing each other without either of us saying a word we don't have to.

"Yeah," I say, "We're already on a first name basis."

Steve laughs at my remark, perhaps a little too loudly. A bad sign, I think to myself. Either he is socially awkward, or he is trying to ingratiate himself with me. Like every other boyfriend that my daughter has ever had, I decide I don't like him before I even get to know him.

Stephanie probably suspects what I am thinking but chooses to ignore it. "Great!" She says as she takes one of my panniers from me and slides it onto the frame on the back of my bike.

I hand her my other pannier. Both are stuffed. I was barely able to close the snaps on the straps that secure the tops.

"These feel heavy, Daddy. Are you sure you want to take this much stuff?"

I can tell she is contemplating opening my panniers and throwing out half of what I have brought.

"Only the essentials," I assure her.

I get that twist of her lips that Steph does whenever I say something that she does not agree with, but she is not ready to challenge me. Not yet, anyway.

She attaches the second pannier and looks over my bike. "I think we're ready to go," she announces.

The three of us are all awkward smiles. The cat busies itself with that incessant feline grooming that cats do.

Steph pecks Steve on the cheek. That communicates two bits of information to me. One, the peck on the cheek is the type of farewell ritual that couples do when they have been in a long term relationship. They have grown comfortable with each other, but some of the passion has seeped away. Second, the peck tells me that this guy is important to her so I had better be nice to him.

I extend my hand again. "Nice to meet you, Steve."

"Nice to meet you, Mr. Reynolds."

We shake hands for the second time. I cannot tell from either his grip or his grin whether his failure to use my first name is intentional or habit.

The cat gets more than a peck from Stephanie. She has picked it up and has buried her face in its fur. Steve and I can hear her mumbling parting endearments to the animal. As cats will do to anyone that feeds them on a regular basis, the furball gives her a few perfunctory licks.

Although I am trying to be on my best behavior, I cannot help myself. I turn to Steve and say, "I think she is going to miss the cat more than you."

Steve nods in bemused agreement. "She will." He pats me on the back. "Hey, youse guys have a great ride."

The "youse guys" expression gives him away. He is from New Jersey — just when I was starting to try to like the guy.

Steph tugs on my shirt. "Let's go. Follow me to the metro station."

"The metro?"

"Yeah."

"With our bikes?"

"We can take them with us before rush hour."

She is on her bike and off before I reach mine. Struggling to get my leg over the panniers and my butt on top of the saddle, I notice Steve and the cat watching me. Steve's face bears an expression of concern, as if he is wondering how a guy who has this much trouble getting on his bike will ever be able to pedal it fifty plus miles a day for six days straight. The cat, on the other hand, is licking its chops in anticipation of me face planting myself in its front yard.

I manage to disappoint the cat, navigate among the cars, and catch up with Stephanie. She is standing next to a glass enclosed structure on the sidewalk.

"I thought we were taking the metro."

"We are."

"Shouldn't we be over there?" I point to what I think is the metro entrance another half block down the street.

"No." Stephanie punches a button on a panel on the glass enclosed structure. Doors open, and I find myself looking at what I believe is the world's tiniest elevator.

I tap a blue and white sign with the universal symbol for handicap. "Isn't this for people in wheelchairs?"

"Yes, and also for people with bikes." Steph squeezes in with her bike. "Come on."

As I don't understand how she was able to fit, I certainly don't see how my bike, my gear, and myself are getting in. "I'll catch the next one," I offer.

"Don't be silly. Get in. I can't hold this door forever."

I do not consider myself claustrophobic, but I hesitate. The elevator had been built for one person in a wheelchair, not two people with two bikes and four fully loaded panniers. Thoughts of being stuck in an elevator broken by too much weight fill my brain.

"Come on." My daughter's voice is issuing a command, not a request.

I slide my bike in first and follow timidly. We jockey ourselves and our rides around until the doors shut. Steph and I are facing each other, my back is to the control panel. The elevator does not move.

"You need to hit the button for the lower level."

"Okay," I say. Easier said than done. I twist and turn, but I cannot get my hand around to reach the panel. Plus, I cannot see which button I would be pressing.

Annoyed by my incompetence, Steph reaches under my arm and hits the button. The elevator lurches and slowly inches downward. Although the trip takes less than a minute, it feels like half an hour. As Steph and I are face to face, I feel the need to talk. I try being complimentary.

"Nice place you have."

"You've only seen the outside."

"True, but it looks nice — from the outside." Something in the tone of her voice tells me she is more comfortable keeping me on the outside — for now.

Steph shrugs. "I'm not there much. When the doors open, go to the right and stand by the turnstile. I'll get your ticket and join you."

The doors open, and I back out of the elevator. As instructed, I make my way to the right against a flood of people passing by the elevator. Somehow, Steph crosses the mass of humanity in the metro station, obtains a ticket from a machine, and then reaches the turnstile before I do. She hands me my ticket and motions for me to follow her. A ticket agent opens a gate for us to walk our bikes through. We stop at a platform. Steph sees me looking around and says, "This is the red line. It will take us directly to Union Station where we will catch the train."

I nod.

She continues, "We need to get on the last car. More room for our bikes, plus Metro rules."

I nod again.

"I'll let you know when it's time to get off."

I give her a big grin. "Sure is good to see you."

"Good to see you, too, Daddy."

I get a glowing return smile.

"I'm going to be hungry when we get to Union Station," Steph says.

"Okay."

"I'm going to want a slice of pizza."

"Plain cheese, right?"

"You remembered!" Steph sounds surprised.

"I never forgot."

"But I don't eat cheese anymore."

"You want to eat a pizza without any cheese?" I ask.

"Yes! They're yummy!"

I wonder why anyone would want to eat a cheese-less pizza, but I say nothing. There is much I need to learn about my daughter.

I glance at my watch. "Time to go. They want us to load the bikes at 3:30."

"Sure."

Steph finishes her cheeseless pizza — which looks like a pile of vegetables on a thin slice of bread — and we head to Gate D. There is already a long line of people waiting to board. An Amtrak agent spots us rolling through the crowd with our bikes and motions us forward.

"Bikes to the front," she calls out.

Nice perk, I think to myself, as I get a few resentful looks from other passengers. I give the same look to First Class passengers who board before me on airline flights, but I am not paying near what they pay.

There are six other people with bikes in a separate line waiting to load. Another Amtrak agent comes forward, unhooks a chain, and points. The train noise is so loud I cannot hear what he says. We move forward. The guy in front of me looks to be his twenties, pretty fit, and like he has done this trip before.

I follow him and Steph follows me. He goes all the way to the end of the train when a conductor steps out of a car and starts waving his arms and shaking his head. We have gone too far, way too far — serves me right for trusting someone in his twenties. Our caravan of bikes turns and makes its way back to almost the other end of the train. A cargo door slides open, and we have to remove our panniers to load the bikes. An agent sporting dreadlocks that reach to the middle of his back appears in the doorway and takes the bikes one by one. I can see through the doorway that he is strapping them to the wall of the cargo hold.

Stephanie tugs at my arm. Train noises and people shouting make it difficult to hear. I follow her to a passenger car. A conductor guides us to our seats.

As a political consultant, I have traveled all over the United States, usually by plane or car. As such, I am totally unfamiliar with trains. When I travel, I am used to being strapped into a confined space while being fed nearly inedible food for a premium price.

The conductor points to my seat. I stare at it believing that some sort of mistake has been made. It is larger than my favorite recliner at home. I sit in it. It is more comfortable than my recliner. As I play with the seat adjustment controls, I attempt to touch the seat in front of me with my foot. I cannot come close because there is so much legroom.

Steph and the conductor are watching me — Steph with an incredulous look, the conductor with a bemused expression.

"Is there something wrong with your seat, sir?" The conductor asks.

"No, not at all," I reply. "How long is the trip to Pittsburgh?"

"Between seven and eight hours."

"Is that all?" I am looking forward to a nice long nap in this chair. "Tell the pilot to take his time."

"Trains don't have pilots, Daddy," Steph informs me. "They have engineers."

"Oh," I reply. "I guess I should know that."

"Sir," the conductor politely interrupts. "What time would you like to dine this evening?"

"Dine?"

Steph shakes her head in disbelief at me. "This train has a dining car. We can have a nice meal on our way to Pittsburgh, or we can get something from the snack bar."

I have a definite preference. Trying to sound sophisticated, I announce, "I think I will dine this evening." I am warming rapidly to train travel. "Will you be able to fit my daughter and I in about eight o'clock?" Without looking at her, I can tell my daughter's eyes are nearly rolling out of their sockets.

"Very good, sir," the conductor replies. "I will make a note of your reservation."

"Is dress black tie or casual?" I inquire.

The conductor glances at the shorts and tshirt I am wearing and smiles. "You are welcome to come as you are, sir. The dining car is three cars forward."

As the conductor moves on, Steph and I settle into our facing seats. Across from us, a large plate glass window will allow us to view the countryside on our way to Pittsburgh.

The setting seems perfect for a long, leisurely conversation. Steph is looking at me expectantly. I take the cue and start the ball rolling.

"I'm glad you called."

Steph shrugs. "So far, I am, too."

I note the emphasis she puts on, "so far."

"I've been wondering ... " I begin but pause.

"Yes, Daddy."

My daughter's tone is expectant, as if she has anticipated my next question.

"What motivated you to call?" I ask hesitantly.

Stephanie replies with a sparkle in her eyes. "I got tired of waiting for you to call."

I have to laugh.

"And I remember," Steph continues, "someone advising me that if I wanted to go out with a guy I should call him, not sit by the phone waiting for him to call me."

I grimace because I know where this conversation is going.

"Do you remember what happened the first time I called a guy based on your advice?" Steph asks.

I say nothing, but I remember all too well.

Steph answers her own question. "The guy started laughing and hung up on me."

I nod and hang my head.

Steph reaches over and rubs the back of my hand with her fingers. "It's OK. Do you also remember what I did after that phone call?"

I nod again, and Steph keeps talking.

"I came to you, and you put your arm around me. You just held me and let me cry."

Looking up, I see my daughter staring intently at me. I start to apologize but she stops me.

"You were — no, make that 'are' — a good father."

Sensing moisture around my eyes, I deliberately try to change the subject. "Steve seems like a nice guy."

———
74

"He is."

"Your cat seems to like him."

"That's a necessity if he wants to live with me."

I smile and nod. "I never let you have a cat," I remind my daughter.

Steph tenses slightly as she responds to my reminder. "That's one of several things I've forgiven you for."

We lock eyes. I see defiance in hers, and I wonder what she sees in mine.

"So what else have you forgiven me for?" I ask.

"It's a long list."

"It's a long train ride."

My daughter shifts her eyes to pretend to look at the scenery rolling past our window.

Without looking at me, she says, "I never appreciated the way you treated my boyfriends." Her voice is almost a whisper. She is challenging me, but I sense that she does not want to push me too far. "You were always so rude to them."

"That's because I didn't like any of them — from the surfer dude to the wanna be hip hop artist to the testosterone laden baseball jock. I thought they were all jerks."

Stephanie looks from the window to me.

"There's a lot of jerks in the world, Daddy."

Yeah, I think to myself, *and you tried to date as many of them as you could.*

We avert our eyes from each other and gaze out the window at the countryside as it transforms from industrial to urban to suburban. As the time and distance expand, I decide to break the silence before the gap between us gets too large. "Look, honey, you need to understand that no boy is good enough for a father's teenage daughter. I was just being protective."

I am only looking at the side of Stephanie's face, but I can tell I need to say more.

"Maybe overly protective," I submit.

I detect a faint curl in the side of her mouth as if she is forcing herself not to smile.

"I was definitely an asshole at times," I finally admit. "And I apologize."

75

That admission earns me a broad smile. Steph turns to face me and pats me on the knee. "Well, Daddy, the problem is that most of them did turn out to be jerks, and I hate it that you were right — about most of them."

I decide not to press my luck by asking which ones I was right about and move the conversation from the past to the present.

"How about this guy you're seeing now?"

Steph withdraws her hand from my knee. "Do you want to know whether he is a jerk?"

"No — I'll decide that on my own. Just tell me a little about him. Like how did you meet?"

"Internet."

I find myself raising an eyebrow. "Is that safe?"

"He hasn't tried to kill me yet."

"You know what I mean."

"No, I don't."

"Guys can pretend to be a lot of things they're not on the internet."

"I had him checked out."

"Checked out?"

"A background check. It's a requirement of my job. I have to clear anyone I associate with."

"Including me?"

At least that got a short chuckle.

"Especially you," she says.

"So what kind of job requires you to run background checks on guys you date?"

"A job in security."

"A company that provides security?"

"No, it's a government job."

"A government job that provides security? Are we talking about the CIA?"

"No, and if I worked there I couldn't tell you."

"FBI?"

"Let's change the subject."

"All right." I figure we can return to her employment later. "Can we talk more about Steve?"

"Sure."

"What does he do?"

"He works for a nonprofit."

"Admirable."

"Very admirable."

I ponder how to phrase my next question. I choose the less diplomatic, more direct approach. "Are you guys married?"

"No."

"Making plans?"

"No."

"Talking about it?"

"Only on trains with my father."

I am getting some information, but I don't feel the conversation is going well. Stephanie has become adept at answering questions by revealing as little information as possible. I sense she has carefully rehearsed this conversation to conceal the real reason she wants to reconnect with me. Therefore, I decide to push her on the subject.

"So why don't you get married? Steve seems like a great guy."

"He is a great guy. But there's more to being a husband than just being a great guy." She looks me squarely in the eye, the way her mother would when she wanted to make a point. "You taught me that."

I am not sure what she means by that, but I blunder on. "Don't you want kids? The biological clock is ticking."

"We live in a messed up world. I want no part of bringing a child into it."

Half of me is shocked; the other half fully understands. "How are we going to fix the world's problems unless we raise children?" I ask.

"With my commitments at work, I have neither the time nor the energy to solve the world's problems." Steph stands up.

"Where are you going?" I ask.

"I need to go pee."

She is direct and to the point, especially about her biological needs.

"Okay," I say. "I feel a nap coming on. Old men need their rest, you know."

"Actually, I don't know." Steph turns and walks toward the front of the train."

As I watch her go, I can tell she is not happy with me. We are talking, but I have no idea how well things are going. Did I push her too hard on the marriage and children issues? I question if I should "be myself" as Katherine had suggested or whether I should start putting a filter on what I say to Steph.

As we have some time before dinner, I settle in for a short siesta. My eyes are barely closed when the chatter of excited female voices rouses me. I open one eye to see three women parading down the aisle: a blonde, a redhead, and a brunette. They are tanned, dressed in shorts and festive T-shirts. I guess that they are in their mid forties. Although I would not describe them as either fat or skinny, none of them strikes me as particularly athletic.

The brunette stops to address me. "I'm sorry. Did we disturb you?"

I open both eyes. "Not at all," I lie. I am a political consultant after all — I make my living telling lies. "You ladies seem very happy to be on your way to Pittsburgh."

"Oh, we're not going to Pittsburgh," the blonde interjects. "We're all from Connellsville, the 'Broken Buckle of the Rust Belt'. That's where we live, and we're headed home."

All three nod in agreement. I detect the hick accent of small town western Pennsylvania. "I've heard of Connellsville," I reply politely. "Isn't it on the Great Allegheny Passage? I think I saw it on the trail map."

"Why, yes, it is." The redhead joins the conversation. "We have just finished biking the Passage."

"And the C & O!" the other two announce loudly. All three giggle in unison, giddy at their accomplishment.

The blonde seems to be the leader of the pack. "We have always talked about biking from Connellsville to D. C., and we have just done it!" she exclaims excitedly.

I suspect that the trio have been celebrating their accomplishment at a local bar before boarding the train. "Congratulations," I say. Although I am not ready to reveal that I hope to duplicate their feat, I am curious. "So what was it like?" I ask.

"Gawd, it was hot!" The blonde complains.

"I have never been so hot in my life!" The redhead adds.

"It was pretty darn hot." The brunette agrees.

I see an opportunity to gather intelligence. "Anything else?"

"Potholes," says the blonde.

"Potholes all over the C & O," adds the redhead.

"Potholes everywhere," agrees the brunette.

"So it's hot and full of potholes," I summarize.

"Oh, and the trees," says the blonde.

"Yes, we should mention the trees," adds the redhead.

"Definitely the trees," agrees the brunette.

Remembering my own encounter with trees while biking, I am intrigued. "Trees?"

"They are down all over the trail," states the brunette.

"I wouldn't say all over the trail," disagrees the redhead. "But there are quite a few down."

"We're just lucky none of them fell on us!" The blonde comments.

For some reason, all three of them think the idea of trees falling on them is extremely funny, and the trio laughs uproariously. I have a different image: of being flattened by a giant oak as I coast along on my bike sweltering in the heat while I dodge muddy potholes.

"Just be sure not to miss the Maryland Rail Trail," the blonde cautions.

"The *Western* Maryland Rail Trail," the redhead corrects.

"Yeah, it's at Lock 56," the brunette adds.

"I thought it was at Lock 46." The redhead suggests.

The blonde shakes her head. "No, it was Lock 59 or maybe 58. Anyway, it is a nice straight, smooth strip of asphalt that runs beside the C & O for about twenty miles."

"Much better than bouncing through the mud!"

"I'll say!"

Again, the trio erupts in gales of laughter. I am reminded of sailors on shore leave who have endured a long, treacherous voyage across an unforgiving ocean and are just happy to still be alive.

"How many locks are there?" I ask.

"We didn't count," admits the blonde.

"Lots," suggests the redhead.

"Lots of locks," adds the brunette.

All three think this comment is the funniest one yet.

Recovering, the blonde apologizes. "Sorry to have disturbed you. We're on our way to dinner."

"Enjoy your meal," I say.

"Oh, we will," the redhead assures me.

"Especially if it's liquid!" The brunette chortles.

With that last comment, the female bikers from Connellsville, Pennsylvania departs for the dining car for further refreshment and celebration.

I check the time and see that I still have a window for a nap before dinner. My conversation with the three women reassures me that I can do this bike ride with Stephanie. If three middle aged, nonathletic women can do it, surely I can.

As I adjust my seat to a more comfortable position, I spot two older gentlemen headed up the aisle. They are dressed in full cycling regalia: colorful padded biking shorts and matching jerseys that make them look like walking billboards. Their legs are covered with mud from the knees down. Their jerseys are soaked in sweat. Their forearms are baked brown from hours in the sun. Their faces are long and haggard. Both men are substantially older than I am.

The one in front nods his head at me in a greeting. I nod back. They stop, and the man in front speaks.

"Sorry for our appearance."

"Doesn't bother me," I say. "You guys been doing a little biking?"

"A little," the man in back snorts sarcastically.

The man in front runs his hand over his bald head. "We just came off the C & O. Didn't have time to clean up."

"If we were to make the train," adds the man in back. He has vestiges of thinning, closely cropped gray hair on his scalp.

"The C & O," I say. "I hear that's pretty tough." I wonder if both men had had full heads of hair before embarking on their trip down the C & O.

The two men both acknowledge my comment as the man in front looks back at his friend. "We've done it maybe a dozen times?"

"Yeah, about that."

"But this time — "

"It pretty much ate our lunch."

"And our breakfast and dinner."

We smile knowingly at each other.

The one in back continues. "Park service is spendings its money on something other than trail maintenance."

"What little money Congress gives it."

"Must have rained hard a week or so ago. Lots of trees down."

"Never seen so many potholes."

"And places where you can just slide off into the Potomac."

"Or a swamp."

I have a vision of me pedaling off the trail on my bike into the welcoming jaws of a swamp alligator.

"At least the weather was nice," the man in the back comments with a wry grin.

"Yeah, right. Temperature got over ninety every day." The bald guy in front shifts his weight as he speaks. "Only thing higher was the humidity."

"Bugs were the worst I've ever experienced," the short gray haired man adds. "Dark clouds of them."

My vision changes to one where just before the swamp alligator snaps its jaws shut over me and my bike, a swarm of giant mosquitoes scoops me up and carries me off to places unknown from which I will never return.

The guy in front seems to sense my discomfiture. "Well, we need to get cleaned up for dinner," he says. "Nice talking to you."

"Nice talking to you," I say. Actually, it was not nice — not nice at all. I was caught between three novice, middle-aged female bikers and two experienced, aging male bikers. All of

81

them had done it, but now I am less sure than ever that I can endure the ordeal that awaits me. Yes, I am thinking of wimping out. Perhaps I have received too much information. I consider whether I should try to jump off the train and walk back to D.C. Fortunately, the luxurious comfort of my train seat causes my innate laziness to kick in, and I elect to try to resume my siesta instead.

Drifting off quickly, I rest fitfully, dreaming of alligators chasing me while I pedal furiously on my bike in a futile effort to get away. No matter how fast I go, the alligators stay right behind me. When a black cloud of giant insects descends on me, I lose my balance and fall off my bike. Just as a particularly large alligator with large crooked teeth is about to swallow me whole, I awake with a start.

Steph is sitting across from me. "Enjoy your nap?" she asks.

"Didn't get much of one," I say, and I do not try to hide my disappointment.

Steph looks at a small screen strapped to her wrist and announces, "It's time for dinner."

"What's that?" I ask and point to the screen on her wrist.

"That," she says proudly as she twists her arm so that I can see it better, "Is an Apple Watch."

"I thought Apple made computers and cell phones."

"It does; it also makes watches now."

"Really? So you can tell the time?"

"The Apple Watch does more than just that. It lets me know when I get a message, lets me play music, sets alarms. Come on. I can show you how it works over dinner." Steph beckons for me to follow her.

Reluctantly, I climb out of my recliner/train seat. "I bet it cost more than fifty dollars," I say as we walk toward the dining car.

"It did," she replies over her shoulder.

"You can get a reliable watch for less than fifty dollars."

"I'm sure you can."

"So how much did you pay?"

"I'm not telling you."

"Why not?"

"Because I want us to enjoy our meal."

We reach the dining car. A waiter greets us and shows us to our table next to a large plate glass window where we can watch the countryside roll past us in the fading light. The table is covered with a crisp white cloth; black cloth napkins accent the layout. Silverware and drinking glasses are impeccably laid out. I have eaten at some of the finest eating establishments in the world courtesy of my political clients, and none of them ever set a table better than this one. Well, maybe Delmonico's.

As we look over the menu, I observe Stephanie twisting her lips — I remember she does this facial contortion whenever something is not right.

The waiter appears to take our orders.

"Are the pork chops good?" I ask.

"Yes, sir."

"I'll have the pork chops then."

"Excellent choice, sir."

I have the distinct impression that I could have ordered Spam on moldy rye toast, and this waiter would still have complimented me on my selection.

The waiter turns to Steph. "And you, ma'am?"

"I don't see any vegetarian options," Steph comments.

"I can have the chef make you a plate of vegetables from the list of sides listed on the menu. Would that work?"

"That will be fine."

Steph makes her selections, and the waiter leaves.

"When did you become a vegetarian?" I ask.

"Actually, I'm a vegan."

"What the hell is a vegan?"

Steph takes a slow sip of water before answering me. "A vegan is someone who does not eat anything that is derived from animals."

"Like meat?"

"Nope."

"Eggs?"

"No baby chick embryos."

"Milk?"

"Only soy milk."

"Cheese?"

Steph shakes her head.

"Just plants then?"

"Pretty much."

"That limits your diet."

"Not really. I can eat vegetables, fruits, legumes, grains, beans, and so on. There's quite a lot of variety."

I tap my fingers on the table top. "What about ice cream? The daughter I knew used to love it when I bought her ice cream."

Stephanie displays a guilty smile. "I make a few exceptions, but there are actually vegan forms of ice cream."

"And you know where to get them?"

"Of course!"

"Why am I not surprised?"

For a brief moment we seem to be connecting — not in how we are alike, but in how we are different.

I lean forward and say: "Show me how your Apple Watch works."

Steph runs through its features until our food arrives. I understand little of what she says, but she seems to enjoy showing off her technical expertise to her Dad. Whatever she paid for the damn thing, it was worth it if it helps us connect.

We finish our food and playfully fight over who is going to pay the bill. I do — of course — I'm the Daddy.

As we return to our seats, Steph says, "You've got a little time to snooze before we get to Pittsburgh."

"Are you going to sleep?" I ask.

"I have some work to do."

"Work? On a train? At night?"

"Just some phone calls." She holds up her cell phone. "I'll wake you."

"Okay," I agree. The thought of a rest after a heavy meal is appealing.

"When we get to Pittsburgh," she reminds me. "We have to retrieve our bikes and ride them to the Hampton Inn."

"In the dark?"

"I have lights for our bikes."

I look around wistfully. "Can't we just take the train back to D. C.?"

Steph ignores my request as she searches for a quiet place to make her phone calls.

I collapse into my recliner of a seat. The sounds and motions of the train lull me into a deep slumber. I do not stir until I feel Steph shaking my shoulder.

"We're here," she advises me.

Groggy from deep sleep, I have no idea where "here" is. She hands me my panniers, and I follow her in a stupor down the aisle. We clamber down steps to disembark from the train. The station is dark, and I do not know where to go. Looking around, I feel a tug on my arm.

"This way, Daddy."

Instinctively, I look down expecting to see a young girl with freckles. My eyes gradually rise to see the adult standing next to me. Stephanie is taller now, and she has lost her freckles. She smiles. I wonder if I am dreaming.

"Come on," she says. "We need to get to the hotel to get some sleep before our big adventure begins.

I follow her, not knowing where I am going. We retrieve our bikes from the storage car, attach our panniers, and walk our bikes down a long corridor. Outside, we cycle through the darkened and empty streets of downtown Pittsburgh. Stephanie finds the Hampton Inn for us, we check in, and then I stumble into bed. I endure fitful dreams filled with giant alligators and swarms of black flies.

Pittsburgh
First Day of Biking
334.5 miles to go

Breakfast at the Hampton Inn is busy. I have justified a second waffle with extra whipped cream on the pretext that I will be burning lots of carbs today. Steph has excused herself to talk to the front desk, and I am left with my thoughts as I work to finish my breakfast. The weather report indicates today is going to be hot, as predicted. A blithering blonde babbles on the television, and I observe that no one is listening. The other customers are too busy checking the weather on their own cell phones.

Although the breakfast area is crowded and noisy, I hear a little voice whispering in my ear. I try to ignore it, but it persists: "It's not too late. Tell her you just got an urgent message. There's a sick friend at home. You need to take the train back to D. C."

I shake my head to silence the voice. I am committed to the trip. I will ride the bike back to D.C. I will do this. Stabbing a large piece of waffle with my fork, I swirl it in a mound of whipping cream and stick it in my mouth to fortify myself.

The voice comes back: "You're not committed until you get on that bike and leave Pittsburgh. The train station is only a few blocks away. You know the way."

I can't, I plead. After eleven years, I owe her at least six days. I promised her that I would do this trip with her.

"You've promised her lots of things, and you've broken those promises. She's used to it, and she'll get over yet another disappointment."

What do I tell her?

"Sick friend. Terminal illness. Stomach cancer."

What if she asks for a name?

"Be creative. Something other than John Smith."

I can't lie to her!

"You've been lying to her that you can do this trip when you know you can't."

I can so do this trip!

The little voice goes away, and I am left alone at the table staring into my plate of half eaten waffles. Getting ahold of myself, I inhale deeply and look up. The young couple sitting at the next table are staring at me. Where the man's eyes are observing me cooly, the eyes of the woman are wide open in amazement. I must have been talking out loud to the little voice.

"Uh, just trying to psych myself up," I try to explain.

Trying not to embarrass me further, both look away.

"It's a psychological trick I read about in a book," I continue. "Apparently, a lot of top athletes use it." Looking down, I spot a dab of whipping cream that has wandered onto my shirt. As I try to wipe it off discreetly, I add, "Not that I'm a top athlete."

The woman has suddenly gotten very interested in her scrambled eggs, but the guy glances back at me. "Uh, huh," he grunts.

I wonder if he is agreeing that talking to yourself was good sport psychology or whether he is agreeing that I was not a top athlete. In either event, I decide that the hole I have dug myself is not deep enough and ramble on.

"Starting the Great Allegheny Passage this morning." I attempt to sound as casual as possible. "Intend to do sixty today."

When that elicits no response, I add, "Plan to go all the way to D. C. in six days."

The woman has the courtesy to ignore me in my disgrace, but the man tilts his head in my direction. His eyes size me up and say, "Good luck, with that, buddy"; however, his lips say, "The Passage is a nice ride — have a good run."

"Thanks." I am saved from further embarrassment by the arrival of my daughter.

"Hey, Daddy, you ready to go?"

The couple sitting next to me glance up at Stephanie and cast sympathetic smiles in her direction. I am sure that they are going to discuss whether I am actually her biological father once we had left.

"You betcha! I was born ready," I reply.

I swear the woman rolled her eyes at me as I follow Stephanie back up to the room. She disappears into the bathroom; it could be the last real one we will see for awhile. I glance at my wristwatch. The time is getting close to eight o'clock. We need to hit the road. Our plan is to cover sixty miles today. I have never biked sixty miles in a single day before, and I am sure that I am going to need every minute of daylight to make our goal As is my habit, I check the drawers and then get on my knees to look under the bed. I hate to leave things in hotel rooms.

"Whatcha doin'?"

I pull my head out from the dust ruffle and glance up. Steph is the epitome of athletic chic with a hot pink jersey and form fitting biking shorts. She has weaved her long chestnut hair into a single braid that lays draped over her left shoulder. In the soft morning light, I think of her mother and how much they are alike.

"Just seeing if I could fit underneath the bed."

Just like her mother used to do when I said something incomprehensible, Steph scrunches her nose. "Why?"

"I was just thinking that if I hid, you might leave without me."

Steph playfully kicks my foot. "Quit foolin' around. Let's go."

I struggle to my feet, wondering if I could claim that I had thrown my back out. She is already standing in the doorway, balancing her bike in one hand and holding the door open for me with the other.

"Okay," I mutter as I push my bike forward. Then I hear her make a clicking noise with her tongue. She points with her chin at my helmet that is sitting in the middle of the bed.

"Might need that," she suggests.

"Yeah, right."

Navigating the narrow hallway, we squeeze into the elevator with another couple. Four humans and two bikes with fully loaded panniers make for a tight fit. We smile awkwardly at each other. Fortunately, the ride is brief. Unfortunately, the lobby is packed.

Some sort of convention must be in town. Young women in trim business suits and men in jackets and open collars mix in small groups. Some sit with laptops in front of them and talk earnestly about marketing plans and business goals. Others gather in clumps, standing between us and the front door. All hold cell phones with large screens which they glance at intermittently hoping for an important call or message to come in as they talk.

I feel more than a little ridiculous navigating between them pushing a bike while wearing shorts and a helmet. The two hotel managers standing behind the front desk act as if people pushed bikes through their lobby all the time. Following Steph — who did not seem to mind the stares from the conventioneers — I just keep smiling and saying, "Excuse me" and "Pardon me".

A guy at the door takes pity on me and holds it open so I can get through.

"Enjoy your ride," he says cheerfully.

I just nod and reply, "Thanks."

The early morning air is refreshingly cool outside. I am more than a little nervous about cycling in downtown Pittsburgh during the day. Last night was dark, but we encountered no traffic. My imagination conjures up images of narrow streets congested with large delivery trucks and long commuter buses. Reality is far different. On Penn Avenue we find a designated bike lane that takes us through the heart of the city. Steph and I take pictures of each other at the cleverly designed bike racks that dot Penn Avenue. One is shaped like rain clouds, another is a replica of a local bridge, another resembles a clock, and yet another appears to be a stack of colorful paper clips. Some are truly artistic as I just cannot figure out what they are supposed to be.

Steph shows me how to take a selfie with my cell phone, but I prefer the old fashioned way: one person poses while the other takes the picture. Nonetheless, she takes some pretty good snaps of us together with silly expressions on our faces. We clown around the way we used to when she was in high school.

We cycle down a serpentine sidewalk that winds its way between cascading streams of water under the convention center. When we exit, we are facing the Allegheny River. Across the flowing tributary I can see Three Rivers Stadium where the Steelers play football and PNC Park where the Pirates attempt to play baseball.

A paved hike/bike trail runs along the waterfront in front of us. Steph glances to the right and to the left; she seems confused.

"What are you looking for?" I ask.

"The Point. That's where the Passage starts."

Like her mother, Steph has no sense of direction. Obviously, we should follow the flow of water downstream to our left, but she insists on pulling out her cell phone and checking the GPS.

I elect to enjoy the view while she fiddles with her technology. As I am waiting, a very fit and attractive woman jogs past us from left to right in an outfit that looks like it was painted on her.

Nudging Steph, I point at the woman and suggest, "Let's just follow her."

Steph gives me a look I haven't seen in over fifteen years: the look a female teenager gives her father when he says something utterly stupid. "Why?" she asks.

"She seems to know where she is going."

"She probably does know where she is going, but that is to the right, and we need to go to the left."

I grin. "Right behind you, boss."

Steph takes off, and we ride along the water to the Point. The Point is short for Point State Park, a spot of deep historical significance for Pittsburgh as well as the western terminus for the Great Allegheny Passage and the onset of our adventure. Reaching the Point, Steph stops at the edge of the fountain that is the centerpiece of the park. I ride around it in a victory lap. We have found the start of the GAP!

Drawing from an underground aquifer that flows underneath it, the fountain spews water 150 feet into the air that falls into a round pool. Stopping when I finish my circumlocution, I gaze at the confluence of the three magnificent rivers. On my left the Monongahela combines with the Allegheny on my right to form the Ohio, which will eventually flow into the Mississippi and then the Gulf of Mexico.

Rather than enjoying the view, Steph is busy tapping a message into her cell phone. I try to peek over her shoulder, but she pulls her device into her stomach.

"Sorry," she says. "I need to pee, and I have to make a phone call."

"Sure," I reply. "I'll stay with the bikes while you take care of your business."

"Thanks."

She walks in the direction of a public restroom, and I am left alone with my thoughts. Rather than consider why she has to make a phone call before we get a mile down the GAP, I ponder random facts about where I am while I extract Hank's going away present out of my panniers. The plastic bear has the same silly grin it had when I had rewrapped it.

Often cited as one of the most livable cities in the world, Pittsburgh is reputed to have the highest number of bars on a per capita basis in the United States. And I will be passing through the city without visiting a single one.

Pittsburgh is a proud city. It is proud of its Steelers (professional football), its Pirates (professional baseball), and its Penguins (professional hockey) but perhaps not its Gladiators, an arena football franchise that folded a few years back. Sports have long been an important part of Pittsburgh culture; the city hosted the first professional football game and the first World Series.

All of Pittsburgh's sports teams wear black and gold uniforms as those two colors are the official colors of the city. They are the official colors because black and gold are used in Pittsburgh's coat of arms which in turn was based on the arms of the first Earl of Chatham. The first Earl of Chatham is better known as William Pitt, the prime minister of England for which the city gets its name.

I attach the tiny biplane piloted by the bear to my handlebars. A man walks past me wearing a black and gold Steeler jersey with the number twelve and the name Bradshaw stenciled on it. Pittsburgh is sometimes called the "City of Champions" because of the titles its sports teams have won, including six National Football Leagues championships (starting with the four won by Terry Bradshaw, a Louisiana boy who did well up north). To date, no other NFL team has won six Super Bowls.

Other nicknames include "City of Bridges" (it has 446 of them, possibly more than any other city in the United States), "Steel City" (because at the end of the 19th century, it was the center of the largest steel producing region in the world), "The Burgh" (the "h" at the end makes it unusual), and "The Paris of

Appalachia" (why any city would want to use this nickname escapes me). Philadelphia sports fans — envious cross state rivals — refer to the city as Shittsburgh.

I see Steph emerge from the bathroom. Standing under a tree several hundred feet away from me, she is listening intently to whatever the person on the other end is saying, with her eyes studying the ground in front of her. As I wait for Steph to finish her phone call, I ponder how this great American city became the second largest in Pennsylvania (after Philadelphia).

The rivers flowing past me and the hills overlooking these rivers hold the answers. The surrounding hills contained vast deposits of iron and coal, necessary ingredients for the manufacture of steel. As the United States expanded westward, business titans such as Andrew Carnegie made vast fortunes by manufacturing and selling that steel to be used in the bridges, railroads, vehicles, and skyscrapers necessary for a modern industrial society.

The Allegheny, the Monongahela, and the Ohio (combined with the railroads that were constructed later) were used to transport the steel and other goods. Control of these waterways was essential to the development of the United States. That control was contested in the middle of the 18th century when France and England fought for world domination in what history calls the Seven Years War. As that conflict spread to North America, the British colonists referred to it as the French and Indian War, as the French had allied with Native American tribes to stop the expansion of the British colonies into the interior of North America.

Steph has started walking in a circle as she continues to talk on her phone. I turn my eyes from the rivers and the hills to the remnants of the fortifications that are preserved at Point State Park.

Both the British and the French tried to establish ownership and control over the Point by constructing forts here. The British had initially started construction of Fort Prince George, but the French drove them off and built Fort Duquesne. In the summer of 1755, a British force under the command of General Edward Braddock and accompanied by a young colonial officer named George Washington marched through the wilderness to capture Fort Duquesne. Braddock, seasoned by years of European warfare, ignored pleas by Washington and other colonial officers to adjust his military tactics to the thick forests of North America and rushed headlong into an ambush. Despite having a force at least twice the size of the French and their Native American allies, Braddock was killed, and his troops were routed. Only the efforts of Washington prevented the entire force from being massacred. Three years later, an even larger British expedition forced the French to abandon the site. In its place, the British built Fort Pitt, named after the current British prime minister, William Pitt. If the British had not been so persistent, Pittsburgh and its surrounding environs may never have become part of the United States.

Steph marches over to where I am standing with the bikes. Her face is grim. As she shoves her phone in her pocket, she barks, "Let's go."

"Problem?" I ask.

"Nothing that can't wait until I'm back in the office."

I can tell she is upset, and I choose not to press the issue. She angrily clips into her pedals and looks around. Her eyes spot the bear peering cheerily up at her from my handlebars.

"What the hell is that?" Steph asks.

"That is a combination navigation, cooling, steering, power, and motivation device."

"I cannot believe that you paid money for it."

"I didn't. It was a gift."

"It looks ridiculous."

"If the shoe fits — "

Stephanie shakes her head in frustration. "Let's go. We've got a lot of miles to cover."

"Which way?" I ask.

"This way," she says and takes off.

I follow.

We leave the park, enter a construction zone, and pass through a parking area. I can tell that we are headed in the correct general direction as the Monongahela remains on our right, but I also know that we have to find a way to cross the river. We are riding underneath bridges rather than finding an entrance ramp to one that goes over the water.

I slow down, but Steph barrels on. The pavement ends and we come to a path that is overgrown with grass and trees. Steph keeps going; I tag along cautiously. We have found an urban jungle in the midst of downtown Pittsburgh. After I spot discarded syringes and broken beer bottles, I stop at a concrete wall that stands next to this trail that seems to be gradually disappearing the further we go. The wall is covered with graffiti which I try to decipher.

While I am standing at the graffiti covered wall, Stephanie returns. "I can't figure out where this trail is taking us," she admits.

I grunt an acknowledgement and point at the graffiti. "As far as I can tell, this says that we should turn around, go back to Point State Park, and let the old guy lead the way."

Steph stands arms akimbo with her bike leaning against her hip. "I doubt that's what it says."

"That's my interpretation. What's yours?"

Pushing her sunglasses up on her forehead, Steph stares at her cell phone screen, taps on it, stares at it again, and then looks around. I wait patiently.

Frustrated, she says, "If you want to lead, be my guest. I can't make any sense of this. According to the GPS, we're on the right route."

I gaze at the foliage that encroaches on us and the garbage that litters the ground around our feet.

"Your GPS might need to update itself, or — " I point to the roadway above us. "We might need to be up there."

"But how do we get up there?

"Follow me," I say. "And try to keep up."

In response, Steph flips her sunglasses down and replies dismissively, "Hummff!"

We bike almost all the way back to Point State Park. I spot a ramp, and we grind our way up to a bridge that crosses the Monongahela. Riding in a bike lane we curve around the opposite shore and run into a large scrum of bicyclists, all wearing the same light blue cycling jerseys. They appear to be raising money for some worthy cause. Steph and I weave our way into their midst, trying to make our way out of Pittsburgh. Our pace slows. We are finally able to navigate through the pack. With Steph in the lead, we break into the open and start reeling off the mileage. That is — until Steph signals she is stopping.

"What's up?" I ask.

She points. A family of geese have waddled onto the bike path. Rather than cross to the other side, they have chosen to march down the center, creating a traffic jam. Steph is tip-toeing her bike behind the geese. The cyclists with the light blue jerseys are piling up behind us.

"Can't you shoo them off the bike path?" I ask.

"They have as much right to be here as we do," she replies.

I start to point out that humans built the bike path for humans, not geese, but I calculate that my protestations will only fall on the deaf ears of a stubborn animal rights activist.

It is almost 11 am. Between the urban jungle, the group raising money for charity, and the flock of geese, I wonder if we will ever get out of Pittsburgh.

But we do, and we leave all shade behind us. It's as hot as Hades — just as Hank had warned me. As I pedal up long ramps over old steel yards in the broiling sun, I remind myself of the old admonition: be careful what you ask for.

Homestead
325 miles to go

Crossing a set of railroad tracks, I take a sharp right turn along the side of a building. This brief interlude of shade from the building provides a temporary respite from the sun which has beating down on us all morning. The trail then returns to the open area along the Monongahela, and I feel myself already sagging in the heat of the first day. Although we have been cycling for hours around Pittsburgh and then getting lost in Point State Park, we are only approaching mile ten of the sixty we are to cover today. I allow the bike to roll to a stop in front of a large brick building with a water tower standing behind it. A sign proclaims that it was the Homestead Pump House. So it was here that it happened, I think to myself.

Stephanie pulls up beside me. "Need some liquids? Have to stay hydrated on a day like today." She offers me her water bottle.

"No, thanks, I've still got plenty. Just trying to absorb a little history."

Stephanie looks around. "All I see are some shops and a few parked cars."

"Well, if we are where are think we are, this was the site of the Battle of Homestead."

"What war was that? Revolutionary?"

"No. Americans versus Americans."

"The Civil War never got this far north."

"Nope. I'm talking about Big Steel versus Little People."

I get a critical look from my daughter,

"You're not going to be stopping every ten miles to give me a history lesson are you?

"But this was a pivotal event in the American labor movement," I protest.

"You live too much in the past, Daddy, and not enough in the present." Stephanie rises on her bike and pedals off down the path. "I'll wait up ahead," she calls over her shoulder.

My daughter is right, of course. I have spent most of my life studying the past, especially the past of other people. It is less painful than studying my own past or trying to live in the present.

I watch Stephanie take off, and then debate whether I should go into the Pump House. Homestead gets only a sentence or two in most history books, but it was a bloody turning point in the relationship between large corporations and the masses of people they employ. I decide to stay where I am as most of the history that had occurred at this spot at about the same time of year had happened outside in the heat rather than in air conditioned comfort.

Toward the end of the 19th century, the area around Pittsburgh was the center of the world's production of steel. The manufacture of steel is hard work that requires hard men.

Iron must be heated to almost 2000 degrees Fahrenheit to remove impurities to make steel strong enough to build the railroads, bridges, and skyscrapers necessary for an industrial economy. Workers had to endure that heat for twelve hours straight seven days a week and would emerge from the mills with blackened faces from the soot generated by the steel manufacturing operations.

By the summer of 1892 Andrew Carnegie and Henry Clay Frick, two captains of the American industrial revolution, had decided that it was time to break the rebellious labor movement that had frustrated their attempts to modernize their operations at the Carnegie Steel Homestead Works. The two were determined to cut the wages of their workforce and eliminate work rules that prevented them from increasing production. Carnegie left the dirty work to Frick and skipped off across the Atlantic for his annual summer sojourn in his native Scotland.

In July 1889, three years before, the Amalgamated Association of Iron and Steel Workers had won a generous collective bargaining agreement after a violent strike. That contract was up for renewal, and the union membership was ready to do whatever it had to do to maintain the hard won benefits of the expiring contract. However, the leaders of the union had not taken into account two significant changes.

First, the economy was sinking into recession, depressing demand and prices for steel. Although the union had amassed a strike fund of $146,000, the company had also prepared for a temporary shutdown of production until strikebreakers (scabs) could be brought in.

Second, management had changed. Frick had taken direct charge of operations at the Homestead steel mill, and he had made careful preparations for what he anticipated would be a violent confrontation. He ordered the construction of an eleven foot high solid wood fence around the plant topped with double strands of barbed wire. Every gate was protected by a high pressure water cannon. Workers laughingly called it "Fort Frick". Frick also made arrangements with the Pinkerton National Detective Agency to hire 300 men to protect the plant. He had used Pinkerton muscle in previous labor disputes, and the mere mention of Pinkerton brought angry responses from workers.

When contract negotiations broke down, Frick started locking workers out of the plant. The union retaliated by declaring a general strike. Frick hired other workers and sent them to Homestead. The union members responded in the thousands as they arrived, using the mass of their numbers to intimidate the strikebreakers, despite the presence of the local sheriff. Workers surrounded the Homestead works but were careful not to enter it. Their sole purpose was to prevent anyone from entering the plant to produce steel at that location.

In the early morning hours of July 6, 1892, lookouts for the workers spotted two barges being pulled upriver by a small steamer named the *Little Bill*. Aboard the barges were 300 Pinkerton agents armed with Winchester rifles. Frick had hired these men and ordered them to sneak into the plant from the Monongahela River, take control, and then protect the strikebreakers that he intended to bring in. Thousands of men, women, and children, all of whom depended on their livelihoods on steelmaking at Homestead, confronted the Pinkertons at the landing wharf at four in the morning. The crowd was estimated at 5000 people.

Both sides were armed, and angry words were exchanged. No one was ever able to determine who fired first, but an initial shot resulted in a barrage of gunfire. The Pinkertons continued efforts to land, but the workers were able to pin them on the two barges. Attempts were made to set the barges on fire. Seven strikers and three Pinkerton guards were killed while dozens more were injured in the fighting.

People on the shore became enraged at the sight of their friends and family members being killed and wounded just as the Pinkerton men on the barges became demoralized by their hopeless situation. Toward evening, the Pinkertons raised a white flag and agreed to surrender, not realizing what lay in store for them.

After they were disarmed, the Pinkertons were marched up the steep shore. Angry workers formed a gauntlet and viciously attacked the Pinkertons. They were kicked, knocked down, and pummeled with clubs and rifle butts. Their clothing was ripped to shreds, and blood streamed down their faces. In desperation, the Pinkertons ran for sanctuary at the Homestead Opera House which was to serve as their temporary detention center. They waited there in terror for someone to rescue them as enraged workers and their families milled around outside. A special train was dispatched from Pittsburgh to retrieve the Pinkertons. It departed from Homestead at 1:00 am on July 7th.

One of the many tragedies of the Battle for Homestead was that workers had been pitted against workers. The 300 Pinkerton agents had been recruited from unemployed laborers in Chicago, New York, and Philadelphia who were only told that they were going to be night watchmen. They did not know their true assignment until they were ordered to disembark from the barges. Suddenly, they found themselves forced to choose between being shot or drowning in the river.

Although the workers had won the battle at the water's edge, they lost the war in the political backrooms. On July 10th, Pennsylvania governor Robert Pattison, a recipient of Carnegie largesse, ordered the entire state national guard, a force of 8500 men, to descend on Homestead and restore order. The soldiers took up positions the next day on both sides of the Monongahela and pointed artillery pieces, Gatling guns, and Springfield rifles at the striking workers. This demonstration of firepower convinced the workers to give up possession of the steelworks. Carnegie and Frick regained control of the Homestead Steel Works, dismissed the old workers, and brought in new workers to resume production. The Amalgamated Association would never again represent the workers at Homestead.

The events in July 1892 at Homestead had a profound effect on steel manufacturing and corporate America. Within eight years, not a single steel operation in Pennsylvania was unionized. As economic circumstances deteriorated during the 1890s, Carnegie Steel relentlessly reduced costs, and then used those reduced costs to undercut the prices of competing firms. When those firms floundered, Carnegie Steel bought their mills at reduced prices allowing it to control 60% of the steel industry by 1900. Workers and managers were never again seen as partners in the production of steel. Management would make the rules, and the workers had to comply or seek employment elsewhere.

Little remains to mark the struggle between workers and owners at Homestead. Scattered exhibits try to describe what happened, but few stop to read them. All of the original buildings, except for the Pump House and the water tower, have been levelled at Homestead. Discarded slag from steel operations has covered the old wharf area where the Pinkerton barge had attempted to land. Today the site of the Homestead strike is a parking lot for a shopping mall where Americans can buy lots of stuff made in China.

Stephanie was right: I did live too much in the past. My problem was that there was so much to learn by studying what had happened before. Taking a large gulp of water, I push off to see if I can catch up with my daughter.

She is not too far ahead. In the early afternoon heat, she is lazily pedaling along. As I come alongside of her, she picks up the pace. I am able to match her for awhile. For maybe a mile we are biking side by side in a friendly race. I catch her glancing at me and grinning.

""What?" I call out over the crunching of the limestone gravel underneath our tires.

She looks straight ahead. "Nothing."

"What?" I insist.

She looks down without slowing. "Not bad for an old man."

"Old man? I'll show you what an old man can do."

It is the first day, and I know that I should be conserving energy, but my male ego has been challenged. I shift into another gear and claim a brief lead. She easily catches me. Although I reach for another gear, the result is the same. She is too young and strong for me. We settle into a fast, side by side pace.

We roll into McKeesport. Since Pittsburgh, we have been following the Monongahela, more or less. Here, another river joins the Monongahela, and we will switch to following it. I stop and stare at the sign announcing the new river. Steph stops next to me.

Although she can read the sign as well as I can, I spell out the name for her. "Y-O-U-G-H-I-O-G-H-E-N-Y. How is anybody supposed to pronounce that?" I ask her.

Steph pronounces the word fluently.

"Can you slow that down for your old man?"

"YAWK." She pauses, smiling mischievously. "e." Another long pause. "gay." Yet another long pause. "nee." I can tell she enjoys her command of the strange name.

I shake my head. "I'll never get that."

Steph shrugs. "Don't have to. Everybody just calls it the 'Yawk' anyway." She clips in and takes off.

"Why didn't you say so in the first place," I yell at her back.

"Come on, we've only covered fifteen miles, and we've got forty-three to go," she replies over her shoulder.

I check the time. The day is two-thirds done, and we are only a fourth of the way to our first night's objective. I suck it up and follow her.

"When are we stopping for lunch?"

Without a break in her rhythm, Steph twists and glares at me. "We don't have time to stop if we're going to make Connellsville before dark."

"Oh."

"Eat a granola bar," she suggests.

"But lunch is my favorite meal of the day," I protest.

"I thought breakfast was your favorite meal."

"It is. They're both my favorites."

"What about dinner?"

"I like that, too."

"You're hopeless."

Remembering my conversations with Katherine, I have to agree. "I think there's a general consensus on that point."

Our tires spin several hundred yards further before Steph suggests a compromise.

"Tell you what. If there's an ice cream shop in West Newton — it's not far — I'll let you buy us both ice cream cones."

We ride on, but West Newton is far — really far for me. Only a few miles further I stop at a pair of sign posts for water and a chance to stretch my legs. My butt is also tired of sitting on that tiny bike seat. Steph notices me pulling over and circles around.

"Got to keep moving, Daddy."

I take a big swig of water before responding. "I know, but I think we took a wrong turn." Pointing at a sign next to the trail, I say, "I'm pretty sure one of those towns is in Massachusetts and the other is in France." The sign reads "Boston 1 mile" and just below it "Versailles 2 miles". Steph cocks her head and says, "Very funny, but I want to get to West Newport for our ice cream, and we are not going to get there anytime soon if we sit around here reading trail signs."

Before I can respond, another biker approaches. He is about a decade younger than me, heavily bearded, and decked out in full cycling regalia that was probably stylish about the time bicycles were invented.

"Afternoon, folks."

"Afternoon," I reply.

"You need help with directions? I live around here and know this area like the back of my hand."

I have always thought that was an odd expression — as if someone asked me how to describe the back of one of my hands, I would not know what to say. Looking at the back of this man's hands, I get an idea.

"We were thinking of cycling over to Versailles to see it," I say. Although I am far from fluent in French, I pronounce "Versailles" the same way a Frenchman would — "Ver-SIGH".

I get a puzzled look from the man.

He responds: "I'm not sure where you are talking about."

So much for knowing this area like the back of his hand, I think. Pointing to the sign, I repeat the name of the local town, perhaps speaking a little louder to help him understand. "Ver-SIGH. Is there an ice cream place there?"

The man looks at the sign. A light of understanding comes on somewhere behind the beard. He chuckles as he says, "Oh, you mean, 'VER-sal-is'. No, there's not much there. Only about 1500 hundred in the town if you count the dogs and the cats."

Steph is looking at me over the man's shoulders trying desperately not to explode in laughter.

I ignore her and ask, "Isn't it named after the famous palace in France?"

"Oh, yeah. That's why it's called — " and again the man cheerfully pronounces "Versailles" as "VER-sal-is". I suddenly have a new appreciation of why the French get so upset when Americans visit their country and proceed to butcher their language while devouring their wine and cheese.

"So where is the nearest ice cream shop?"

The man looks up and down the Passage before responding. "I would say your best bet from here would be West Newton. Yeah, there's a nice place in West Newton, but it's a fer piece from here."

I glance over at Stephanie. She is jerking her head for us to get going.

"Thanks," I say. "We better get moving then."

The man is correct: West Newton is a "fer" piece. Fortunately, the heat of the day has passed, and cool air flows up from the river below us. We roll along in the shade of tall trees. Still, I am dead tired, and I have to stop and get Stephanie to take a picture of me lying down in front of a sign that states, "Dead Man's Hollow" — an appropriate title considering my present physical condition.

On we go, though. Whenever I slow down, Steph announces loudly "VER-sal-is" which causes me to laugh and speed back up. That and the thought of a cold, creamy reward gets me through Greenock, Buena Vista, Industry, Blythedale, Sutersville, and Smithdale. In West Newton, we find a place called Scoops N'at.

My muscles are tired and stiff; I have trouble getting my right leg over my bike seat and panniers. Watching me, Stephanie looks concerned.

"Are you okay?"

"I'm fine," I fib. "Nothing two scoops of ice cream won't cure."

"Only two?" She laughs, and we go inside.

The shop is small, but the list of available flavors is long. A small window air conditioning unit blows chilled air over us as we make our selections. After obtaining tiny tasting samples from a young woman behind the counter named Alicia, I cannot decide between Creamy Coconut and Boysenberry Blast, so I ask for a scoop of each in a cup.

Like the little girl I used to know — except that I don't have to give her a boost to see the flavors — my daughter carefully studies her options through the display glass. The decision of which ice cream to get always had to be carefully thought through — all possibilities and combinations given full consideration. Watching Stephanie contort her face as she tries to decide, I chide her. "I thought vegans didn't eat dairy."

Steph wrinkles her nose. "They don't."

"But ice cream on a hot day is an allowed exception?"

Unwrinkling her nose and twisting her lips as she continues to look through the display glass, she replies. "No, not an allowed exception."

"So you're falling off the vegan wagon, so to speak."

"Not at all. I told you that there is such a thing as vegan ice cream."

"How can you possibly make ice cream without milk that comes from an animal?"

"Use milk that comes from plants." She turns to Alicia and asks, "Do you have coffee ice cream made with soy milk?"

"We do. It's one of our top sellers." Alicia replies cheerfully.

"I'll take two scoops in a cup, and do you have a non-dairy chocolate sauce?"

"Yes. It's fifty cents extra."

Steph glances at me. "Does our travel budget allow for chocolate sauce?"

The entire purchase was adding up to less than one double latte at Starbucks. "I think I can clear that with the home office," I say and nod my okay to Alicia.

She looks at me strangely, but delivers two scoops of vegan coffee ice cream to my daughter. I pay and give her a small tip. Steph and I sit at a small table inside to enjoy our ice cream and the air conditioning.

"Your mother loved coffee, you know," I say.

"I remember." The answer is noncommittal. Just the way she was when she was younger, Steph is absorbed in enjoying her ice cream.

"She would have a cup every morning," I continue.

"Did she like coffee ice cream as well?"

"Only if was covered in chocolate sauce."

"Are you telling me I am just like my mother?"

I study my daughter with her braided hair flattened by her bike helmet. From what I can tell, she is wearing no makeup other than sunscreen. The light from the window reflects off her chestnut brown hair and sparkles in her brown eyes. Sitting in that tiny ice cream shop in West Newton, she is the very image of her mother — the woman I had loved with all my heart, the woman I had lost so long ago.

Rather than tell my daughter what I am feeling, I choose a time honored political tactic; I deflect and dissemble. "I think you are your own person — despite my best efforts." We share a smile. "Are we done for the day?" I ask hopefully.

Steph starts putting her cycling gloves back on. "Nope. I think we can easily make Connellsville today.

"How far is that?"

"Only twenty-five."

"Is that miles, kilometers, or yards?"

She does not answer me as she exits the ice cream shop. I try to follow her, but my legs have trouble straightening. In the few minutes we have been sitting, my lower back and thighs have stiffened. I extract an Advil capsule from the bottle Hank gave me, pop it in my mouth, and stagger outside.

I should be refreshed from our break, but I have trouble regaining my rhythm. Steph lets me take the lead, and we cruise on a smooth path through the forest. Gradually, my muscles loosen and stop complaining enough for me to pick up the pace. Steph pulls abreast with me, and we talk about nothing in particular. It feels so good to be enjoying the day with her that I do not notice a change in the consistency of the gravel underneath our tires. Both of us pump harder, but we both slow as our wheels sink into the surface. The once solid track has become a slushy goo. Our rear tires make deep ruts from the weight of our panniers. We come to a stop to assess the situation.

"Connellsville, huh?" I say.

"We can still make it," Steph replies confidently. "We just have to hoof it for a while." She dismounts and pushes her bike onto the grass on the side of the Passage. Her tires gain traction. "Come on. It won't take long. It's just a section they haven't rolled and compacted yet."

I nod reluctantly and follow her lead.

That is when the gnats attack. They swarm about our heads in dark gray clouds trying to fly into our mouths, nostrils, and ears. Holding our handlebars with both hands as we struggle through the grass, we are defenseless. Our only hope is to get to a place where we can get back on our bikes and out run them.

Jogging next to my bike actually feels good. My butt is getting a break from the bike seat, and my legs like the different motion. However, my ankles persistently bang against either my bike pedal or my panniers. Steph has the same problem, but I notice that she solves it by leaning the top of her bike toward her at a forty-five degree angle. I follow her lead. Although I am able to move faster, the bike is harder to steer.

Still, we race along until we reach a large roller that straddles the entire bike path. We work our way around the giant machine and see that the slushy gravel has been compressed on the other side. As quickly as we can, we remount and pedal as hard as we can to escape the gnats. We do not slow down until we are a safe distance. Even then, fear of the gnats makes us keep up a steady pace.

We are cruising along when we spot a man climbing up from an embankment next to a bridge. Curiosity gets the better of me, and I slow. He greets us, and I return the greeting.

"Great swimming hole down there," he says.

Stopping on the bridge and looking down, I see nothing but thick foliage.

"Can't see it from up here," he continues. "Only the locals know about it. But if you've been biking all day and would like a break, it's a great little spot. You have to take this little trail around to the right and down." He points to a small opening in the trees.

"I think I've earned a break," I announce. Turning to Steph, I ask, "Do we have time?"

She shrugs noncommittally.

I awkwardly swing my right leg over my panniers and lean my bike against a tree. Steph pulls her bike next to mine, and we chain them together to the tree.

"Thanks for the tip," I tell the guy.

"No problem," he replies.

He watches us descend down the trail. It is steep and slippery. I have to bounce from one tree to the next to make it down.

About halfway down, Steph stops and says, "I think I left something up top. I'm going to go get it."

"What?"

"Something I think I'll need."

"What?" I persist.

"You'll see."

She heads back up the trail. I watch her go, not looking forward to the time when I will have to ascend. However, that will not be until later, and I can hear the sound of flowing water. It draws me down. I come out on top of an enormous boulder that projects into a pool of crystal clear water. Above the pool, water flows over a ledge.

My shoes and socks come off. Finding a comfortable rock near the water, I dangle my overheated feet in the icy water. The air is cool and refreshing. After sitting on a narrow bike saddle all day, my bottom relishes the broad if hard surface of the rock.

Stephanie reappears; she is carrying a crimson scarf that I recognize immediately. This idyllic spot — I think to myself — is as good as any to start the conversation.

I shift over to give Steph room to sit next to me on the rock. Instead of sitting next to me, she steps past me and wades into the water. It covers her ankles. As she carefully steps around the small pool, my daughter ties the red scarf loosely around her neck. Although the rock and the pool have suddenly become uncomfortable for me, I fold my fingers together as I sit patiently waiting for her to build up the courage to start the conversation.

Steph completes three laps around the pool before she begins. "I want to talk about Momma."

"Okay," I reply. "I recognize the scarf. It was her favorite. I didn't know you kept it."

"I bring it out when I miss her."

"I don't ever remember seeing you wear it."

Standing in the middle of the pool, my daughter fingers the scarf around her neck. "I never wore it when you were around. I was afraid it would upset you."

I had to admit that seeing my daughter wear Nancy's scarf stirred up feelings inside me that I had buried long ago. Those feelings took me to dark places. My mind drifts into the past as memories of my wife flood my brain.

"Daddy?"

Steph's voice jolts me back into the present.

"What? Huh? Yeah? Sorry." I stumble through single word responses as I struggle to regain my composure.

Stephanie moves closer to me and asks, "Are you okay?"

I try to stand, but she gently presses against my shoulders and says. "I think you ought to stay where you are."

"Right. Okay," I mutter. "I'm fine. What do you want to talk about?"

Stephanie folds her arms and stands in front of me. "My mother. Your wife."

"Sure," I say. "Ask me anything you want." The air around the pool no longer seems as cool as it was.

"We never talked about her when I was growing up."

"Of course, we did. She came up all the time."

"She came up alright, but we didn't talk about her."

"We didn't?"

"No, you would go off somewhere in your mind the same way you just did now."

"Oh, well, uh, okay." I place my hands on my knees to steady myself. "Ask away."

"I don't have anything in particular to ask at the moment. I just want to be able to talk about her without you getting weird on me. I want to know things about her, and you're the person who knew her best."

Rubbing the rough stubble on my chin, I think about that last assertion. Had I really known Nancy?

"All I can say," I offer, "is to tell you what I know about your mother — from my point of view."

Steph nods and throws her arms around my neck. "Thanks, Daddy. I knew I could count on you."

Her reaction surprises me, but we hug awkwardly. I am sitting on my rock, and she is standing in the pool of water. My nose is buried in my dead wife's scarf. Stephanie must never have had it cleaned because I can still smell Nancy in it. I pull away before memories overcome me.

"I'll be glad to talk about your mother," I lie. "But I will always be weird — no matter what we talk about. It's my natural state."

"Oh, Daddy!"

I receive a light push on the shoulder and then an admonition from my daughter. "We need to get back on our bikes if we are going to get to Connellsville before dark."

We collect our stuff, put our shoes back on, and climb back up to our bikes.

As we strap our helmets onto our heads, I say, "I'm glad you kept that scarf of your mother's. We should always remember her."

I do not tell Steph about the wedding ring that I am wearing on a chain around my neck under my shirt.

A large curved sign that stretches over the Passage greets us when we arrive at the outskirts of Connellsville. My thigh muscles and butt cheeks feel relieved as they have reached their limits, and my stomach is rumbling. Steph is waiting for me at the sign. Fortunately, we have enough daylight left to take the obligatory photos. I force a smile onto my face as if I am having the time of my life.

"You look tired and hungry," Steph comments.

"That's because *I am* tired and hungry." I reply.

"We can try to stay there." Steph indicates some Adirondack style shelters close to the bike trail.

I like their proximity, but my body aches for a real bed. "Let's head into town and see what we can find," I suggest.

"Okay."

I did not realize that going into town meant climbing up a hill. My thigh muscles scream at me to stop at the very first hotel we come to. It is an old wooden clapboard establishment sorely in need of fresh paint. The sign is so faded that I cannot read the name. However, a large neon sign in a window flashes the word "Vacancy" in bright yellow letters. That is all I need to know.

Steph gives me a doubtful look. "Are you sure? This place looks just like the one they used in that movie *Psycho*."

"The Bates Hotel?"

"Yeah, I guess."

"Nah. It's more like the one they used in *The Shining*."

I didn't care as I could not pedal the wheels of my bike another revolution. All I wanted was a square meal, a hot shower, and a soft bed. Dismounting, I tell Steph, "Wait here. I'll see if the presidential suite is available."

When I grab the doorknob on the front door, it comes off in my hand. I do not need to turn my head to see that Steph is shaking hers. Not to be denied, I reinsert the knob and gingerly jiggle the door open. Inside, I am greeted by a large entry with furnishings that must date from around the Spanish American War. It is drab and dark, but I have committed myself. I walk over to a plate glass window that is at least three inches thick. Cracks in the glass indicate that someone had once unsuccessfully tried to break it.

I see an elderly woman sitting in a chair at a desk. Her eyes are closed and she holds her hands folded in her lap. She appears to be napping. I rap lightly on the glass.

Her eyes open, and she seems genuinely surprised that she has a customer.

I smile as I say, "Hi, I was wondering if you have a room for tonight."

"What? I can't hear you!"

Still smiling, I lower my head until it's close to the small opening near the bottom of the glass. "Do you have any rooms available?"

"Yeah, lots." The woman speaks loudly, the way people who are hard of hearing talk. "How many do you want?"

"Just one. Two beds if possible."

"How many nights?"

"Just tonight."

The woman looks disappointed.

"$75," she yells. "Cash only. No checks or credit cards."

At this point in our conversation, Steph enters, looks around, and asks, "Do they have a room?" I can tell from her voice that she is hoping the hotel is booked solid for the whole week.

"Yes, honey," I reply.

When I turn back to the woman, she has a knowing look on her face. She tells me, "It's $75 whether you use the room for an hour or all night. Cash. Payable in advance."

The woman obviously has the wrong idea about my relationship with Steph. All she sees is an old man with a young woman trying to get a hotel room. I could try explaining to the woman that Stephanie is my daughter, but that probably doesn't matter to her way of thinking. This is the backwoods of western Pennsylvania after all.

I shell out four twenties and slide them through the small opening. In return I get a small key with a gigantic fob attached. I wait for my change, but the woman only stares placidly at me.

Finally, I say, "I thought you said the room was $75?"

"It is, but there's also a $5 key deposit."

I think to myself that I was lucky I hadn't slid the woman a hundred dollar bill. The key deposit might have risen to $25. "Can you suggest a place nearby to eat?" I ask.

"Yes."

I wait. When no further information is forthcoming, I ask, "Can you tell me the name and give me directions?"

"The Broken Buckle down the street. They've got pretty decent food." The woman pauses. "For a sports bar, anyway."

"Thanks."

The woman does not say "You're welcome" as Steph and I depart to look for our room for the night.

We find it at the end of a long hall. Fortunately, it is on the first floor and near a fire exit. We smuggle our bikes in through the exit and then clean up.

Steph goes into the bathroom first.

I sit on the edge of one of the beds to take my shoes off. My butt sinks almost to the floor. At least the bed will be soft I think to myself. Between the two beds and our two bikes, there is little space to maneuver in our room.

I hear a distinct gasp come from the bathroom.

"Are you okay?" I call to her through the closed door.

"I'm pretty sure I saw a rat."

"Where?"

"There's a hole in one of the baseboards. I think I saw it run into it."

"Probably just a mouse."

"Rat — Mouse — Whatever! I don't do well with rodents where I am trying to sleep."

I poke my head into the bathroom. There is indeed a hole in the baseboard.

"Hand me a towel," I say.

Steph hands me a threadbare piece of cloth.

I look at it and shake my head. "No, I need a towel, not a washcloth."

"That's all I see in here."

After a quick glance around, I have to agree with her. "Okay, I guess I'll have to make this work." I get down on my hands and knees to examine the hole in the baseboard. It looks larger up close. Twisting the piece of cloth into a knot, I stuff it into the hole. I have to get Steph to hand me another "towel" which I knot and jam alongside the first piece to plug the hole.

"There," I say as I admire my handiwork. "That should keep the rodents at bay — at least for tonight."

"What are we going to use to dry off?" Steph asks.

"There were only two towels?"

"I think the word 'towel' is a generous term."

Scratching my head, I look around the room. "Maybe we use our bed sheets?" I suggest.

My daughter makes a face at me. I make a face back. We laugh.

"Let's go eat," I say.

She agrees.

We set out on foot at my suggestion. Our hotel host had indicated that The Broken Buckle was not far, and I was tired of sitting on a bicycle seat. We walk and walk and walk. Apparently, the expression "just up the street" in Connellsville means that something is almost a mile away. Still, the evening is pleasant, and Steph and I recount the adventures of the first day of biking as we walk.

The sun has set by the time we reach a flashing neon sign that proudly proclaims, "The Golden Buckle".

"Do you think this is the place she meant?" Steph asks.

I shrug. "Let's go in and see."

We enter. The odor of stale cigarette smoke wafts over us as our eyes adjust. Customers fill less than a quarter of the seats. Three guys are huddled together at the bar. A handful of couples are eating on side tables. A single, rather small TV screen displays a baseball game. No one is watching. People talk quietly among themselves.

"I thought she said this was a sports bar," Steph comments.

"She did," I reply.

I walk over to the bar and catch the bartender's eye. He is about my age and height, which means that he is older and shorter than I would like to be.

"Do you serve food here?" I ask.

With one large towel draped over his left shoulder, the bartender walks toward me drying a beer mug with another.

"Best burger and fries in Connellsville!" he announces jovially.

"Works for me," I say. When I look over my shoulder at Steph, she has a concerned look on her face.

"May I see a menu, please?" she asks.

"Sure," replies the bartender. He hands Steph a placard with the word "menu" emblazoned at the top and little else. Food choices are limited at this fine dining establishment.

I watch Steph's face contort into various expressions as she peruses the fare of The Golden Buckle. She looks up at the bartender. "Do you have a veggie burger?"

The bartender looks puzzled. "What is a veggie burger?"

"A hamburger made out of vegetables."

"Who would want to eat that?"

"I would," Steph replies coolly.

"Oh," says the bartender. The name "Stan" is stitched on his shirt.

I intercede and explain: "She's a vegan."

"What's that?"

Steph answers: "A person who doesn't eat meat."

I can tell from her tone that she is irritated. Even when she was little, she was easily irritated when she was hungry — just like the people in the Snickers commercials.

Stan smiles amicably. "Oh, sure. How about a nice personal cheese pizza? You can add whatever vegetables you like."

Before Steph can launch into lecturing Stan on the non-dairy aspects of the vegan diet, I raise my hand.

"How about just a plate of vegetables?" I suggest.

"I need more than that — like some carbs." Steph adds.

The three guys at the other end of the bar have stopped talking and are listening in on our conversation.

"I've got just the thing," Stan says as he raps his knuckles on the bar. "Would a large plate of sweet potato fries work for you, little lady?"

He is rewarded with a smile from Steph, although I doubt she likes being called a "little lady".

"That would be great!"

Stan seems pleased with himself. "Okay, what can I get you two to drink? How about something tall, cold, and frosty?"

"Sounds like a woman I used to date," I remark.

Steph rolls her eyes, but I get a guffaw from Stan.

"What's on tap," Steph asks.

"Yuengling," Stan answers. "And Yuengling Light for us older fellers." Stan grins at me.

I smile back politely.

Stan continues. "It's the local brew. Pretty much everybody around here drinks it."

"Damn good American beer!"

The boisterous recommendation came from the three young males who have been listening to our conversation with Stan. They raise their three mugs and toast us. I would guess that all three are in their late twenties. The one closest to us sports a mop of black unruly hair. His eyes lock with mine. I sense that he's angry about something.

Steph and I acknowledge their toast with nods.

Turning to Stan, Steph states: "I'll have one of those."

"How tall?" Stan asks as he extends his palm about a foot above the bar.

Steph raises her palm a couple of inches above Stan's. "This tall," Steph answers.

"And you?" Stan asks me. "The same?"

I shake my head as I pick up the menu. "I will take some of the local water and something a little more exotic. Did I see that you offer Beck's?"

I hear hissing from the trio at the other end of the bar.

Stan turns toward them and playfully shouts, "Hey! Pipe down! I've got paying customers I'm working with here!"

He turns back to Steph and me. "That Beck's comes in a bottle, is that okay?"

"Sure," I answer as I notice the guy with the unruly black hair staring at me.

Tearing a sheet off his order pad, Stan waddles through the kitchen door and then returns. He pops off the top to a Beck's and pours a tall glass of Yuengling. Setting the beers in front of Steph and me, Stan leans in over the bar. He tells us in a low voice: "Don't mind them boys at the other end of the bar. Some foreign conglomerate came in and bought out the company they worked for. Started letting people go left and right. They've been laid off from the mines for going on three months now."

"Mines?" Steph asks loudly.

"Coal mines. Their Dads and their Granddads all had jobs in the mines. Connellsville was once known as the Coke Capital of the World."

"Coke?" Steph looks puzzled. "What does a sugary carbonated beverage have to do with coal production?"

Loud exclamations explode from the other end of the bar.

"Without coke, lady, you can't make steel."

"Without steel, you can't build cars."

"And without a car, you can't get to your fancy city job."

Steph pivots sharply on her stool. "I'll have you know that I ride my bike or take the subway to work. And although my job is important, it is far from fancy."

Sensing trouble, Stan intervenes. "Okay, gentlemen, that's enough. Finish your beers and go home. You've been here long enough."

"But, Stan —"

"Don't 'but Stan' me. I've got a business to run. You boys need to go."

While two of the three stand, the former coal miner with the unruly black hair does not move. The glass in front of him is empty. He looks at Stan and then at me. He says rather slowly: "I want another beer."

Stan places his left elbow on the bar in front of the guy, and says, "Ricky, I don't want any trouble." From where I am sitting, I can see that he is holding a baseball bat in his right hand below the bar. Bartenders always need to be prepared for trouble.

Ricky remains defiant; he turns his eyes from me to Stan. "I ain't done drinking."

Stan lowers his voice, but we can still hear him. "Another beer isn't going to get your job back. Or your Mustang the bank repossessed. And it certainly isn't going to get Shirley to come back to you."

116

Flames seem to shoot out of Ricky's eyes.

Steph and I look at each other; what have we walked into? I see Stan's grip on the bat handle tighten. A quick glance reveals that there is only one way in or out of this bar. The three former coal miners — young, healthy, and angry — are between us and the exit.

Still speaking in a low voice, Stan keeps talking to Ricky. "I've got your father's cell phone on my speed dial. Do I need to call him?"

"Come on, Ricky," one of his drinking buddies pleads. "Let's go. There's lots of other places we can get more beer."

Sullenly, Ricky rises and follows his friends toward the door.

"Shall I add this round to your tab?" Stan asks.

Ricky stops and glares at Stan. "You know I'm good for it — as soon as I get my job back."

Stan relaxes his grip on the baseball bat. "Sure, Ricky. As soon as you get your job back."

Ricky moves his glare to me. "Enjoy your foreign beer, Mac."

Knowing that correcting Ricky's reference to me as a "Mac" might further inflame the situation, I let it pass. Instead, I foolishly tip my beer bottle in his direction and say: "Indeed, I shall." With that, I take a long drink of my Beck's.

I believe that Ricky would have gone after me then and there, but both his buddies grab his arms and drag him outside.

Stan quietly restores his baseball bat to its hiding place underneath the bar. Addressing us, he says, "Sorry about that, folks. I've known those boys since they was in diapers. They're alright kids. Come from good families. But times are hard in these parts. Whole economy was built around coal production, especially coke for steel production."

"What's coke have to do with coal and steel production?" Stephanie asks.

"Coke is a special kind of coal. It's burned down like charcoal. They used to make it in little beehive ovens. You probably saw some on the hillsides around town."

"Small piles of brick?" I ask.

"Yeah. That's a pretty good description."

"We saw them as we were biking on the Passage." I say.

"Yeah, you can see them from the bike trail."

"I still don't understand what coke has to do with making steel," Steph persists.

Stan chuckles. "Everything. The coke burns hot enough to melt the iron ore to make steel with fewer impurities. The better the coke the better the steel. Connellsville was once a leading center of coal and coke production that was used in steel manufacturing in the Pittsburgh area. Unfortunately, the less steel they make, the less coke they need, and the fewer jobs we have around here."

We hear a female voice call out from the kitchen. Stan goes through the door and returns with my burger and Steph's vegetables. Steam rises from both meals. He sets them on the counter in front of us.

Looking over Stan's shoulder, I spot an unusual photo behind the bar. A half dozen men are running in shorts on a track in front of a large crowd. The picture is in black and white, is taken from the side, and is slightly faded. Most of the runners in the picture are white. In the foreground, a tall scrawny black man with long legs is running in an outside lane trying to get to the front of the pack. Etched on the photo are the words "Berlin 1936".

"Huh," I grunt. "Is that Jesse Owens in that picture? What's his connection with Connellsville?"

Stan glances back briefly and says, "That's actually an enlargement of a trading card issued by the Muratti Cigarettes Company of one of the greatest foot races in Olympic history." Stan lifts the picture off its hook, flips it over, and shows us the backside. Printed words appear to describe the photo on the obverse side.

"A cigarette company issued sports trading cards?" Steph is dumbfounded at the thought.

"Yep," Stan replies. "Sounds weird today, but that was seen back then as a way to sell tobacco products."

"It's all in German," I remark, noting the language on the back of the photo.

"That makes sense," Stan muses. "Muratti was a German company." He returns the picture of the trading card back to its place of honor on the wall.

"I suppose there is a story that goes with that photo," I say.

"That there is," Stan replies.

Yanking a dish towel off his shoulder and employing the long slow strokes bartenders use when they have a tale to tell, he starts wiping the counter.

"Just about everybody knows the story of Jesse Owens at the 1936 Olympics held in Berlin, Germany. Them goose stepping Nazis thought they would use the Olympics to show the world they was better than everyone else. Aryan white supermen, or some nonsense like that. Jesse won four gold medals: in the hundred, the two hundred, a relay, and —"

Stan stops talking and wiping as he tries to remember the fourth event.

"I think it was the long jump," I suggest helpfully.

"Yeah, that was it. Thanks." Stan resumes his wiping. "Thing is, that ain't Jesse Owens." He looks up and grins at us.

"Who is it then?" Steph asks. "Somebody wrote 'Berlin 1936' on it."

"People forgit. Jesse Owens weren't the only black man to win a gold medal at the '36 Olympics. *Five* African Americans won gold medals. That there is Long John Woodruff. His race was the 800 meters, and he was from Connellsville. Used to come in here all the time when he was in town. He moved to New Jersey and then out to Arizona when he got older and couldn't handle the northern winters no more."

Stan finishes wiping the bar.

"How's the food?" he asks.

"Good," we both mumble between mouthfuls. The burger is tasty, but I am so hungry anything would have tasted great.

Stan picks up a bar glass and starts polishing it as he continues with his story about John Woodruff.

"Ol' Long John almost never became an Olympic runner. He grew up in hard times — the Great Depression. People think times are hard now, but back then people had to worry about getting enough to eat, not just buying fancy new clothes.

119

When John was sixteen, a bunch of his white classmates left school to get factory jobs. John's Daddy only had an eighth grade education; his Momma just got through the second grade. Not bad for them cuz *their* parents had been slaves in Virginia. John's family needed money, and he had reached high school — further than his parents had gotten. So, he trotted down to see if he could get himself a job. The plant manager was polite to John — he was a likeable kid — but told him the company was not hiring Negroes."

"How racist!" Stephanie blurts out.

I almost choke on my burger.

Stan just chuckles. "Times were different then, but I can't blame the plant manager."

"Why?" my daughter demands.

"The plant manager was *my* Grand Daddy. He loved to tell that story. Would always kid Long John about that — said he was the reason for his success."

"How so?" Steph is not going to let even *ancient* discrimination pass. She ignores my stern fatherly looks to do so.

"It forced Long John to go back to school. He started playing football. Every day after practice, the whole team had to run up to the cemetery on the hill and back. Long John always came back first. The track coaches noticed, recruited him for mid distance running, and then got him college scholarships. The rest is history. He was the only member of his family — I think they had a dozen kids — to graduate from high school. If he had gotten that job at my Grand Daddy's factory, Long John would never have been a track star and gone on to college."

"Hmm." Steph reluctantly accepts Stan's story — at least partially. "Why do you keep calling him 'Long John'?" she asks.

Stan seems startled at the question. "Cuz that was his nickname," he says. "That boy stood six foot three — maybe four. Look at the picture. He's all arms and legs. His stride was measured at over nine feet!"

I look again at the picture. Long John is a head taller than the rest of the field, and his legs seem a foot longer than those of his competitors.

"Is this the gold medal race?" I ask.

"It is. He loved that picture. He had won the semifinals by twenty yards, but he had to face experienced runners in the finals. One of them was an Italian who was the reigning European champion. That feller in front?" Stan waves the bar glass he is holding at the photo. "Some Canadian doctor who was at his third Olympics."

Stan puts away the bar glass and grabs another to polish.

"Long John had just finished his freshman year at college. He had run just a handful of international races. I bet you this bar that those other runners sized up the situation and figured that they had to gang up on him if any of them hoped to win."

"So why is he running so far outside?" I ask. "Seems like a hard way to win a race."

"It is. You have to cover more ground when you run on the outside. What happened was that Canadian doctor jumped to an early lead with Long John right behind him. The doctor set a slow pace allowing the other runners to box Long John in. He couldn't use his long strides, and he was afraid of fouling and being disqualified."

Stan pauses his tale, looks at our plates, and asks, "Are you finished?"

"Uh, yeah," I say.

"What did he do?" Steph asks.

Picking up our plates, Stan turns and heads for the kitchen. "I'll tell you when I get back."

Steph leans into me with her palms outstretched. "Can you believe this guy?" she whispers. "He leaves us in the middle of the story."

I laugh. "He knows he's got us hooked."

Stan returns. "Dessert?" he asks.

"Sounds good," I reply.

"I would like to hear the rest of the story," Steph says defiantly.

"I don't think he's going to tell us the rest of the story unless we order dessert," I say as I look at our bartender/waiter for confirmation.

"Or more beer," Stan says with a grin.

"Can we see a dessert menu?" I ask.

"Sure." Stan picks up an index card, writes something on it, and hands the card to me.

All the card says is "apple pie".

I peruse the index card carefully, as if I have a number of delectables to choose from. When I show the card to Steph, she makes a face.

"You actually have two choices," Stan admits.

"Really?" I say.

Stan smiles. "Yes. You can have apple pie, or — you can have apple pie with a large scoop of vanilla ice cream."

"I don't see any prices on this menu," I caution and wave the index card in the air.

Stan is nonplussed. "A buck fifty for the pie; two bucks even with ice cream."

I was going to resist the temptation of dessert, but I cannot pass such a deal. "It's a difficult choice to make, but I think I'll have the apple pie — with the ice cream."

Stan assumes the hauteur of an Italian waiter who has been given an expensive wine order. "Excellent selection, sir, and the little lady?"

Steph bridles at the use of the term "little lady", but I can tell she wants to hear more about Long John. "Just a slice of the pie," she says.

"Coming right up." Stan disappears into the kitchen.

While Stan is away, Steph extracts her cell phone.

"Who are you calling now?" I ask.

"No one," she answers."I'm going to google this guy and see if this bartender is pulling our legs."

"So what if he is? He tells a good story," I say dismissively.

Steph works her fingers over the screen. "He's not pulling our legs. There really was a John Woodford, and he won a gold medal at the 1936 Olympics. There's even a YouTube video of the race."

At that moment, Stan returns with our pies. They are huge slices, and I have a generous portion of vanilla ice cream on mine.

Stan restarts the story as he sets the slices of pie in front of us. "With a little over half of the race to go, Long John is crowded in by the other runners. He has no place to go. Then he does the most amazing thing. Picture this: you're a young guy — about twenty-one years old — in the race of your life — the Olympics — and what does he do? He stops running! How can you win a race without running as fast as you can the whole way? Some people say he just slowed down, but Long John always claimed that he stopped and let all the other runners pass him. Then he moved two lanes to the outside and chased them down one by one. Absolutely incredible."

"And he won the race," I say to conclude the story.

"But it was far from over. Not by a long shot. That Canadian doctor was a cagey fella. After Long John got the lead, the Canadian made a little sprint to get back ahead. As they came down the stretch, the Canadian protected the inside of the lane and ran so as to push Long John wider and wider especially as they came around the final turn."

"That forced Long John to run a farther distance."

"Exactly."

"What did Long John do?"

"He just kept to the outside and used that long loping stride of his to win going away. The Italian made a last ditch effort to catch Long John but could only come in second."

"Wow!" Steph exclaimed.

"Yeah, it was pretty amazing," Stan agreed.

Steph held up her phone. "There's a video of the race on the internet. It's pretty much as you described it."

"Really? I don't use that internet thing much," Stan admitted. He turns to me. "The Nazis gave every gold medal winner an oak sapling from Germany's Black Forest to take home with them. To get across the Atlantic back then, you had to go on a boat. Weren't no airplanes flying that far. Imagine keeping a baby tree alive all the way across the ocean and back to Connellsville! To show you what kind of man Long John was, he planted that tree right outside of the high school football stadium where he got his start running. He did that so that all of Connellsville could share in his victory over those Nazi bastards. You guys can see it if you like. It's still standing."

"An oak tree planted in 1936? It must be huge by now!" Steph has warmed to the story — probably because the internet had confirmed it *and* it involved a tree.

"Yep. I think the last time they measured, it was eighty feet tall."

"Did he run in any other Olympics?" Steph asks.

Stan shakes his head sadly. "There was not another Olympics until 1948 — twelve years later. Little scrap we had with the Nazis called World War II kept Long John from being known as the greatest distance runner of all time. He finished his collegiate racing career setting world records and never losing a race. Then he served his country by enlisting in the fight with the Nazis and then in Korea."

"Is he still alive?" I ask.

"Fraid not," Stan answers. "Passed away a few years ago. Say, you folks need anything else? Time for me to stop yakking and close up."

I settle up with Stan. The check is so small that my tip is almost more than what the food, the beers, and the dessert cost. Stan gives me a funny look when he sees how much money I have left on the bar.

"For the story," I say.

He nods in appreciation.

"You can always put it toward Ricky's tab," I suggest.

He laughs.

We are the last customers to leave The Golden Buckle. Stan locks up behind us as we head back to our hotel. The streets are deserted. A few cars are parked along the street, but the buildings look vacant with no signs of activity inside.

It feels good to stretch our legs after the day's biking and sitting at the bar. The air is cool and refreshing.

"So, how many miles did we cover today?" I ask Stephanie.

"Officially?"

"Out of the 334 point five that I have to do to get back to D.C."

"68."

"That many? Not bad for an old fart." I have to brag on myself. For the first time, I am starting to believe that I can complete this trip. ""What's the mileage for tomorrow?"

"42."

"Is that all?" I was feeling cocky. This bike trip was starting to look like less of a challenge.

Steph cast a sideways glance at me. "That's it, but our big mileage day is the day after tomorrow. We have to cover 73. I'm sure you can handle it without any problems."

At least my daughter has confidence in me I think to myself.

With no traffic, we walk in the middle of the street, quietly sharing the events of the day and planning tomorrow's ride. The light is dim, and I cannot see clearly. I do not notice the three figures emerge from a side street. I think nothing of it until they are almost on us and the figure in the center shouts at us.

"Ain't nothing wrong with American beer!"

I recognize Ricky's voice from the bar. He and his two friends have been waiting for us.

Steph whispers to me, "Just ignore him and keep walking."

I glance sideways at her and whisper back, "That might be difficult."

We keep walking, but the three of them spread out and block our path. Stephanie and I are forced to stop. Nervously, I look around, but no one else is in sight. We are alone with three intoxicated men on a deserted street in a dilapidated old town.

Despite having lived in large metropolitan areas most of my life, I have never been mugged. At least not until now. Friends and acquaintances have been mugged, but not me. They have shared their awful experiences with me, and they have uniformly advised me to give the muggers whatever material possessions they want. Just hope that the

125

confrontation will not turn violent. Resisting will only add physical pain to the humiliation and financial loss.

Ricky, the drunk in the middle, addresses me directly. "So what you think is so wrong with American beer?" He is holding something in his right hand, but I cannot make out what it is.

"Nothing is wrong with American beer," I say.

"Oh, you say that now, but back at The Golden Buckle you said a lot of bad things about American beer."

"All I did was order a Beck's because that was what I was in the mood to drink tonight."

"Oh, an American beer wasn't good enough for ya, huh? I guess that makes you a Conny Sewer?"

The three of them laugh at his play on the word "connoisseur".

"I guess it does," I say. All I want to do is get out of the street and to the relative safety of our room. Unfortunately, we are several blocks from the hotel. "Please excuse us."

I try to step around Ricky, but he moves to block me.

"Not so fast, Mac." Ricky pushes my chest with the palm of his left hand.

Not resisting the push, I step backward. I have no idea why he thinks my name is 'Mac', but for some reason I find it irritating — more irritating than being pushed.

"You need to apologize," Ricky demands.

"Fine," I say. "I'm sorry if I insulted you."

"Not to me, you moron," Ricky hisses. "To my beer." He raises his right hand, and I can see he is holding a half empty bottle.

"Okay," I say. "I am sorry, Mr. Beer, if I insulted you."

Ricky shakes his head. "That ain't good enough."

He sets the beer down on the asphalt between us. "You gotta kneel down, and ask the beer fer forgiveness."

I am incredulous. "You want me to get down on the ground and ask a bottle of beer for forgiveness?"

"That's right, sucker," one of Ricky's companions interjects. "And make sure you get your head lower than the top of the bottle."

The other companion says, "Ricky, you put it in the wrong spot." He picks up the bottle and places it on the side of a water-filled pothole opposite to where I am standing. "That's where he should apologize."

The intent is for me to place my face in a muddy hole as I say that I am sorry. As I contemplate this humiliation, I wonder how far these three thugs with push the situation. Will they be satisfied, or will they beat me up, take my money, and assault Steph? Out of the corner of my eye, I think I see Stephanie slowly move her head from side to side telling me not to comply.

"Look, guys, how about I give each of you twenty bucks as an apology?" I suggest. "You can buy a lot of great American beer at The Golden Buckle with the money."

Rick sneers. "Oh, we'll get to the monetary compensation, but first we want to hear your heartfelt apology with your nose in that mud puddle. And in front of your girlfriend," he adds.

"She's not my girlfriend," I protest. "She's my daughter."

"No way," one of Ricky's friend sneers. "You're too ugly to be the Daddy of a hot babe like that. Say honey, let me be yo Daddy tonight." He steps toward Steph.

To my dismay, my daughter smiles at the guy. I hear her say in a soft sultry voice that I have never heard her use: "Sure, baby."

She keeps smiling at him as he walks over to her and starts to put his arm around her. *What is she doing,* I wonder.

As the miscreant reaches toward her with his right hand, she grabs it with both her hands. Steph seems to have clenched his thumb in one fist and his pinkie in the other. Twisting violently, she jerks the guy's arm upward. I hear a loud pop, and the guy screams in pain. Although there is not much light, I can see that Stephanie has a hold of his pinkie and is bending it backwards at an awkward angle. His knees buckle, and he crumples to the ground.

Ricky steps toward Steph and says, "What the f — "

Steph abruptly terminates his question with a roundhouse kick to his jaw. I hear the smack of tennis shoe against human flesh, a grunt, and the thud of Ricky hitting the pavement. He is out cold.

Ricky's remaining friend whips out a switchblade. He flicks it open, waves it around, and says, "I'm going to cut you up, bitch!" Steph steps back as he slashes at her.

I grab the beer bottle by its throat and smash the bottom on the asphalt. The liquid inside splashes me and the surrounding pavement. "Hey," I yell out in an attempt to distract the hoodlum.

He looks over his shoulder at me and sees that I have an improvised weapon. The distraction is just enough for Stephanie to make her move. She grabs his forearm with one hand and his wrist with the other. A sharp twist and the knife drops. Using her body weight, she bends his arm back and then up. The derelict sinks to his knees. Steph jams her foot into his armpit and yanks his arm. He cries out.

Steph lets go of his limp arm, and it sinks to the ground. With eyes darting around, she starts walking at a quick pace. "Let's go," she whispers to me. Ricky is out cold on the ground. One of his friends is in obvious pain, kneeling and holding his right hand with his left. The other is writhing around pawing at his right shoulder. I see no one else, and no lights come on.

I follow behind my daughter. She is walking so fast that I am almost trotting. I ask, "Where did you learn to — "

She cuts me off. "Let's not talk about that now. We need to create some space between us and them. Quickly and quietly."

"Shouldn't we call the — "

Again, she cuts me off. "No. Contacting the locals will create complications for me at work. *And* for our trip. I'll make some calls when we get back to the room."

We say nothing more until we are safely inside our hotel room.

Rather than talk, Steph yanks out her phone and sends out a flurry of texts. The room is stuffy, and the window air conditioner does little to alleviate the situation. While she is busy, I go into the bathroom and get ready for bed. I make sure the towels are still stuffed into the hole to keep the rats from crawling all over us during the night.

When I emerge, Steph is quietly sobbing on the edge of her bed.

"Are you okay?" I ask.

"I'm fine," she claims. "I just don't like hurting people, even if they *are* assholes."

I have more questions to ask her: about her frequent phone calls, about her job, and about where she learned her martial arts skills. However, I sense that she just wants to get to sleep, and we have several more days to talk.

"Daddy," Steph says without turning to look at me. "Thanks for distracting the last one. I did not anticipate that he would have a knife, and I was sure that he was going to cut me before I could get it away from him."

"Uh, sure, honey."

"Just don't ever try to negotiate with terrorists. They will just keep making more demands."

"They weren't terrorists; they were just drunk, unemployed coal miners."

"They were using violence or the threat of violence to obtain their goals. In my book, that's terrorism, and there is only one way to deal with terrorists."

I do not ask what she meant or why she felt so strongly about terrorists. Nor do I make a crack about how they were merely beer aficionados who wanted me to appreciate the quality of an American formulation. No, tonight I need to keep my big mouth shut.

What a first day I think to myself. I have biked as many miles in a day as I usually do in a week. I have spent the whole day with my only offspring, and we have not gotten into a major argument. And I have discovered that my vegan daughter is a martial arts expert.

Stephanie sits on the side of her bed with her back to me. I see her broad shoulders and the well toned muscles of her arms before I turn off the lights. I lie down in a strange bed in a strange town and ponder how I do not know who this woman is that claims to be my daughter.

Second Day of Biking
Leaving Connellsville
Still 275 miles to go

An odd sound wakes me, and I suspect something is wrong. I look over at Stephanie; she is still sound asleep. The night had been rough with doors slamming and truck traffic that I could hear even over the racket made by the window air conditioning unit. I am still shaken by the encounter last night. With another long day of cycling ahead of me, I try to stretch while lying in bed. Every muscle below my waist screams at me to stop and go back to sleep.

My first attempt to touch my toes barely gets me past my knees. I hear the noise again. With the bikes filling all available floor space, I crawl over the bed to the window, bend the slats of the cheap venetian blinds, and peek out. Fog envelops the parking lot, but I can see the source of the odd noise. Rainwater is leaking through a rusted out gutter and hitting a row of clay pots.

A light drizzle descends from the overcast sky in every direction I look. From the elevation charts I know that today we will be biking uphill all day. To my immense joy, we will apparently be doing it in the rain.

I let go of the blind. It is covered in decades of dust. I wipe the dust off my fingers on the bed covers. Steph is up and staring at the screen on her phone.

"What's it like outside?" she asks.

"Bright sunshine," I lie.

She looks up. "That's not what my weather app says."

"Who ya gonna believe?" I ask. "Me — your father — or some weather app?"

Without hesitation, she replies, "My weather app."

I grin at her. "Smart girl."

Steph puts her phone away. "It should clear up in an hour."

"So we leave in an hour?" I ask hopefully.

"Can't count on the rain stopping in an hour. Need to hit the trail, but I think I found a shortcut."

"I like shortcuts."

We dress rapidly, pulling out our rain gear for a soggy day of biking. While Steph checks our tire inflation and lubes our gears, I try to stretch. Neither of us mentions breakfast so I stuff two granola bars into my mouth.

Before we exit the room, Steph says: "I know we need to talk about last night, but I'm not ready yet. I got confirmation this morning that those three jerks received medical treatment. We don't need to worry about them or what happened."

"But how do you know that?" I ask.

She holds up a hand. "Just trust me. I do."

"Okay." I don't press the issue although my fatherly instincts scream at me to dig further into the issue.

We leave the room. Under the small awning outside, we pause. The morning mist obscures most of our vision. It is not raining hard, but I wonder if this moment is the last time I will be dry today.

Steph pushes off, and I follow. We pass sleeping homes, taking one back road after another. At least we are going downhill which means that we are headed back to the Yough and that I can coast. However, the slick pavement makes some of the steeper sections slightly treacherous.

We reach a massive stone railroad overpass that towers at least a hundred feet above us. The small trees and shrubbery growing out of it indicates that it has not been used for years. I want to take a picture, but neither one of us is willing to risk pulling out our cell phones in the light drizzle.

After the overpass, we encounter a river and a road that runs along the river. It must be the Yough. Unfortunately, there is no sign of the Passage. A car passes us carrying a commuter to her job. The driver stares at us as she goes by, wondering what kind of fools would be out biking in the rain this early in the morning. Not only are we biking in the rain, we are *lost* biking in the rain.

Steph pulls up under a tree that provides some protection. I squeeze in next to her. She extracts her cell phone and stares at the screen.

"According to this, we should have crossed the Passage by now," she states.

I think for a moment. "Maybe we went under it," I suggest.

"How could we have done that?"

"Remember that overpass?"

"Yeah."

"The Passage could have been above us."

"I didn't see a way to get up there."

"I didn't either. That's one of the problems with taking shortcuts on electronic maps. They leave out important details."

"Am I about to get a fatherly lecture?"

I squint as I look about. "I don't think under a tree during a downpour is the proper place and time for a fatherly lecture."

"I agree."

We stand over our bikes contemplating our situation. Retracing our route would mean biking — additional miles — uphill — in the rain.

"So what are we going to do?" Stephanie asks.

I point to the river. "If that's the Yough, doesn't the Passage follow it?"

"I guess."

"This road we're on runs alongside the Yough. I suggest we follow it upstream until we find the Passage."

"How do we know which way is upstream?"

"Your question informs me that I have failed miserably in my duty to give my sole offspring appropriate instruction on riparian hydraulics."

My daughter gives me her look.

"Which way is the water flowing?" I ask.

Steph examines the river and points. I direct her in the opposite direction.

"We go the other way to go upstream," I instruct her.

Our eyes lock momentarily. Rainwater is dripping off the edges of our helmets. I can tell my daughter is evaluating whether she can trust my judgment of the situation.

"Okay," she says cautiously. "We can always turn around."

"We won't need to," I say with false bravado. "Shall I lead?"

"Be my guest."

Before she can change her mind, I am off. Almost immediately the rain slackens and then stops. Clouds still loom above, but droplets are no longer pelting us. We ride the potholed asphalt with the river flowing in the opposite direction on our left. On our right, a steep embankment rises over our heads, covered with trees and thick underbrush. About a mile later we come to an eight foot high chain link fence with a padlocked gate. Through the links we can see a workyard filled with construction equipment. We have hit a dead end with no sign of the Passage.

"What does the map on your phone say?" I ask.

"According to this stupid app," she taps the screen, "We are on it." She looks up at me. "But we are obviously not."

I grimly nod in agreement.

"Shall we turn around and go back to Connellsville?" Steph asks. I can see disappointment in her eyes. She trusted my judgment, and I failed her.

Before I could answer her, rays of sunlight break through the parting clouds. The rain has stopped completely, and the sky is clearing. I look up. Above us — through the mass of leaves — I detect the brief flash of light glinting off moving metal. Then I see a head encased in a biking helmet scoot past.

"There's someone on a bike up there," I say.

Skepticism covers Steph's face. "I don't see anyway to get up there," she says.

"Stay here," I say. I dismount and lean my bike against a tree. A narrow muddy path leads straight up through the foliage. Grasping the trunks of small trees, I pull myself up hand over hand for about ten feet. When I poke my head through some branches, I see a level path of crushed limestone. A guy on a bike whizzes past me.

I clamber back down to Steph and tell her what I have seen. She nods thoughtfully. We study the vertical muddy path leading to the Passage. Getting the weight of the panniers off the rear of our bikes will help, but navigating our handlebars and gears through the dense underbrush lining the trail will be difficult.

"Look at the bright side," I say. "It could be raining."

133

I get a smile.

She unhooks one of my panniers and hands it to me, and I start climbing. We work as a team. Steph takes the panniers off our bikes and carries them up the mud trail. She hands them to me about midway up, and I take them the rest of the way to the top. Only one pannier can be transferred at a time. A free hand is necessary to get up the path. For every two steps I take going up, I slide down one. Tree branches brush across my arm, legs, and face. I find myself breathing heavily, and we still have a long day of biking ahead of us.

"Last one," Steph says.

I take the last pannier and without thinking say, "Thanks, Squirrel."

My daughter freezes.

I freeze.

When she was a tyke, she loved to scurry around the yard imitating the bushy tailed rodents that overran our yard, She had the motions and mannerisms down pat: the short hops, the tail shakes, the curled up front arms, the chirping noises.

Like all first time parents, Nancy and I adored and encouraged every notion of our daughter. We would chase her around the house and the yard, pretending to be frustrated cats and dogs trying to catch her. Rather than Easter egg hunts, we would search for "acorns" filled with chocolate. Her bedroom was decorated with a squirrel theme: dark brown carpet, walls painted with trees, and — of course — multiple stuffed squirrels in assorted sizes.

My nickname for her — entirely affectionate and appropriate in my opinion — was "Squirrel". She loved it for years, but — several years after I became a single parent — when she had started junior high — she sat me down one afternoon and told me that she no longer wanted me to call her "Squirrel". Period.

She gave no reason. There were no histrionics or accusations: just a calm and mature request.

Shocked, I had agreed. Until today, I had kept my agreement. Reflecting on that moment over the years, I had realized that was her first step away from me. I had deferred to her request because I wanted her to be her own person.

Watching her scurry back and forth this morning with the panniers reminded me of her as a little girl — full of energy. Climbing up and down with the panniers had been exhausting and made me forget my agreement with her.

"I'm sorry, Steph. I know you hate that nickname. It just slipped out, I'm tired, I — "

I stop in mid sentence. Steph is staring at me with a bemused expression on her face.

"It's okay, Daddy," she says. "You can call me 'Squirrel' if you want."

"But you asked me not to."

"I was a teenager going through puberty. I was trying to go from being a child to being an adult. I didn't want you to slip and call me that in front of my friends, that's all."

"But you made it clear that I was not to call you that at any time."

"Let's just call it insurance."

"Insurance?"

"I didn't mind if you called me Squirrel if it was just the two of us, but never in public."

"But that wasn't what you told me."

"Right. Insurance. If you never called me Squirrel, I didn't have to worry about you calling me Squirrel where someone would hear you."

"Insurance. I see."

"You ready to get the bikes up?"

I examine the muddy trail and the thick foliage through which we will have to retrieve our wheels. Not looking forward to the task, I say, "What if we just walk the rest of the way?"

"You can walk, but I'm going to ride."

Steph walks her bike up to the beginning and struggles to push it up. I go over and help her. It takes us working in tandem to get each bike up to the Passage.

At the top, we reload and push off. We are soaked from the earlier rain and muddy from hauling our bikes and gear up the path. Nevertheless, we are back on the crushed limestone of the Passage gliding through a thick forest. Above us, the limbs overhead almost touch, forming a green canopy for us to ride under. The Yough stays on our left, and we are pretty much in the shade. I catch glimpses of rafters on the river below us.

I lose myself enjoying the scenery — so much so that I almost do not notice that Stephanie has stopped in the middle of the Passage. As I start to go around her, I suddenly see why she has stopped, and I brake hard.

A large white ash tree has fallen across the bike path, completely blocking our route. I can see no way around it, as the massive trunk extends from where its roots came out of the ground on one side of the trail to where the steep embankment falls off toward the Yough.

Steph gives me a sideways glance. "Don't even think of suggesting we turn around."

"Thought never crossed my mind," I say breezily. "I'm just waiting for you to pull your chainsaw out of your pannier and get to work clearing a path for me."

"Ha!" Steph dismounts and leans her bike against the tree. She wades between the leaves and the limbs, scouting out a path for us. My daughter disappears from view, but I hear her voice: "There, I think we can get through here. We'll have to hold back the branches for each other."

We laugh and joke as Steph takes photos and videos of us struggling over and through the fallen tree. On the other side, we regroup.

"Wonder why it fell, "Stephanie asks.

"Looks like it's been raining a lot," I answer. "Wet ground, shallow roots." I point to the base of the tree. "All it takes is a strong gust of wind and over she goes. Usually, they land on a house or a car."

We push off and settle into an easy cadence, side by side. Steph looks around at the forest that surrounds the bike path. "Not too many houses or cars around here," she comments.

"True," I agree with a grin. "But one could easily fall on us in a rainstorm. The daughter of a friend of mine got caught in a thunderstorm running from one house to another. Huge tree fell on top of her. Doctors said that if it had landed either six inches to the left or right it would have killed her. She still walks with a limp."

"Pleasant thought," Steph remarks.

"Good thing we're wearing these helmets." I tap the side of my head.

Steph shakes her head. "Like that would help." She speeds up and makes me eat her dust.

We click off the miles. I know she can go faster — much faster — but she sets a reasonable pace for her old man. As the air warms, our clothes dry out.

Before long, we reach a bridge that crosses the Yough. We stop to admire the view and take some pictures. Two male bikers approach us from the opposite direction.

"Hey," I call out to them. "Would you mind taking a photo of my daughter and me?"

In a low voice, Steph chastises me. "Daddy, don't bother them. I can take a selfie of us."

"No problem," the one dressed in red and black answers. He dismounts, and I hand him my cell phone. His friend, decked out in yellow and green, stops and greets us.

"Is this your first time here?" he asks.

"It is," I admit.

"You're in for a real treat then."

"Why is that?"

"Right now, you're on the High Bridge. A little further down the passage you will cross the Low Bridge. Then you'll see Ohiopyle. But between here and there is the most beautiful hundred acre spot in the world — the gem of Pennsylvania."

The guy in red and black teases us as he lines up the shot. "Try to look like you're enjoying yourselves."

Steph and I smile; he takes several snaps, adjusting the angle on each one.

"There you go," he says as he hands my cell phone back to me.

"So what is this 'gem' of an area your friend is talking about?" I ask the guy in red and black.

"Oh — that's the Ferncliff Peninsula. The Yough — the Youghiogheny — makes a loop forming an unusual spit of land that is covered with what they call a late successional forest."

"What is a late successional forest?"

"Lots of mature and old-growth trees. Unusual for this area. Plants used to warmer weather in Maryland and West

Virginia washed down the Yough. The way the river bends and the low elevation allowed them to thrive. Early settlers around here cut down most of the trees. Ferncliff was spared because it became a tourist destination. People would pay a dollar to ride the train down here from Pittsburgh. The area was covered with hotels and support buildings."

"All of that is gone now," the guy in yellow and green chimes in. "There's a trail that will take you along the perimeter of the peninsula. About halfway around, there's a great view of the Ohiopyle Falls."

"Ohiopyle — that's an unusual name," Steph comments.

The guy in black shrugs. "It's a Native American — Lenape — word supposedly meaning white and frothy, which accurately describes the rapids."

The guy in yellow and green interjects, "It also describes the faces of people who go through those rapids."

Both of them laugh. "You'll understand when you see the falls," says the guy in red and black.

My ears have perked up: I have this thing about waterfalls. "Can you see the falls from the Passage?" I ask.

Both guys shake their heads. "Nah," the one in red and black says. "But there's a short hiking trail. You'll see the signs up ahead."

I look expectantly at Steph. From her expression I can tell that she remembers my thing about waterfalls, but she also wants to make Rockwood before dark. If it is an impressive flow of water, I could spend the rest of the day staring at it.

"How long is the trail?" she inquires.

The two guys look at each other; both shrug. The guy in yellow and green speaks. "Maybe a couple of miles if you do the whole loop. Lots of side trails. You might want to pick up a map from the visitor center before you start hiking so you don't get lost."

"Thanks," I say to them as we separate.

Steph and I coast off the bridge as the Passage reenters the forest. A light drizzle starts, and the air turns misty.

I stop at a sign that reads "Ferncliff Natural Area" next to an inviting hiking trail. My butt pleads with me to get off the bike and walk.

Stephanie pulls up next to me. "So you want to do a little hiking?"

"You know me and waterfalls."

"I do, but those guys on the bridge suggested we cycle up to the visitor center in Ohiopyle and get a map."

"How far do you think it is?"

"A mile or two."

I do a quick calculation. A mile or two round trip would add two to four miles to the day's mileage. My butt screams at me that I do not need a map. Getting a map would be the sensible thing to do, but what is sensible about an overweight man in his sixties trying to cycle 334.5 miles?

"We don't need a map," I assert confidently.

As we line up our bikes and chain them to a tree, the rain intensifies. It is an ominous warning. We throw a tarp over the bikes and strap a bungee cord around the tarp to keep it from blowing away. Although we will get soaked, our rides and gear will stay relatively dry.

We start walking. The tree branches overhead partially shield us from most of the rain. Around us, the forest glows in luminous shades of green. Moss covers rocks. Ferns flourish underneath the oaks and the hemlocks and the tulip poplars and the black birches. Raindrops drip from leaves. Bright orange and red mushrooms sprout next to fallen trees.

Hearing sounds of rushing water and occasional human voices brimming with excitement, I guess there are quite a few people enjoying the rapids in the rain.

We come to a split where a short side trail leads to a craggy overlook. Through the leaves I can see large volumes of water cascading over a rocky ledge. The precipitation has made the area slippery, but we venture out to get a better look.

The same rain coming down on us has made the Yough a roaring mass of angry water. Although hard to tell without a point of reference, I estimate that the Ohiopyle Falls are about twenty feet high.

As I position myself to take a photo, Steph calls out. "Look!"

Out of the mist hovering over the Yough, I catch a glimpse of a person in a kayak hurtle over the falls. He (or she)

---

clears the foaming base that most likely would have sucked him (or her) under. A testosterone laced victory shout rolls over the water toward us. Definitely a male.

Another kayaker appears just above the falls. This kayaker is furiously using the paddle for positioning. The kayak lands in the midst of the boiling cauldron of water at the base of the falls. Digging frantically with his paddle, the kayaker barely pulls himself away from the thundering wall of water behind him.

A third kayaker shoots through. Barely dipping his paddle in the water, this kayaker confidently leaps over the falls. The nose of the kayak submerges briefly on the landing but then reemerges. The kayaker raises his paddle over his head and pumps his fists.

The show is over; no more kayakers appear. Steph and I rejoin the main trail and continue walking. We reach a trail sign. Our options are to continue on the Ferncliff Trail or take the Fernwood Trail. We discuss and decide on the Fernwood. As we pass a plaque, I stop to read it. It marks the site of the Ferncliff Hotel that once stood at that spot in the 1880s. The plaque also mentions a dance pavilion, a boardwalk, a bowling alley, ball fields, tennis courts, and fountains. I look around and see no evidence of any of these structures amidst the foliage of the trees. The area must have been the definition of rustic luxury in its heyday, but little remains of it now. The forest has reclaimed its territory. A dozen or so steps further up the Fernwood we see a sign for the Oakwood Trail. With no landmarks to guide us and the rain starting to intensify, we take the Oakwood. Further down the Fernwood we stumble upon the Buffalo Nut. The Ferncliff Peninsula is a labyrinth of intersecting trails.

"Should have gotten the trail map." I admit.

"Yep," Steph agrees.

To avoid getting hopelessly lost, we retrace our steps back to where we first set off on foot. Our short side trip has turned into a hiking marathon.

We unwrap our bikes and climb back on them. The rain has stopped — for the time being. We cycle through the rest of the forest and onto the Lower Bridge across the Yough. At the end of the bridge is Ohiopyle. The Visitors Center, a former railway station, sits beside the trail.

Ohiopyle
258 miles to go

We dismount and go inside. I pull a Ferncliff Peninsula trail map from a rack and show it to Steph.

"Looks like we were almost around to where we started when we turned around and retraced our steps," I say to Stephanie.

"So we walked twice as far as we were supposed to?"

"At least. Sure would have been easy to run down here before we started."

"Yep."

Yes, it would have been easy to have fetched a trail map before we wandered in the rain all over the Ferncliff Peninsula, but then we would have missed an adventure.

"Hungry?" Steph asks.

"Do I get to eat lunch today?" I reply.

"I think you earned it after that hike."

We lock the bikes near the visitor center and cover them with the tarp. Although it is not raining at the moment, the clouds swirling above us look heavily laden with moisture.

I drift toward the aroma of smoked barbecue emanating from a building to our right. Steph grabs me by the elbow and steers me away. She points at a rambling structure up the street.

"Let's try that cafe," she insists. "The woman in the visitor center recommended it.

I allow myself to be dragged away from carbonized beef covered in a cholesterol packed sauce toward an uncertain — but healthy — meal. We find seats at a table on an outdoor deck overlooking the Passage and the Yough. I pull out two menus tucked between the condiments and hand one to Steph.

The beer on the menu is tempting. My body could use both the calories and the anesthetic effects, but I have to keep my wits about me for the miles I have to pedal today.

"Can I get you something to drink?"

I look up. The question is from a waitress: young, pert, and braless. I avert my eyes: definitely not cool to stare at a pair of nipples poking through a thin tank top with your daughter present. My menu suddenly becomes very interesting.

"Do you have any herbal teas?" Steph asks.

"Oh, yes. There's a list here." The waitress leans over to show Stephanie where on the menu to look, giving me a clear and up close side view of her ample anatomy.

"I like the carrot chamomile myself," she offers.

"That sounds good," Steph says. "And I'll have the veggie wrap."

"Cool. And you, sir?"

I studiously examine my menu as I cannot figure out how to look up at the waitress without stopping at her chest.

"Do you have anything with meat in it?" I mumble.

"Oh, yes. How about a roast beef wrap stuffed with avocado and bean sprouts in a tomato and oregano tortilla?"

"Uh, huh," I say noncommittally. "That sounds nice." I pause. "Can I have it without the avocado and the bean sprouts?"

"Sure."

"And can you leave off the tomato and oregano tortilla?"

The waitress laughs. "So all you want is the roast beef?"

"That would work nicely."

"Okay. How about some sweet potato fries to go with your roast beef?"

I hesitate, thinking that I would prefer regular fries.

"They're soaked in an organic beer batter," the waitress adds seductively.

I feel she is smiling at me, but I refuse to look up. "That sounds good," I admit, although I am not sure about the organic part. I start to put my menu down, but then I remember that I need it as a prop to keep from staring at the waitress's chest.

"And to drink? Would you like some of the carrot chamomile herbal tea as well?"

"I prefer to eat carrots rather than drink them."

My comment comes out sounding grouchy, but it does not phase this temptress.

"We have great lemonade — fresh squeezed."

"Fine. I'll have the lemonade."

Thankfully, the waitress leaves.

Stephanie leans forward and whispers, "Growing up, I was taught to always look at a person — even a wait person — when talking to them."

She is grinning from ear to ear at me. I feel my face redden.

"Whoever raised you," I reply, "taught you correctly."

"So, 'Do as I say, not as I do'." My daughter is teasing me mercilessly.

"Sometimes there are exceptions."

"Such as."

"Such as inappropriately dressed waitresses at health food cafes."

"She's just trying to improve her tips."

I consider how my daughter learned how a waitress would improve her tips by wearing revealing clothing. Rather than ask if she knows from personal experience, I decide to change the subject.

"I see the rain has stopped now that we are under cover."

"Probably will start back up again when we leave," Stephanie suggests.

"Yeah."

From where we sit, we can see groups of rafters and swimmers playing in the Yough.

"Do you remember teaching me to swim?" Steph asks.

I reply, "Haven't thought about it in a while, but, yeah, I remember."

"I was sitting around a pool earlier this summer watching a father trying to teach his daughter how to swim. It wasn't going well. The little girl was terrified, and the dad was losing his patience."

"Let me guess: the child had her arms around his neck in a death grip."

"Pretty much. "

"And the father kept asking the child to trust him."

"How did you know?"

I shrug. "That's the way our first swim lessons went."

"Really? I have a different memory. You were very patient with me, and with your help I was a much stronger swimmer than the rest of my class."

"That was only because I took your grandfather's advice."

"Which was?"

"As he saw it, I had two options: I could just toss you into the deep end of the pool and let you figure it out or I could trick you with a few mind games."

"I don't remember you throwing me into the pool."

"I didn't. If you had been a boy, I would have."

"That's sexist of you."

"Guilty as charged."

"So what mind games did you trick me with?"

"Hard for me to remember," I fib as I rearrange my napkin in my lap. "What I do remember is that pink frilly swimsuit you loved to wear."

"I don't recall that."

"A two piece. Your mother bought it. You put it on in June that summer and didn't take it off until August."

"I'm sure you exaggerate."

"Only slightly." I gaze at my daughter and remember how she looked: hair the same color but shorter and curlier. Same sparkling eyes. "We built a sand castle."

"That I remember. Rehoboth Beach."

"Very good." I remember the little girl who ran in terror from the foot high breakers. The woman sitting across from me would never run, even if a tsunami was rolling toward her

Our food comes. Without a menu to distract my eyes, I rearrange my silverware until the waitress departs.

As we start to eat, I ask, "Where are we headed from here?"

"Confluence. It's supposed to be a nice little town."

"It is — or at least it used to be."

Steph stops eating her pile of organic vegetables. "When were you in Confluence?"

"I took your mother there once. To a little bed and breakfast. Before you were born."

"I didn't know that."

"It was for our anniversary. For some reason, she was a big fan of Frank Lloyd Wright. Wanted to see Fallingwater and Kentuck Knob. Both are not far from here."

"I didn't know that either."

"Your mother was a complex woman."

"Tell me more."

"She was very excited — one of the few times I truly surprised her."

"Why was she so interested in Fallingwater?"

"Beats me. A better name for it would be Falling-in-the-Water. Don't get me wrong. It's stunning to see, positioned as it is right over a waterfall. It has these huge concrete decks that extend out as if they are floating in the air."

"Concrete?"

"Yeah, Wright loved to work with concrete. Did some pretty amazing things with it. Problem was, Wright ignored the engineer's recommendations when it came time to build Falling-in-the-Water."

"Why?"

"Probably — like most talented, famous architects — he was stubborn. He had come up with a unique design and didn't want to alter it. Anyway, the owner — a department store magnate named Edgar Kaufmann — the engineer, and the contractor conspired behind Wright's back to secretly insert extra supports. Otherwise, the whole structure would have fallen into the creek long ago. Kaufmann complained to his friends about the persistent mold problem; living over a waterfall means constant moisture. Both the roof and the windows constantly leaked. Although I don't know if he was complaining so much as bragging that he owned a Frank Lloyd Wright house."

"But Mommy liked it?"

"Every square inch. And it is amazing — but I could never live in a place like that."

"You don't like leaky windows and roofs?"

"Not just that. From what I understand, Wright insisted on designing even the furniture for the houses he built."

"How was that a problem?"

145

"Wright was only about five foot seven, and he specified the dimensions of the furniture to fit him. I tried some of the chairs and they were the most uncomfortable things I ever tried to sit in. Way too short. I could never have gotten my legs underneath the built in desks. Felt like I was in a dollhouse."

Steph starts laughing.

"What's so funny," I demand.

Between chuckles, my daughter says, "I'm just trying to imagine you trying to sit in a chair built for a midget, that's all."

We finish our meals, and the waitress with the clingy tank top convinces us to order the fresh-homemade-gluten-free-all natural-organic-locally grown strawberry rhubarb pie. I doubt that anything that healthy sounding will taste very good, but I agree to order a slice to share with Stephanie — mainly to get the waitress to leave.

When the pie arrives, I am surprised at how good it is, but Steph eats at least two-thirds of it. I make a mental note not to share any more desserts with my daughter for the duration of the trip.

When I settle the bill, the waitress gets a larger tip than I usually give.

Back on the Passage, we ride through a portion of the 20,000 acres of the Ohiopyle State Park. The rain resumes, but tree tunnels partially shield us from the intermittent downpours. These tunnels are formed by the interlocking branches of trees that arch over the bike trail. This portion of the Passage is on the right of way abandoned when the Western Maryland Railroad went out of business. Completed in 1986, this section of the old railway was the first to be put into use as a bike path.

We encounter two more fallen trees. None of them are as large as the first obstacle we had to overcome. We easily navigate both. Miles click off, and the gentle rain fails to dampen our spirits.

"I love your rooster tail!" Steph shouts as we pedal along.

"My what?"

My daughter laughs. Rather than try to explain, she points behind me.

I glance over my shoulder but see nothing. Shrugging my shoulders, I say, "What are you talking about?"

Speeding up slightly, Steph calls out. "I bet I have one, too."

Indeed, she does. The rear wheel of her bike is picking up mud from the trail and spewing it backward in the shape of — the tail of a rooster.

We motor our way to Confluence, proudly raising our rooster tails.

I have pleasant memories of Confluence. Before my daughter was born and the problems with my wife started, I had surprised Nancy on our second wedding anniversary with a weekend trip to a charming little bed and breakfast just outside of town. We had visited Kentuck Knob and Fallingwater — Frank Lloyd Wright's masterpieces. Nancy — who had once aspired to be an architect — was enthralled with the structures.

Nancy and I were still madly in love then, and Steph was probably conceived on that trip. That little detail I do not reveal to my daughter. That — and other details — I am not ready to divulge.

We do not slow down until we reach the outskirts of Confluence, and I am ready for another break.

Confluence
247 miles to go

"My gears aren't changing when I want them to," I complain to Steph.

She looks sideways at my chain. "Probably the grit coming up from the bike trail is messing up your shifter. Your legs are covered with it. Maybe we can find a place in town where we can hose our bikes down."

At that moment, I spot a cyclist flying toward us from the opposite direction. He is tanned, muscled, and decked out in a mud-splattered red, white and blue cycling outfit. I swear it is The Bike God in all his glory — or a close relative — or at least a patriotic version. Traveling fast with a smooth pedaling motion, I expect that he will give us a curt nod as he blows past.

Instead, our All American Cyclist stops and asks, "Problem?"

Stephanie answers. "My Dad's having an issue with his gears."

"That's probably the junk from the trail getting into the mechanism. Happens to me all the time. There's a great bike shop here in town where you can hose both your bikes off. In fact, my ride needs a rinse."

"You done the Passage before?" I ask.

"Lots of times. You?"

"It's our first. Where are you from?"

"D.C. Left there yesterday morning."

I do some quick mileage calculations in my head. "You've covered almost 250 miles in two days?" I do not try to hide my incredulity.

The All American Cyclist shrugs. "Sure. Fairly flat. Smooth surface once you get to the Passage. The C & O is a different animal. Hard to get any speed there before you hit a pothole. Gnats and flies were ferocious this year. Had to fight my way through them."

He grins at me.

I force a grimace in reply: another warning about what awaits me once we reach the Potomac.

The All American Cyclist continues. "But three days is what it typically takes me to get from D.C. to Pittsburgh. How about you?"

I am too embarrassed to give this patriotic version of The Bike God an honest answer, but Stephanie has no qualms. "We're doing it in six days. My Dad likes to check out all the historical stuff."

"Lots of that. I've never bothered with it."

This Bike God is friendly, but cocky. It must come with being immortal.

I ask, "So, are you going to take Amtrak back to D.C. once you reach Pittsburgh?"

I receive a haughty shake of the head in reply.

"Nah. I'm just gonna turn around and cycle back. A buddy is getting married this weekend."

I do more quick mileage calculations in my head. This guy is going to bike almost 700 miles in six days, and I have been whining about doing half as many miles in the same time frame. Resisting the impulse to bow down and worship at his feet, I ask, "Can you tell us where this bike shop is?"

"Confluence Cyclery? I'll take you there."

He and Steph take off. I follow but struggle to keep them in sight. Two turns and we arrive. Our All American Bike God disappears into the bike shop and returns with a faucet handle.

I start to make a comment about needing more than a faucet handle — like a hose and a water source — but I remember whose presence I am in and bite my tongue — hard.

He leads us around back to an alley where he fits the handle on a spigot. Offering an end of the hose to me, I wash off my bike and Steph's bike. I also rinse our legs. When I start to turn the water on his bike, he grabs the hose from me. I am obviously not worthy of cleaning the chariot of a god.

Once the All American Bike God is satisfied with the state of his ride, he turns the hose on himself, laughing as he does so. He removes his helmet and then runs the water over his head, shoulders, and legs. Done, he turns off the water, removes the faucet handle, and flips it to me.

"Can you give this back to Brad?"

Catching the handle, I reply stupidly, "Brad?"

"Brad's the owner. Great guy. Supports the biking community. Buy some gear from him." The All American Bike God pauses and fixes me with a cool stare. "Whether you need it or not."

I offer a fake smile.

He laughs. After shaking excess water from his arms and legs, he straps his helmet back on his head and takes off.

I watch his red, white, and blue colors disappear around a corner.

Stephanie has already walked her bike to the front of the store. I follow. Entering the store, I spot a man with white hair standing behind a counter. Around him, a group of a half dozen young male cyclists have gathered. They are chatting and laughing amongst themselves. They stop as I approach.

"Are you Brad?" I ask the man with white hair.

"That I am."

"I was told to give you this." I hand him the faucet handle.

"Thanks." Brad takes the handle and drops it in a drawer. "If you need a restroom, help yourself." He points to a sign at the back of the store.

After casually glancing at my attire and sizing me up, the group of cyclists decide to ignore me and resume talking amongst themselves.

"I'll do that," I reply. "Right now, it feels good to be off the bike and walking around." The room I am standing in is cavernous. Large plate glass windows allow natural sunlight to brighten the interior and the display cases "This place feels more like an old-fashioned department store than a bike shop," I comment.

Brad smiles. "That's because it *was* an old-fashioned department store before my wife and I bought it 2006. It was originally built in 1905, and it took us about two years to repurpose it."

"You did a nice job," I say as I look around.

"Appreciate that. Are you riding the Passage?"

"Yep. Headed to D.C."

Brad regards me carefully before speaking. "That means you'll be riding the C & O."

I nod as I swear I hear ominous music in the background.

"Ever ride the C & O before?" Brad inquires in a cautionary tone.

"Can't say that I have."

My answer stops the conversation of the group of cyclists. Several turn so they can hear my exchange with Brad. They have grave expressions on their faces.

Brad inhales and lets out a low whistle. "It can be tough this time of year with the heat."

"And the humidity."

"And the bugs."

"And the potholes."

"Don't forget the mud."

"Or the trees down across the path."

One by one, each cyclist adds to the list of the challenges facing a cyclist on the C & O in the dead of summer. I detect sympathy in the eyes of some of them. Others display skepticism that I will be able to make it to D.C.

"Look," Brad says. "When you get to Cumberland — that's where the C & O starts — the bike path will have two tracks. On the Passage, you can ride anywhere, but you will have to make a choice between the right side or the left side on the C & O. Once you're in that track, you pretty much have to stay in it."

The advice sounds odd to me, and I shrug. "Wouldn't I just stay to the right to avoid oncoming cyclists?"

"Of course," one of the cyclists lounging behind Brad says. "Unless you come up on a hole that is going to bounce you into the Potomac. Then you want to get to your left."

Another cyclist chimes in. "But on the left, you are liable to slide into the old canal. Given my druthers, I would rather end up in the Potomac rather than that slimy sludge in the old canal."

"My preference would be not to end up in either one," I reply.

My response gets a few chuckles.

"One more thing about biking the C & O," Brad says. His steel gray eyes lock with mine. "Storms can come up quickly on the Potomac. Sun can be shining and ten minutes later you can find yourself in the middle of a raging thunderstorm. Has happened to me quite a few times."

"Thanks," I say appreciatively.

"Hey, maybe you can help us," one of the cyclists suggests.

"Yeah," another one says. He points at a large sign on the wall. The word "T-H-U-L-E" appears in large letters. It is obviously the brand name of foreign manufacturer. "How do you pronounce that?" he demands.

Brad eyes the guy. "Don't start with this," he cautions.

"Hey," the guy protests, "We have a legitimate controversy here that he could help us resolve."

151

I look around for Stephanie to give me some guidance, but she has retreated to a far end of the store and is studiously examining a display of biking gloves. Turning back to the group, I admit my ignorance: "I have no idea."

My response elicits gleeful cackles from the group. Apparently, there is little to do on a rainy day in Confluence other than sit around a cycle shop and argue about the pronunciation of the name of a foreign company.

"How about you give me some choices?" I suggest.

The group seems to like this idea, and one of them starts.

"Most people unfamiliar with this company say: 'Thool'. Rhymes with fool. As in you would have to be a fool to pay this much."

"I'm pretty sure the English translation is 'X-PEN-SIVE'."

"Have you tried calling the company to see how they pronounce it?" I suggest."

"Oh, yes. We were arguing this same point about a month ago and thought that would settle the issue. In fact, all six of us called."

Apparently, there is not much to do in Confluence even on days it is *not* raining. "So what did the company say?" I ask.

One by one, each cyclist rattles off an answer.

"Ta-hoolie."

"Tooly."

"Thoo-yeee."

"Too-yuh."

"Too-yah."

"Two leer."

The cyclist who started the round playfully mimics someone with a lisp: "Hey, jutht becauth thome of uth have a little lithp doethn't mean you need tuh make fun of how thilly Thool thounds."

The whole group erupts in laughter.

Brad raps his knuckles on the counter to interrupt them. "Fellas, I know you like to come in here and chit-chat, but if I have a customer walk up to this counter with a credit card in his hand, and he wants to actually buy a $500.00 roof rack system, he can pronounce 'T-H-U-L-E' any damn way he wants."

By this time, Steph has made a decision on a new pair of biking gloves. She completes her purchase with Brad, and we leave the bike shop and the group of cyclists as they continue to debate the pronunciation of 'T-H-U-L-E'.

Back at our bikes and out of their hearing, I ask her, "How do you pronounce it?"

She does not look at me as she tests out her purchase. Her answer: "I avoid the issue by using Yakima." Satisfied with the fit of her new gloves, she gracefully swings her leg over her panniers and saddle and pushes off.

As we leave Confluence, the rain picks back up. It's as if a master plumber is watching from upstairs — turning on a faucet whenever we mount our bikes and turning it off whenever we dismount. On we go — in the rain — uphill.

Five miles or so outside of Confluence we cross a long bridge. The rain lets up, and we stop to check our maps and take a few photos. I see a glimpse of the sun peeking behind a cloud and get my bearings.

"I know you're the navigator on this journey, but shouldn't we generally be going in a southeasterly direction to get to Washington?"

"Generally. I guess. What's the problem?"

"At the moment, I think we're headed almost due north."

"Could be." Steph's fingers fly over the face of her phone. "We can head south if you like."

"Really? Is that a shortcut?"

"Possibly. We just have to bike over the highest point in Pennsylvania — Mount Davis — that's all. Are you up to climbing to 3213 feet?"

I groan.

Steph continues, "Looks like we are skirting Mount Davis. What river is this?" she asks.

I pretend to study my map and then look over the railing. Water rages far, far below us. Rubbing the stubble on my chin, I say, "I would guess the Mississippi at flood stage from the looks of it."

Steph gives me a brief sideways glance before examining the map on her phone. "More likely it's the Casselman River. If we're on the High Bridge, we're almost to the Pinkerton Tunnel."

"A tunnel? How exciting!" I deadpan.

Steph puts away her phone. "Try to curb your enthusiasm."

"It will be difficult."

"There are five major tunnels on our route: four on the GAP and one on the C & O. This is the first one."

"Why can't we just keep following the river? I find it rather scenic."

"Before they reopened the Pinkerton Tunnel last year, the Passage took a mile and a half detour. We can still do that if you're afraid of the tunnel."

I shudder at the thought of any additional mileage — even less than two miles — and shake my head. Drops of rainwater fly off my helmet. "No, thanks," I say. "I'll suck it up and do the tunnel."

Stephanie takes a quick shot of me on the bridge and then puts away her phone. I follow her off the bridge, and we come to the entrance. Across the top of the entrance the word "Pinkerton" with the number "1911" underneath have been cut into the stone.

The information that I had read online indicated that the Pinkerton Tunnel had been dug out in 1877 as a shortcut through the Pinkerton Horn, a sharp bend in the Casselman River. Originally supported by a wooden framework, a timber fire within the tunnel two years after it was built shut it down for six years. The 849 foot long tunnel was completely rebuilt in 1885, this time using hand cut stone. Deteriorating supports over the years led to rock falls, and the tunnel was closed in 1975. For decades, barricades obstructed both entrances. A two million dollar rehabilitation project reopened the Pinkerton Tunnel in 2015.

I have no idea who Pinkerton was or why the date 1911 appears on his tunnel, but he must have been somebody to have a tunnel *and* a bend in the Casselman River named after him. The interior of the tunnel is lined with corrugated sheet metal. As we enter, Steph lets out a shriek of joy, and the sound of it echoes from one end of the chamber to the other.

The air temperature must drop ten degrees inside. Near the exit, I stop at a bench and climb off my bike to take a break and enjoy the moment.

Steph is silhouetted in the sunlight that pours through the opening. She is standing astride her bike taking pictures. I watch her and wonder if it is time to bring up something that has been on my mind all morning.

Walking her bike back to me, she asks, "You ready?"

"Kind of hate to leave this spot," I reply. "A bridge, a tunnel, and is that another bridge I see up ahead?"

"Yep. Lots more to see, so we need to keep moving."

"But this place is so beautiful," I plead.

"It is, but it's also not raining right now, and we could lay down some tracks before it starts again."

"I predict that it will start raining the second we leave the shelter of this tunnel. Let's enjoy the moment."

Stephanie smiles. "Okay, Daddy." She sits next to me, and we gaze out at the trees swaying in the afternoon breeze.

"I guess this would be a good time for a father-daughter chat," I suggest.

My daughter turns her head toward me and playfully frowns. "There is *never* a good time for a father-daughter chat."

"Why do you say that?"

"The last one — the one where you tried to explain the birds and the bees to me — remember that one?"

"Yeah," I grimace. It was one of many, many conversations I had had with my adolescent daughter when I had wished for Nancy.

"Well, that little conversation set my sex life back ten years. There was no way I was going to let a boy touch me based on your description."

I perk up. "Excellent. That was the whole point of the conversation."

My little Squirrel shakes her head as she turns it away from me. I get a face full of braided ponytail.

She talks quietly. "I don't think that's supposed to be the purpose of a sex talk with a teenager, especially all the stuff about the complications of pregnancy and the difficulties of giving birth."

I consider lecturing my daughter on how she might feel differently when it came time to talk to her own daughter about sex, but I refrain. I have a more immediate concern.

"This father-daughter conversation is not about sex."

"Good, because you stink at that."

I wonder what else she thinks I stink at but press on. "I would like to know where you learned that kung fu you demonstrated on those three guys last night."

Steph drops her head and stares at the ground. She paws at the ground with her cleated bike shoes as she talks. "That wasn't kung fu, and I really can't talk about it."

"Whatever it was, you put the hurt on those guys."

Steph sharply snaps her head at me. "I used reasonably necessary non-lethal force to extract us from a dangerous situation."

My head jerks back at her explanation. Her words are couched in legalistic terms to justify what she had done. "You broke that one guy's arm," I state.

"I only dislocated it. If I had needed to break it, I would have."

"But you didn't wait for the police to explain that. Nor did you offer medical assistance to them."

Steph drops her eyes. "I did not want to deal with the paperwork, and it would have interrupted our trip."

"Are you into police work? You sound like a cop."

"In a manner of speaking."

"Who do you work for then?"

"I can't tell you."

"Can't or won't?"

"Same difference."

I persist. "FBI?"

"No."

"CIA?"

"You've asked me that before. The answer is still no."

"One of the arms of the Defense Department?"

"Hell, no." Steph looks at me coolly. "You're not going to give up, are you?"

I scratch my cheek and shake my head "no".

"Fine. I work in security for the State Department."

My head recoils involuntarily. "The State Department? I didn't know we sent diplomats out to kick the crap out of jerks."

"That's not what I do."

"That's what you did last night."

"I oversee the security for State Department overseas installations. At times, self defense exercises are offered, and I have taken a few."

"How many?"

"Seventeen, if you count weapon training." she says without hesitation.

I let out a whistle. "Wow!" I look around to see if any other bikers are coming along the Passage and lean closer to her. "The State Department has embassies all over the world. How many of these installations are you in charge of?"

"All of them."

"How many are we talking about?"

"If you include the consulates, 272."

"And you provide the security for *all* of them?"

"I don't physically stand guard outside them. No. I allocate resources and make recommendations as to improvements to compounds. It means I travel — a lot. I have to be available 24/7/365. If any State Department facility is attacked or compromised anywhere in the world, I'm the person who gets the call."

"Hmm," I muse more to myself than to my daughter. "That explains all the phone calls."

"Some of them are personal. Steve has wanted to know how things are going."

"With us?"

"Yep."

"What did you tell him?"

Steph does not answer my question. Instead, she stands up and changes the subject. "We need to check out the view on the Lower Bridge."

"You know it's going to start raining again just as soon as we leave this tunnel."

"It's a chance we'll have to take."

She is off before I can say more. I sense she has just as many questions for me as I have for her, if not more. Unfortunately, neither one of us is ready to ask the questions, much less hear the answers. After stretching a bit, I follow her onto the Lower Bridge. I feel the first raindrop while we are taking pictures of each other with the Casselman River in the background.

Intermittent rain showers keep us cool in the afternoon heat. We are pedaling above the Casselman and catch glimpses between the trees of the river below. Across the water a locomotive pulling a motley collection of freight cars and tankers roars in the opposite direction on a track that must have replaced the one that we are on.

By the time we roll into Rockwood eight miles further down the trail, we are soaked and filthy from riding in the rain. All the grit that we had washed off in Confluence has reattached itself to us. I am ready for a shower as I follow Stephanie off the Passage and over a set of railroad tracks. She leads me to building with recently applied red paint. I read the sign outside: "Rockwood Mill Shoppes and Opera House".

"We're sleeping in an opera house tonight?" I ask.

"If you want to," Steph replies. "Myself, I am going to sleep in the hostel next door. We just check in here."

I am relieved. If there is one thing I cannot stand, it is listening to a fat lady sing in Italian as if an anvil has just been dropped on her foot. Actually, opera is one of many things that I cannot stand.

Next to the front door, a small plaque informs us that the building is on the National Register of Historic Places. Originally constructed in 1898 as a lumber and feed mill by Penrose Wolf — an early leading citizen of Rockwood — he added culture in the form of an opera house in 1904. Brought in by the adjacent railroad, high class entertainment came to Rockwood including plays, minstrels, vaudeville acts, and the New York Concert Company. After Penrose passed away, the opera house faded away between 1918 and 1921. The lumber and feed mill lasted until 1938, probably a victim of the Great

Depression. For decades the building sat vacant until it was reopened in 2000 after extensive renovations.

Two young girls of high school age cheerfully greet us as we enter.

"Do you have two spots open in your hostel for tonight?" Steph asks.

"Sure do," they answer in unison.

"Great," I say, "We'll take three."

I get blank stares from the two girls. The one on the left leans toward Steph, points at me, and asks, "Is he with you?"

"Afraid so," Steph replies. She tilts her head forward conspiratorially. "He's my father."

"Oh!" the two girls exclaim in understanding. The three of them nod at each other in complete comprehension of how fathers say dumb things trying to be cute but only end up embarrassing themselves and their daughters.

Looking around, I ask, "What sort of entertainment do you offer here?"

"Tonight, we have a murder mystery!" offers the young girl on the right.

"And tomorrow night, we have a musical tribute to John Denver!" chimes in the young girl on the left.

"So I have a choice of death by murder or death by singing?" I ask and enjoy the puzzled looks on their faces.

"Just ignore him," Stephanie suggests. "Do you have linens for us?"

One of the two young girls retrieves a double set of towels and sheets; she leads us over to the hostel and shows us around.

"Is there a place we can lock up our bikes for the night?" Steph asks.

The young girl takes us downstairs to a room that was once a garage and then leaves us. We have everything we need: a bike rack and a garden hose. After unpacking, we hose our bikes and then each other. Steph takes particular delight in running the cold water up and down my back. Halfway clean, we go upstairs to use the washing machine and dryer. With our clothes in the laundry, I retreat to the shower. I adjust the temperature as hot as I can stand it and contort my body to let the warm water soothe my aching muscles.

As my body relaxes, I hear my wife's voice faintly over the sound of the water coming out of the shower head.

"When are you going to tell her?"

"I haven't decided," I reply.

"Haven't decided when — or if — you're going to tell her?"

"I'll tell her when the time is right." I bury my face in the stream of water, but I cannot drown out the voice in my head.

"There is no 'right' time. You just have to sit her down and tell her."

"Why are you always so angry with me?" I ask the voice.

"Because I blame you for what I did. You were supposed to save me."

"I tried. I couldn't," I say.

"I know. You failed me."

I slam my palm against the side of the stall. "What was I supposed to do?" I demand.

The voice does not answer. I shut the water off and grab a towel. After dressing, I come out of the shower clean, but emotionally and physically drained. Stephanie is decorating our sleeping area with damp laundry.

"Feel better?" she asks cheerfully.

"I'm not sure I feel anything right now."

"Is that a good thing or a bad thing?"

I feel my thighs gingerly. They don't hurt right now, but I wonder if I will get cramps during the night. "At the moment, I would say it is a good thing," I say.

"Great! Tomorrow is a big day."

"I thought today was a big day."

"It was, but tomorrow will be even bigger. Our longest day of the trip: 72 miles."

I swallow hard, thinking about how much I have struggled on the two days so far with far fewer miles. "Looking forward to it," I say without conviction. "We better get up early."

"Yeah," Steph agrees sleepily. "Can't oversleep."

Both of us are out as soon as our heads hit our pillows.

During the night, a train seems to chug through every half hour on the tracks that run immediately behind the hostel. I suspect that whoever makes the rail schedule has determined the precise amount of time that people need to return to sleep after being awoken in the middle of the night — and sends a train through at the exact moment you are about to go back to sleep.

Rockwood
Third Day of Biking
228 miles to go

We oversleep in the morning.

I shake Steph awake.

"Hey, it's 7:30. We need to get a move on."

She grumbles but gets up.

We pull down our semi-dry clothing and pack silently. Everyone else in the hostel is asleep. Tiptoeing out, we stop by the Rockwood Mill Shoppes looking for breakfast. Steph gets her coffee, and I order an enormous cream cheese pastry and a matching blueberry muffin that I hope will get me through the morning. On our way out, I spy a bucket of cucumbers sitting next to the door. A large handwritten sign proclaims: "Take me! I'm free!"

"Hey," I say to Steph. "Want a cuke for the road? These things are huge."

My daughter scrunches her nose. "I don't care for cucumbers."

"Neither did your mother," I comment.

"Is that surprising?"

"Not at all. You remind me of her all the time."

Steph pauses in the doorway. "Is that a good thing or a bad thing?"

"It's just a thing." I shrug. "Neither good nor bad."

Her eyes narrow, and I know she wants to say more. She decides to save it, at least for now.

I grab the shortest cucumber in the bucket — which is at least a foot long — and follow her to the bikes.

For once, it is not raining.

"What's the weather forecast?" I ask.

Standing next to her bike, Steph is scrutinizing her cell phone screen again. "Don't know, yet. Going through messages."

I try to look over her shoulder, but she quickly slips her cell into the back of her biking jersey. Looking around, she says, "I'd say partly cloudy and cool all day."

"Perfect weather for our big biking day."

"Yep."

"Ready?"

"Yep."

We start off slowly through the streets of Rockwood back to the Passage.

As we pedal side by side, I ask, "Besides the ridiculous mileage today, what makes today so big?"

"Two viaducts and three tunnels."

"Big bridge and tunnel day, huh?"

"We also cross the Continental Divide, highest point on the Passage, and — the Mason Dixon Line."

"Okay."

"And we start the C & O."

I shudder involuntarily causing my bike to wobble.

When we get back to the Passage, Steph picks up the pace. My legs handle the gradual uphill grade fairly easily, and a gentle breeze seems to be pushing me along. Eight miles down the trail, we pass through the tiny town of Garrett, Pennsylvania.

I see the first wind turbines erected in southwestern Pennsylvania on a ridge overlooking the quiet little hamlet. I count eight of them. At this distance, they are not very impressive, but the towers are 200 feet high, and the blades of each turbine are 95 feet long and weigh five tons.

Watching the blades slowly spin, I try not to think about the horrible events of September 11, 2001 as I cycle. About 25 miles due east of here is the Flight 93 National Memorial, marking the spot where the United Airlines flight crashed nose first into the ground killing everyone aboard. Forty-four people died. As the plane had been redirected toward

Washington, D. C. — possibly targeting the Capitol — many more would have died except for a combination of factors: the flight was delayed in taking off due to traffic congestion, one of the intended hijackers was apparently missing, and the four hijackers present delayed the start of their attack. Those factors gave the crew and passengers time to prevent an even greater tragedy by resisting and then attacking the hijackers.

Now my daughter has the job of protecting American embassies and consulates around the world from similar attacks. I did not want to think about that or the Memorial, but I should. I have never been to the Memorial. Like every American, I should go, but I don't want to. The memories and the stories are important but painful. I know I should go. I will. Some day.

Just beyond Garrett we reach the Salisbury Viaduct — a 1908 foot long bridge across the Casselman River Valley. Originally built in 1912 for the Western Maryland Rail Company, the Viaduct handled train traffic until 1975. In 1998, it was renovated for trail use with a special deck added for cyclists, hikers, and equestrians. I hope no one is out on a horse today as I do not fancy encountering a rider and a large animal while riding a bike between two handrails.

Soaring a hundred feet above the ground below, the bridge provides an incredible view of the Casselman River Valley. It spans the river, the old two-lane US #219, the modern four-lane US #219, and the CSX Rail Line.

Steph and I dismount to stand against the railing. We stand side by side to enjoy the view.

"Didn't you have a sister?" my daughter asks.

The question catches me by surprise.

I glance at Stephanie out of the corner of my eye. She is not looking at me.

"Yeah," I reply.

"What was her name?"

"Kimberly."

"You never talked about her."

I hesitate before I respond, contemplating where this conversation is going. Quietly, I say, "She died when she was very young."

"How old was she?"

"Let's see, I was sixteen — just starting high school. She was not quite twelve."

"Wow, she was young. You both were."

"Uh, huh," I agree cautiously. Somehow, I get the sense that my daughter has carefully rehearsed this script.

"What happened?" Steph asks.

Again, I hesitate. Stephanie immediately backs off — or pretends to.

"You don't have to talk about it, if you don't want to."

"No, I don't mind telling you what happened." That is my first lie: it bothers me a great deal to dig up this part of my past. "It just happened a long time ago, and the details are foggy." My second lie: the details of that day are still vivid in my memory even after forty years.

"What was she like?"

"Pesky — like you." Steph and I share a knowing smile.

I continue. "She was a typical little sister. Five years younger than me. I got stuck looking after her alot. Then she started tagging along after me. That just wasn't cool for a teenage boy to have his little sister with him. Plus, she would tell our parents everything I did. In fact, I think that's why my parents made me take her with me."

"And that bothered you?"

"Sure did. Once I took her to a park, put her in a swing and started pushing her. Got her going really high. She was having a great time — squealing her head off."

"Sounds like a sweet big brother."

"Hardly. As soon as I got her going high enough. I took off. She had no way of stopping that swing. Probably took her a minute or two to realize I was no longer·behind her."

"You just left her?"

"I'm afraid I did."

"So, she was stuck in that swing until it stopped?"

"That was the idea. Not a good one, but it worked."

"Your parents must have killed you when you got home."

"They never found out about it."

164

Stephanie stares at me incredulously. "You left her all alone. You ran off. How could they have not found out about it?"

"Kimberley never told them." I fold my hands in front of me on the railing and use them as a focal point as I continue. "When I came back to the park about an hour later, she was sitting against a tree. I could tell she had been crying. Her face was red — redder than usual — and her nose was running everywhere. When she saw me, she jumped up and hugged me so hard I thought she was going to break one of my ribs. She didn't yell at me, or berate me, or fuss at me. She was just happy to see me. I couldn't understand her babbling at first, but she thought that God had taken me away."

"God?"

"We went to Sunday School on a regular basis. Old school religion. I spared you that indoctrination."

"Thanks, but why would God have taken you away?"

"There's this belief in certain Christian circles that the 'good' people on earth will be taken to heaven by God before the end of the world. It's called 'The Rapture'."

"And somehow she thought the brother who had left her swinging in the park was a 'good' person?"

"Yeah."

"But the prodigal brother returned."

"Look, I'm not proud of what I did. Probably shouldn't have told you that story, but I felt — well — constrained." I look up from my folded hands at my daughter. "I used to call her my ball and chain."

"Why did you call her that?"

"Because that was what she felt like. Once upon a time, prisoners would have a heavy iron ball chained to one of their ankles. A prisoner could still move around, but he couldn't get very far — very fast."

"And you wanted to get away from your parents?"

"Oh, yeah. Just like any other red-blooded American teenager."

"I know that feeling." My daughter smirks at me.

"Touche," I say. Sensing an opportunity to escape, I remount my bike. "I hate to leave this view, but I think we need to keep moving."

Stephanie nods in agreement. "I'm sure there are more good views ahead."

Meyersdale
216 miles to go

Our conversation on the bridge seems to have energized my daughter. She races ahead, and I lose sight of her.

A couple of miles later I coast into Meyersdale. On my right is a reconditioned caboose painted blue. I always thought they were supposed to be red. Just beyond it is the restored train depot.

Steph waves to me from the rear of the caboose. I pull up.

"I think my bike needs a break," I suggest.

"Your bike needs a break?" My daughter asks skeptically.

"Yeah, it's tired and cranky."

"It's not you that's tired and cranky?"

"Nah, I'm fresh as a daisy — a daisy that needs some water and a leg stretch."

We walk around, reading the historical signs and exploring the gift shop. Steph finds a picnic table and sits. I find a freezer filled with ice cream novelties. Selecting two oversized ice cream sandwiches, I join my daughter. As I sit across from her, I toss one of the ice cream sandwiches in her direction. She catches it to keep it from sliding off the table.

Ripping open the wrapper covering my sandwich, I watch her examine the list of ingredients on the packaging.

"Don't worry," I say. "I made sure that it wasn't vegan."

My daughter playfully glares at me. "You're a bad influence." She opens her sandwich and nibbles at it the way a squirrel would.

"You used to love these things," I comment.

"I remember. You would take me to the park and buy me one from that convenience store on the corner."

"That's right."

"And then you would push me in one of the swings."

"Uh, huh."

"The way you pushed your sister."

An alarm bell goes off in my head. My ice cream sandwich suddenly loses all of its flavor. "I knew I shouldn't have told you that story. It's not the same. I'm older. It's different with a daughter than a sister."

Stephanie leans across the table toward me. "Do you miss your sister?" she asks.

"I do."

"Do you miss Mom?"

The questions are surprise double punches to my gut. I miss both of them. "Yes. Very much."

"Did you miss me?"

I feel like a novice boxer who has been set up and tagged by an experienced pro. Two body blows followed by an over the top punch to the exposed chin. If I had not already beaten myself up with the same feelings, I would have toppled off backwards off the bench I was sitting on.

"Yes, I did," I say weakly.

"And I missed you," Steph replies.

We stare at each other across the table. Although we say nothing, our faces accuse each other with the same unspoken question: Then, why didn't you call?

Steph extends her hand across the table, and I take it.

"I'm glad you called," I say.

"I'm glad you answered," she replies. "I tried several times. Dialed all the digits except the last one. Then I would hang up."

"That would explain why I never got the call."

"I even wrote you letters. Long letters."

"I don't recall getting those either."

"That's because I didn't mail them."

"Do I get to read them now?"

"Afraid not. I filed them in the trash."

"I would have liked to have read them."

"I think not. I said some pretty angry things. Mean things."

"You had a right to be angry."

167

"I did. I felt abandoned. First, my mother had left me. Then my father."

"I'm sorry. I — " My voice trails off. I do not know what more to say. We have stopped eating our ice cream sandwiches; the sun is melting them while my daughter and I try to patch our relationship back together.

"It's okay," Steph reassures me. "That's all in the past. We're talking again, and that's all I care about." She gets up and grabs some paper towels to clean up the mess we have made with the melted ice cream sandwiches. I help her, and then we are back on our bikes riding the GAP.

As we cruise over the crushed limestone, I review our conversations in my head. I agree with my daughter that our lack of a relationship is hopefully in the past, but what she does not realize is that things from the past have a way of coming back and biting you — very hard — in sensitive places.

After Meyersdale we find ourselves crossing the Casselman River yet again on another bridge. At 909 feet, the Keystone Viaduct is less than half the length of the Salisbury Viaduct, but it is still impressive. Constructed in 1911 for the Western Maryland Railway, the viaduct curves toward a massive rusting truss. Knowing that the oxidized metal would eventually turn the restored deck red, the renovators wisely chose to paint it reddish brown.

Yelling like maniacs, we roar through the hundred year old girders that crisscross around us. Steph whips out her cell phone and takes a selfie of us as we ride. For a brief moment, I forget about my aching muscles.

After the Keystone Viaduct, the Passage resumes its steady climb towards its highest point at 2392 feet. We are about to cross the Eastern Continental Divide. Flaugherty Creek runs alongside us. Fortunately, I can handle the grade.

Barely.

I see the divide from a long way off. It is uphill, of course. And it's actually an underpass for McKenzie Hollow Road. Colorful murals decorate both sides of the entrance. Steph and I stop beneath the underpass at an elevation chart that depicts the entire Passage. I look at the chart and point to where we are — the apex of our journey.

"All downhill from here," I say.

Steph is rapidly texting on her cell phone.

"Shit!" She exclaims.

I am startled by her response. "I thought going downhill would be a good thing."

My daughter is still texting. "No, no. Not now." Unsure whether she is talking to me or saying what she is texting, I look over her shoulder. She has texted what she just said. The reply comes in: "He is on his way."

I do not know who "He" is or what is meant by "on his way". We are on a bike path in the middle of nowhere.

"Problem?" I ask.

Disgusted, Steph shoves her cell phone in her pocket. She starts talking as if I am not standing next to her. "All I wanted was one week — one week. But — no — it can't wait. It never can."

My impulse is to bombard her with questions, but I resist. Katherine said the best thing I can do is listen so that is what I decide to do.

Steph catches herself and looks at me. She has regained her composure. "We're getting a visitor. Not my choice."

"Uh-huh," is all I say.

"But we're going to push on."

"Okay."

"We've got three big tunnels coming up. Let's go."

I just nod; this listening thing is hard for me.

The first one we reach is the Big Savage Tunnel. We approach it through a thick forest. It appears as a small hole between the trees in the mountainside that gradually grows larger. I am reminded of the haunted Halloween attractions where you enter with no idea where — or if — you will come out.

We stop for pictures just outside the entrance. I notice two large doors on either side of the portal.

"They're not going to close those after we go in, are they?" I say pointing at the colossal barriers.

Steph shakes her head. "They only close them during the winter. I think from December to April. It protects the tunnel from ice damage."

I peer into the dark interior. Dim lights in the ceiling barely illuminate the cavern we are about to enter.

"We've got flashlights," Stephanie assures me.

"How many?"

"Two: one for each of us."

"Can I have both of them?" I plead.

Steph chuckles. "Scared of the dark?"

"Yeah!"

"Daddy, don't be a coward! Now, hurry up. We need to get through this tunnel before they close the gates."

"That's four months from now."

"At the rate you're going, it will take you four months to get through it."

"Fine. You lead the way. I'll be right behind you."

As we enter the Big Savage, the air temperature drops twenty degrees. It is like rolling into a walk in freezer. The cooler air gives us a break from the late morning heat. The clash of warm exterior air and the cooler interior air generates a fog. The lights above us cast an eerie pall on the sides of the tunnel. Our flashlights barely make a dent in the darkness. Other cyclists whizz by us going in the opposite direction. I cannot make them out until they are nearly on us. Our bicycles make a swooshing sound as we pass each other in the tight confines of the tunnel. I try not to think about the consequences if I happen to hit one of them — or if one of them hits me!

At 3294 feet, the Big Savage Tunnel is the longest of three tunnels (Savage, Borden, and Brush) which were constructed for the Connellsville subdivision of the Western Maryland Railway. Restoration of the tunnel cost $12.5 million, but the price paid was crucial to the success of the Passage. Without it, cyclists would have to haul their bikes over a tree-covered ridge.

The tunnel burrows through Savage Mountain, named after John Savage, an early surveyor of the area. The story is that a Lord Fairfax had commissioned Savage to find the headwaters of the Potomac River to settle a boundary dispute. Savage and his party set out in 1736 traversing the rugged terrain and establishing boundaries. During the winter of that year, severe weather and depleted stores led to serious starvation. As the leader of the expedition, he magnanimously volunteered his emaciated body as food to sustain the rest of his party. Fortunately for Savage, the group refused to accept his self sacrifice. Some accounts state that a flock of wild turkeys had the misfortune of stumbling into the camp just as the group was about to take Savage up on his offer. The altruistic Savage returned to civilization in 1737. Hopefully, Lord Fairfax had a good meal prepared for him. For his troubles, the name Savage was used for several landmarks in this area, including a mountain, a river, and a town.

Steph and I reach the brilliant shaft of light at the end of the Big Savage. A wave of hot air slaps us across our faces as we exit. We do not care as we are treated to a magnificent view of rolling farmland that unfolds before us. We can see three states: Pennsylvania, Maryland, and West Virginia. If Delaware were not so small, we could probably see it as well.

We find a bench where we can enjoy the view and snack on granola bars.

"Daddy, I have to meet someone." Steph says.

I give up on just listening and revert to questions.

"Is this the 'He' in your message?"

"Wait — did you — "

I could see my daughter was starting to get upset. "Hold on, Squirrel. I just saw a brief text. I don't know anything else, and I don't need to know who he is."

"Good."

"So who is 'He'?"

"I thought you didn't need to know."

"I don't need to know, but I would like to know."

Steph frowns. "I can't tell you his name. All I can say is that he will be here any minute, and you need to find something to do while I meet with him."

"Okay," I reply as I glance up and down the Passage. "Which way will he be coming from?"

"He won't be coming on a bike."

I raise and open my palms in confusion. "How else can he get up here? Only bikers and hikers are allowed on this trail. What's he going to do? Just drop out of the sky?"

"He used to do that — when he was in the 82nd Airborne. Now, he uses slightly more conventional transportation."

At that moment, I detect the distant whirling sounds made by a helicopter in flight.

I look up in the sky and then back at my daughter. "Some guy is flying up here in a helicopter to meet you? This 'He' must really want to talk to you."

"Apparently so." Steph sighs resignedly. "He's not used to being told 'No' — or 'Later' — for that matter."

"Is this guy your boss?"

"Not exactly, but I have to work with him."

I can see the helicopter circling above us. The pilot is scoping out his landing zone. The chopper is painted the dull dark color of a military Blackhawk.

"This guy is army?" I ask.

"Head of Special Operations. When one of our embassies gets into trouble, he decides who to send to save our butts."

"So you need to stay on his friendly side?"

"He doesn't have a friendly side."

"Oh."

"Look, Daddy. This shouldn't take long. He just prefers to talk face to face, especially when he has to deliver bad news."

My fatherly anxiety level rises. "Are you in trouble?" I ask.

"I'll know more after I talk to him. Right now, I need you to find something to do. A couple hundred yards down the trail is where it crosses the Mason Dixon Line." Steph directs me away from where the Blackhawk is coming in for a landing. "Lots of history there to keep you occupied."

I reluctantly nod in agreement and cycle away.

I see a stone pillar on my left marking where the Mason & Dixon Line crosses the Passage at a sharp diagonal. To my right, eleven rectangular blocks trace the boundary; each bears a letter of "Mason & Dixon". I stop and park my bike.

Looking back, I watch the Blackhawk land. Four armed and helmeted soldiers exit the aircraft just as its skids touch down. They disperse about the area, taking positions where they can observe any activity and interdict anyone who attempts to approach. I have seen this exercise before, but usually in movies where a chopper has landed in hostile territory — not on the border of Pennsylvania and Maryland.

The boundary between Pennsylvania and Maryland was not always so peaceful, primarily because of mistaken geography. My mind wanders back hundreds of years rather than contemplate what my daughter has gotten herself into.

Charles I of England granted a royal charter to the Calvert family in 1632 that included land north of the Potomac River up to the 40th parallel. The 40th parallel runs north of Philadelphia, which would have made the future City of Brotherly Love part of Maryland. Almost fifty years later, in 1681, his son, Charles II, granted a royal charter to William Penn to establish the Pennsylvania colony that included most of present day Maryland. Part of the problem was that father and son used different maps of the New World. Like proper English gentlemen, the Calverts and the Penns took their claims to court where the matter languished for years.

Exasperating the situation further, Maryland colonists were primarily Catholic and those of Pennsylvania Quaker. As settlers moved into the area, disputes broke out between the two disparate groups. A Marylander named Thomas Cresap figured prominently in some of these conflicts; consequently, the dust up became known as Cresap's War. Both Maryland and Pennsylvania sent militias to the area in the mid 1730s to settle the matter by force of arms but apparently could not find each other in the wilderness.

Weary from the squabbling among his subjects, King George II intervened and forced the two parties to compromise. In 1763 they agreed to establish the Pennsylvania-Maryland border on the latitude line fifteen miles south of the southernmost house in Philadelphia. To lay out this line as well as the boundary for neighboring Delaware, the English team of Charles Mason and Jeremiah Dixon was commissioned to perform the survey. American surveyors were not considered up to the task because of their inadequate training and lack of proper scientific instruments. I am sure that English snobbery had nothing to do with the selection of Mason and Dixon.

The survey took three years for Mason and Dixon to complete, from November 1764 to October 1767. Both men were astronomers and had previously worked together to observe and record the transit of Venus in 1761. To accomplish their task in the wilds of North America, the pair transported across the Atlantic the latest scientific apparatus. Some of their equipment included a transit and equal altitude instrument, a telescope with a precision adjustment screw, a theodolite plumb bob, a spirit level, a Hadley quadrant, and a zenith sector to measure the precise position of stars. The zenith sector was considered so delicate that it was transported on a feather stuffed cushion in a box supported by springs. In addition, Mason and Dixon loaded up boxes with survey telescopes, 66 foot long Gunter measuring chains, logarithm tables, and star charts. Mason and Dixon also brought stones over from England — hundreds of them. These stones were set every mile: hence, the term milestone. One side had a "P" for Pennsylvania, and the other had an "M" for Maryland. Every five miles, a special crownstone was set into the ground so that the family crest of Penn faced Pennsylvania and the family crest of Calvert faced Maryland. These crownstones became collector items in later years and "disappeared" over time.

To accomplish the task of hacking through a wilderness while conducting the scholarly activity of drawing an accurate straight line on a map, Mason and Dixon had to assemble a force of about one hundred guides, cooks, axmen, laborers, and trailblazers. I would have hated to have been in charge of their Human Resources department.

As surveys at this time were done by using a chain and pole method, a reference point was established using astronomical measurements. With a pole marking that spot, measurements would be made using a long, heavy chain from point to point. To determine accuracy, a survey would be conducted back to the original starting point. Usually, errors would be random; however, Mason and Dixon encountered systematic errors, meaning that they were consistently off in one direction. This observation lead to the startling discovery that the gravitational pull of the Allegheny Mountains was affecting their measurements.

For Mason and Dixon to accurately make the measurements, they had to clear a path thirty feet wide in twelve mile chunks. Without power tools, they had to cut down trees, clear brush, and cross rivers and creeks before they could even start their surveying work. While they worked, they had to keep a vigilant eye out for hostile natives who might object to white men crossing into their territory.

The invaluable service completed by Mason and Dixon might have been lost in the voluminous survey work that was done as the North American continent was settled and divided into states. However, the state of Pennsylvania abolished slavery in 1780. With Maryland still allowing slavery, the Mason & Dixon Line became the demarcation between north and south — free and slave — in the United States.

I know all of this information about a survey that was done 250 years ago seems irrelevant, but boundaries are important — both those on the ground and the ones between people in a relationship. They are difficult to determine, but they have long term consequences. While I was trying to establish new boundaries with my daughter, I felt lost in the wilderness of my broken promises.

Returning to the present, I watch Stephanie walk toward where the helicopter has landed. Still wearing her bike helmet, she stops short of the rotor wash. One of the soldiers approaches her. They talk with their helmeted heads almost touching. I see the soldier nodding and then gesturing back at the helicopter.

The soldier takes a dozen steps in my direction and then kneels to the ground, his head pivoting from side to side. A thin man hops out and walks toward where Stephanie is standing. Even at this distance, I can tell from his bearing that he is career military. Although the rotors have slowed, he leans over until he reaches Steph. They do not shake hands.

The thin man starts talking. My daughter listens with her arms akimbo. Occasionally, she nods. When he gives Steph a chance to speak, she shakes her head from side to side as she does. Even from this distance I can tell that she does not like what he is telling her. She paws the ground with the cleat of her bike shoe like a horse eager to run away.

The thin man keeps talking. He is trying to convince her of something. I see his left arm reach out and grasp Steph's right bicep. She does not pull away. I can tell she is accepting what she is being told, even though she does not like it. They shake hands and separate.

I watch the thin man jump back aboard his helicopter. The four soldiers follow him, and the Blackhawk takes off. It turns and heads back to where it came from.

My eyes switch to my daughter. She strides purposely to her bike, mounts it, and slowly pedals toward me. I guess that she is anticipating the questions that I will bombard her with and how she will answer: What sort of man travels around the United States in a military helicopter with armed soldiers? Why would he meet with her in person in the middle of nowhere, interrupting our bike trip? What was so important that it could not wait until she was back at work next week?

Although I am dying to ask her those questions and more, I stifle my fatherly curiosity and concern.

"Ready to ride?" I ask.

"You betcha."

I laugh. It is one of my expressions. She glides past me. I follow her.

The Passage drops rapidly after crossing the Mason & Dixon Line, from almost three thousand feet in elevation to six hundred feet in a little over twenty-five miles. With trees on our left and an old rail line on our right, we literally fly. The wind whistles through my helmet. We occasionally pause for a picture of some rusting train equipment or an abandoned piece of machinery, but our goal is to reach Cumberland as fast as possible. I squeeze my brakes far more than I push my pedals on the way down.

Coasting into Cumberland, we are hot and hungry. The temperature has spiked with the rise of the sun and the drop in altitude. Cumberland marks the end of the Passage and the beginning of the C & O. I am ready to celebrate with a burger and a beer — and put off starting the C & O as long as possible. As usual, Steph has different ideas.

I point hopefully at a sign for a restaurant that reads: "Uncle Jack's Pizzeria & Pub". It proudly advertises the establishment's Black Angus burgers.

Stephanie shrugs indifferently. "Let's walk around," she suggests.

"Why not?" I reply. "This is the 'Queen City of Maryland' after all."

"What are you talking about?"

"It was once the second largest city in Maryland. Gateway through the Appalachian Mountains via the Cumberland Road."

"Whatever."

Dismounting, we lock our bikes in a shady corner. The sun is scorching the pavement underneath our feet. Waves of heat rise from the concrete and asphalt to greet us. I tap a sign proudly proclaiming the town's motto: "Come for a Visit, Stay for Life".

Stephanie shakes her head. "I hope not."

We wander aimlessly around the middle of downtown Cumberland. Its buildings portray a prior prosperity. Its streets have been converted to a pedestrian mall designed to attract tourists. There are quite a few who stroll past us braving the oppressive humidity. Steph is looking for something to eat that comes out of the ground; I would prefer eating something that had once walked on top of it. She seems indifferent to the heat; I am hallucinating about finding a cool, shady place with frosty drinks and a working air conditioner.

I settle for a seat in the shadow of a building next to a fountain. My daughter wanders away. In relative comfort, I watch her until she disappears around a corner. I turn my attention to the flowing water beside me. This little oasis relaxes me and takes my mind off my aching muscles and growling stomach.

"You're doing it again."

The voice is familiar and feminine. Startled, I desperately scan the knots of pedestrians meandering around me. I don't see her.

"You lost her once, and you're about to lose her again."

"Nancy?" I say out loud.

A woman stops next to me and talks to a small child in the stroller that she has been pushing. To shield her face and half the county from the blistering sun, she is wearing a bright pink hat in the style of a Mexican sombrero. She eyes me warily from underneath the brim of the hat and replies, "Are you talking to me?"

"No — sorry." I apologize as I look past her into the crowd.

The voice returns. "She needs your help. That is why she asked you on this miserable bike trip."

It hasn't been so miserable, I think to myself.

"You were almost mugged, you're soaked in sweat from the heat, your legs are covered in mud, and every muscle in your body is screaming at you."

"All part of the adventure," I reply aloud, knowing full well that Nancy never understood the concept of adventures.

The woman in the hat the size of Texas glances up at me from where she has been attending her child. I ignore her.

The voice continues: "You need to find your daughter and talk to her. She needs you. And no more of your silly historical trivia."

"Okay, okay," I say as I reluctantly rise from my seat. "I'll go find her, but I think she can take care of herself."

Seeing me stand and hearing me talking to myself, the woman in the enormous hat quickly puts as much distance as she can between me and her child. She scurries off, pushing the stroller in front of her and glancing back at me.

I have to walk several blocks before I see Stephanie walking toward me. We reunite in front of Uncle Jack's.

"Find anything?" I ask.

"No."

I can tell my daughter is frustrated. Taking her arm, I turn her toward Uncle Jack's. "I'll bet old Uncle Jack will cook you up a nice plate of vegan pasta," I suggest.

Stephanie reluctantly allows me to steer her inside. A wave of freon refrigerated and burger infused air washes over us as we enter. Inhaling deeply, I know we have found the right place.

We seat ourselves in a booth, away from the other customers. The waitress takes our orders and then brings us our drinks — beers and waters.

I reach for my beer mug to propose a toast. Stephanie anticipates my toast and takes the beer away from me. She pushes a glass filled with water toward me.

"Hydrate,' she commands.

Pretending obedience, I take a small sip of water and then reach again for my beer. Steph pulls it further away from me.

"All of it." It is a direct order.

"I feel like I'm a marine in Desert Storm," I comment.

Steph says nothing; she glares at me instead.

Dutifully, I down the entire glass of water. Stephanie slowly slides the beer toward me.

"I think you've been hanging around military types too much," I remark.

"Comes with the job," my daughter replies matter of factly.

Although I am feeling a bit bloated from all the water I have just downed, I take a long satisfying draw on my beer before I speak. "I would guess so. You being in security for the government."

Stephanie says nothing.

I take another drink before I ask what has been on my mind for the past twenty odd miles. "So what did the captain want?"

Steph turns her head away from me as she speaks. "He's a general, not a captain."

"Of course not. Captains don't fly around in helicopters with armed guards."

Steph turns her head back toward me. "No, they don't."

"You guys talk about the weather?" I ask.

I get a brief smile and a shake of the head.

"Sports?"

This time I receive an eye roll.

"Must be something happened at the office," I guess.

"You could say that."

"And it involves you?"

"I made a call, and I have to take responsibility for it."

"Oh."

We sit in silence until our food comes. I observe my daughter while we wait; she avoids my eyes, suddenly interested in the decor of the restaurant.

The plates of food are large, but we devour everything on them and then order dessert. When the waitress departs, my daughter meets my gaze.

"Look, Daddy, I can't tell you very much because most of what I am involved in is classified."

"Understood."

Steph pauses and rearranges her silverware. "Ever heard of Benghazi?"

"Port on the Mediterranean. North coast of Africa. Second largest city in Libya."

Steph nods. "Yeah, but it has a different meaning for me. Libya has been involved in an ongoing civil war since Gaddafi was ousted from power."

"Didn't he die in a gun battle?"

"Officially, yes."

"Unofficially?"

"No. He was captured and executed by multiple blows from blunt objects and stabs with sharp instruments."

I grimace at the thought of such a cruel death, even for a dictator known for his brutality.

"Immediate cause of death was a bayonet inserted into his rectum by one of his captors. Unconfirmed reports stated that Gaddafi had ordered the execution of one of the man's relatives in a similar fashion."

I grunt as I squirm involuntarily in my seat.

"Dozens of Gaddafi's followers were disarmed, beaten mercilessly, and then shot."

"Executing prisoners is a serious war crime," I remind Stephanie.

"I'm afraid that is only one of hundreds in Libya."

"That, and only the losers of conflicts are prosecuted for war crimes."

My daughter shrugs. "My issue started the year after Gaddafi died. We have X amount of resources and X plus Y security needs. My job is to make assessments and recommendations about where to allocate our limited resources. The security situation had deteriorated in Benghazi. We knew that, but there were other places in worse circumstances."

"And Benghazi was a consulate, not an embassy."

"True, but the real complication was a request that we keep a low profile in Benghazi. Adding security would have raised the profile."

"This request came from another government agency?"
"Yes."

"First federal agency that comes to my mind that likes to keep a low profile would be the CIA."

"I cannot confirm or deny that assessment."

"Spoken like a true spook."

"I am not a spy," Steph hisses at me.

"Okay, okay. Just seems strange that the CIA would be running an operation out of Benghazi at that time that it wanted to keep quiet."

"I did not say it was CIA."

"But you didn't deny it either." I ponder for a moment. "Lots of weapons floating around after a civil war. Weapons that are difficult to trace back to their origin." I scratch the stubble on my chin. "Question would be where the CIA would want to send them in 2012." I snap my fingers. "Of course, Syria! The civil war was just starting to heat up."

I know that I am right when I see the color drain from Stephanie's face.

"I never told you —" she starts, but I cut her off.

"Of course, you didn't. These things aren't that hard to figure out when you've been around as long as I have. They pulled the same stunt back in the eighties with Iran-Contra. They've done it in Africa, Asia — just about every continent except Antarctica."

Our dessert arrives: a thick chocolate brownie topped with several scoops of ice cream and covered in a thick fudge sauce. I could have done without the fudge sauce, but it is Steph's favorite. She did not ask if the ice cream was vegan — a sure sign she is stressed.

As I watch her devour most of "our" dessert, I try to recall what I had read about Benghazi.

"There was an attack on our consulate in Benghazi on the anniversary of the 9/11 attacks." I say, half to myself.

Stephanie stops eating and pushes the mostly eaten dessert in my direction.

"That's right. And another facility about a mile away."

I pick up a spoon. "I thought it was a spontaneous riot triggered by some video."

"That is the official State Department line."

"I take it that it was not exactly spontaneous."

"Two separate United States facilities were attacked within hours using automatic weapons, rocket propelled grenades, and mortars."

"That type of coordination and those types of weapons usually require more than a little preparation," I suggest.

"And there was not a soul outside the gates before the attacks."

"So no angry crowd to start a riot."

"Nope."

"Some people died," I say softly.

Steph folds her hands together on the table and stares at them as she speaks. "Yes. Chris Stevens — the first US ambassador killed in the line of duty since 1979. Sean Smith, an IT guy who should not have been there. I knew them both personally. Plus two CIA guys I did not know: Glen Doherty and Tyrone Woods. There would have been a lot more Americans killed if some very brave men had not broken rules and risked their necks to get to the scene."

182

I push away the remains of our dessert. Thinking about the sacrifices these men made has cost me my appetite. "So they're going to fire you because someone has to take the blame."

"The powers that be won't let me off that easy — they want me to testify before Congress."

"That's a fate worse than death. A bunch of smug politicians showing off in front of the cameras at your expense."

"I have two choices: I can testify and be assigned to a desk preventing polar bear attacks on our embassy in Canada or I can refuse to testify and be assigned to a desk reviewing a mountain-sized pile of passport applications."

"Either way, you will need to hire an attorney and have a big bill at the end of it all."

"Yep."

"You could resign," I suggest softly.

"I love my job too much."

I nod as I swirl the dregs of my beer in the bottom of the glass. "I thought Secretary of State Clinton took responsibility for what happened at Benghazi?"

"She has. In a way. She has said she is ultimately responsible as Secretary of State, but that she relied on her security professionals."

"And you would be one of the security professionals she relied on?"

"Yep."

"At least the one they picked as a sacrificial lamb?"

Steph does not respond. I can tell she is sinking into a funk, but I have to get one more piece of information. I lean across the table to get her attention. She looks at me.

"When are you scheduled to testify?"

"Next week."

"That explains the general's helicopter visit. Some Senator is probably holding up funding for one of his favorite projects until he offers a victim."

"Have no idea, Daddy. You know I get petrified talking in front of people. Have since I was little. But I will do what is asked of me."

I rap the table with the knuckles of my right hand, realizing that I have raised a young woman who is ready to take responsibility not just for her actions, but the actions of others. That is a dangerous trait in the viper den of Washington politics.

"Are you ready to go?" Steph asks me.

I can tell that she is tired of talking about her situation and is ready to get back on her bike. "As soon as I pay the bill. We only have a couple of miles more to go today, right?" I inquire hopefully.

"More like thirty."

"Thirty?" My spirits sag. I doubt I can do three more miles, much less thirty.

"Are you up for it?"

"Sure, sure," I lie.

"There's a unique place in Paw Paw I want us to stay. A biker friend told me about it."

I pay, and we leave. The day has not cooled down much, but I feel revived as we get back on our bikes. I temporarily forget that we are about to start the part of the trip that I have been dreading. We pedal through Cumberland on a paved bike path, pausing at a sign that marks the end of the Great Allegheny Passage and the beginning of the C & O for pictures.

We pass by the restored red brick Western Maryland Railway station which has been turned into a museum. I long to stop, retreat into its air conditioned environs, and admire the mockup on its lower level of a mule-powered canal boat that once plied the C & O, but we still have thirty miles to pedal before the sun sets. The fear of trying to navigate the treacherous C & O towpath in the dark drives me to cycle on.

As we exit Cumberland, the asphalt rapidly transitions from crushed gravel to packed dirt to slippery mud. We find ourselves slipping and sliding on top of an embankment that steeply slopes into either the old canal on the left or the Potomac on the right. The scenery is fantastic, but I dare not take my eyes off the ground below my tires for long. If I do not pay attention, I will find myself careening down one side or the other. As Brad at Confluence Cyclery had cautioned me, the C & O soon splits into two tracks. Although I try to stay to my right, I often find myself wandering over to the left to avoid large water-filled potholes and overgrown areas. It is as treacherous as advertised.

I also remember Brad's warning about the unpredictable weather: sudden heavy rainstorms can unload on bikers at any moment. I glance up quickly, but all I see are innocent looking fluffy clouds drifting across the late afternoon sky.

As I waggle between muddy tracks, my mind wanders onto the origins of the path that I am on. Between 1803 and 1850, thirty-six major canal projects were constructed in the United States. Prominent men of the new nation, such as George Washington, believed that canals were essential to American economic development, as they offered safer and faster movement of cargo and passengers than overland wagons or stagecoaches.

Two of the most famous of these projects were the Erie Canal in New York state and the Chesapeake and Ohio (C & O) Canal that was to run next to the Potomac. The Erie connected New York City and the Hudson River to the Great Lakes via Lake Erie. Construction of the Erie from 1817 to 1825 and its subsequent success motivated backers of the C & O to push for their own route to the growing American frontier west of the Appalachians. In fact, the first engineer for the C & O — Benjamin Wright — had been the engineer for important sections of the Erie Canal in New York.

The idea was to connect the Chesapeake Bay with the Ohio River (hence the name: Chesapeake & Ohio Canal) by digging a narrow channel running from Georgetown on the Potomac to Pittsburgh on the Ohio and fill it with water. This man made waterway would run beside the Potomac to avoid seasonal flooding and the large numbers of cataracts in the river that made navigation challenging.

Before he became the first President of the United States, George Washington had founded the Potowmack Company with a similar ambition. It constructed five skirting canals around the major obstacles on the Potomac: House's Falls, Payne's Falls, Seneca Falls, Great Falls, and Little Falls. In the days before steam engines, the boats would merely float downstream. To return, the boats would have to be pushed against the current by men with poles. With the formation of the Chesapeake and Ohio Company, the assets of the Potowmack Company were folded into the new project.

A canal separate from the Potomac was deemed necessary because of the hazards of trying to navigate an unpredictable river. In the spring, the Potomac would often flood while in the summer water levels would drop so low that cargo laden vessels could not stay afloat. Parts of the Potomac would freeze solid in the winter. Whirlpools and strong currents threatened to wreck boats anytime of year.

The C & O was built between 1828 and 1850. It is essentially a long ditch with locks every so often to adjust for changes in elevation. A dirt towpath runs next to it so that a pair of mules could be driven to pull the boats along. To create the ditch, thousands of unskilled laborers dug with picks and shovels and hauled the dirt away with wheelbarrows. Horses and mules were employed where possible, but most of the dirt and rocks were removed by hand.

To obtain enough workers, the Canal Company resorted to indentured servants from Germany, Ireland, Holland, and England starting in 1829. The groups did not speak the same language or share the same cultural habits; consequently, they did not get along well with each other. Despite the offers of meat three times a day, vegetables, and a "reasonable allowance for whiskey" in addition to their pay, workers resented the long hours of hard manual labor in slavelike conditions. They would often take their frustrations out on each other.

Completion required the construction of 74 locks to raise and lower boats, eleven aqueducts to cross major streams, and at least 240 culverts to cross the minor ones. In addition, a tunnel of over 3,000 feet had to be bored through the hills around Paw Paw. All of this engineering work required skilled laborers including stonemasons, mason, carpenters, and blacksmiths.

Problems plagued construction of the C & O from the beginning. The initial price estimate came in at $22 million, more than four times the anticipated cost. Rather than abandon the project — which was deemed of national importance — the investors hired another expert to prepare a lower estimate. As a result of this lower estimate, cost overruns constantly plagued the construction of the Canal as the original estimate — although less than the actual cost — was far more accurate. In fact, all construction stopped from 1842 to 1847 when the Canal Company ran out of cash to fund operations. To reduce the cost of excavation, the width of the Canal gradually narrowed: it is eighty feet up to Lock 5; sixty feet from Lock 5 to Harpers Ferry; and a mere fifty feet above Harpers Ferry. The last few locks constructed on the Canal were made from cheaper composite materials with supporting wood structures that have deteriorated over time.

Construction problems were foreshadowed at the groundbreaking ceremony. President John Quincy Adams had to make three attempts against the rocky ground before he could successfully turn over the first shovel of dirt to start construction.

Competition from railroads and the high cost of creating a navigable canal in the mountains forced the abandonment in 1850 of construction plans to extend the Canal. Today, the C & O only runs from Georgetown to Cumberland, having fallen 150 miles short of its intended destination.

At mile 181 we come upon Evitts Creek Aqueduct, the first of eleven aqueducts that we will cross on our way to D.C. At one time the aqueducts held water that boats could float on as they crossed creeks that flowed into the Potomac. An aqueduct is basically a water bridge over a stream of water. This afternoon, we can pedal our bikes either on the dry bed of the aqueduct or on the towpath above. Steph takes the lower route while I elect to stay on the towpath for a better view.

Construction of the Evitts Creek Aqueduct was started in 1839 but stopped in 1841 when the Canal company ran out of money. The aqueduct was finally completed in 1850. Inadequate funding for construction — a persistent problem for the company — led to the use of substandard material in building the aqueducts. The National Park Service has struggled to maintain them, but the Fossiliferous Tonoloway Limestone used to erect the aqueducts erodes easily. I can see rusting iron supports that the National Park Service had installed in 1979 and 1983 to stabilize the structure.

At seventy feet in length, the Evitts Creek Aqueduct is the smallest of these structures along the C & O Canal. My perch on top offers a great vista of Evitts Creek emptying into the North Branch of the Potomac River.

Evitts Creek and nearby Evitts Mountain are named after one of Allegany County's earliest settlers. It's said that old man Evitts wandered into this remote (at the time) area to "contemplate his bachelorhood." As I rest astride my bike, I contemplate my own self-imposed bachelorhood.

Steph has paused to take a photo of me. As I watch her, I think about how I had devoted my life to my daughter after her mother had died. I felt I owed her that much. After Nancy, other women did not interest me. I did not have to retreat into the wilds of western Maryland; instead, I created my own wilderness by erecting emotional barriers.

"So, how did that work out for you?"

It's Nancy's voice I hear, soft but challenging.

"Fine," I reply.

I hear her chuckle. "That's always your answer — no matter how dire your situation is. Remember that time we had a leak in the pipes in the basement?"

I groan at the memory.

"I stood at the top of the stairs and called down to you to ask how things were going. You came to the bottom of the stairs. You were soaked, standing in ankle deep water with a wrench in one hand and a hammer in the other."

"I was trying to fix the leak," I plead.

"Do you remember your reply?" The voice pauses momentarily. "All you said was 'Fine'."

It was my turn to chuckle. "Thankfully, you called a plumber before the whole house flooded."

"At least one of us had common sense."

Steph waves to me, and I wave back. She motions for me to come on, but I raise my hand to tell her I need more time. Impatient, she turns her bike around and pumps up the incline to where I am.

188

"Sunlight isn't going to last forever," Stephanie comments when she reaches me. "How are you doing?"

"Fine." I grin at her as I reply.

"What are you doing?" she asks.

"Just thinking about the history of this place," I say untruthfully. "In August 1864, during the Battle of Folck's Mill, Union forces halted a raiding party of Confederates who had burned Chambersburg, Pennsylvania a few days earlier. They were on their way to Cumberland but unable to cross the bridge at Evitts Creek. The Confederates were forced back to Oldtown where they eventually fought their way across the Canal and the Potomac."

"More history. Great. Let's go."

Steph is off, and I follow. Back on the towpath, my thoughts return to the history of the canal we are cycling along. Thinking about history keeps my mind off my aching butt.

A trip from Cumberland to Georgetown on the C & O typically took seven days. Families would tend each boat and every member was expected to put in an eighteen hour day, seven days a week. The design of the canal boats emphasized large cargo areas separated by three cabins. One of the cabins served as a stable for the mules; one acted as a storage bin to hold hay for the mules, and one provided living space for the family. The family would cook, eat, and sleep in a single twelve foot by twelve foot room.

Canal boatmen were an insular and obstinate lot. They stuck to themselves, forming their own separate communities even during the winter when the Canal would close for the season. Children raised on the boats would work and marry on the Canal as adults since they knew of no other life. Pilots would fight for almost any reason: to get ahead of another boat at a lock, to resolve a perceived insult, or just to get some exercise.

Coal was the most profitable and important cargo. Unfortunately, dust from the coal would often enter the living quarters of the family inflicting respiratory ailments on young and old alike. Boats pulled by teams of mules transported coal east, and on the return west carried furniture, produce, and fertilizer. Other types of cargo included sand, lumber, wood, and flour. Between the dust from the coal and the odor from the mules, the boats could not have been a pleasant place to live.

In 1889 a devastating flood forced the Canal Company into receivership. To keep the Canal's right of way from falling into the hands of its competitor, the Western Maryland Railway, the B & O Railroad acquired the Canal.

By 1923, competing forms of transportation (railroads and trucks) had decimated traffic on the C & O. Only five boats carrying sand from Georgetown to Williamsport were reported to have operated on the Canal in 1924. Later that year another catastrophic flood damaged bridges, breached dams, and washed away masonry up and down the Canal. Operations ceased. Communities started dumping sewage into the Canal, and the stagnant water became a breeding ground for mosquitoes.

During the depths of the Great Depression, the federal government received the abandoned Canal in exchange for a loan that the B & O Railroad needed from the Reconstruction Finance Corporation. Jobs for the unemployed were offered to restore the Canal as a recreation area. After World War II, proposals were made to turn the Canal into a road parkway, but concerns about flooding delayed implementation of the proposals.

After challenging newspaper reporters to join him, US Supreme Court Justice William O. Douglas organized an eight day hike in 1954 down the canal towpath from Cumberland to Georgetown in an effort to save it from being converted to a parkway for cars. Although only nine men (including Justice Douglas) covered the whole 184 point five miles, the persistent efforts of Douglas (sometimes referred to as "Wild Bill" for his efforts to preserve the environment) succeeded. In 1961 President Dwight Eisenhower designated the Canal a National Monument, and in 1971 the Canal became a National Historic Park. It is about the only productive thing a Supreme Court justice ever accomplished I muse to myself.

To punish me for that thought, I fail to avoid a pothole and I bounce hard on the seat of my bike. My bottom objects to this additional abuse, and I focus my attention on the part of the Towpath we are now on. It does not seem to be maintained at all. Dodging rocks, roots, and fallen limbs slows us down. We see turtles sunning themselves on logs, deer peeking out through the foliage, and a large blue heron stalking its afternoon snack. Fortunately, no bugs bother us although we pass large bodies of stagnant water in the old canal covered in blue-green algae. Stephanie is relentless with the pace.

The only thing that stops her is a large tree that has fallen across the towpath. It extends from one side of the trail to the other. I pull up next to Stephanie. We stare at the wall of green leaves in front of us.

"Looks like it fell recently," Steph comments. "Must be all the rain."

"Good thing it didn't fall on one of us," I reply.

My daughter gives me a sideways glance. "Always with the positive thoughts," she chides me. "Let's get through this."

We dismount, find a narrow opening in the branches, and continue on. Steph easily resumes her pace, but my energy stores are depleted. A gap grows between us as I struggle to keep my legs moving. Watching her backside glide away from me as if I am standing still discourages and infuriates me. I glance to my right and left to make sure that I am indeed moving forward. Then I summon my last reserves, rise up on my pedals, and try to accelerate to catch up with my daughter.

I do not see the tree root running across the width of the Towpath until it is too late. A cautionary thought floats lazily through the lactic acid filling my brain: Going over the handlebars is not a recommended biking experience.

My front tire hits the root and halts. Although my bike has stopped, I do not. Time slows as I take stock of my situation. My butt rises in the air, and my feet come off the pedals. To compensate, my hands instinctively latch onto my handlebars in a death grip. The result is that I am inverted, staring at a plastic bear in a biplane waving happily at me. My feet are where my hands should be and vice versa. My sunglasses fall away. My water bottle flies past me chased by a half eaten granola bar that I had stuffed in my shirt pocket.

Another warning drifts through my mind from the days when I took a few flight lessons. A takeoff can be fine, but the landing not so much.

The ground closes in on me quickly. A brief recollection shoots through my brain as I realize my situation. This experience is what those young Olympic gymnasts must go through when they perform somersaults on a balance beam. What was it I had yelled at the television? Stick the landing! Stick the landing! Should be much easier for me than them. They only had a four inch wide piece of wood to land on. I had the whole C & O Towpath.

I do not stick the landing, but my legs fly over enough so that I am able to land feet first rather than face first. My heels skid out from underneath me, and I more or less make a three-point landing: on my feet and my butt.

Stephanie rolls up next to me as I sit in the middle of the Towpath. Trying to gather my wits, I stare at a large mud puddle just in front of me that I could have landed face first in.

"Daddy, are you okay?"

In a daze, I look up at my daughter and ask, "Did I win the gold medal?"

"What? I happened to look back and see you go over your handlebars! You should be asking if you broke any bones. How did that happen?"

Without responding, I try to get up. Steph will have none of that.

"Stay right where you are," she orders. "We have to make sure you're okay first."

Obediently and gratefully, I sit back down. I feel relieved to still be breathing and not sitting on a bike seat. Steph peppers me with questions, asking me to move each of my limbs in turn. She gently presses on various parts of my body, asking if I feel any pain. I watch her face as she examines me. It feels good to have someone genuinely concerned about my well being. Once she has determined that I have inflicted no permanent damage to my body, I get the lecture.

"You have got to be more careful. You could have seriously injured yourself. We are miles from the nearest emergency room. There is no way I could have — "

My daughter stops in mid sentence and breaks into tears. I am sitting in the middle of the muddy C & O Towpath; she is crouched next to me. Slipping my arms around her, I pull her in to comfort her. We are two lost souls in the middle of a wilderness.

After a minute or two, Steph pushes me away and punches me in the shoulder.

"Don't do that again!" she orders.

"Believe me, I don't plan on it," I promise.

"You're the only father I have."

"You're the only daughter I have."

"I'm glad we've got that straight. Now, let's check out your bike."

Steph helps me up, briefly hugs me, and then retrieves my bike. It is in the same condition that I am: old, battered, but still rolling.

We remount, and I discover some new sore parts of my body as we start pedaling. Only the thought that our evening destination is not far keeps me going. Fortunately, Steph takes pity on me and slows the pace.

To get to Paw Paw, we have to cross the Potomac into West Virginia. I force my weary legs to pump the pedals to get up the bridge. A small sign next to the road proudly pronounces the population: 508. I wonder if that census included cats, dogs, and squirrels. We enter the town: a handful of buildings straddling the highway. The sun is just above a row of mountains to our right; we have made our destination just before dark.

I turn to Steph. "Exactly where are we staying?" I ask.

"We have to find Hoop," she replies.

"Hoop?"

"Hoop."

I wonder if Hoop is a place or a person. Steph goes into a convenience store to inquire, the only place we see with any activity. I am tired, dirty, and hungry; I see no place where I can rest, shower, and eat.

Coming out of the convenience store, Stephanie points to the other side of the highway at an old clapboard house. I can see someone lying in a hammock on the side porch.

As we cross the road, a head pops up out of the hammock.

"Hey, are you Stephanie?"

"Yep," my daughter replies. "Are you Hoop?"

"Yes, ma'am. I've been awaitin'. Come around to the side here." Hoop vaults over the porch railing landing neatly between two large shrubs, a gymnastic feat he must do on a regular basis. It's the sort of stunt I would do when I was in my twenties.

"Do you have a place where we can hose off our bikes?" Steph asks.

Hoop sizes us up. Our legs, backs, and bikes are all caked in mud from riding the C & O. "The two of you could use a little hosing off," Hoop cackles.

I could find this guy irritating, but his friendly small town directness is refreshing. He unwinds a hose, turns on the water, and watches us remove layer after layer of trail grit from each other and our bikes. After he secures our bikes in a small shed, he leads us to where we will be spending the night. It is a small building. Inside, four bunk beds constructed of two by fours and plywood are jammed together in a single room. Plastic inflatable mattresses with sheets stretched over them have been laid on the plywood. A minuscule closet in the corner has a sink and a shower crammed into it to serve as a bathroom. The floor is smooth — but bare — concrete. There are no windows. Fortunately, Hoop will have no other guests tonight. Eight people in this space would be more than a little tight.

Steph and I step inside, absorbing all of the available floor space. She seems pleased with the set up. I refrain from making my usual sarcastic comments. Based on what I have seen of Paw Paw so far, this arrangement is the best — if not the only — overnight lodging this tiny town has to offer.

As there is no room for him inside, Hoop stands in the door and points out all the convenient features of our evening's accommodations, including a coffee maker and an assortment of magazines. I don't drink coffee, and the latest magazine I see is seven months old. Hoop mentions that he has done all the work himself. Glancing up at the ceiling, I see a large opening where insulation has been hastily stuffed to fill it. I test the sturdiness of one of the bunk beds with my right hand. The rough hewn wooden bed does not budge. I cannot recall ever sleeping on a plastic air mattress, but I doubt that it will matter: I am beyond bone tired.

From the way Hoop is beaming, I can tell that he is quite proud of his creation. I just hope the local fire marshall does not drop by during the night and kick us out before we leave in the morning.

Hoop offers us grilled cheese sandwiches and sweet potato fries for dinner. I will eat anything right now, and Steph is so hungry she says nothing about being a vegan. All we demand is cold beer, which Hoop assures us will not be a problem.

After he departs, Steph asks, "What do you think?"

"It's the Ritz Carlton of Paw Paw," I proclaim.

"Well, I call first dibs on the shower."

"Be my guest," I say. I let myself outside so that Steph has a little privacy. In the fading light, I spot Hoop heading over to the convenience store. It is probably the only place in town still open. Everything else looks closed for the evening. I pull out my cell phone and try to make a call, but there is not a single bar showing on the screen. Apparently, I will have to wait until we get closer to modern civilization before I can reach out to my old political contacts. I need a little more information before I can figure out how to help my daughter.

While I am pondering her situation, Hoop returns. He has the sandwiches and the fries wrapped in aluminum foil. More importantly, he has a styrofoam cooler packed with ice cold beers. Figuring that the food will stay warm enough in the foil, I pull out two of the beers and offer one to Hoop. He readily accepts. We sit outside in the gathering darkness at a red picnic table and discuss small town life and the dreams he has for his small boarding enterprise. I am relieved to hear that the fire marshall is a friend of his, but disturbed that the building inspector is his brother. That would explain all the blatant code violations I saw. Hopefully, we will not have a fire tonight. Hoop and I finish our beers and say goodnight.

I poke my head into our room. Stephanie is coming out of the shower: one towel wrapped around her torso and another wrapped around her hair. She is wearing the two towels the same way her mother did. The little twist at the top of the towel that covers her torso keeps it in place while the towel wrapped around her head struggles to contain her hair. She stops, bends over, lets her hair fall, and then shakes the towel out. Starting at her forehead, Steph wraps the towel around her hair giving it a little squeeze and folding the towel in so it stays in place as she raises her head.

Watching her brings back vivid memories of Nancy and reminds me of how much I still miss my wife and the life we had together. But this is my daughter, not my wife. This is now, not twenty-five years ago. Fortunately, Steph's greeting knocks me back into present reality.

"Hey, Daddy."

"Hey, Squirrel."

"Is that our food!" She attacks the bag I am carrying that contains our dinner. There is no place to sit in our room except by leaning over while perching on the edge of a lower bunk. We sit across from each other — knee to knee — as we eat our sandwiches and drink our beer. I am dirty still wearing my biking clothes; she is clean wearing two towels.

We devour our dinner as if we are two starving lions sharing the carcass of a zebra. Between bites, we talk about the day, but I can tell something is weighing on my daughter's mind. When we are almost done, she sits back and says casually, "You never finished telling me about Kimberly."

"Kimberly?"

"Your sister. She would have been my aunt."

My daughter is nothing if not persistent — a trait she no doubt inherited from me. She wants to know about another memory from my past: faded but still vividly painful. I am not anxious to delve into this area. "What do you want to know about her?" I ask just before I stuff my final bite of sandwich into my mouth.

"I don't know. Tell me what she was like."

"She was five years younger than me. She was my bratty little sister that was always hanging around when my friends came over."

"You told me all that before."

I shrug. "So what else do you want to know?" I ask.

My daughter sighs and ponders my question for a second before asking, "What was her favorite color?"

"I dunno know. She liked to wear turquoise bracelets and necklaces. We went on a family vacation to New Mexico once, and I think she bought every piece of turquoise jewelry in the state."

"Did she have a boyfriend?"

"Better not have. She was only twelve when the — " I stop in mid sentence, not sure of the words to use. I did not want to talk about a tragedy that had happened forty years ago. A tragedy that had taken me years to come to terms with. I had only come to terms by no longer having to talk about it. But if Stephanie and I were going to discuss her mother, I would have to talk about my sister.

Stephanie is watching me closely, and I stare back at her.

"Accident happened," I finally finish my sentence. I choose these words because I think they are safe — at least a safe place to start.

My daughter's eyes shift away from me for a moment and then return. "Can you talk about the accident?" she asks. Steph was direct and to the point. Just like her mother.

"Sure, I can talk about it," I lie. I try to sound nonchalant, but I feel my pulse quicken.

Stephanie waits for me to continue, but I am not eager to begin. After a sufficient period of silence passes, I ask, "What do you want to know?"

"Everything — or at least what you're comfortable telling me."

I drain the remnants of my beer, and open a fresh one to help me tell this story as quickly as possible. Although I am not comfortable sharing the details of that day with anyone, I feel a need to share it with my daughter. Perhaps she will trust me again if I tell her the whole story; perhaps, she will not.

"That day it was raining," I begin. "Hard. My mother — your grandmother — asked me to take Kimberly to her dance lesson. I didn't want to do it. It just wasn't cool to chauffeur your little sister around. However, my mother was insistent and informed me that if I wanted use of the car that weekend — I had a big date on Saturday night — I had better get my butt behind the wheel and take my sister to and from her dance lesson. Although I was not happy about the task, the thought occurred to me that I could just drop my little sister off at the front entrance to her dance studio and then I would have free use of the car for an hour until I had to pick her up."

I pause for some liquid fortification, and Steph does the same.

"What I did not realize," I continue, "was how hard it was raining. It just wouldn't stop. The rain sounded like someone was beating on the roof of the car with drumsticks. Water was flowing in the street about a foot deep. We were barely out of our driveway when I turned to Kimberly and asked her if she really wanted to go to her dance lesson. She started chattering on about how she had a recital coming up and how her teacher expected everyone to attend class and how important it was to rehearse. The only thing I heard was the dreaded word 'recital'. I had already been forced to attend several, and here another one was coming up. They were long, god awfully boring fiascos that lasted forever. I knew my parents would play the 'your sister sat through your baseball games so you can watch one little dance recital' card. Plus, you need to support your younger sister. She looks up to you. Plus, a little artistic culture will do you good. For the life of me, I never saw anything artistic or cultured about my sister's dance recitals. Mothers would dress up little girls in frilly costumes, plaster them with makeup until they were nearly unrecognizable, and then parade them across a stage to make other mothers envious."

"Wow, I never knew how strongly you felt about recitals," Stephanie comments. "I guess that explains why I never took dance lessons."

"You did for a year, until I convinced your mother it wasn't a good idea."

Stephanie nods, but she steers the conversation back to what she is interested in. "So, you're driving. It's raining. There's water on the road."

My daughter will not let me digress about dance recitals.

"I drive very slow. Windows are fogging up. It's raining really hard. I can barely tell where the edges of the road are. There's a few other cars out, and they are all making wakes the same way speedboats make wakes on rivers."

I pause in my narrative to take another sip; Steph patiently waits for me to continue.

"I am almost to her dance studio when we get to a low water crossing."

"What's a low water crossing?"

"The road dips down to allow water to come over it."

"Why not have a bridge so that the road goes over the water?"

"Good question. Bridges cost a lot more to build than just lowering the road."

"Shouldn't the water flow underneath the road. Doesn't it cause a problem when it flows over the top."

"Only when it rains."

"And it was raining that day."

"Was it ever, and flood water was pouring over the road."

I take yet another drink. My daughter has set her beer down.

"So what did you do?" Steph asks.

"I drove into it. What else could I do? It was the only way to get to the studio."

I pause again as I am approaching the painful part of my narrative.

"What did you do when you got to the other side?" Steph asks.

I sigh. "We never made it to the other side. A huge pickup truck came roaring in the opposite direction when we were in the middle of the crossing. It had a jacked up suspension and oversized tires. We were in a Chevrolet Impala. Not a small car, but it sat a lot lower than that monster. Water from the truck's wake rolled over the hood. Kimberly screamed. I probably shouldn't have, but I instinctively braked. The car stalled out. We were stuck in the middle of the crossing with the water rushing all around us."

While I talk, I focus on a small knot in the wood of the bunk bed just above Stephanie's head. As close as we are sitting, I am doing my best to avoid eye contact.

"Did you call someone to come get you?" Steph asks.

"Call? There was no telephone booth in the car. This was long before cell phones."

"Did you try to get out of the car?"

"If we had tried to open one of the doors, the water would have come rushing in. We were trapped. All I could think to do was to try to restart the car, but it wouldn't. Kimberly started crying hysterically — saying she didn't want to go to her dance lesson anymore — that all she wanted was to go home."

"What did you do?" Steph asks.

My eyes travel from the knot in the bed above Stephanie's head to the smooth concrete floor, quickly glancing at my daughter in transit.

"Like a stupid big brother," I say sheepishly, "I yelled at her to shut up."

"Oh, no, Daddy!" Steph exclaims.

"Afraid so," I admit. "But it worked. For a little while anyway. Then pieces of wood and other debris started knocking against the side of the car. Every time something hit the car, it would set her off again. Then the force of the water started pushing the car sideways off the road."

"Oh, no."

"Oh, yes. The rain had slackened, but the water kept rising. I was afraid the Impala was going to flip over or that the water would drown the car. We couldn't open the doors, but I got my window open. I told Kimberly to follow me as I climbed out to get on the roof of the car. After I was on top of the car, I looked back in. Kimberly hadn't moved. In fact, she had fastened her seatbelt and was clutching her dance bag on her lap. No matter what I said, she refused to budge. And she was sobbing uncontrollably."

I feel Steph place her hands on mine and hear her say, "I am so sorry, Daddy."

With a deep breath, I forge ahead. "Two men came toward us in a rowboat. They drew alongside. Rain was still coming down, but I told them my sister was still inside the car. One of them stuck his head in the window and tried to coax Kimberly out. He tried to reach through the window to unbuckle her seatbelt, but he couldn't reach it. While he was trying to calm her down, a wall of water hit us. I don't know where it came from, but it knocked the rowboat against the side of the Impala. Both the boat and the car rolled over. Both men and I were dumped into the water, "

I stop at this point, wondering if I should go on — if I need to talk about the frantic struggles of myself and the two men to get our heads above the swirling water or the frenzied efforts of the two men to try to get to my trapped sister or the last time I saw my sister's face pressed against the glass of the car window.

I decide to omit those details and simply summarize the outcome. "Kimberly never made it out of the car. The two men got me to a nearby house where they dried me off. Calls were made to the police and to my parents."

My mind drifts back to when I sat for hours wrapped in towels in a strange house. Memories flood my brain of people I did not know asking me questions that I could not answer — of my father picking me up and not asking me any questions — of my mother locking herself in her bedroom and not coming out for months, not even for the funeral.

I feel Stephanie gently squeeze my hands.

"Thanks for sharing with me, Daddy. I know it must have taken a lot for you to tell me about — " Steph pauses as she searches for the right words to use.

I let her off the hook. "You wanted to know, and I didn't see why you shouldn't know."

"I'm sorry I brought it up. Still seems painful after all these years. I wouldn't have asked if I had known."

"Don't be sorry," I say. Steph hugs me, and I hug her back.

I stand and excuse myself to get ready for bed. In the shower, I scrub myself extra vigorously not just to remove the grime of the day, but also the memories of that day when my sister and I were caught in a stalled car in the middle of a rainstorm.

In telling my daughter about the accident that claimed my sister's life, I admit to myself that I omitted a few details — details I am truly ashamed of — details that only I and Kimberly know. I do not know how long we sat together in that flooded car. It was probably only minutes, but it seemed like hours. I had screamed at my sister in the beginning. I had screamed at her for wanting to go to a dance lesson. I had screamed at her for wanting to go out in the rain. I had screamed at her for being my sister.

I can make excuses for my behavior — that I was scared myself, that I was immature, that I was afraid of getting in trouble for messing up my mother's car.

But there really is no excuse for how I reacted that day.

I begged and pleaded with my sister to climb out the window while I lay on the roof. The rain pelted down on me while she sat looking anxiously around. Kimberly would not unbuckle her seat belt and leave the car because she was more scared of me and my anger than the flood waters swirling around her. My anger trapped my sister in that car more than the water.

Did I lie to my daughter by not telling her everything that happened? Can I lie merely by omission? Do I have an obligation to divulge all my secrets?

When I come out of the shower, the lights are out, and Stephanie is snoring softly. I feel my way through the darkness to my bed. Although I have never slept on an air mattress laid out on a sheet of plywood, I am so physically exhausted from the day's biking and emotionally drained from talking about my sister that I fall asleep quickly.

Paw Paw
Fourth Day of Biking
156 miles to go

I wake up hungry and looking forward to a good breakfast. Hoop has promised us eggs, bacon, and pancakes —

all made fresh by his wife who he asserts is an excellent cook. I dress and step outside. A light drizzle greets me. Looking around, I see no lights on in the main house. Further, I do not detect the cooking sounds of pots and pans being jostled or the cooking smell of frying bacon. My stomach growls in disappointment.

As usual, Steph is way ahead of me. She has already walked over — probably in search of coffee — and is now walking toward me.

"Hoop says his wife is not feeling well this morning. Says he's going to run over to the convenience store and get us some muffins and juice."

"Probably something wrapped in plastic and a week after the expiration date," I comment ruefully. "Not exactly the meal I was anticipating."

"It gets worse. His coffee maker is broken."

"That is a real crisis."

Steph ignores my sarcasm as she checks her panniers. "I'm going to run over to the Dollar General and see what I can find."

"I didn't know Dollar General had a vegan section."

My crack earns me an early morning scowl.

"You're welcome to wait for the stale muffin. But we have to cover sixty miles today, and it looks like we're going to get more rain. I don't want to sit around. Hoop moves even slower than you do."

"Thanks."

"You're welcome." Steph is off. She is grouchy when she is hungry and without coffee.

I stuff gear into my panniers. The drizzle lifts, and the sun comes out. Hoop appears with the sunshine. He shuffles over to me.

"You sleep alright?" he asks sheepishly.

"Great," I say. "Ready for another long day in the saddle."

"Sorry about the breakfast. Wife just wasn't up to getting out of bed this morning."

I just nod.

"I'm going to fetch you and your daughter a little something to eat."

Without looking up, I say, "Don't worry about that, Hoop. My daughter has already taken off, and I need to catch up with her."

"But you paid for a breakfast."

I look up at Hoop; he meets my gaze. He is a young, small town guy trying to make an honest living; I am an old codger living off a 401k.

Smiling, I extend my hand to shake his. "We enjoyed our stay, but I have to go. I'll get that breakfast next time I pass through. In the meantime, I'm going to tell my biking friends what a great place this is to stay."

Hoop brightens. "Why, thanks."

"Now hold this bike while I try to get on it."

"Sure."

With a final nod to Hoop, I exit his parking lot. My knees are creaking this morning as I head out. I go slow for them to warm up in the cool morning air.

Finding a quiet spot not far from Hoop but still away from Stephanie, I glide to a stop, pull out my cell phone, and check my reception. Not a full slate of bars but hopefully enough for my purpose. I dig deep through my contacts to find the number I need. The phone is answered on the first ring.

"Senator Mallory's office. Clifford speaking."

I take a deep breath before I launch my gambit. It will be a miracle if it works.

"I cannot believe that you still work for that old cuss," I growl into my phone.

"Pardon me, sir." The voice on the other end of the line is polite, but defensive. I recognize it, but the speaker does not recognize me. Yet.

"I thought you'd have found a more respectable line of work by now. Something like loan sharking — or maybe kidnapping newborns from their mothers."

The person on the other end pauses. I fear that he will hang up on me, but a memory synapse fires somewhere deep in his neocortex.

"Reynolds? Is that you?"

"Who else would be calling you this early in the morning acting like a jerk."

204

"About half of Senator Mallory's constituency."

"Can I quote you on that?"

"Of course not. Tom, how are you?"

My muscles remind me of how many miles I have biked and how many more I will have to pedal.

"Couldn't be better," I lie. "And you?"

"Busy as a beaver."

His reply gives me the opening I need. I don't have much time to get my request in.

"Yeah, you must be busy. I hear you have some big hearings coming up next week."

"That's right. Dealing with security issues about our embassies. The Senator is passionate about the safety of our diplomats."

"I'm sure he is. Are you in charge of the witness list?"

The voice became guarded. "I have some input. Do you know someone who would like to testify?"

"Just the opposite. I know someone who is not interested in testifying."

"Oh — uh — hang on."

I hear the rustling of papers and the clicking of a computer keyboard.

"Are you pulling up your witness list?" I ask.

"Yeah, I got it here."

"See the name 'Stephanie Reynolds'?"

"Yeah."

"See the key on the upper right of your keyboard?"

"Which one?"

"The one that says 'Delete' on it?"

"Yeah."

"Hit that a bunch of times."

"Hang on there, Tom. I can't just remove the name of our star witness."

"Sure you can. I just told you how."

"It's not that simple. The Senator has made these hearings into a big deal."

"I'm sure he has, but he's going to have to find someone else's career to ruin."

"Wait — Reynolds — same last name. Did you remarry?"

"Nope."

"Relative?"

"Daughter."

"Oh." Over the phone, I hear a chair creak as the Senator's aide leans back in it. "I am really sorry. Your daughter has gotten herself into a shitstorm of trouble."

"I don't like hearing the term 'shitstorm' used in the same sentence with my daughter. The way I hear it, she was just doing her job. The Senator — or someone else — needs a scapegoat. I suggest you find someone else."

A hear a low whistle over the phone. "I understand where you're coming from, Tom. I really do. But like I said, the Senator is really passionate about the security of our diplomats."

"The same way he was passionate about coaching those young men on that high school wrestling team?"

I hear a sharp thud over the phone as the aide's chair bangs forward into his desk.

"You agreed that we were never to discuss that issue again," the Senator's aide hisses.

"I did. And I don't plan on discussing it further as long as you start hitting that "Delete' key."

"You're asking a lot. Your daughter was in charge of security. An American ambassador was killed."

"Yes, a good man died doing his duty because he didn't have sufficient security. Tell me, did the good Senator approve the funding the State Department requested for security for its embassies?"

"The Senator has a fiscal responsibility to the taxpayers of this country."

"Yes, he does, so I'm sure he won't mind explaining where those funds came from that went to — let's see, I think there were several names on that wrestling team that I can recall — if you give me a minute." I pause before adding, "Do you want me to recall those names?"

"That won't be necessary," the aide mumbles into the phone.

"So you're going to start hitting that 'Delete' key?"

"It's not quite that simple. I have to talk to the Senator and make some phone calls."

"Alright," I say slowly. "When can I expect confirmation of our arrangement?"

"I'll start on it as soon as we get off the phone."

"Then I won't keep you. You still drinking that French Chardonnay you like so much?"

"Every chance I get."

"I'll send you a case. Consider it a peace offering."

"You might need to send me two cases to deal with the headache you've just given me."

"That's what old friends are for," I say as I hang up.

Spotting the Dollar General sign, I cross the street and start heading toward it. At the edge of the parking lot to the Dollar General, Steph has stopped to talk to two men standing next to an old truck.

I pull up to see a jumbled display of fresh fruits and vegetables that have been arrayed on the tailgate.

Steph does the introduction thing. "This is my Daddy that I was telling you about. Daddy, this is Jerry and Dave. They're local farmers who are selling their produce."

The one that Steph indicates is Farmer Jerry says to me, "You really biked all the way from Pittsburgh?"

"Yes, and I have the saddle sores to prove it," I reply.

"Here, you deserve a taste of this then." Farmer Jerry cuts off a slice from a loaf of bread and hands it to me. I usually don't take food from the hands of strangers, but I am desperately hungry and we are still in West Virginia. No need to upset the locals.

"Wow," I say after I take a bite. "That's pretty good. What is it?"

"It's my wife's apple cinnamon bread."

Steph swipes the rest of the sample from me and eats it.

"Hey," I object. "That's not on a vegan diet."

"Sure it is," she mumbled with a full mouth. "Can we get a whole loaf of that?"

"Sure 'nuf." Farmer Jerry replies with a proud smile.

"What the hell is that?" I say, pointing at what looks to me like a deformed yellowish-green potato. I feel one of

Steph's sharp elbows dig into my ribs, trying to remind me of my manners.

Farmer Jerry only laughs. "That there is known as the 'poor man's banana' — what this town is named after — the paw paw." He pulls out a knife and slices the paw paw open lengthwise. Inside is a row of six shiny brown seeds surrounded by a dark yellow filling.

"Is that edible?" I ask as I move far enough away from Steph to avoid another elbow.

"Sure. Nothing like a fresh paw paw in the morning." He expertly uses the tip of his knife to flick out the six seeds. Then he carves out two slices, offering one to Steph and one to me.

"Hmm," I remark. "Tastes like a banana custard." I turn to Steph. "What do you think?"

"I like it."

Savoring the tropical flavor of the paw paw, I gesture at the half dozen buildings around us. "So this great big metropolis was named after this little bitty fruit?"

"Yes, sir."

"I don't think I've ever heard of a town named after a fruit."

"That's because the paw paw is special. In fact, there's quite a few towns named after it besides this 'un. Hey, Dave, what states are those towns in."

Farmer Dave pulls on his short beard as he speaks. "Well, let's see, I knows they's one over in Michigan. Maybe Kentuck."

"What about that feller from — where was that?"

"Oh, yeah, the Okie. He said there was a Paw Paw in Oklahoma."

"That's right."

"Them town's all over. None very big so you got's to keep yo eyes peeled for 'em."

I swallow my mouthful full of paw paw and say, "So besides tasting pretty good — I have to admit — what's so special about the paw paw?"

"It's chock full of protein," Farmer Jerry says.

"And vitamins A and C," Farmer Dave adds.

"As well as antioxidants," Steph contributes this last little bit of information as she studies the screen on her phone. She has found a webpage on the internet dedicated to the fruit "Says here," she continues, "That it grows in 26 states from the Gulf Coast to the Great Lakes. It's also the favorite host plant to the zebra swallowtail butterfly."

"Really?" I remark in mock disbelief.

"Yeah, it's larvae like to feed on the leaves. Native Americans and early European settlers ate paw paws. At least two U.S. presidents liked paw paws: George Washington enjoyed them for dessert and Thomas Jefferson grew them at Monticello."

"Fascinating," I say. "And I had never heard of them before this morning. Shall we get a bag of paw paws for breakfast?" I ask my daughter.

"Sounds good to me. And how about some of those strawberries?" Steph points. I agree, and we add a carton of raspberries and a large cantaloupe to our shopping order.

Farmer Jerry collects our items and stuffs them into a couple of plastic bags. "How about a loaf of paw paw nut bread to go with the apple cinnamon bread? Dave's wife made it."

"It's pretty good," Farmer Dave comments as he chews. Apparently, he is eating a slice himself. "And neither of us can go home until we sell all the bread our wives' done made."

"Or we eat it ourselves," Farmer Jerry laughs.

"Why not?" I say grinning. "Don't want you guys to stay out here all day. So what does all this come to?"

Farmer Jerry proceeds to make his calculations by literally counting on his fingers. Steph and I exchange a glance.

"That comes to seven fifty."

I stare blankly at Farmer Jerry. Just one of the loaves of bread would surely cost seven dollars and fifty cents in a store. We just bought two plastic bags filled with fresh produce plus the two loaves of bread. Rifling past the fives and tens in my wallet, I pull out a twenty and say, "All I've got is this picture of Andrew Jackson. Don't worry about the change."

"Oh, no, we got change," Farmer Dave assures me. He and Farmer Jerry start pulling dollar bills out of their pockets.

Looking at Steph, I flick my head in the direction of the Passage. She nods in understanding. We each grab a bag, mount our bikes, and race off.

Farmer Jerry and Farmer Dave call out for us to come back for our change.

"Do you hear anything?" I ask Steph.

She tries to hide the smile on her face. "Nope," she says.

We cross from West Virginia back over into Maryland. Truck and car traffic is light. After pumping hard on the overpass, I enjoy a long glide back to the Passage. Making a sharp right turn, I bask in the streams of early morning light filtering through the canvas of leaves overhead. Cool, crisp air fills my lungs. Today's ride is starting pleasantly, but I am only able to enjoy it for a mile or so. I can see where the water of the canal disappears into a dark, foreboding hole in the cliff ahead. Our bike journey descends directly into that abyss.

"The Paw Paw Tunnel!" Steph shouts behind me. I pause at a safe distance from the opening, not ready to take on such a challenge this early in the day. Holding her cell phone in one hand and steering her bike in the other, she gleefully films a video as she passes me. This tunnel is one of the top highlights of the C & O for her.

I pretend interest in the signs posted along the trail describing the tunnel, postponing the inevitable. To continue on the trail, I knew I had to go through the tunnel, but I prefer to linger hundreds of yards from the entrance rather than approach.

I already knew what the signs are telling me. The Paw Paw Tunnel was the largest structure on the C & O Canal and was an engineering marvel for its day. At only 3118 feet, it was never one of the longest tunnels in the world, but it possesses a colorful history.

When construction of the C & O reached this part of the Potomac River in 1836, the engineers were faced with a major topographical problem. High cliffs on the Maryland side meant that they would have to hack the towpath out of the rock face. Known as the Paw Paw Bends for the abundance of pawpaw trees that grew in the area, the Potomac folded upon itself in five horseshoe-shaped turns over a six mile stretch.

The board of directors were aghast at the anticipated cost and time required by this part of the project.

A new engineer, Charles B. Fisk, suggested a different solution. He proposed digging a tunnel that would cut directly across the bends in the river and shorten the towpath by several miles. Hoping to save money, the board approved the tunnel proposal, based on Fisk's promise that it would be completed in two years (by July 1838) at a cost of $33,500. In fact, the tunnel was not completed until 1850 and nearly bankrupted the canal operation with its final cost of $616,478.65. I am pretty sure Fisk was fired at some point during the fourteen years of construction.

A Methodist minister turned contractor, Lee Montgomery, was hired to build the canal tunnel. He had previously built the Union Canal Tunnel in Pennsylvania. Starting work in June 1836, Montgomery confidently predicted that he could bore seven to eight feet a day. Crews worked from either end, blasting away rock with black powder and hauling the rubble away with horse carts. Montgomery immediately ran into labor problems. The Irish workers who had been digging out the canal up to that point were not skilled tunnel builders. Despite working crews in three shifts daily, Montgomery could only manage to bore ten to twelve feet a week.

When Montgomery brought in other workers (English masons, English and Welsh miners, and "Dutch" or German laborers) to complete the tunnel, the Irish — as they often did when they felt slighted — took exception and started rioting. They continued rioting off and on for the next three years, burning the living quarters of other workers and destroying a tavern in Oldtown. Financial problems of the Chesapeake and Ohio Canal Company stopped construction from 1842 to 1847. In November 1848, another company, McCulloch and Day, was brought in to complete the tunnel which it did in October 1850.

The problems of the Paw Paw Tunnel convinced the board that tunneling north through the Allegheny mountains would be impossible. Consequently, the C&O terminated at

Cumberland, rather than continue on to Pittsburgh — conceding defeat to the Baltimore and Ohio Railroad.

Completion of the Paw Paw Tunnel did not end strife at the site. Its narrow channel did not allow for passing or turning. Only one boat could operate in the tunnel at a time, with the first to arrive at either end having the right of way. Captains — being captains — would sometimes argue over who arrived first and refuse to yield, leaving two boats in the middle of the tunnel blocking each other — and all commerce moving on the canal. Although a loaded boat headed downstream was supposed to have the right of way, more than one fist fight broke out. One dispute lasted several days until a canal supervisor tossed green cornstalks into a roaring fire at the upwind entrance and forced the downwind boat to retreat.

Maintenance costs, floods, and rockslides plagued the Paw Paw Tunnel almost as soon as it opened. Bricks often fell from the ceiling without warning. A major flood on the Potomac in 1852 — two years after the tunnel opened — severely damaged the canal. Rock slides in 1858 and 1889 interrupted navigation for months.

As canal traffic grew in the early 1870s, disputes and delays increased proportionately. The Paw Paw Tunnel gained a reputation as a major bottleneck on the C & O Canal. Still, millions of tons of lumber, stone, coal, agricultural products, and industrial goods passed through the tunnel until the C & O was closed in 1924.

Steph calls out and waves for me to join her at the mouth of the tunnel. Knowing the star-crossed history of this engineering marvel, I approach it with trepidation. I slowly roll in her direction, eyeing the arched entrance. Three huge mud holes have to be navigated to get to the tunnel opening. Weathered stone steps climb either side. More large mud holes fill the pathway leading inside.

"You know," I suggest timidly, "There is a trail that goes around this tunnel. It's only about two miles long." I point at a trail marker on my right. It is helpfully labeled "Tunnel Hill Trail".

A puzzled look spreads across Steph's face. "Why we would take that?"

I stare past her at the yawning tunnel opening that is about to swallow us. "I don't know. It's such a nice day out."

Her eyes narrow. "Is there a problem?"

"No, no. It's just — " I pause, not wanting to explain the reasons for my hesitation.

"What?" my daughter demands.

"It's just so — so sinister looking."

Steph turns her head to look at the tunnel entrance and then back at me. "Coward," she teases me as she bounces off her bike and walks it forward. "Take my picture."

I have to take quite a few pictures because Steph poses at the entrance with her bike and without it. Then she climbs up on the steps that run up the side of the tunnel opening so that I can snap a few more. While she is coming down, I approach the tunnel entrance on foot. The towpath narrows to just a few feet across, barely wide enough for two bikes to pass. I peer into the darkness, but I cannot see the end of the tunnel, much less oncoming bikers or hikers. On the left side, a wooden railing separates the towpath from the canal. The black water in the canal swirls ominously below, hiding whatever creatures are about to leap out and eat us for breakfast. On the right side, the brick-lined tunnel curves immediately over our heads.

Stephanie wheels up next to me. "Ready?" She does not try to hide her exuberance.

I point up to the bricks over our heads and ask, "I wonder which one of those is going to fall and bean me on my head?"

She shrugs, "That's why we're wearing helmets."

"Good point," I admit.

Stephanie leans over her handlebars and gazes up at the ceiling and curved wall. "Whoa, that's a lot of bricks. Wonder how many?"

"5.8 million."

She gives me a look of disbelief.

"You know I read a lot," I remind her.

'Yes, I do. Too much, in fact. But I think you are making up the 'point eight' part."

"We can count them, if you like," I offer.

"No, thanks." She inches forward still straddling her bike. "It's really dark in there. I think I see the end, but I'm glad we brought our flashlights."

I feel my face break into a smile. Stephanie is a little kid again about to ride her first roller coaster. "Do you remember?" I ask.

"Are we going to play that game again?"

"Why not?" I want us to remember the good times as well as the other times. "Do you remember the time we rode The Big Bad Red Wolf together?"

"The hanging roller coaster at Busch Gardens?"

"Yes."

"That is something no terrified nine-year-old would ever forget."

"You did not want to ride it, but I coaxed you into doing it. Screamed your bloody head off during the whole ride."

"I do remember that. Distinctly."

"And do you remember what you said to me after that first ride?"

"I asked you if we could do it again."

"Right. We rode that ride eight more times, and you screamed your head off every time. I was deaf for a week."

"I think you're still deaf."

"Thanks."

"But what does that have to do with us going through this tunnel?"

"Nothing," I answer aloud; everything, I think to myself.

Stephanie flips on her handlebar mounted flashlight. The beam of light is quickly swallowed by the darkness. "Okay, I'll lead." Her bike is moving before I can stop her. She makes it about ten feet into the Paw Paw Tunnel before her bike bounces into the brick wall on the right and then violently jerks sideways toward the wooden railing.

"Steph! Are you okay?" I try to jog my bike forward, but it bucks up and down off the uneven floor of the towpath inside the tunnel. My light reveals layer upon layer of ruts.

"I'm fine, but I thought for sure I was going to end up in the Canal."

I glance over the railing at the stagnant, soupy water below. "Glad you didn't. I don't think there's enough antibiotics at John Hopkins to kill the germs down there."

After helping her up, I suggest I take the lead. She agrees.

The exit to the tunnel is a tiny pinprick of light in the distance. We move slowly along, walking our bikes and trying not to stumble on the uneven path. Gradually, the tiny pin prick grows larger. The beams of our headlights illuminate only narrow portions of the path underneath our feet. And the curving brick wall leans against our right shoulder. About halfway, Steph asks to stop. We stand in the middle of the Tunnel, listening to drops of water land in the Canal.

Steph points up. "It looks like someone drilled holes in the ceiling."

"Those openings would be weep holes. Allows for water to drain. Otherwise, the water pressure would build up and cause the tunnel to collapse." I place my left hand on the railing next to us. "This railing has grooves worn into it. Must have been rope burns from the towlines being dragged across it."

"What are those brass plates for?"

"They put them in every hundred feet to mark the vertical shafts they dug — probably for light and air as they worked."

"Oh." Steph gazes at one end of the tunnel and then the other. No other bikers or hikers are in sight.

""Let's turn off our flashlights!" she suggests.

"Why we want to do that?" I ask.

"To see what it's like in here without any light."

We turn off our lights, and the darkness immediately closes in on us. I imagine hearing the steady trod of mule hooves as the animals pulled the boats through the tunnel and the slap of water against the sides of the canal from the wake of the boats. No wonder the boatmen would sing as they passed through to keep their spirits up. There is very little sound for us to hear except for our own breathing and an occasional, ominous drip of water.

"Okay. Enough of that," Steph says after less than a minute. She flicks her flashlight back on, and we continue toward the sunlight streaming in from the far end. We exit the

Paw Paw Tunnel onto a boardwalk that takes us past a sheer rock wall. Our tires rattle on the wood.

With each pedal stroke away from the tunnel, the towpath grows more treacherous. The bike path on the other side of the Paw Paw Tunnel had been wide and groomed. On this side, the trail narrows leaving less room to maneuver. No matter where I steer a bump or a rut is lying in wait for me. To my left, a steep embankment leads into the algae infested remains of the C & O Canal. On my right are trees. I alternate from one side to the other dodging the encroaching foliage and the mud holes After three days of biking, my butt feels like it is breaking with each bump I hit. A gentle rain starts, making the path slippery. Several times I find myself sliding part way down the embankment. Fortunately, I am able to right myself before catastrophe strikes.

Still I keep going, following behind Stephanie: what choice do I have?

A few miles down the path the rain lets up, and rays of sunshine poke through the clouds. I increase my speed, but another biker easily glides past me from behind. He is riding a road bike on a trail seemingly designed for four-wheel-drive dune buggies. Its narrow tires easily navigate between the potholes. His skinny legs propel him effortlessly past me until he is abreast of Steph. He slows slightly, and I see his helmeted head turn toward Steph. I hear her laugh.

Although I cannot hear what they are saying, they engage in an animated conversation. As they talk, their pace picks up. I would be left in their dust, except there is only mud for me to eat. All I can do is stare at the backside of his black and white cycling outfit. He carries no gear so he must be out for a day ride. While I have to keep my eyes glued to the trail to avoid the obstacles, he seems to have a built in radar for them. His head is turned toward Steph as much as it is pointed straight ahead.

We cycle in this arrangement for miles with the gap between myself and Steph and this new Bike God growing ever larger. My male ego will not allow me to call out and admit my inability to keep up. The only thing I can do is try to keep them in sight.

When I am not able to do that, I decide to enjoy the scenery and the beautiful day. The temperature is in the low eighties, and the sun is shining. I am surrounded by green forest. All I have to push out of my mind is that my daughter is off riding with another man. I am confident that I will eventually catch up with her — somewhere between here and D.C.

My confidence is rewarded a few miles later when I spot Steph patiently waiting for me on the side of the towpath.

"Where's your boyfriend?" I ask.

She looks at me quizzically. "In D.C.," she replies slowly.

I shake my head. "I was talking about today's boyfriend."

"Who? Lanny? We were just talking. In fact, he told me of a great place for us to have lunch. He called it the most unique restaurant experience in Maryland."

I look around skeptically at the forest that surrounds us. "Squirrel, there's not much civilization between Paw Paw and Hancock. A restaurant out here in the middle of nowhere? I think that guy was pulling your leg."

"He said he'd wait for us at the place. It's up ahead on the left. We go under an overpass, and it will be on our right. Can't miss it."

"Does this restaurant have a name?"

"Bill's Place."

"Do we get to meet Bill?"

"Maybe. All I know is that Lanny recommended the cheeseburgers."

The mention of one of my favorite foods after a long morning of bouncing up and down on a hard bike saddle makes me involuntarily salivate like one of Pavlov's dogs. Although I fear a major disappointment, I gamely push off. I seriously doubt we will find any sort of decent eating establishment in this wilderness.

We reach a turnoff for Little Orleans and go under the overpass. There on the right is a long rambling wooden structure. A wooden sign swinging from a stanchion proudly proclaims that we have found "Bill's Place". The sign mentions beer, boats, and bait. Burgers have been omitted. I am so hungry I am willing to eat bait in a boat as long as I have lots of beer to wash it down with.

Steph and I park our bikes along a low stone wall and climb a set of stairs to the front door. We enter a cavernous room. A long L-shaped bar dominates the left side. Worn chairs and tables provide seating for half the population of Maryland. Memorabilia and stuffed animal heads decorate the walls.

I nudge my daughter and point up. The entire ceiling is covered with one dollar bills. Each one has been autographed and appear to be glued in precise rows and columns.

"That's a lot of Washingtons," I remark.

Steph tries to direct my attention to various spots on the walls. I cannot discern what she wants me to see.

"What?" I ask.

She leans in close to my right ear. "The Confederate battle flags."

Indeed, there are quite a few interspersed between the plaques and pictures.

"Was not expecting that north of the Potomac," Steph whispers.

"Well," I reply, "We are south of the Mason Dixon line."

We see Lanny sitting at the bar. He spots us and waves us over.

He has taken off his helmet, revealing a mass of thinning gray hair. Now that I can clearly see his face, I am guessing that we are close to the same age. However, Lanny is in much better shape than I am. He is as skinny as a rail and propels his bike much faster than I do mine.

I had resented Lanny before; now, I downright dislike him. I had assumed from his build and the pace he generated on his bike that he was at least half my age.

Steph introduces us. We shake hands. I pretend to be friendly.

"My daughter says you recommend the cheeseburgers here."

Lanny grins. "I do — just had one." He points to his empty plate. "Also recommend the sweet potato fries."

"I prefer onion rings," I say, more out of orneriness than anything else.

My rudeness does not faze Lanny; he remains friendly and good natured. "They have those as well," he replies with a smile.

I look at the menu display over the bar. Nothing high tech: a white felt board with black plastic letters. It is a relic that I have not seen in decades. The prices come from the same era.

"A cheeseburger is really three dollars?" I say dumbfounded.

"Yeah," Lanny comments. "Hard to believe, isn't it?"

"Must be the size of a walnut."

Lanny laughs. "I needed both my hands to hold mine." He motions to the man sitting on a stool behind the bar. "Jack, come over here. My friends here are hungry."

Jack rises slowly — very slowly — from his perch; he is in no hurry to serve a customer. "Yeah, who isn't around here," he says. "What'll ya have?"

I order a cheeseburger and onion rings; Steph asks for an extra large platter of sweet potato fries.

As Jack saunters slowly away from us, I turn to Lanny. "Is there a Bill?"

I can tell from the puzzled look on Lanny's face that he does not catch my drift.

"It's called 'Bill's Place'," I explain.

"Oh." Lanny's countenance brightens with understanding. "There was. He passed a few years back." Lanny nods at our surly waiter. "Jack is his son. Took over after his old man died."

"I see he continues the tradition of fast, cheerful service," I remark sarcastically.

Lanny laughs. "Hey, Jack is ten times faster and friendlier than his father ever was."

"You knew Bill?" Stephanie asks.

"I did. I've been coming here every summer for the past ten years — since I retired."

Thinking that Lanny and I are about the same age, I ask, "You retire early?"

"No. I had to stick it out to sixty-five to get my full pension benefits. Nearly killed me, but somehow I survived."

I do the math. Ten plus sixty-five makes Lanny at least seventy-five. He's fifteen years older than I am, and he left me eating the mud kicked up from his tires back on the towpath. My dislike for Lanny turns to complete and utter enmity.

Lanny stands. "Sorry to leave you guys, but I need to head back. You enjoy your time on the C & O."

Steph and I tell him goodbye.

"Nice guy, huh," Steph comments as Lanny exits the front door.

"If he were any nicer, I'd have to punch him in his mouth," I reply.

Before my daughter can ask me what I mean, our food arrives. We are so hungry we devour our food without talking. The cheeseburger and onion rings refill my tank. Although I am ready to get back on the trail, Steph insists on autographing a dollar and posting it on the ceiling before we leave.

Back on the Towpath, I regret my eagerness to get back to the biking. Deep ruts have been excavated into the trail, and I ricochet from root to rock to root to rock. Fortunately, my bouncing only lasts for two to three miles until we reach Lock 56. I see Stephanie veer to her left off the towpath and up a steep incline. Chugging along, I follow her thinking it is much too soon for a break.

I catch up with her at an open yellow gate. Beyond the gate is a glorious stretch of smooth, black asphalt extending as far as my eyes can see. It is flat and straight. Compared to what we have been on, I think I have died and gone to bicycling heaven.

"What is this?" I ask.

"It's the Western Maryland Rail Trail," Steph replies. "Lanny suggested we take it."

"If Lanny were here, I would kiss him."

"Really?" Steph gives me a puzzled look. "I thought you hated him."

Ignoring my daughter, I ask hopefully: "Does it go all the way to D.C.?"

"Not all the way, but I think we should enjoy it as long as we can."

"I agree."

We take off. A mile clicks off. Then another. As we cruise, I glance off to my right. Down below — between the trees — I can see a pair of bikers struggling through the swamp that is the C & O in this area. I am glad that I am up here, but I pity their plight. Perhaps running into Lanny was worth the humiliation — at least, for the few miles the Western Maryland Trail runs.

My thoughts shift suddenly from what I am riding on to what I am riding under. A large raindrop smacks me in the face. I look to my left and watch dark gray clouds billow over the trees. More rain is coming.

I catch up with Steph and pull alongside her.

"We better pick up the pace," I say as I point over my shoulder.

Stephanie's eyes follow my finger. She sees the darkening sky and shrugs.

"Afraid of getting wet?"

"I'm not, but you might melt," I warn her.

She scoffs and pedals faster. I match her, but I don't know how long I can.

The rain starts coming down in sheets. I see nothing to shelter us ahead, and we have not passed anything that would protect us from the downpour. We are caught in the open with nothing else to do but keep cycling.

After stopping briefly to stow our cell phones in plastic bags and don what rain gear we have, we set out at a fast clip. We ride side by side, laughing at our predicament. In minutes we are literally soaked to the skin. The rain fails to dampen our spirits; instead, it invigorates me.

My daughter and I roar across the asphalt, knocking off the miles. The trail is narrow, and we would normally be riding single file. However, we don't see any oncoming riders so we ride side by side with the ends of our handlebars almost touching.

Although the bike path we are on is smooth, I keep an eye out for an errant rock or tree limb that we might hit. Running into anything at this speed and on this slippery surface would be disastrous.

With little room or time to maneuver, I spot the small lump directly in the way of my front tire. It rises suddenly and sharply about four inches above the surface and about six inches wide. I see no way to avoid it. Hitting it would be like striking a street curb. My front tire will hit this object, and my rear tire will rise, catapulting me into the air. My bike will stop, but I will keep going. I imagine myself flying over my handlebars and landing face first on the rain soaked, unforgiving asphalt. I am not sure I will be as lucky as I was with my first tumble over my handlebars.

Steering to my left would crash my bike into Stephanie while veering to my right might send me careening down the embankment into the trees. Hard braking would not stop me in time. With no options, I brace myself for the impact and the inevitable consequences. Instead, I flash by it. Somehow, I have miraculously avoided a disaster.

"What was that?" I shout through the rain at Stephanie, knowing she must have seen the lump.

"A turtle."

A turtle had decided to hunker down on the pavement and weather out the rainstorm directly in my path — a hazard I had not anticipated.

"I thought I was going to hit it," I say.

"I thought you were, too," she replies. "How did you miss it?"

"I don't know."

Remembering that we are riding through Maryland, I chuckle to myself. The mascot for the University of Maryland is the terrapin. I still recall attending the 2002 Final Four when Maryland crushed perennial collegiate basketball powers Kansas and Indiana to win its first and only national championship. The sea of Maryland fans wore red and black T-shirts emblazoned with the warning: "Beware the Turtle". At the time, it was humorous. After all, who would fear a team with a terrapin as its mascot? Now, I know to fear the turtle when I am in Maryland.

With no place to take shelter, we ride on for miles in the downpour. Finally, we reach an underpass and stop to wait for the storm to exhaust itself. We are soaked, but our gear has remained dry for the most part. I retrieve a couple of granola bars and hand one to Steph.

We sit next to each other on a concrete support and watch the rain come down. I can tell that Steph has something on her mind and is trying to figure out how to bring up the subject. Digging in my pocket, I extract a penny and hand it to her.

My daughter smiles. "A penny for my thoughts?"

"I'll gladly pay more," I offer. "Go ahead, Squirrel. Tell me what's bothering you."

"It's not really bothering me. I'm just curious. That's all."

"So, what are you curious about?"

Stephanie looks down at the gravel between her feet and asks, "Why didn't you ever remarry?"

It's my turn to examine the gravel between my feet. "I wanted to avoid the Hansel and Gretel issue."

"What does a fairytale about two kids lost in the woods have to do you with why you never remarried after Mom died?"

"If I remarried, then that would mean that you would have a stepmother."

"So?"

I made a circular motion with my hand trying to get her to think through the issue.

Steph only gives me a blank stare.

"I didn't want you to have to deal with a 'stepmomster'."

"A what?"

"Have you forgotten the role of the evil stepmother in the Hansel and Gretel story?"

"Not all stepmothers are evil."

"I must've only read you the politically correct version of the fairytale. Another failing of my parenting skills."

"How does the politically incorrect version go?"

"Well, in the original version told by the brothers Grimm, a woodcutter lives next to the forest with his two children. Their mother has passed away, and the woodcutter has remarried. Times are tough. The stepmother convinces him after much persuasion that they cannot afford to feed Hansel and Gretel, and therefore leads them out into the forest to get them lost."

"Stepmothers are portrayed as the bad guys in a lot of fairy tales. They're getting a bad rap."

"True," I agree, "but I did not want to put you through the process of adjusting to another woman in the house. I was fine with just you and me. In fact, I preferred it that way. It led to a much less complicated life."

"Are you saying that women make life complicated?"

"Most definitely. The more women you have in your life, the more complicated your life is."

"But a far less interesting life, I bet."

"I won't argue that point."

"Is that why you never remarried after I left for college?"

"Partly," I admit. "I like living a simple lifestyle. Also, I had gotten pretty set in my ways. I didn't want to go to the trouble of breaking in a new wife."

"I thought it was the other way around: that wives train their husbands."

"That's another way to look at it. I'd been trained one way by your mother, and I didn't want to be retrained by a different woman."

"Ignoring your blatant sexism, did you ever consider that I might have wanted another adult — especially a female adult —around to bounce ideas off while I was growing up?"

"Uh, there was your Aunt Margaret," I suggest timidly.

"Mom's sister? She's the complete opposite of my mother. I don't even see how the two of them could have ever been related."

I nod in agreement. Nancy and Margaret were like vanilla and chocolate. Both female, but vastly different in flavor. "She offered to move in after your mother died."

Steph looks at me aghast. "Why?"

"For the same reason you just mentioned: to have another adult help raise you."

"Thanks for turning her down."

Again, I nod. What I don't tell my daughter is that her aunt had suggested that I turn over custody of Steph to her — a suggestion that had led to a brutal argument over my fitness as a father. Margaret and I have barely spoken to each other since.

Hancock
124 miles to go

The rain lets up. Our clothes have gone from soaked to damp. We peer out at the sky above to see if the weather is only trying to lure us out to try to drown us. Reluctantly, we venture from our refuge. The pavement is littered with leaves and small branches from the storm, but the hard smooth asphalt underneath gives us great traction. We elect to try to get to Hancock before the next wave of rain.

Besides being one of the oldest settlements in Maryland, Hancock occupies a unique spot in the state of Maryland — it's located in the narrowest part of the state with less than two miles separating Pennsylvania from West Virginia. Started as a trading post in the early 1700s, it grew with the construction and operation of the C & O Canal. George Washington supposedly visited the area on several occasions; that guy really got around. We breeze through the small town past hanging baskets stuffed with colorful flowers, stopping only briefly at the visitor center and the charming local bike shop — C & O Bikes.

After Hancock we encounter the Tonoloway Aqueduct. Both walls of the aqueduct are gone. Instead, a narrow bridge crosses the creek. Its wooden beams groan under my weight as I cross.

Locks 51 and 52 pop up next: large stonewalls that rise out of the ground without any sign of water. After the locks, I start hearing the roar of car and truck engines at high speed. The sound of Interstate 70 traffic will be with us for the next few miles.

We reach a large body of water called Little Pool. "Little" implies that we will soon encounter an even larger body of water. Turtles crowd onto logs that line the banks. As we cycle past, a heron flies away from us skimming low over the surface of (not so) Little Pool.

Only the upstream wall of the Licking Creek Aqueduct has collapsed. Supposedly, this aqueduct consists of the largest stone arch in North America. I just hope the rest of it does not collapse while we are on it. As I do not want to land in the muddy water of Licking Creek either by wandering through the yawning gap to my left or crashing through the suspect remaining downstream wall on my right, I stay in the center as we cross.

Beyond Licking Creek Aqueduct, we indeed find the larger body of water: Big Pool. It extends for a mile and a half, paralleling the Potomac River. From the number of anglers we see, I gather that it has quite a number of great fishing spots.

We take a quick spin through Fort Frederick, a massive pre-revolutionary fort constructed from 1756 to 1757 to protect early settlements in the area during the French and Indian War. It consists of a large square with diamond-shaped bastions at each corner, a design typical of eighteenth century fortifications. The walls are made of native sandstone. I would like to tarry a bit and explore the barracks, but Steph directs my attention upward. More rain clouds are gathering above us.

The gathering storm chases us through an area known as Four Locks — where, oddly enough, there are four locks: Locks 47, 48, 49, and 50. As the Potomac makes a large loop here, the canal engineers decided to dig a shortcut across the neck of the loop rather than follow the river. My thighs are grateful for the reduced mileage.

I glance at my map. Only nine more miles to Williamsport where we plan to find a hotel for the night. The anticipation of a hot shower and a warm bed spurs me on. I start loudly singing the lines of the old Carly Simon song of the same name — at least the lines that I remember. My performance earns me a puzzled backward glance from Steph, who no doubt believes that her father has lost the last vestiges of his sanity.

Just north of Williamsport we encounter the Conococheague Aqueduct. It is one of the more decrepit ones that we have had to navigate. Completed in 1835, the upstream stone wall collapsed three times. The last time — in 1920 — a canal barge smashed into the side of the aqueduct and then plummeted through the opening into the Conococheague Creek below where it remained stuck for sixteen years until a flood washed it down the Potomac. A wooden wall was hastily reconstructed in order to get the aqueduct back in service. This fix remained in place until the canal ceased operation four years later in 1924 after back to back floods.

Today, we rumble across the crumbling stone floor of the aqueduct. Thick tufts of grass jut out from between the joints. The ground slants decidedly to the left. No barrier would prevent us from sliding into the murky brown water lying in wait for us below. A rested, cautious person would walk a bike across. Tired, I remain on my bike seat and hug the wall on our right as I continue to pedal.

Once across the aqueduct, we approach the Cushwa Basin. At one time this area bustled with boats lined up to load and unload cargoes of coal, lumber, and grain. It was one of the few places where a boat could turn around on the canal. A restored warehouse — painted bright rusty red — has been converted into a visitor's center and overlooks the basin. This afternoon, only a few geese lazily float in its waters.

Two unique bridges attract my attention, but Steph is waving vigorously for me to join her. I pedal over to where she is studying a map of Williamsport. She points at a spot near the center of downtown.

"I think this hotel is the closest to the Towpath," she offers.

I nod. "Closest sounds good to me."

On the map, the hotel does not seem far away. What the map does not tell us is that the road to the hotel goes straight up a hill. Nor does it tell us about the traffic.

While Steph powers ahead of me, I gear down to the lowest one I can find on my bike and struggle behind her. Cars roar past us, ejecting foul emissions that we have to breathe in. I am so fatigued that my front wheel wobbles as I limp onward and upward. My daughter stops at every intersection and waits for me.

When I reach her, she asks, "Are you okay?"

I respond with a grimace, "Never felt better."

She shakes her head at me and then leads us on.

We repeat this exchange five times at five intersections. At the fifth intersection, she offers words of encouragement.

"It's not much further."

"How much further?" I gasp.

"A little over a mile."

A large pickup passes us, honking its horn.

I stare up at the hill still rising before us. The thought of biking uphill for another mile overwhelms me. Then I catch Steph grinning at me.

"Relax," she laughs. "The hotel's right there."

She points to it across a wide parking lot.

I start to scold her for teasing an exhausted old man; instead, I follow her quietly to the front door. Leaning my bike to my left, I try to dismount by swinging my right leg over my panniers. It is too stiff, and I am too tired. My foot catches the top of my right pannier. My bike and I keel over in a loud clatter onto the sidewalk.

Steph pulls my bike off me and helps me stand up.

Trying to look respectable, I push through the front door. The receptionist cheerfully greets me as I enter the front door. No doubt she has just observed my gymnastics outside. She is young, smiling, and looks freshly scrubbed. Her smile fades as her eyes travel from my bike helmet to my windbreaker to my shoes.

My legs are covered in mud, and I am leaving a track of footprints.

Looking behind me, I apologize. "Sorry."

"No problem."

But I can tell there is a problem. Someone — most likely her — will have to clean up the mess I have made.

I get a room, the wifi code, and the location of a faucet where we can hose down ourselves, our bikes, and our stuff. We have established a routine: after removing our panniers, we wash our bikes, brush off the exterior of our panniers, and then Steph takes great delight in mercilessly spraying me with the hose.

After hot showers and a change of clothes, we wander over to a nearby Chinese restaurant. It is located in a small, out of the way strip mall. The table is set with inexpensive flatware and paper napkins. Plastic flowers serve as decoration. I have eaten in many similar Chinese establishments, and — despite the lack of expensive decor — I have never been disappointed in the food.

Famished, we start ordering: chicken egg rolls, wonton soup, sweet and sour pork, and broccoli beef for me; vegetarian egg rolls, dumplings, sesame noodles, and Kung Pao tofu for Steph. For something to drink, we are both feeling fruity. Stephanie orders a Redd's Black Cherry Ale; I opt for the Blueberry version.

We are the only customers in the place. The waitress — who is also most likely the proprietor — was probably expecting a slow night. Her eyes widen as she runs out of room on her order sheet.

Steph and I settle back with our drinks while we wait for our food.

I watch my daughter take a long pull on her ale. "When you were little," I remark, "your mother used to sneak into your room after you had gone to sleep and whisper what she called 'positive energy' into your ears while you slept."

"Really?" Without asking permission — but knowing she has it — Steph reaches for my ale to sample it. "I don't remember that."

"After she left us, I used to do the same for a while."

"I know."

"What?" I am surprised. "You remember me whispering in your ear but not your mother?"

After taking a healthy sample of my ale, Steph comments, "That's good, but not as good as mine." She slides her ale toward me.

While I take a quick sip of her ale, Stephanie continues.

"You weren't very good at sneaking in. Kind of like a water buffalo walking on bubble wrap. I would hear you, but pretend to be asleep. But you would tell me that you loved me

— that you would always take care of me — that everything's gonna be alright."

I feel the muscles in my throat constrict. "Yeah, I did," I admit. "I felt you needed it."

"I did, and I loved it when you said those words — because you never did when I was awake."

I shrug helplessly — another failing of my parenting.

"But then you stopped coming into my room at night."

"Yeah."

"Why?"

I shift nervously in my chair. "I didn't think it was appropriate."

"Not 'appropriate' to tell your only daughter that you loved her?"

I feel my face flush, and I wonder if the restaurant air conditioning has suddenly broken. "No. It was the part about sneaking into your room at night. You see, you were starting to — uh — develop." Avoiding my daughter's gaze, I stumble on. "The thought occurred to me that it was kind of creepy for a grown man to slink into his adolescent daughter's bedroom at night."

Steph does not reply. When I look at her, I see a broad grin stretching across her face. She is enjoying my discomfiture. As she starts to take a drink, she says, "Yeah, that does sound kind of creepy. Especially if that's the only way you can tell your daughter that you love her."

We lock eyes. I know the appropriate response is for me to say the three little words my daughter wants to her, but I cannot bring my lips to form the syllables.

Steph lets me off the hook by changing the subject.

"So, how are you holding up?

"Other than the fact that my butt is black and blue, I think I'm doing fine." I reply.

Our food arrives. It is delicious. We order refills for our ales. Back at the hotel, we sleep like two people who have biked 235 miles over four days.

Stephanie and I find a local pancake shop in the morning and gorge ourselves with carbs for the day ahead. The terrain of our mileage today is saturated with Civil War history. I know that I will have to struggle with Steph to get her to slow down so that I can absorb it all.

I finish my third waffle and gaze out the window. For once the sun is shining brightly. Steph has her nose buried in her cell phone.

"What's the weather report?" I ask.

"Scattered thundershowers."

"Perhaps we should make hay while the sun is shining," I suggest.

Steph looks up at me. "What's that supposed to mean?"

"It's an old farmer's expression."

"When were you ever a farmer?"

"That's not the point."

"What is the point?"

"That we should get a move on."

"I agree, but what has that do with hay?"

"Nothing," I admit.

Steph cocks her head and lifts her palms up in frustration with me.

I try to explain. "Farmers used to make hay by cutting it and letting it dry in the sun, that's all."

Shaking her head, my daughter rises from the table and states: "You are a walking encyclopedia of useless information. I'm going to check the bikes."

Taking a last slurp of orange juice, I follow her. We load our bikes, not speaking much. I am afraid to even mention the word history, wary that it will set her off.

Steph tugs on her gloves, mounts her bike, and turns to me with an impish grin. "Ready to make some hay?"

I smile back. "Sure."

We snake our way back to the Canal towpath through the early morning rush hour traffic of Williamsport. About fifty yards short of the Cushwa Basin, I stop. George Washington once considered Williamsport for the capital city of the newly born United States, and a stone was laid to designate the proposed Federal Square. Miller's Lumber Company is across the street, and I look for a cut in the stone wall between the two houses. I am finally able to discern the marker: an X carved into a stone laid in the ground at the middle of the cut. How different this area would be today if our nation's capital had been established here rather than farther down the Potomac.

Once a Native American passageway between what is now New York and the Carolinas, the Williamsport area was host to a wealth of historical events. Thomas Cresap, an early American pioneer, built a spring house in the area in 1692, and this structure is thought to be the oldest permanent building in Washington County. Following the American Revolution, General Otho Holland Williams settled in the area and established Williams Port. The C & O Canal came to Williamsport in 1834 and created an important commercial route that extended to Washington, D.C. and beyond to the Chesapeake Bay.

About forty miles north of here lies the small town of Gettysburg. Today it is a peaceful college town. Back in July of 1863, it was the scene of three of the bloodiest days of fighting of the American Civil War. The number of casualties on both sides exceeded 50,000 men, or roughly a third of the troops that were engaged. Robert E. Lee, the Confederate commander, desperately sought to win the decisive victory he hoped would end the war. Having failed to destroy the Union forces arrayed against him, he now had to extract his army, his wounded, and the precious provisions that his men had liberated from the Pennsylvania countryside. Years of fighting had stripped his native Virginia of the food and equipment that his men badly needed. Prior to invading the North, the soldiers of the Army of Northern Virginia were surviving on a quarter pound of salted meat each per day.

On the afternoon of July 4th, Lee dispatched a wagon train with the captured supplies and 10,000 wounded to Williamsport — the same town where Steph and I had spent last night. This train extended seventeen miles in length and departed in a blinding rainstorm — probably similar to the kind of rain that we had been riding through. Union cavalry harassed the train during the entire forty mile trip. Although the train was supposed to immediately cross the Potomac, it had to stop at Williamsport because the rains had flooded both the river and the parallel C & O Canal. Lee's army followed. Trapped by the rising water, Lee and his men had no choice but to dig in and pray for the Potomac to go down. They had to wait a week, which must have weighed heavily on the tired, hungry southerners.

The Union army under George Meade followed them cautiously, like a hunter tracking a wounded but still dangerous tiger. The bulk of his forces did not arrive until July 12th. The next day, the level of Potomac fell enough for Lee to send most of his army, wounded, and supplies across at Williamsport and a pontoon bridge further downstream at Falling Waters. On July 14th, Meade ordered his Union army to attack the rear guard Lee had left behind. Although hundreds of Confederates were captured, the bulk of the Army of Northern Virginia escaped to continue the war for almost another two years. Lee is seldom given full credit for his ability to keep his forces intact despite its deprivations.

We leave Williamsport and pass Falling Waters. The Potomac is high up on its banks from the recent rains, and I try to imagine what it was like to be trapped with a sworn enemy bearing down on me.

Not much further down from Falling Waters, we stumble upon a mobile home park that stretches along the towpath. Most of the trailers are set on cinder blocks and possess all the creature comforts of home: air conditioning, decks with lounging chairs, satellite television, and golf carts. Many have boats on trailers parked next to them. What a Confederate soldier would have given for one of those boats back in the summer of 1863.

At Lock 43, green algae covers the water, the stones, and the disintegrating remains of the swing gate. In contrast, the lock house wears a fresh coat of white paint, a new cedar shingle roof, and bright green shutters and door. A small sign proudly announces that it marks the midpoint of the C & O Canal. I give myself a pat on the back for making it this far. I get the feeling that I just might make it the whole way.

Lock 41 marks the beginning of a section of the C & O known as the Big Slackwater. Boats headed southeast would enter here; boats moving northwest would exit. Rather than blast a canal and towpath through a ridge, engineers decided to dam the Potomac and create a calm slackwater area without strong currents and protruding rocks. Boats would be towed out of the Canal into the Potomac for about three miles.

We reach a picturesque red barn situated on a stone foundation above a babbling brook and adjacent to a striking waterfall. Stopping for pictures, I ask a couple standing nearby the name of the barn.

"McMahon's Mill," the fellow answers confidently.

"That's not entirely right," his female companion corrects him. "Says here, it was also known as Avis Mill, Charles Mill, Cedar Grove Mill, and Shaffer's Old Flouring Mill."

"Yeah, but everybody calls it McMahon's Mill."

"But that's not entirely true."

"Why do you always feel the need to correct me? The man asked me a simple question, and all I did was answer him."

"But what you told him wasn't correct."

"It wasn't the whole story, but he didn't ask for a complete Wikipedia entry, just the name."

"Why are you getting upset with me? You were the one that gave him the wrong information."

"I did not give him incorrect information, only incomplete information — in your opinion."

The couple are so engaged in their argument that I find it easy to slip away quietly on my bicycle. I feel guilty that with a simple question I have ruined what must have started as a beautiful morning of sightseeing for them.

Steph is waiting for me at the edge of a winding boardwalk that extends along the edge of the Big Slackwater.

"What's this?" I ask.

"This part of the trail has only been open a couple of years. Two severe floods in 1996 washed away large parts of the old towpath, and it took them fifteen years to raise the money to fix it."

We set out again. With no holes or mud, we are able to set a fast pace. However, new hazards arise as I try to take in the magnificent views without cycling over the edge of the boardwalk into the Potomac or smashing into the sheer limestone cliffs on our left.

As I keep stopping to take a photo or read a sign, Steph gets far ahead of me. Confident that she will wait at some point, I don't worry that I have lost sight of her. Besides, we can always contact each other on our cell phones.

The boardwalk ends, but the scenery continues. Sunshine brightens the day; lots of people are out enjoying it. I stop at the Ferry Hill Visitor Center to replenish my water and see what it has to offer. The two story columns in front remind me of an old plantation house, which it was before it became a visitor center. Although I expect to catch up with my daughter here, there is no sign of her.

From the information displays, I discover that the river that I have been riding beside for the past two days has had several spellings over the years: from "Patawomeke" (according to Captain John Smith) to "Patawomeck" (a Native American tribe that lived in present day Virginia) to "Patowmack" (which was used by an early canal company started by George Washington). Not until 1931 did the United States Board on Geographic Names settle on "Potomac" as the official spelling.

Native Americans used two different names for the Potomac, calling the portion of the river above Great Falls the Cohongarooton (meaning "honking geese") and the portion below the "Patawomke" (meaning "river of swans"). Apparently, they gave weight to the type of waterfowl on the different sections of the river. Considering the fact that our nation's political capital now dominates the lower portion of the Potomac, I wonder if Native Americans would switch the

235

designations to reflect the human honking geese that populate Washington, D.C.

I also learn about the surrounding area and its local towns. Sharpsburg lies on this side of the Potomac with a population of 705 according to the 2010 census. Joseph Chapline settled here around 1740. After the conclusion of the French and Indian War in 1763, he founded a town he named "Sharps Burgh" in honor of his friend Horatio Sharpe, who was also the governor of the Province of Maryland. Helps to have "friends" in high places I muse to myself.

Shepherdstown — which sits on the opposite bank of the Potomac from here — is more than twice the size of Sharpsburg with 1,734 people counted in the 2010 census. Originally named Mecklenburg (no one seems to know why), it is the second oldest town in West Virginia. The Virginia House of Burgesses approved the charters of Mecklenburg and Romney on the same day (December 23, 1762), but Romney is listed first. Mecklenburg changed its name after the Civil War to Shepherdstown in honor of Thomas Shepherd, who had started the town.

In 1787 James Rumsey demonstrated the first boat propelled by steam power on the Potomac between Sharpsburg and Shepherdstown. Although technically successful, the country would have to wait until Robert Fulton demonstrated the commercial viability of steam power in 1807.

George Washington considered the region around Sharpsburg and Shepherdstown in 1789 as a possible site for the United States Capital but eventually chose the area closer to Georgetown. The Georgetown site was, after all, closer to his plantation home at Mount Vernon.

The C & O Canal arrived in the area in the 1830's, providing employment opportunities and a boost to the local economy.

I do not know why I find such tidbits of information fascinating; perhaps, because I lead such an unfascinating life.

Returning to my bike, I think I see Steph ahead of me on the towpath. I pedal like a madman, but when I get to within a hundred yards I realize that it is just another woman on a bike with long braided hair. For the first time, I get a little concerned. I shake away the crazy thoughts that start filling my head about what can happen to young females alone in isolated areas. Chuckling, I remember how she handled the three punks in Connellsville. Rather than worry about her, I should concentrate on taking care of myself.

I push on to the Antietam Aqueduct before stopping. It resembles the Conococheague Aqueduct, stretching about 140 feet over three arches with the center one larger than the other two. I lean over the side and gaze at the water running clear and swift underneath me. On September 17, 1862, the color of this water was much different. Upstream along Antietam Creek a force of 87,000 Union soldiers under the command of General George B. McClellan clashed with 40,000 Confederates under General Robert E. Lee. On a single day, over 23,000 men and boys were left killed, wounded, or missing in action. This carnage remains the most costly one day tragedy in U. S. history — even more so, because it was Americans trying to kill Americans. This same creek that I am standing over ran red with the blood of those casualties.

Looking back on the Towpath, I wonder if Stephanie is behind me — waiting patiently for me to appear. Although I think I would have seen her, she could have turned off somewhere where I missed her. I consider circling back, but quickly reject the idea. The mileage of each day is exhausting me, and I am barely able to make the minimum without any extra. Not sure of what I should do I decide to cycle on. The foliage of the trees thickens and seems to press in on me as I pedal. A thorny vine rakes across my right forearm, and I cuss at it. Stopping to inspect the damage, I feel a burning sensation in my arm. Blood seeps from shallow scratches and my skin is covered with red blotches as if I am having an allergic reaction.

Great, I say to myself, enough is enough. I stop and lean my bike against a tree. Pulling out my cell, I try to call my daughter. The call fails; the screen displays zero bars. I start to fling the phone into the Potomac.

"Don't do that!"

"Why not?" I answer angrily. "What good is the damn thing if the technology doesn't work when you need it?"

Nancy's voice is calm and analytic as always. "The problem isn't with the technology of the phone. The problem is that you've got your head stuck in what happened a hundred and fifty years ago to people you never knew rather than paying attention to what is happening today to people you care about."

"What am I supposed to do?" I ask in frustration. "I haven't seen her in two hours and fifteen miles!"

"Get back on your bike and find her."

"I don't know where she is!"

"Get back on your bike."

"Which way do I go?"

"Get out of your head and follow your heart."

I mount my bike. "Fine. I'll follow my heart."

"And one more thing," the voice adds softly.

"What's that?"

"Be sure and yell at her when you find her."

I ignore the sarcasm in my dead wife's voice. "Don't worry about that. She's in for a royal chewing out."

My fury supplies the adrenaline I need to push my bike forward. I pump as hard as my weary legs allow until I come to an open meadow. At the far end, I spot my daughter sitting on a picnic table, chatting amiably with two other women in cycling clothes.

Seeing her safe and happy, I slow. I practice a parental speech where I calmly express my concerns about her safety while admonishing her lack of responsibility. To give myself more time to cool off, I dismount and walk my bike toward her and her two new friends. My lower body rejoices at the break from biking. Alternating feelings of relief and anger course through my veins as I try to get a grip. However, I sense my feelings of anger overcoming all my other feelings, and I am ready to explode.

Stephanie has not seen my approach as her back is to me, but one of the women points and says something. Steph turns and jumps up.

"Hey, Daddy!"

I march my bike toward her, my hands fiercely gripping the handlebars. Her face radiates, and I can tell that she is happy to see me. Behind her, I see the two strangers watching our reunion. I stop a foot away from Steph and stare at my daughter. Her eyes dilate as she realizes how upset I am. I am about to unload when I see her lower lip quiver. Releasing the death grip on my handlebars, my bike crashes to its side, and I throw my arms around my daughter. I say nothing as I hold her tight to me, and she responds by hugging me back. I close my eyes tight to keep from crying.

"Daddy, I thought you were ahead of me."

I hear my daughter talking, but another voice inside my head is telling me, "Never let her go." My fury subsides as I realize that I have gotten her back. Feelings of relief dissolve my anger into puddles of joy.

"I thought you were ahead of me so I rode as fast as I could to catch up with you, but then I ran into Karen and Frieda." Steph keeps chattering. "They said they had been riding since Harpers Ferry in the opposite direction and had not seen anybody that would fit my description of you. So I decided to hang out with them for awhile until you came along."

I loosen my grip on Stephanie slightly. Pulling back, I glance at Karen and Frieda and then regard my daughter. "How did you describe me? Like Robert Redford on a bike?"

I hear the two women chortle. They are as fit and trim and young as my daughter.

"Not exactly," Steph admits.

"More like John Travolta," one of the women offers.

I consider that comparison for a moment before asking, "And do I fit that description?"

"Oh, definitely," the other one exclaims, "Except better looking."

"I like your new friends," I tell Steph.

Sitting down and sharing snacks from our panniers, we talk and explore each other's lives. Karen and Frieda live in Bolivar, just outside of Harpers Ferry and frequently bike the C & O Towpath. I enlist their help in convincing Stephanie that we should cross the Potomac, get off our bikes, and explore Harpers Ferry.

I open my gambit with a simple question: "What's there to see in Harpers Ferry?"

My daughter gives me a suspicious side glance. She suspects I already know about everything there is to see in the town.

"Lots of quaint old buildings," Karen offers. "If you're not into all the historical stuff, the scenery is fantastic."

I can tell from Frieda's smile that she has caught on to my little ploy. She comments, "My art history professor in college claimed Harpers Ferry was the 'most painted town in America' because of its scenery. It's definitely a place to see if you've never been there before."

From Steph's noncommittal air, I can tell that she is taking in Karen and Frieda's remarks and not buying a word of it.

"Uh, oh," Karen utters as she glances over my head.

We all turn to see what she is looking at. Billowing dark clouds drift over the treetops. They are moving in rapidly from the west.

"We better get moving," Frieda suggests as she collects the refuse from our afternoon picnic. "We don't get these storms often — but when they hit — you do not want to be caught outside."

"Especially on a bike," Karen adds.

We exchange hasty goodbyes and depart in opposite directions on the Towpath.

"Didn't it rain about this time yesterday afternoon?" I ask Steph.

"Yep."

We have the rain routine down: cell phones into sealed plastic bags, panniers secured, rain gear on.

The once clear blue sky has transformed into multiple shades of gray. It starts to bombard us with heavy pellets of water that sting our faces, shoulders, and backs. The rain beats on our helmets like drums.

I turn my head to look at Steph riding slightly ahead of me. Over the thumping noise the rain is making on our headgear, I shout, "Good thing we're wearing these helmets!"

She turns back to look at me, grinning from ear to ear, and yells, "Yep!" I can tell she is loving every minute of this ride in the rain.

Shortly before we get to Harpers Ferry, the Appalachian Trail joins the C & O. For about three miles, the two routes share the same track. We chug past backpackers trudging through the downpower. Clumps of day hikers — out for a leisurely stroll so that they can claim that they have "hiked a portion of the Appalachian Trail" — cluster together wherever they can find a semblance of shelter. Unfortunately for them, they are no dryer than Steph, me, or the backpackers.

We roll along searching for a way across the Potomac to get to Harpers Ferry and a respite from the rain that is pounding us. Steph stops to talk to a group of hikers that have gathered around a stone column. She has to shout to make herself heard over the downpour.

I hear her ask, "Do you know where the bridge is?"

I see a few faces turn to her. They are framed by hoodies drawn tight to keep heads and bodies dry. In unison the hikers point upward.

Steph and I stare up at the underside of the bridge towering above us. Four flights of stairs separate us from the ground and the bridge. We will have to carry our bikes with the weight of the panniers up these stairs in the pouring rain. The steps look treacherously slippery. Plus, hordes of people are clambering up the stairs seeking the shelter of the buildings in Harpers Ferry.

"Still want to visit Harpers Ferry?" she inquires with a mischievous grin on her face.

"I hear it's quite quaint," I reply, mimicking her grin. "And scenic."

Looking up at the gray overcast skies above us, we laugh.

People passing by look at us as if we are idiots.

We abandon our bikes, unhook our panniers, and carry them to the top of the stairs. Getting off the bike and climbing the stairs the first time is a relief. I am able to use different muscles, and the panniers are not that heavy even with water dripping off them. My footing is a different matter. Stephanie bounds nimbly up the stairs with her panniers. I stumble a few times on the way up with my load. She offers to help me, but my male pride forces me to decline her assistance.

At the top, we drop off our bags and turn around to fetch our bikes. We now encounter a new problem. As the rain continues to pound the area, masses of people are fleeing up the stairs. On our ascent, we were moving with them, so we travelled with the flow. Now we had to fight our way down the steps to get back to our bikes. Steph lets me run interference for her until we reach the bikes.

At the bikes, we have a major disagreement. She wants to carry both bikes at the same time with one of us at the front and the other at the rear. I prefer that both of us take one bike at a time. Without the panniers, the bikes are not that heavy, but they are awkward to carry up a flight of slippery stairs. Rather than argue in the rain, I give in. Up we go, with me in the rear and her in the front. We only make it to the first landing when Steph stops and suggests we switch. My male pride has been washed away by the rain, and I humbly comply. People pass us as we slowly stumble to the next landing. This time, my daughter decides to agree with me. Leaving my bike behind on the landing, we take her bike up and then return to fetch mine.

Reloading our bikes, Steph points at my left leg. Blood trickles down my shin but quickly washes away. I had scraped it on one of the bike pedals on the way up.

"Does that hurt?" she asks.

"Only if it stops raining," I reply.

At that precise moment, the downpour abruptly ceases. Rays of sunshine break through the clouds and dance across the surrounding hills. We stand on the bridge taking in the magnificent views of the Shenandoah River as it flows into the Potomac. A brilliant rainbow arcs across the sky.

"Scenic," I remark.

"Yep," Steph agrees.

We walk our bikes on the bridge toward Harpers Ferry soaking in the view as we dry out.

In the town, we read the signs and look at the displays. I have the annoying habit of reading every word, trying to soak up as much knowledge as I can. At least, I can tell that my habit annoys my daughter. She skims through the exhibits and then doubles back to where I am standing.

"Let's get something to eat," Steph suggests.

"Sounds like a good idea," I reply. "Did you want to get a burger or a steak?"

She ignores my jab at her vegan diet.

"I spotted a salad bar up the street."

"Sounds nice," I say noncommittally as I continue reading the display in front of me.

Steph wraps her left arm around me and leans her head on my shoulder. "I'm really hungry," she cautions me quietly.

I have to take her warning seriously. My daughter's empty stomach can turn her into a raving monster.

"Almost done," I say.

"What are you reading about?"

"Shepherd Heyward."

"Who?"

"Shepherd Heyward." I repeat.

"You're reading about a sheep herder?"

"Not exactly," I laugh. "Shepherd Heyward was a free black man living in Winchester, Virginia in 1859. Owned a house there and worked as a baggage handler for the Baltimore and Ohio Railroad."

"Wasn't Virginia a slave state? How could he be a free black man, own property, and have a paying job?"

"Slavery — as southerners would sometimes describe it — was a 'peculiar' institution. Not all African Americans labored under the hot sun picking cotton. Some held paying jobs and could own property before the Civil War."

"But not many?"

"Only a few."

"So what did a guy who lived in Winchester have to do with Harpers Ferry? That's about twenty-five miles from here."

"The train he was working on arrived in Harpers Ferry on October 16, 1859 about the same time as John Brown showed up with his group of abolitionists. Brown planned to seize the federal armory here and issue a call for slaves to join him in a revolt. The weapons in the armory were going to be used to arm escaped slaves. He believed that only violence would ever free the southern slaves."

I pause as I gaze down at the display.

"Anyway," I continue, "Shepherd spotted them and turned to run away. Brown's men were afraid that he would raise an alarm so they shot and killed him."

"So men who had come to free enslaved blacks ended up killing a black man who was already free. How ironic."

"History is full of irony."

Stephanie shrugs. "Great, let's go get something to eat."

With that, we walk our bikes up the street in search of Steph's salad bar while I contemplate the history of the town.

While most people associate Harpers Ferry with John Brown and his attempt to instigate a major slave rebellion in the South, there are so many other notable names and "firsts" associated with the town. George Washington made Harpers Ferry the first stop on his first surveying expedition when he was just 17 years old. Thomas Jefferson, upon seeing the confluence of the Potomac and Shenandoah Rivers for the first time proclaimed that the view was "worth a voyage across the Atlantic." Two of our country's greatest explorers, Meriwether Lewis and William Clark, began their famous westward expedition here. Stonewall Jackson's first command was at Harpers Ferry and the site of origin for the famous Stonewall Brigade. Storer College was the first real academic college for African-Americans and educated freed slaves in the pursuit of higher learning. Harpers Ferry has been visited by no less than eight American Presidents throughout its history.

We select a booth where we can talk in semi private and sit across from each other. I attempt to share all of this valuable historical information with Steph over lunch, but she is not interested. Instead, she seems preoccupied. I shut up and wait for her to tell me what is on her mind.

We eat most of our lunches. Only a few bites remain when Stephanie looks up at me and asks, "Can we talk about the accident?"

I am puzzled by her request. "I think I told you everything I remember the other night," I begin, but the expression on my daughter's face tells me that she is referring to a different accident: an accident that affected her directly; one that happened a long time ago; but not as long ago as the one that killed my sister.

It was a fair question. Of all people, she had a right to know what had happened; a daughter had the right to know how her mother had died. It surprised me though. After all these years, I dreaded reliving those moments that changed both our lives. I turn slightly away from Steph as I gather my thoughts. Out of the corner of my eye, I can see her watching me.

"You know," she continues, "The accident where — "

I cut her off, perhaps a bit too curtly. "I know which accident you're talking about." I nervously rub my hands together; suddenly, they feel sweaty. "It's been a long time since I've talked about it."

"I just thought that since you were able to talk about the accident with your sister you could also talk about the one with Momma."

Sentence fragments form in my head, but I cannot get my lips and tongue to utter them. Images of that night flicker through my head. Two accidents decades apart tore two women out of my life. The most important woman in my life right now wants to know what happened in the second, because it involved her mother. I can only stare blankly at my daughter.

245

Steph shifts uncomfortably on her side of the booth. "We don't have to talk about it right now," she offers. "I know talking about it has got to be painful. Just at some point — " Her voice trails off.

"No — I mean — yes." I stumble over my words. Pausing to take a deep breath, I start over. "Yes, we should talk about it." I smile nervously at my daughter, and she smiles back. Glancing around the small restaurant, I note the mid afternoon crowd is thinning out. Although not an ideal situation, the booth gives us some privacy. My brain tells me this is the perfect time to tell my daughter everything that happened that night, but my heart is pounding so loudly I can barely hear what my brain is saying.

"Your mother and I were —" I begin. Suddenly, I feel my throat constricting, and I cannot get any more words out. I start coughing. To stop, I drain the last of my water glass. Steph slides her water glass toward me. I take a long draught from it.

"Are you okay?" Stephanie asks.

I cough again and then drink more water. "I'm fine," I hear myself saying.

"You don't look fine."

She is right. I don't feel fine; I feel light-headed.

"Daddy!" Steph exclaims. "Take a breath." She jumps around to my side of the booth, grabs my forearms, and raises them over my head. "Take a deep breath now!" she commands.

I obey. The urge to cough subsides, and oxygen starts to flow back into my brain.

Stephanie lowers my arms and slides in next to me in the booth. "Look, we don't have to talk about the accident right now. We'll talk about it another time."

"No, I'm alright," I insist. "I can tell you what happened."

After another sip of water, I begin. "Your mother and I were coming home from a party. It was late. Very dark. The road was not well lighted. We both had had a little too much to drink. Something — a night critter, a small animal of some sort — darted into the road. The car swerved and hit a tree. I don't recall much after that. You probably remember that I was in the hospital quite a while afterwards."

"All I knew was that my mother and my father were gone for a long time," Stephanie says quietly. "Eventually, my Daddy came back, but my Momma never did." My daughter pauses before adding. "And he was a different man."

"Yeah," I agree. "I had quite a few operations. Lots of reconstructive surgery."

"Not as different on the outside as the inside."

I nod in agreement. "I had to make adjustments. Everything in the house reminded me of her."

"Including me?" Steph asks.

"Especially you," I reply and give her a squeeze. "The hardest thing after the accident was sleeping alone. Except I couldn't sleep — not for weeks."

"Thanks, Daddy."

"For what?" I ask, puzzled.

"For talking to me about Momma's accident. I know it was difficult."

The waitress interrupts us to see if we need anything. Steph asks her for a recommendation for a place to stay tonight. After informing us that all of the places in town are probably booked, she suggests a place just outside of town. She then launches into a long, complicated set of directions that make me feel it would be easier just to bike the remaining 61 miles to D.C. rather than try to find this place. I realize halfway through her monologue that she thinks we have a car. Stephanie, in the meantime, has found the place on her GPS.

"Thanks," she dismisses the waitress. "I found it."

To me, Steph says, "It's just on the other side of the river a mile or two and not far off the trail."

"We have to go over that bridge and down those stairs again?" I whine.

"You're the one who wanted to visit Harpers Ferry," she reminds me.

I drop my head. "True."

We settle the bill and retrace our steps back through town to the bridge.

"And you know where this place is?" I ask.

"Got it right here," my daughter says, confidently waving her cell phone in the air.

We cross the bridge, unload our panniers, carry them down, retrieve our bikes by climbing back up the stairs, reload the panniers, and resume our cycling.

With only a few miles to go, I slow my pace. The rain has cooled temperatures off, and the weather has become quite pleasant. Although I enjoyed the diversion to Harpers Ferry, hauling our bikes up and down the bridge staircase has sapped my remaining energy. Talking about Nancy's death has drained me emotionally. I am ready for a long hot shower, a long cold beer, and a long deep sleep.

I poke along gazing at the steep hills around me until I catch up with my daughter. She is standing astride her bike in the middle of the trail with her cell phone out which she is agitatedly jabbing with her finger.

"How much farther?" I ask.

"Not far," she replies.

I stop next to her and try to read her screen. Unfortunately, I cannot make heads or tails out of it. Looking around, I see the Potomac to our right. To our left is a heavily wooded ridge that rises almost straight up.

"Problem?" I ask.

"A slight one," she replies. "According to my GPS, the hotel the waitress recommended is that way." My daughter does not point down the towpath or to the right; instead she points up and to the left.

I let out a groan, thinking that there is no way I can pedal to the top of the ridge.

"Is there an escalator?" I ask.

Steph shakes her head. "Not on my GPS."

I stare at the green wall of trees that stands between me and my place of rest.

"I see a road that goes up to the hotel," Steph continues. "We just need to find a path through the forest, but that is not the real problem."

Looking in front of and behind us, I see no break in the overgrowth.

"So what is the real problem?" I ask.

"Between the road and this line of trees is a railroad track."

"No big deal." I shrug.

"We'll see," Steph warns.

We pedal further down the Towpath, scouting for a break. I do not see anything but thick overgrowth.

Stephanie stops and points. "There."

"All I see are leaves and vines waiting to swallow us whole," I comment.

"C'mon."

She disappears into the underbrush and then pushes branches aside to reveal a narrow trail that only a rabbit could use. Reluctantly, I follow her.

As we slog our way through the thick foliage that we cannot see through, I remark, "I told you we should have brought machetes."

My daughter ignores me.

Shortly, we come to a small creek. We lift our bikes and portage them across, carefully stepping from stone to stone. I am almost to the other side when my right foot misses its mark and lands squarely in the water. Stephanie turns sharply at the sound of the splash.

"I meant to do that," I assert.

She shakes her head and resumes pushing her bike.

We start climbing, working our way upward. A branch slaps me in the face. Then another. Finally, we break into the open. The rains have stopped for the day. The late afternoon sun burns through the clouds.

In front of us — stretching as far as we can see in both directions — is a solid wall of concrete blocks about four feet high. Another four-foot high wall of concrete blocks runs parallel to it. In between the two walls lies a railroad track. Large signs warn against trespassing or attempting to cross.

"I guess we have to turn around," I say.

"To hell with that," my daughter replies. "Hold my bike."

I watch as she walks up to the first wall. Steph nimbly vaults over it and turns to face me.

"Hand the bikes over to me one at a time," she commands.

"What if someone sees us?" I ask.

"Hurry up so that no one does."

"And if a train comes along while we're between these concrete barriers? There's no room. We'll be squished."

"All the more reason to hurry."

I nervously glance to my right and left before letting out a deep sigh. Lifting my bike over first, I pass it to Steph, and she bounces it over the tracks to lean it against the second wall. She returns for her bike to repeat the process.

Now it is my turn to get up and over the concrete barricade. I place both my hands on top and jump. My stomach reaches near where my hands are and then bounces off. On my second attempt, my stomach lands on top of the barrier. I flail my arms and legs trying to get the rest of me over, but I am hopelessly stuck.

Steph comes to my rescue, pulling me over.

"Would you quit clowning around," she scolds me.

"I wish I was clowning around," I reply.

My daughter then effortlessly catapults herself over the next wall. I lift and hand over first her bike then mine. While she is checking our bikes and extracting leaves and vines from our gears, I size up the second wall. Although I know that it is the same height as the first one, I am exhausted from my earlier exertions and do not want to get stranded on top of this concrete wall. I use my feet to tamp the gravel into a launching pad. Backing up a few steps, I take a running start to catapult myself over. I accomplish my goal too well, sailing over the wall and landing head first on the other side.

"Daddy! Are you alright?"

I lay on my back on the ground and give her a thumb's up. "Couldn't feel better!" I lie.

"You could have hurt yourself," Stephanie protests.

"I had my helmet on," I counter as I pull bits of gravel out of my forearms.

We remount our bikes and amble along a crumbling asphalt road that runs beside the railroad tracks. The sun dips just below the trees. Birds chirp. A cool breeze refreshes us. An occasional house nestles into the wooded ridge on our left.

"We're almost there," Steph comments.

"No rush," I say. "I'm enjoying this part of the ride."

"I don't think you will like the next part," she warns.

The road turns sharply left and shoots straight uphill.

I coast up the incline until my bike stops. "Oh, well," I sigh. "I was ready for a walk."

While I push my bike up, Steph slips into a lower gear and grinds her way to the summit. She soon disappears from view.

I soak in the smell of pines as I walk alone. Although tired beyond belief, I feel accomplished to have made it this far.

"One more day." Nancy's voice is accusatory.

"Plenty of time," I reply.

"You always wait until the last minute."

"I have to find the right moment."

"You had the 'right moment' and you choked."

"I couldn't help it."

"No more excuses. Just get it over with. You didn't tell her what was going on in our relationship."

"She doesn't need to know."

"Our daughter deserves to know that our marriage was over."

"It was not over. We were just going through a rocky period."

"Bullshit. You didn't even tell her who was driving."

To block the sound of Nancy's voice out of my head, I start humming loudly. I would whistle, but I am a terrible whistler. Not that I am a much better hummer, but my humming accomplishes the task, and I am able to finish my hike up the hill.

At the top, I gingerly remount my bike and coast down to the hotel. Stephanie is waiting for me with a hose in hand. She delights in knocking the mud off our bikes and then me. When I offer to return the favor, she playfully declines, saying she does not trust me with the hose. I tell her she is a wise woman. Reasonably clean, we check in for the night.

My last thought before I lose consciousness is that tomorrow will be our last day of biking, and I pray that it will be an uneventful one. I have had enough adventure for one trip.

My eyes open, and I stare at the strange ceiling above me. One more day to go I think to myself. I can tell by the soft light peeking around the curtain over the window that it is early morning. Just one more day, I repeat to myself.

Inching my legs one muscle at a time to the edge of the bed, I pull my phone off its charger to check the weather. The forecast is for light precipitation with possible thunderstorms in the afternoon. How can there be any more rain in the clouds after yesterday, I wonder to myself.

Steph stirs in the other bed. I grasp my right thigh with both my hands and move my leg off the bed. Then I grasp my left thigh in the same way and move it off the bed. Slowly, I roll up to a sitting position. My body makes cracking noises, and I hear myself grunting with the effort.

I notice that my daughter is staring at me.

"Good morning," I say.

"Good morning," she replies. Her greeting sounds unusually melodic.

"You're sounding chipper," I comment.

"I'm feeling pretty good."

"That so?" I do not tell her how much my body hurts.

"Yes, I just got a text message from my office. Apparently, my testimony next week has been cancelled."

"Really?" I turn away from my daughter so that she will not see me smiling. I am glad for her, even though I know the stunt I pulled on Senator Mallory will cost me a case of ridiculously priced wine. "Did they reschedule the hearings?" I try to make my voice sound as innocent as possible.

"No, the hearings are still going on — just I won't be a part of them."

"How nice."

"It's odd is what it is. There was all this pressure for weeks to get me to testify. A ton of phone calls and emails. Threats of a subpoena."

"And a helicopter visit," I add.

"Yep," Steph agrees. "That, too. Then right after we talk about the situation — poof — it all goes away." My daughter spreads her fingers up in the air. "It's like some fairy godmother came along, waved her magical wand over the situation, and made it all go away."

Or a fairy godfather, I think to myself. Shrugging, I say, "Sometimes, Washington can be a magical place."

Out of the corner of my eye, I catch my daughter eyeing me suspiciously.

"Not in my experience," she replies. "Unless you are talking black magic."

"One person's black magic is another's white."

"Maybe so," Steph admits. She bounces out of bed while I am still trying to summon the strength to stand.

"Are you ready?" she asks.

"Ready for what?"

"The last day."

"The last day of my life?"

"No. The last day of our trip."

"Is it?" I feign ignorance — something I am very good at.

"We can turn around and bike back to Pittsburgh if you like," she teases me.

"No problem," I fib as I gingerly rise to my feet. "But you have to get back to work, young lady. I didn't raise a slacker." I head to the bathroom with more grunting and creaking noises emanating from my joints.

We pack quickly and are out the door. I check the time: 8:16 — our earliest start yet.

At breakfast we sit next to four men in their early thirties. They are wearing heavy hiking boots, cotton shirts unbuttoned down to their navels, and extremely short shorts. I would guess that they were a gay outdoor group, but there is nothing effeminate about them. They are eating copious amounts of scrambled eggs and bagels without touching the bacon on their plates.

I lean over and whisper to my daughter, "Should I ask them where they get their shorts?"

Stephanie glances over at the four men and then shrugs. "Why?" she asks.

"So I can get a pair."

Shaking her head in disbelief, Steph gets up and says, "I'm going to get more cereal and find some soy milk."

I hear the men talking. It is not hard as they are loud. However, I cannot understand what they are saying as they speak a language that seems familiar but foreign. One of the men rises and looks around. He walks over to where I am sitting.

"My I borrow your salt?" he asks politely with a thick accent.

"You can *have* my salt," I reply as I hand it to him.

"Thank you."

I decide to initiate a friendly conversation. "Where you guys from?" I ask.

The man pauses before he answers. "Israel. Is that a problem?"

Not only is he staring at me, but the three other men have stopped eating and have their eyes glued on me. I sense there will be a problem — for me — depending on how I answer.

I smile.

None of them smile back.

"Of course not," I say. "What brings you to the States?"

One of the men still sitting at the table says something in what must be Hebrew. The only words that I can decipher is the name: "Robert Redford". All of them laugh including the man with my salt. I look at him for a translation and an explanation.

He shrugs as he gestures with the salt shaker in one hand. "We are here because of one of your American movies."

"An American movie with Robert Redford in it?" I guess.

Grinning, he nods. "Crazy, yes?"

Not as crazy as the biking adventure I have been doing for the past five days, I think to myself.

The other three men relax and return to eating. I quickly run through a list of all the Robert Redford movies that I can remember and ask, "Which one: ***Butch Cassidy and the Sundance Kid? The Sting? The Way We Were? The Great Waldo Pepper*?"**

All the Israelis shake their heads at the mention of each movie. One of them states, "We have not heard of these movies. Is Robert Redford in all of them?"

"Yeah," I reply. "And a lot more. He was the Leonardo DiCaprio of his era."

Impressed, the men nod.

"So what Robert Redford movie got you to come here?" I ask.

"***A Walk in the Woods,***" came the reply.

"The book by Bill Bryson?"

"No, the movie by Robert Redford," the guy who borrowed my salt says. "We are hiking the Appalachian Trail because of that movie."

I vaguely remember seeing something about Redford making a movie based on Bryson's book. I elect not to suggest to my new Israeli friends that they should have read the book rather than just watch a movie.

"The Appalachian Trail? That's at least 2000 miles," I comment. Suddenly my 334 point 5 mile trek on a bike seems puny in comparison. "You traveled all the way across the Atlantic to hike over 2000 miles?"

Three of the men start laughing and pointing to the fourth. "Yes," one of them says, "This *schmuck* told us it was 2000 *kilometers*!"

I know the difference between a kilometer and a mile, but the guy who borrowed the salt leans toward me and explains, "A kilometer is a little over half a mile, so we are having to hike twice as far as we thought."

Another Israeli adds, "He also forgot to tell us how much it rains, how much the path goes up and down — up and down — and that there are no McDonalds on the trail!"

"Oyeh," the guy they are all pointing at admits. "If I had told them the truth, my friends would not have come."

Stephanie catches my eye. She is standing by the door and motions for me to follow her.

I wish the Israelis luck and depart.

Outside, Steph is standing next to our loaded bikes ready to go, helmet and gloves already on.

"Hate to tear you away from your new friends," she comments.

"Just trying to improve our international relations," I reply.

"Our relations with the Israelis are fine. At least they were until you started insulting them about the length of their shorts. Let's go."

She is off before I can lodge a formal diplomatic protest. We make our way back to the towpath. The sun warms the air around us into a beautiful day.

We pass quickly through Brunswick. Once a small community of a few hundred people, it grew quickly with the arrival of first the C & O Canal and then the B & O Railroad. Limited for space by the Catoctin Mountains, the Canal and the railroad fought furiously over right of way. Brunswick supposedly had the largest rail yard in the United States at one time; it got its name because so many of the construction workers on the railroad hailed from Brunswick, Germany.

A few miles after Brunswick, we cross the Catoctin Creek Aqueduct. Its wide center arch collapsed in October 1973 and was not restored until 2011.

At Point of Rocks, a narrow wooden bridge leads us into town where we admire the quaint railroad station while ignoring the dilapidated homes. The town gets its name from an unusual rock formation in the nearby Catoctin Mountains.

We reach the Monocacy Aqueduct, an impressive 500 foot, seven arch, stone bridge that once carried the canal over the Monocacy River. The aqueduct took four years to build and was completed in 1833. Only the Paw-Paw Tunnel surpasses this structure as an engineering marvel on the Canal.

I pause halfway across and watch a great blue heron lazily wading through the brown water, patiently stalking a mid morning snack. Although the Monocracy is wide, it does not seem very deep — not much of an obstacle to cross. Further upstream — just south of present day Frederick, Maryland — and 150 years ago, it was quite an obstacle.

By the summer of 1864, the Confederacy was in dire straits. Three years of constant fighting had drained the South of manpower, money, and munitions. Its capital — Richmond — was besieged by Union forces. To relieve the pressure and force the North to seek peace terms other than unconditional surrender, Robert E Lee dispatched his Second Corp under the command of Jubal Early to invade Maryland and attack Washington, D.C.

The daring move caught the Federals off guard. Major General Lew Wallace — who would author the novel **Ben Hur** after the war — scrambled to gather sufficient troops to stop the rebel advance. Outnumbered two to one, Wallace chose the banks of the Monocacy to make his stand. Despite fierce fighting, the men under Wallace could not stop the Confederates. However, they delayed the rebels for a day — just enough time for reinforcements to reach Washington. Early reached the federal capital but after leading a few skirmishing charges against Fort Stephens and Fort DeRussy decided to order a retreat.

Wallace's defense along the Monocacy is credited with saving Washington from the wrath of the rebels under Early.

Once we leave the Monocacy, the Towpath deteriorates into an abysmal mess. Potholes that had made a checkerboard pattern that we had to dodge now merge into one long mud hole that we have to pedal through. Our pace slows as we slog our way along.

Hot and tired, I stop where a strip of asphalt crosses the towpath and take several slurps of water. A small sign identifies the pavement as Whites Ferry Road. Steph stops next to me.

"A ferry?" she asks. "I didn't know there were any ferries on the Potomac."

"Let's check it out," I suggest. I will do (almost) anything to take a break from the muddy Towpath at this point. After a hundred yards, we ride under a red, white, and blue sign that welcomes us to "Historic Whites Ferry". The smooth asphalt that leads to the ferry is a refreshing relief; it runs straight down into the river. The ferry — basically an over-sized raft with room for three lines of vehicles — is docked next to the car in the water. It is attached to a steel cable that extends across the Potomac. A sign erected over the deck proudly proclaims the name of the craft in large dark blue block letters: "GEN. JUBAL A. EARLY". Just off the edge of the pavement, I see the rear end of a dark blue BMW sticking out of the water.

I roll up to a young guy that I take to be one of the deck hands for the ferry.

We exchange "Good mornings".

"I thought cars were supposed to go *on* the ferry," I ask, pointing at the trunk of the BMW poking above the surface of the water.

"Yeah, most of 'em do, but every once in awhile we have some fella that thinks he can just drive across."

We share a chuckle.

"Is the driver okay?" I ask.

"Oh, yeah, he sobered up real quick once he hit the water." The guy removes his Home Depot baseball cap and scratches the top of his head. "Hope you aren't in a hurry to get to the other side. It will take awhile for the tow truck to get here. We can't operate until that car gets pulled out of the way."

"Oh, we're not planning to go across," Stephanie interjects. "My Daddy just likes to stop whenever he can and chit chat."

I detect a note of irritation in my daughter's voice.

"I'm a history buff," I admit sheepishly.

"Lots of that here. There's been a ferry at this spot ever since 1782. The bend in the river slows the current down so it's easier to cross. Once there were hundreds of ferries up and down the Potomac to help people get from one side to the other. The Jubal A. Early here is the last one still operating."

"So your boat is named after the Civil War general?" I ask.

"Sure enough. There's a statue of him over yonder." The ferryman points to a lonely figure surrounded by an iron fence next to a copse of trees.

"But I thought this was called Whites Ferry," Steph asks.

"Interesting story there," the ferryman says as he coils a rope. "Elijah Viers White was born not far from here in 1832 —

on this side of the river. After spending a year out west fighting in the border wars between Missouri and Kansas, he came back at the ripe old age of 24 and bought a 355 acre farm just across the Potomac in Virginia. When the Civil War started, Lige — that was his nickname — joined the cavalry on the southern side as a private. Fought in quite a few big battles — his unit was one of the first to reach Gettysburg. Worked his way up in rank to Lieutenant Colonel in charge of his own unit. Called themselves White's Comanches because of the way they would holler when they charged."

The ferryman finishes coiling the rope and hangs it on a hook. "After the war, Lige returned to Leesburg and became a successful businessman. Served as sheriff for four years, ran a bank, and bought this ferry. Everyone called it Whites Ferry 'cuz he owned it, but he named his boat after his favorite commander — General Jubal A. Early."

"Fascinating," I say, truly interested.

"Yes, fascinating," Steph echoes, her voice dripping with sarcasm.

Lights flashing, a tow truck rumbles toward us.

"You folks have a nice day," the ferryman wishes us. "Looks like I've got to get to work."

As Steph and I turn our bikes around to return to the towpath, Steph nudges me. She points at a three story building painted blue next to the road.

"Looks like a country store," I say.

"Do you see the three black lines?" she asks.

Just below a third floor window is a black mark with the word "Flood" next to it and the date "6-24-72" underneath it. Just below those words is another black mark and the date "1-21-86", and just below that is yet another black mark and the date "11-07-85". The marks are at least ten feet over our heads.

"What do those marks mean?" Steph asks.

"I imagine that's how high the water got during floods," I reply.

We both glance nervously over our shoulders at the Potomac flowing calmly behind us.

"No way," Steph comments.

"Just in case it starts raining again, we better get moving."

We push off. The sign that welcomed us to Whites Ferry now thanks us for visiting. As we rejoin the soupy marsh that the towpath has become, I notice that the old canal bed, or prism, has disappeared in the foliage. Trees, shrubs, and grass have overgrown the area. Nature has reclaimed its territory.

I take a slug of water and realize that my bottle is almost empty. Steph is just ahead of me, and I call out to her, "How much water do you have left?"

She does not turn her head back to me, but keeps it down as she works her way through the slop we are in. "I just finished mine, but I'm sure we can refill up ahead."

Indeed, we have found numerous places along the Towpath to replenish our water. And on most days it has rained so that we have gotten air delivery of our hydration needs. So far, no rain has fallen from the clouds scattered above us.

We continue on. I offer Steph some of my water, but she refuses to take any until I insist. Soon my water is gone; yet, the Towpath seems to stretch endlessly before us.

Searching for a potable water source, we pause at one of the many campsites established by the Park Service along the Towpath. Most are positioned next to the Potomac so that campers can set up their tents close to the river and enjoy views of the water. Today, the water is flowing directly *through* the campsite. Rain from the past few days has caused the Potomac to jump its banks, inundating tent pads, picnic tables, and fire pits.

Surveying the scene, I remark dryly, "Too bad we're not camping."

"Yep," Steph replies. "This is one of the spots where I thought we could spend the night." She points at the top of the picnic table; it is inches above the level of the water. "We'd have to sleep on top of the table to keep from floating downriver."

I shake my head and silently thank Hank for convincing me not to try to camp on this trip. The plastic bear in the biplane attached to my handlebars nods its head in agreement.

Back on the Towpath, we have to navigate a soupy mix of gravel and roots. Just as I consider the prospect of trying to drink from the muddy potholes around us, Steph shouts, "Finally!"

She has spotted one of the ancient pumps that the Park Service maintains along the Towpath. The water is treated heavily with iodine which leaves a distinctive odor but makes the water safe to drink.

I work the long pump handle, and Steph holds our water bottles in place. We ignore the water's peculiar flavor, taking gulps between refills. Fully hydrated, I watch Steph fuss with the straps of her panniers. I wonder why she is going to such trouble as we do not have that many more miles to go, and it is only early afternoon.

Then I hear the distinctive rumble of thunder. Through the trees, I see angry grey clouds rolling toward us. They extend across the entire northwest horizon and extend up into the air like floating skyscrapers. We are about to transition from not enough water to too much.

"We need to get a move on," I suggest to Steph.

She looks at me, and I point in the direction of the clouds. She nods in agreement.

The wind picks up and pushes us down the Towpath. Unlike the rainstorms of the previous few days, this one pounds us relentlessly. At first, I am not concerned. We have endured a daily soaking every day of the trip. All we have to do is keep moving. Eventually, the rain will stop, and we will dry out. This time, however, long rows of billowing clouds unleash their anger on us with a fierceness we have not experienced. I hear more thunder.

Stephanie is riding ahead of me, and I am trying to keep up.

"We need to find shelter!" I shout. "I don't want to get hit by lightning!"

I see the helmet on her head bob up and down in agreement.

Unfortunately, there is no shelter to be had. The Towpath opens up, and we are exposed to the full fury of the storm. We race across a small wooden bridge. I glance to my right. Water is pouring over a large spillway in huge torrents, creating a loud roar.

We enter a wooded area, but there is no place out of the rain that will protect us. Water is pouring down from the clouds and splashing up from the Towpath. We are beyond soaked. In the distance, I think I see a building.

Again, I shout at Stephanie, but she is farther ahead of me, and I doubt that she hears me. I start to shout one more time when a bolt of lightning strikes just ahead of her with a thunderous roar. It hits a tree just to our right. The brilliant jagged light almost blinds me as it seems to rip apart the air around it. I watch in horror as the tree topples across the Towpath and on top of my daughter.

Staring at the scene unfolding in front of me in disbelief, I momentarily freeze and stop pedaling. Stephanie had been riding hard in front of me and then within a second has disappeared underneath a dense pile of foliage. The tree looks huge, and its trunk extends all the way across the Towpath. Large raindrops bounce off the Towpath as I frantically resume pedalling toward the fallen tree.

Questions race through my mind: Is she alright? How can she be? As I get closer the fallen tree seems to grow in size. It has massive branches that extend from its think trunk. There is no sign of Stephanie.

More questions: If she is pinned by one of those branches, how will I get her out? Only a chainsaw could cut through them. Or what if she is under the trunk? I shudder at th thought of what I would fin if that ere the case. Maybe she only has a broken arm or leg?

Nancy chooses this moment to insert herself: "You've really done it this time."

"Not now!" I plead.

Ignoring my request, she pelts me with questions of her own: "What are you going to do if she has broken an arm or a leg? You are in the middle of nowhere. How are you going to transport her?"

"I'll figure something out."

"Sure you will." Nancy's voice drips with sarcasm. "What are you going to do? Strap her on top of your handlebars and pedal fifty miles to the nearest emergency room?"

"That's enough!"

"Why are you even out here in a thunderstorm for chrissakes?"

"I need to concentrate on helping our daughter."

"The way you helped me? You couldn't save me. Why do you think you can save our daughter?"

"Shut up, Nancy!" I yell in exasperation.

Reaching the fallen tree, I toss my bike down in the middle of the Towpath. My right ankle catches a pedal, opening a gash which I ignore. The fallen tree has created a giant green wall of soaking wet leaves. I call to Steph repeatedly, hoping that I will hear her respond that she is okay, but I hear nothing from her. As I start clawing my way through the limbs searching for any sign of life, I keep calling her name, but I cannot find my daughter. Pushing and breaking limbs when I can, I encounter the trunk. It is wet, slippery, and chest high. As I try to hoist myself over, I think I hear a sound to my left over the rain. My grip gives way; the left side of my face scrapes down the rough bark; and I hit the ground with a grunt.

"Steph?" I call out in frustration, praying for a response.

My prayer is answered when I hear Stephanie reply.

"I'm over here, Daddy!"

"Are you okay?"

"I don't know, but I think so."

"Don't move," I order as I clamber toward her.

"I'm fine."

"Stay put. I'll find a way to get to you."

From the sound of her voice, I can tell that she is on the opposite side of the trunk from where I am. I work my way up the trunk; fortunately, the limbs seem to be getting smaller. Still my forearms are being raked raw as I fight my way to my daughter. I reach a spot where a limb has broken underneath the weight of the trunk, but the stub is holding the trunk above the muddy ground. There is just enough room for me to squeeze under the trunk and through the muck.

Popping up on the other side, I spot a helmet among the leaves.

"Steph?"

The helmet slowly turns in my direction. I hear a soft chuckle.

As I work my way through the last few branches, I ask," What are you laughing about?'

"Daddy, you're a mess. Your face is all scratched up. You're covered in mud. And you're bleeding."

I glance down at my ankle. Blood is trickling into my shoe.

"Don't worry about me. Let's focus on you."

"I'm fine." Steph tries to pull herself up.

"Sit." I command.

Reluctantly, she complies. As my daughter plops back down; she seems dazed. Her helmet is slightly askew, and her cycling jersey has a large rip running vertically down her back.

Remembering how she had thoroughly checked me out after I had taken my tumble on the Towpath outside of Paw Paw, I drill her with the same questions and ask her to raise and extend her limbs the way she had directed me. She dutifully complies. About halfway through my examination, something about the process tickles Stephanie, and she starts giggling. Her amusement lets me know that she is indeed alright, but I caution her to be serious. She apologizes. I resume. She giggles. I scold her. The cycle repeats one more time until I give in.

Relieved that Stephanie has escaped serious injury, we laugh together, ignoring the rain pouring down on us until we notice that it has stopped. Rays of sunshine pierce the clouds.

"Better find your bike," I suggest.

We dig through the leaves and branches until we spot it. Somehow, the major limbs of the tree missed Steph and her bike. Extracting them from the tangled mass takes some effort. Then we have to wade through the fallen tree again to retrieve my bike from the other side.

With the rain over — at least for the moment — Steph retrieves a fresh cycling jersey and stuffs the wet, torn one into one of her panniers. She sports a large bruise on her right forearm, but is otherwise uninjured. Her bike has also escaped serious damage. I consider it a miracle and say so.

Steph grins and replies, "Not as much of a miracle as my old man cycling 334 miles."

"334 point five," I remind her.

She nods in bemused agreement as she asks, "On to Great Falls?"

"To Great Falls."

Great Falls
14 miles to go

The Great Falls on the Potomac River in Maryland normally discharge 207,000 cubic feet of water per second; in comparison, the more famous Niagara Falls on the Niagara River discharge a mere 100,000 cubic feet of water per second. Today — with the heavy rains — I estimate at least a half million cubic feet of water flows past me each second.

I lean against the railing and watch the convoluted torrents of water twist through the gorges. Although I could stay and watch the water flow past me for hours, I know that I have to rejoin my daughter and complete the journey to D.C. Walking back to the Towpath, I see her standing next to a wooden railing.

Stephanie calls out to me: "Hey, Daddy! Take a picture of me with Dolly!" My daughter is literally nuzzling a dark four-legged beast standing next to the railing. It resembles a horse, but its ears are excessively long. It hardly has a mane, and its head is enormous compared to its body. "Squirrel! Get away from that thing before you get fleas or it bites you!" I call out.

Steph ignores me. I figure that the only way to quickly get her away from the brute is to take a picture as fast as I can. *Why do I have a daughter who instantly adores any animal she sees,* I ask myself.

I abandon my bike and half sprint to where I can get a hasty shot. Having spent the last few days sitting on a bike, my legs have forgotten how to move in a non circular motion. I probably look like Festus from the old Gunsmoke TV show as I hobble over.

As I am lining up the shot, a park ranger ambles past. "Would you like for me to take a picture of you and your daughter?" he asks.

"Oh, yes, Daddy!" Steph exclaims. "Let's get a picture of us together with Dolly!"

The ranger chuckles at her excitement.

I eye the creature that my daughter has fallen in love with and turn to the ranger.

"What is that thing?" I ask.

"Thing?" the ranger looks puzzled. "Oh, you mean Dolly? Dolly's a mule."

"A mule?"

"Yeah," the ranger says as I hand him my cell. "A mule is a cross of a male donkey and a female horse. "

I contemplate this unnatural abomination and shake my head.

The ranger continues. "Just like humans inherit certain traits from each one of their parents, so do mules. From the father — the donkey — mules get intelligence, long ears, and small hooves — important for sure-footedness. From the mother — the horse -- mules get a cooperative demeanor, strength, and endurance."

"Sounds like I'm a mule," Stephanie laughs. "A horse for a mother and a jackass for a father."

"Hey," I protest.

The ranger ignores us as he is in full instruction mode. "Mules were the engines for the packet boats on the C & O. They were cheaper to buy and keep than horses and less likely to get injured or sick. Mules are also more sure-footed than horses and less likely to trip and injure themselves pulling heavy loads. Skin is thicker so they are less likely to get sores from their harnesses. And stronger, too. One mule can pull the equivalent of one and a half horsepower."

"Guess they got great gas mileage," I comment.

"You bet. Just feed them grass hay. And you don't have to feed them as much as a horse. Plus they live longer, too. If a canawler took proper care of his mule, that mule would pull his boat for twenty years."

"What's a 'canawler'?" I ask.

"Oh," the ranger laughs. "That's a slang term for the boatmen. I think it is a run together term for 'canal hawler' because that is what these boatmen did: haul freight on the canal."

"I'm guessing some of these 'canawlers' did not necessarily take good care of their mules," I proffer.

"One of the hardest jobs for the mules was getting the stationary boats out of the locks. Some boatmen would overload their boats and then use whips to drive the mules relentlessly."

"How horrible!" Stephanie exclaims.

"Yeah," the ranger concurs.

Dolly tosses her head vigorously up and down in agreement.

"What kind of care did the mules need?" Steph asks as she strokes Dolly's cheek.

"The children of the boatmen usually took care of the mules. Brushing them down, feeding them, making sure that they had plenty of water, mucking their stalls on the boat. Biggest job was greasing and oiling the harness so that it would stay supple. Mules weren't just work animals, they were pets and companions. After a 'trick' — that's the term the boatmen would use for a half day of pulling — they would need to be curried — brushed down. There was a saying among the old canawlers: If you treat a mule right, she'll treat you right."

As I edge closer to where Steph and this creature called Dolly are standing, I notice that the mule is watching me closely with its large black eyes. Its ears are pointing directly at me like a bull's horns.

"Come on, Daddy!" Stephanie urges me.

At a safe distance, I address the animal. "You're not going to bite me, are you?" I ask it.

I swear the mule winks at me.

"How close should I get?" I ask the ranger.

"Just stay on this side of the fence and don't ever walk behind her," the ranger cautions me.

"Why's that?" Stephanie asks.

"A maintenance worker startled her, and she gave him a pretty good kick. Knocked him clear across the Towpath."

"Was he in the hospital for a while?" Steph asks.

"Didn't have to go. Nothing broken. He was just sore for a few days."

While Stephanie and I are standing on either side of Dolly posing for the picture, I feel a warm, wet nudge on my right arm. Startled, I jump halfway toward where the ranger is standing. Another mule, smaller and lighter in color, has decided to join us. It has white patches around its eyes and nostrils. Steph and the ranger find my reaction hilarious.

"Nell justs wants to get into the picture," the ranger claims.

"How many of these critters do you have?" I ask.

"A total of six: all female. Besides Dolly and Nell, there's Eva, Lil, Ada, and Molly."

"Why are they all female?" Steph asks.

"We find females easier to work with. Every mule has her own little idiosyncrasies — what she likes and doesn't like. The females tend to work it out among themselves."

"Whereas the males fight over the females?" I comment.

"Something like that."

"Leaving the females to do all the hard work," Steph adds.

The ranger smiles. "These mules have it pretty easy these days. Their predecessors on the Canal would typically pull a 140-ton boat eight hours a day, seven days a week. Dolly and Nell pull at most a twenty-eight ton boat, two hours per day, four days a week. If you hurry, you can book a seat on the *Charles F. Mercer,* our replica passenger packetboat. It'll give you a little taste of what it was like to travel on the canal back in the day." He points at a boat floating in the canal not far away from where we are standing. It has two decks: The lower deck is an enclosed cabin; the upper deck is open with a canvas canopy. Across its bow is stenciled its name — "Charles F. Mercer" — in bold black letters.

"Who was Charles F. Mercer?" I ask.

"He was the first president of the Chesapeake and Ohio Canal Company."

"Fitting," I reply.

"We're lucky to have her: it's popular with most visitors. After thirty years of faithful service — oh, I think it was in 2003 — we retired the previous replica. It was a freight boat called the Canal Clipper III. Park Service commissioned a study for a replacement, but no funds were available to build it. Typical problem for the Service."

"Billions for aircraft carriers but not a dime for anything historical," I complain.

"Where did the money come from to build it?" Stephanie asks.

"Interesting story there. A third grade class at the Seven Locks Elementary School thought it was unacceptable not to build a new replica canal boat just because of a lack of money. In the spring of 2004 — all by themselves — they raised $2000."

"That's impressive for a bunch of third graders," I remark. "But I doubt $2000 even paid for the canopy."

"Nope, the final cost was well over half a million, but the fact that those little kids were able to get that amount of money inspired — or in my humble opinion: shamed — adults to dig into their pockets and come up with the necessary funds."

The thought of leisurely floating on the Canal during the heat of the day with a cold beverage in one hand is tempting, but I can tell from my daughter's expression that it is time to get back on our bikes and complete our adventure. We part ways with the ranger after thanking him, remount our bikes, and get back to pedaling.

At Fletcher's Boathouse, Steph directs us off the towpath onto the Capital Crescent Trail. I spot a mile marker that indicates we have three miles to go. I am focused on completing the Towpath without any scenic side trips. My aching legs will not allow any extra mileage on my itinerary. I ask her why the route shift.

"Less traffic and better surface," she answers. I ride the Crescent all the time. It runs parallel to the C & O until we reach the Francis Scott Key Memorial Bridge."

I decide to save what little energy I have left for biking rather than argue with her. We descend into a thickly foliated area, trading the crushed gravel of the towpath for the smooth asphalt of the Crescent. Occasionally, I catch a glimpse of people above us walking or biking on the C & O towpath. They must be at least thirty feet above us. I enjoy gliding along on the pavement, but I am wary that we may eventually have to climb back up.

My fears bear fruit at the Francis Scott Key Memorial Bridge when Steph takes a sharp left and starts heading almost straight up. I dismount and walk my bike, humming the Star Spangled Banner to myself to keep my mind off the cramp in my right thigh.

When we rejoin the towpath, it is crammed with people. We weave our way through the narrow area lined with small shops on a red brick walkway.

With a water-filled portion of the canal on our right and a bush-lined building on our left, we pass Lock One. Normally, I would stop to investigate, but I have seen enough locks over the past few days. My mind keeps reminding my aching body that we are almost done.

We bounce along a brick paved path as we approach the back of a large brown sign. Ahead of me, Steph pauses and turns to read the sign. Then she looks to her left at a green plaque mounted on a rock beneath a large trip. I see her smiling, and I know that we have done it. More specifically, I have done it and survived. I have ridden six days and 334 point 5 miles on a bike through mud and thunderstorms, and I am already looking forward to gloating over my accomplishment. Hank is going to be picking up the beer and burger tab at Tomfoolery for months.

I read the large brown sign and the green plaque. They are filled with information about the C & O Canal, but I already know everything they say. With a foot on either side of my bike, I crab walk over to where Stephanie is standing.

I awkwardly give her a one-armed hug.

"We did it, Squirrel. We biked the whole Passage and the Canal. I have to admit that I wasn't sure I could do it."

Stephanie looks at me blankly.

I babble on. "I mean, I knew you could do it, but quite a few people told me I was crazy to try to do this trip."

My daughter looks down at the screen on her phone. "We're not done," she says quietly.

"But — "

"This is not mile marker zero. We still have a ways to go."

"But the signs — "

Follow me," Steph commands. "And stay close. It gets tricky."

A muscle in my left calf twitches, but I have no choice but to follow her. We take a sharp right onto a bike path that parallels Rock Creek Parkway. Rush hour traffic inches along beside us as we ride. Passing underneath K Street, we navigate busy intersections until we reach the Thompson Center parking lot on our right. We veer left onto a bridge that crosses the Canal and then left again into an area filled with rowing boats. A crew of eight young women are cheerfully carrying their boat toward the water. They are fit and trim as they prance in front of us wearing the least possible amount of clothing. I am too tired to admire how their outfits conform to the contours of their bodies.

Unable to pass them, we dismount and walk our bikes behind them. They stop every few feet and discuss their options. Finally, Steph squeezes around them, and I follow. We skirt a rack of rowing boats that forces onto the loading ramp that slants into the Potomac. I think we have reached a dead end, but Steph takes us onto a gravel path that runs past a storage area. We come to a historical marker, but I am too tired to read it. Rattling over a wooden bridge, I see the C & O Canal zero mile marker standing obstinately by itself. Below it, deteriorating slowly in the waters of the Potomac, are the remains of the "watergate". Boats would enter and exit the C & O at this point.

Georgetown/Washington DC

Hovering above us is the Watergate office and hotel complex, and my thoughts drift back to the summer of 1974. I hum the Lynyrd Skynyrd song *Sweet Home Alabama* that had been released in June of that year. Just out of high school, I had listened to that song constantly.

Stephanie looks at my oddly. "That's a strange tune to be singing," she comments. "We're nowhere near Alabama."

I grin at her, point at the blue skies above us, and keep singing. My daughter shakes her head at me.

At that point in my life, I had been a staunch Republican, and I had believed Richard Nixon when he had claimed that he was not a crook. I also had believed that it was my duty as an American male to serve my country, even if it meant risking my life in a jungle in southeast Asia. Stephanie had not grown up during Watergate and Vietnam; her faith in her country and government had not been shaken the way mine had been.

I get to the part of the song and recite the lines that had forever changed by political beliefs: "Now Watergate does not bother me/Does your conscience bother you?/Tell the truth". Richard Nixon resigned in disgrace on August 8, 1974 — less than two months after the release of the song I was singing.

Stephanie is watching me closely now — certain that our six day bike trip has pushed me over the edge.

I decide that I owe her an explanation. "Without the courage of two investigative reporters, a federal district judge, and a snitch at the highest levels of the FBI, our democracy would be in worse shape than that watergate." I point at the rotting remnants of the C & O watergate sticking out above the surface of the Potomac. "A 'third-rate burglary' in an office at that Watergate — " and I direct her attention to the building near us " — led to the resignation of the President of the United States — a man who ruthlessly used the power of his office for his own personal gain. We should never forget that."

Steph nods in understanding, but I am sure that she still thinks that I have gone crazy.

Standing next to the marker zero — what I believe to be at last our final destination — we enjoy the view of the

Watergate Complex, the Kennedy Center for the Performing Arts, and the Potomac River flowing lazily past us. I know now that I have reached my physical limit. Although exhausted, I feel euphoric at having completed the trip — and reconnected — with my daughter.

"Can we call Steve now to come pick us up?" I plead.

Steph is examining her phone. She glances briefly at me and then returns her focus to her screen. "Oh, we're biking back to my place."

"We are?" My voice is tinged with disbelief. "How far it that?"

"Just a few more miles."

My legs start screaming at me that they have no more miles left in them.

"But first, we have to spin by the Lincoln Memorial," my daughter adds casually.

"The Lincoln Memorial?"

"Yep, it's not far."

"But isn't it further away from your place?"

"A little. Not much." Steph is already turning her bike around for us to retrace our route.

I try to form my lips and tongue to voice a protest, but my whole body goes into shock at the thought of riding through D. C. traffic on wobbly legs to tour the Lincoln Memorial and then pedal to Steph's townhouse.

Dutifully, I follow Stephanie back across the wooden bridge to the gravel path, around the storage area and the rack of rowing boats, and through the parking lot. Turning right, we get back on the bike path that runs next to the Rock Creek Parkway and cycle past the Watergate complex and the Kennedy Center. The day is warm and sunny, and I would enjoy the ride along the Potomac if my body did not hurt so much. I wonder if reconnecting with my daughter would be the death of me.

That fear is confirmed when we have to dart across several lanes of traffic. Cars, trucks, and buses are fighting each other to get to the Arlington Memorial Bridge. I am convinced that the Republican drivers think that I am a Democrat and the Democratic drivers think that I am a

Republican because all of them seem to be accelerating to try to hit me — although they are probably just typical government workers who want to get home at the end of the day.

Unfortunately, we still are not done when we reach the sidewalk on the other side. We are on the backside of the Lincoln Memorial and Stephanie wants to take pictures of us holding our bikes aloft over our heads in front of the reflecting pool.

Around we go. We clamber around on the steps scouting for the best location. Steph climbs up on a pedestal with the reflecting pool and the Washington Monument in the background. I nod my concurrence and roll her bike over to her. Before I hand it up to her, I ask, "Do you want to lift it with or without the panniers?"

The weight of the panniers is more than double the weight of her bike.

She gives me a sweet smile. "Without. I don't like to show off."

I remove her panniers and hand the bike up to her. Stepping back, I get ready to take the photo. Like an Olympic weightlifter, she deftly snaps her bike over her head, and I snap the photo.

Setting the bike down, Steph announces, "Your turn."

Envisioning myself toppling off the pedestal if I try to lift my bike over my head, I try to think of a reason not to attempt to copy her feat, but I have run out of excuses. Instead, I take her place on the pedestal and somehow lift my bike the same way she did — just not as gracefully.

Afterwards, we sit on the steps of the Lincoln Memorial sipping from our water bottles and watching the hordes of tourists mill around us. They come in every size and shape. I hear Japanese, German, Spanish, and several languages I do not recognize. Some women are dressed in skimpy summer outfits that reveal acreages of skin. Several women from India are dressed in full length saris that cover their bodies from head to foot. There are far more foreign tourists than there are American.

Stroking the short stubble on my cheeks, I examine my legs and arms. They are covered with bruises and scratches, but nothing that looks permanent. Although I am tired and grungy, Steph seems as fresh and clean as when we started. That is a talent she somehow picked up from her mother. Stephanie pops up and starts kicking a soccer ball around with some little kids.

I ease back against the stone steps and wonder where she gets her energy. Looking up, I cannot see a cloud in the sky after the deluge we had survived earlier that day.

A soft voice whispers in my ear.

"Perhaps all the rain this week has washed away your sins, Tom."

I snort in reply and respond to Nancy in my mind: *It will take more than a few rinse cycles to cleanse me.*

"Perhaps some soap would help."

That and a good hard scrubbing with a steel brush, I say.

We share a laugh as I watch our daughter play soccer.

I say out loud, "I wish you could see her now. She's all grown up and seems happy."

"I can. She is happy, but she is missing some things in her life."

Like what, I respond in my mind.

"Like her parents."

Are we back to that again?

I press my palms against my temples, trying to squeeze Nancy's voice out of my head — but she stays.

"You did good, Tom."

What did I do?

"You took a big risk. We both doubted you could make the whole trip."

Did I have a choice? I ask.

"You always have a choice. This time you made the right one."

***This** time?*

"I don't think that I have to remind you of when you have not made the right choice."

You don't have to, but you like to, I muse to myself.

275

The voice in my head ignores my musing and continues. "She still needs you. Keep talking to her."

I watch my daughter laughing in the midst of a crowd of tiny soccer players and admit to the voice: *I haven't told her everything.*

"She's not ready. Not yet. She's still trying to figure out how much she can trust you."

The way I trusted you, I accuse the voice.

It does not respond. Instead, I hear a noise I have not heard in almost a week. My cell chimes. It is Katherine's ring tone, and I answer it.

"Hello."

"Oh, I finally got you. I've been trying all day. How's the trip going?"

"Great."

"What's all that noise I hear in the background? Where are you?"

I watch a large group of hispanics pass by where I am sitting. Their guide must have a megaphone surgically implanted in her throat from the way she is loudly describing what the group is seeing in Spanish. "Based on what I am seeing, we're just outside of Mexico City," I say.

"Mexico City? But didn't you start in Pittsburgh?"

"Yeah, I think we took a wrong turn."

Katherine laughs softly. "So you won't be back in time for dinner tonight, I take it."

"No, but maybe tomorrow night. I could use a good meal. I've probably lost thirty pounds."

I hear Katherine emit a low growl. "Oh, boy. I'm looking forward to checking that out."

Rubbing at a patch of mud that has attached itself to my calf, I say, "I will probably need a good cleaning with a power washer first."

"How did the trip go? Are you close to finishing?"

I grimace as I stretch out one of my legs. "We're not done — yet — I think. She keeps adding to the trip."

"Maybe she doesn't want it to end."

"Possibly, but I'm ready to get back to you."

"Good. See you tomorrow."

"Tomorrow."

I hang up and see that Stephanie has returned. I ask, "How far is it to your place?"

"Not far."

"That seems to be your standard answer for this trip whether it's one mile or twenty."

"Yep," she grins at me. "But the good news is that it is all *uphill*."

"Wonderful," I say as I take a long slug of water and pretend that it is a Yuengling lager. Then I look seriously at my daughter and tell her, "I'm glad you called and invited me on this little excursion."

She grins at me. "I'm glad you accepted." Her eyes drift away from me toward the Lincoln Memorial as she asks,"So what are we going to do next summer?"

"Next summer?" I smile. "Next summer, I am thinking we go on a cruise with a large swimming pool, an all you can eat buffet, and lots of frozen fruity drinks with tiny little umbrellas."

Steph scrunches her nose. "You would really want to do that?"

I remember the rain, the bugs, and the pedalling we had just endured for 344.5 plus miles and compare that to a luxury cruise in the Bahamas. *Yeah,* I think to myself, *I would.* Then I look into the eager face of my daughter and make the mistake of asking, "What did you have in mind?"

"I was thinking we might bike the Natchez Trace."

"The Natchez Trace?"

"It's a national parkway that runs from Tennessee to Mississippi."

"I know what it is," I reply, slightly irritated, "but it's a highway for cars."

"Not strictly for cars," Steph corrected me. "According to the National Park Service, it is ideal for road biking."

And what does the National Park Service know about road biking, I think to myself. "And you want to go end to end?" I ask, knowing full well what her response will be.

"Yep." She nods so vigorously that I can see her braided ponytail bouncing behind her. It's the same ponytail I had observed on a little girl that I once called Squirrel a long time ago. I know what my answer will be.

"And how far will we have to bike?" I hear myself asking, as if the distance that I will have to endure matters.

"444 miles."

I feel my jaw drop.

"That's al-almost a hun-hundred miles fur-further than what we j-just did," I stutter.

"Yep."

Enjoy *Biking the Passage?*

In today's book market, reader reviews are critical to the success of independent authors. Without strong reviews and ratings, work such as the one you just read will sink into oblivion, and further efforts will be stifled. I would be extremely grateful if you would post your review or comments on Amazon, Goodreads, or any other preferred site.

The adventures continue:

Biking the Trace

A novel of recovery

Coming Fall 2019 — unless lightning strikes another tree

A few parting shots from the author...

Some of the events described above are partially true. If I have not completely discouraged you from biking the Great Allegheny Passage and/or the C & O Towpath, may I suggest some further reading:

Bike Trail Guide for Great Allegheny Passage (GAP) and C&O Canal Towpath Trail // Pittsburgh to Washington DC by Ed Quigley

It covers the whole distance and comes highly recommended.

Biking the GAP: A comprehensive, visual guidebook to bicycling from Pittsburgh, PA, to Cumberland, MD, on the Great Allegheny Passage by Brian J Krummel

Before you start screaming at me that you will never pay $45 for a paperback book, consider the great photographs and the fact that the author grew up in the Pittsburgh area

The C&O Canal Companion: A Journey through Potomac History Paperback by Mike High

A fairly thorough guide to the history of the C & O, if you're into that sort of thing.

Trail Guide, 14th edition,

This is the official, authorized guidebook for the Great Allegheny Passage and C&O Canal Towpath, covering two scenic trails and one amazing journey. It is constantly being updated. Available from the GAP Trail Store

A few websites:

Official website Great Allegheny Passage:
https://gaptrail.org/

Official website of Chesapeake & Ohio Canal National Historical Park
https://www.nps.gov/choh/index.htm

Youtube is full of videos of people who have recorded their trips on both the Passage and the C & O

And — of course — because there is an app for just about everything these days:

C&O Companion iPhone App

Note: "Author has no time or plans for an Android version."

A Shout Out

Sections of the Great Allegheny Passage are managed and maintained by local volunteer organizations. Without their dedicated efforts, the Passage would not be the smooth ride that it is. Some of these organizations are:

Friends of the Riverfront
McKeesport Trail Committee
Mon-Yough Trail Council
Regional Trail Corporation
Somerset County Rails to Trails Association
Steel Valley Trail Council
Westmoreland Yough Trail Council
Whitsett-Fayette Yough Trail Chapter
Yough River Trail Council

Made in the USA
Columbia, SC
23 June 2020

12175890R00171